# Shortening Shadows

# Shortening Shadows

A Novel

**Tom Woodward**

All rights reserved. This is a work of fiction. All of the characters (other than public figures and those persons whose names are drawn from the news stories of the time period), events, and settings (other than buildings set forth as real) described in this novel are imaginary, and all character names and descriptions are fictional. In all cases, any resemblance between the characters in this novel and real people is purely coincidental.

Real public figures, products, places, businesses, government agencies or other entities are depicted fictitiously in this novel for purposes of entertainment and comment only. No affiliation, sponsorship or endorsement is claimed or suggested.

The author and publisher shall have neither liability nor responsibility to any person or entity with respect to any loss or damage caused, or alleged to be caused, directly or indirectly, by the contents of this novel.

Copyright © 2016 Tom Woodward
All rights reserved

ISBN: 153059118X
ISBN 13: 9781530591183
Library of Congress Control Number: 2016906196
CreateSpace Independent Publishing Platform
North Charleston, South Carolina

# Dedication

*This book is dedicated to memory of Dan Parrish,
who grew up in Atlanta, Georgia,
and who, like the author, at one time worked in the "newspaper game."
Our world lost a good man when he passed.
And, in this world, that's no small thing.*

> "Evil is always more dangerous when it takes the cloak of familiarity."
> — UNKNOWN

# Note To The Reader

This book was written as an author would have created it at the time in which it takes place, 1935. As a result, the narration and dialogue contain terms and slang words as they would have been used by the characters and authors at the time. A number of the words and their usage in this context have passed from the common language. A **Glossary** is provided at the back of this book to assist the reader.

# CHAPTER 1
# The Boardinghouse

Matthew Grimes awoke from a very pleasing, yet unsatisfying dream. Even so, it was such a pleasant, almost decadent vision that he felt his face redden at its recollection. The dream he'd had was of Jean Harlow. She was on his mind a great deal lately and now had invaded his sleeping hours. Matt had seen Harlow in *Red Dust* several years ago, and the scene of her bathing in the rain barrel was still etched in his memory. He lingered in his bed for a time relishing the reverie. Gable sure had more willpower than I would have had at that moment, Matt thought with a smile. And now Harlow's coming to the Loew's Grand this Friday in a movie intriguingly titled *Reckless*. A photograph of Harlow and William Powell, the lucky dog, snuggled cheek to cheek, had appeared in the newspaper this past Thursday. Her glowing loveliness spurred his desire to see the movie even further. Unfortunately, his girlfriend, Evelyn Nash or Evie, as he called her, wanted to go see something called *Mississippi*, a musical comedy with Bing Crosby and Joan Bennett. It opened at the Paramount the same day. Great! A musical! Can't wait for that one! Matt brooded. That Evie had a crush on Crosby and his warm bass-baritone voice had nothing to do with Matt's feelings about the prospect, he told himself. Joan Bennett was something to look at all right, but didn't do for Matt what Jean Harlow did.

# SHORTENING SHADOWS

Stirrings down the hall and on the floor above him brought Matt back to the present with the realization that he needed to get out of bed and start moving. Even though some things were looking better, jobs were still hard to come by in the Great Depression spring of 1935, and he couldn't afford to lose his at the newspaper. Matt untangled himself from the sheets, sat up, and put his feet on the room's area rug. Despite the rug, he could still feel the coolness of the hardwood floor through the fabric. The young man realized that temperatures were still below normal for this time of year in Atlanta. He stepped to his room's radiator and basked momentarily in its welcomed warmth.

Matt sat back on the bed and sleepily stared at the green-and-white plaid bathrobe draped over the foot of his bed. Evie had given it to him for Christmas. A bathrobe seemed an unnecessary extravagance. The garment was something he'd never owned nor would have bought for himself. Matt hadn't had the heart to tell her that he didn't like the color green, except those hues produced by Mother Nature or printed by the U. S. Government. He and Evie had been seeing each other for a while, but the topic of color likes and dislikes had simply never come up. More to the point of not speaking his mind about the color of the thing was that the cost of a bathrobe certainly surpassed that of the lady's handkerchiefs, even monogrammed, he'd given her. Buying a gift for a girlfriend was difficult, he recalled. The present can't be anything too personal, he'd decided, yet has to be thoughtful and loving. Evie had insisted, correctly, of course, that, living in a boardinghouse, Matt absolutely needed a robe when roaming the hall to the bathroom at night and in the early-morning hours. Matt smiled briefly, wondering whether her real motive might have been to prevent him being accidentally "seen" in some "compromising way" – in his pajamas? – by the women boarders who lived on the floor above the men, but who still had to make their way up and down the single, open stairway at the end of the hall.

Reaching with his left hand, he groped for the robe and stood, stretching his six-feet-three, two-hundred-plus pound frame like a cat. Pulling the robe on and cinching it, he walked to his bureau and picked up his bar of Lifebuoy soap. Red, he considered, as he sleepily sniffed the bar's fragrance. Now that's a color he could go for. Red was the color of automobile he'd wanted when he bought the gray '32 Ford Tudor he now drove. But the gray model was the one available which he could afford at the time. Old Chester Gray, he thought they called it. A drab gray, yes, but that V-8 motor really hummed down the road. Next time, a red one, he assured himself. He looked in the bureau mirror and ran his fingers through the thick blond hair that sprouted above his face, one that Evie called boyishly handsome. Picking up his shaving gear, toothbrush, Squibb dental cream, and towel, he made his way down the hall to the bathroom door, which was closed, indicating the space was occupied. As he turned to go back to his room, Matt barely heard his name being called. It sounded more like a question than anything.

"Matt? Is that you?" Mr. Fleming, the husband half of the couple who owned and ran the boardinghouse, was using a stage whisper to get Matt's attention from his bedroom.

Matt walked the short distance farther down the hall to the Flemings' open bedroom door. Rhamy Fleming was sitting on an oak Windsor chair in the corner, putting on his boots, preparing for the day at a butchers' abattoir where he worked over on Brady Avenue near the stockyards. Freckles, the household canine of "indeterminable ancestry," as Mr. Fleming jokingly put it, sat by her master's side. The Flemings' twelve-year-old son, Cliff, had given the dog her unusual name based on the many spots across her puppy's belly when she was found as a stray some five years earlier. The dog looked Matt's way and wagged her tail several times, acknowledging his presence. After a moment's contemplation, she got up and strolled to him to get her ears nuzzled before returning to her master. She sat next to Rhamy as he finished pulling his second boot on.

His face reddening as he bent over his paunch to draw his boot over his left foot, Mr. Fleming looked up at Matt. "How are you this beautiful mornin', young fella? What's new in the world of crime?" Matt smiled but, before he could answer, Mr. Fleming continued, "Anything new on that story about the police raid of the house where they found the dynamite and safecrackin' stuff and arrested those four folks Saturday night? I heard that the one who tried to go out the back door ran straight into the arms of a cop, but had to be knocked down several times before he was overpowered."

Matt marveled at the extent of Mr. Fleming's knowledge of the incident. Maybe I need to go to Mr. Fleming before writing up my stories, he thought. "There's nothing new other than the charges being drawn up against the four. I understand they'll be presented to the Grand Jury today. The Macon police want the one who escaped their custody, that Joel Randall fella, back for a trial there, but Assistant Solicitor Hudson is determined to try him and his codefendant for the grocery store holdup here first." As Matt spoke, the bathroom door down the hall opened and, another boarder, Melvyn Briggs, darted across the hall to his room and closed the door. Matt wanted to rush to the available bathroom but waited until Mr. Fleming finished their conversation.

As he heaved himself from his chair, Mr. Fleming embarked on a new topic. "Well, today's the big day – openin' day for the Crackers' season. The Knoxville Smokies are supposed to have a pretty fair team this year."

"Yes, yes they are. Should be a great game, too." Matt glanced again at the open bathroom door. "I'm very sorry to cut this short, Mr. Fleming, but I really need to grab that empty bathroom and get going."

"Sure, sure, Matt, I understand. I didn't mean to slow you down none," the older man said with a wave of his hand. "You go on 'bout your business. I'll see you down at breakfast." With that, Matt walked down the hall and made his claim on the second-floor bathroom.

Rhamy Fleming went about his last bit of preparation for the day ahead, running a comb through his dark-brown hair with a touch of distinguished graying at the temples. As he did, he thought about the pleasure he derived from talking with Matt. The Flemings had lost a ten-year-old son very soon after Thanksgiving, 1918, to the influenza outbreak. Tom would have been about Matt's age now. Rhamy enjoyed the time spent with the young reporter, moments that somehow seemed to help fill the void. Tom's loss was even more difficult a subject for the family than might otherwise have been expected, owing to the deaths of one of his wife's sisters to the same pandemic and of one of her brothers earlier in the same year as he fought in the Great War in Europe. Rhamy looked around the bedroom and in their private bathroom one last time before he closed the doors to his chifforobe. His wife had enough to do managing the boardinghouse without cleaning up after him all the time. Rhamy called to Freckles, closed the bedroom door, and headed downstairs.

---

A short time later, Matt was ready for the day. The aroma of ham and coffee, wafting from the busy kitchen, greeted him as he descending the stairs. His landlady, Mrs. Fleming, was hovering over the stove as usual for this time of the morning. The plump but firm woman wore a faded floral-patterned housedress with a bib apron tied around her waist. Her gray-black curly hair was knotted on her nape. "Mornin', Matt," she called out, glancing in his direction as he walked to a pot of coffee sitting on the kitchen's porcelain-top side table. The tube of a cream extractor ran from a bottle of Aristocrat Dairy milk to a glass jar next to the coffeepot. Also on the table was an open bag of My-T-Pure flour with the remnants of some type of food preparation. Biscuits this morning, Matt reflected with a grin.

Taking one of the mugs already set out there, he poured himself a cup.

"Good morning! Sure smells great, Miss Dixie." Mrs. Dixie Fleming, matron of the boardinghouse at 71 Houston Street, was known to everyone, from her boarders and her preacher to the milkman and the black man, Adolphus, who did odd jobs around the house from time to time, as "Miss Dixie." Mr. Fleming was always just that, more a show of respect for his "advanced age" of forty-seven and the teachings of the general Southern upbringing than anything else. Not that Miss Dixie was a pushover in any respect. She was a kind, understanding, everyone's-favorite-aunt manner of woman, but she had strict policies about her boardinghouse, and God help anyone who didn't follow the rules, family included.

Foremost among the house rules was her version of the "Mason-Dixon Line" or, as she referred to it, the "Mason-*Dixie* Line." That policy decreed that the third floor of the house, the women's domain, was off limits to all the men of the household, *all* men, meaning boarders and family, with one exception. The only time Mr. Fleming was allowed on the third floor was for routine maintenance work, and only after his appearance there had been preceded by a "man on the hall" warning from Dixie, followed by her presence during the work. If the job called for Adolphus or some repairman to be there, the same warning was issued to any female boarders present, and then the work would be under Mrs. Fleming's supervision at all times. This, she said, was for the repairman's protection as much as that of the lady boarders. The Mason-Dixie rule applied equally to a woman's presence on the second floor, except the very brief time it took a woman to descend the stairs between the third-floor and first-floor levels. No dawdling, no conversations. If you wanted to speak to a member of the opposite sex at the boardinghouse on Houston Street, there was a parlor for such, or the dining table, or the front porch. Again, she emphasized, this rule was in everyone's best interest.

Miss Dixie would brook no "mess" from anyone, as was the hard lesson learned by one Miss Laverne Wells, who, after repeated warnings about lingering on the staircase in the second-floor area to speak to male boarders, suddenly departed the residence at Miss Dixie's "urging." The landlady said nothing about the unexpected exit, holding to her belief that 'the least said the soonest mended.' If Laverne's name ever came up in passing, all Miss Dixie would say was, "Well, bless her little heart!" Considering Miss Wells's behavior and deportment, everyone in the household expected to see the voluptuous young woman's name on the marquee at the Capitol Theater, next to Davison's over on Peachtree Street any day now, headlining one of their advertised late-night, vaudeville-style "intimate girl revues." If that actually came to pass, Matt had decided that he might just take in a show. Of course, that would *only* occur on a slow news day and *only* in the interest of supporting an old acquaintance. At least that's what Matt told himself.

The second major rule of the household was timely attendance at supper, served promptly at six thirty in the evening. If, for whatever reason a boarder could not attend the meal or had some activity planned, they were to notify Miss Dixie as early as possible about the conflict. Missing supper without telling the landlady ahead of time was as bad to a good Baptist lady like her as not tithing: unforgiveable. Miss Dixie prided herself on offering what she considered the cleanest and best-fed boardinghouse, for the price, in all of Atlanta. She maintained that one way to do so was not to waste food. The other circumstance that aided her in her money-saving pursuit was the ability of Rhamy to bring home generous cuts of beef and pork from the slaughterhouse. Rhamy Fleming was a hardworking man and had many friends and customers of the abattoir who were happy to show their gratitude. Miss Dixie's kitchen held the very biggest and best appliances she could manage to help her in her quest. Of course, in Matt's opinion, no one was more adept at planning a menu so today's leftovers, if any, provided a delicious soup, stew, hash, et cetera, tomorrow. And no one was a better cook than Miss Dixie. Not even his momma.

As Matt was stirring his coffee, Cliff came into the kitchen from the backdoor entry through the pantry. He carried a large basket full of eggs and was followed closely by Freckles who dutifully crossed the room to the underside of the table where Matt stood. The youngster had made his morning rounds in the chicken coop that adjoined the old barn-carriage house which stood behind the residence. He sported his usual shock of unruly hair. "Great day in the henhouse, Momma! Good mornin', Matt." Before Matt could respond, Miss Dixie gave her son a stern look, which caused Cliff's face to flush and immediately correct himself. "Uh, I mean, good mornin', Mr. Grimes."

Matt grinned at the boy. "Good morning, Cliff." Matt didn't mind the boy calling him Matt, but he knew better than to countermand an instruction from Miss Dixie to her offspring. Matt had already innocently crossed that bridge once, and, based on Miss Dixie's strongly expressed determination to bring her son "up proper," he would not address the issue again. For his part, Matt didn't use the pet name Cliff's father often used with him. No one else did either.

Rhamy Fleming, ever the wry wit, had nicknamed his twelve-year-old son "Hafta" soon after his birth and referred to him by the moniker on occasion. The name came about in a peculiar way. Cliff's late entry to the family, though a happy addition, was a surprise. When Mr. Fleming was celebrating the boy's birth with his coworkers, one of the men, who had something to do with kosher meats, told Rhamy that the Hebrew word for "surprise" is *hafta'a*. Whatever the true Hebrew pronunciation, Rhamy's broken-Hebrew-southern articulation of the word came out "hafta." Upon christening his newborn son with the epithet, Rhamy jokingly said that, though he might be a "surprise baby," we "hafta" keep him. Rhamy Fleming was known for his dry, odd sense of humor and playful nature with words. The exception to the running gag was when the young man was in trouble. Then, his father used his full name, Clifford Emanuel Fleming.

Watching Cliff carefully place the eggs in a bowl in the large, double-door monitor-top refrigerator, only one of the better-quality appliances Miss Dixie's kitchen proudly possessed, Matt decided to wait for breakfast in the dining room across the hall. Before leaving the kitchen, though, he reached down to pet Freckles under the side table, the only spot in the kitchen she was allowed by the strict Miss Dixie. Matt spoke her name, nuzzled her ears, and rubbed her fur, made soft and clean by the weekly bath given her by the Flemings' son. The regular bathing was an absolute requirement by Miss Dixie for the dog's continued presence in the household. As the landlady had put it when the dog made her initial appearance, followed by the careful begging by Cliff to keep her, "I'm running a boardinghouse, not a kennel for critters." With that said, she finally relented with the understanding about feeding and regular bathing to be done by her son. The latter was an at-least-once-a-week obligation. Rhamy suspected that the puppy's enthusiastic licking of Dixie's hands and the pooch's playful nature had something to do with his wife's decision to keep her.

When Matt stepped into the dining room, Mr. Fleming was there, sitting in his usual spot at the head of the table, sipping coffee, and scanning the sports page of the *Constitution*. Also at his regular place at the table, next to Mr. Fleming so they could exchange the morning newspaper sections as they read, was the other boarder Matt had seen hurriedly leaving the bathroom earlier, Melvyn Briggs.

Melvyn was a salesman for a local piano company. In his middle thirties, by Matt's estimation, Melvyn was a mousey, shorter-than-average, balding man who tended toward plumpness. He had an open cherubic face and dark, brooding eyes. Melvyn seemed fairly dowdy, too fastidious, and quiet. He appeared to everyone as such until he sat at a piano keyboard, which Matt had to admit, he handled with certain aplomb. Suddenly, those dark eyes, set wide on his face, would shine with laughter as he played. Melvyn seemed to think his ability at the ivories made him more appealing to women, especially to one boarder. So, he entertained the Flemings and the other residents at every opportunity, much to Matt's chagrin. Matt called those episodes "room and 'bored'." Melvyn was about to display another habit, which produced even more vexation in Matt. The piano salesman had an irritating tendency to read the competition's newspapers with an unnecessarily loud flare when straightening or turning the pages, especially when Matt was around. Irksome only to Matt. To the casual observer, Melvyn's actions would not have seemed anything unusual, but Matt took them as an intentional rub aimed at him and his third-ranked city newspaper.

"Are you covering the upcoming little boy's marbles championships for the paper, Matt?" Melvyn asked with a tinge of derision from behind the front section of the morning edition. At this, Rhamy lowered his newspaper ever so slightly and peered over it.

"No, that comes under the banner of the sports page. Why? Are you entered, Melvyn?" Matt inquired, stressing his name as Mel-*vyn*. The only response Matt's sarcasm garnered was a louder than usual rustling of the newspaper as the now red-faced Melvyn turned the page. But, somehow, even that weak reaction gave Matt some satisfaction.

For his part, Mr. Fleming enjoyed quietly watching and listening to this thrust-and-parry word game. He thought that, for whatever reason, these two could be like two cats with their tails tied together and draped over a clothesline, all hissing and claws. As Matt and Melvyn finished their verbal jousting, he shook his head slightly, smirked, and took another sip of coffee behind his sports section. Other boarders started making their way into the dining room.

Diane Keller was the first to appear. The heart-wrenchingly pretty, tall, long-legged Diane took the seat between Matt and Melvyn, a welcomed buffer from Matt's perspective. Diane was a friend of Evie's and worked with her at Davison's, although on a different floor. She had introduced Evelyn and Matt to each other and relished the idea that her matchmaking had stuck thus far. A native of the village of Smyrna in nearby Cobb County, Diane had a very outgoing, playful nature. Her boyfriend, Dave, several years older than Diane, was something of a mystery to the household. Diane said very little about her guy and usually met him elsewhere for their dates. On those rare occasions when he did appear at the boardinghouse to pick her up, he never came inside, but waited at the curb behind the long hood of his black 1934 Brewster Ford Town Car. Fortunately, Diane occupied a front bedroom on the third floor, from which she could see and hear Dave's arrival and never kept him waiting for very long. Miss Dixie did not approve of this behavior, but she recognized that she was not the girl's mother. When leaving for her dates with Dave, Diane would dance through the first floor of the residence, all dolled up, doing her best Ginger Rogers impersonation, dancing and singing the Cole Porter favorite "You're The Top," which had immortalized the maker of her boyfriend's automobile, the Brewster. Diane smoked a bit and drank a lot, another few things Miss Dixie frowned on. Miss Dixie said, with a hint of disapproval, that, if Diane had been born ten years earlier, she would have been a flapper! "No Agnes Scott girl she," the landlady would occasionally add.

As she settled into her seat at the table, Diane gave Matt a playful elbow to his right arm. Mindful of the apparent "friendly" friction between Matt and Melvyn, as was the rest of the boardinghouse, Diane could not restrain herself from asking, "Are the boys behaving this morning, Mr. Fleming?" At the verbal jab, Melvyn noisily shuffled the newspaper with a grunt, while Matt merely rolled his eyes and returned a nudge to Diane. Mr. Fleming quietly smiled but didn't respond, conceding that the answer was the same as always.

Meanwhile, another third-floor resident, Amanda Hardin, and Joshua Green, the third and final male boarder of the house, entered the dining room together. Amanda had Joshua engaged in close conversation. This pairing was somehow appropriate because both Amanda and Joshua were each enigmas. Amanda and Joshua stood behind the chairs opposite Matt and Diane as they quietly continued their discourse.

Closer in age to Melvyn than the other boarders, Amanda was raven haired and attractive but, obviously, had been very beautiful once. She now appeared world-weary beyond her years, often with bags under her eyes that face powder could not hide. Lines were beginning to show around the corners of her mouth and eyes. Amanda's faded beauty was like a heavyweight boxer aging, going a touch soft. The impression was still there, but the effect had been diminished slightly. Even so, Amanda was still a head-turner. She was employed as a receptionist in the relatively new W. W. Orr Doctor's Building over on Peachtree Street, just above Pine Street. Although she was outwardly friendly to the others sharing the house, she remained a bit reclusive. Rumors quietly swirled about a sudden end to Amanda's first marriage in Savannah some time before she moved to Atlanta. Matt simply attributed the innocuous gossip to her withdrawn manner and the inevitable speculation that can follow one of such a solitary nature.

A kindred spirit with Amanda for a taciturn nature, Joshua Green was even quieter and more remote from the everyday carryings-on of the household. He would readily participate in the mealtime discussions and gather with the group around the radio on most evenings, but generally kept to himself. Always smarty dressed, Joshua was a tall, thin, and very neat young man. His tidiness was an attribute of which Miss Dixie was particularly fond. What little was known about him in the boardinghouse consisted primarily of his employment at a local haberdashery in the business district. The consensus was that he was in his late twenties.

Rhamy Fleming was of the notion that Joshua might be of the Jewish faith, not that it mattered. His feeling was based largely on the fact that Joshua would disappear for long periods on Saturdays, the Jewish

Sabbath, or Shabbat, as Rhamy had learned from his fellow worker at the slaughterhouse. As if to point out the assimilation of his people into the southern culture, Rhamy's coworker had begun to greet him with a greeting of "Shalom, ya'll" periodically, after Rhamy posed some friendly questions about his religion. The man's words always brought a smile to Rhamy. Notwithstanding Joshua's routine, he did not seem to follow the dietary practices of his faith, as Rhamy understood them, when it came to mealtime in the boardinghouse. Again, Joshua's background, whatever it might have been, was immaterial to everyone in the home. He was part of the "family" residing at 71 Houston Street.

Amanda and Joshua were trailed by Victoria Wilson and Teresa Rossetti. The two girls spoke in low tones as they tried to plan some evening out together soon. They stopped just inside the dining-room door as they spoke.

Victoria, a graduate of a local business college, was employed in the Canada Dry Ginger Ale offices in the Candler Building. Slightly on the pudgy side, she stood five-feet-seven, had deep-blue eyes, and striking auburn hair. Victoria's laugh, never very far from the surface, was infectious to all around her. Some might have called it a flirtatious giggle but for her otherwise quiet mannerisms. Just to hear her chuckle, Mr. Fleming would often tease Victoria, particularly about the paradox of a rival soft drink company's offices occupying a building constructed by Asa Candler, of Coca-Cola fame. The landlord was also quick to point out the additional irony of each company's beginning and growth having been largely the efforts of pharmacists. When she laughed at his jokes, the whole room lit up.

Teresa was the olive-skinned, dark-haired beauty of the household. Unlike the other women of the boardinghouse and contrary to the fashion of the day, she allowed her long, silky tresses to fall naturally down her back. The look, combined with her beautiful smile, produced an alluring effect on every man and boy. If allowed to do so, Cliff would have followed her around like an adoring puppy. Miss Dixie kept that from happening in a manner that only an embarrassed and apologetic parent could understand. Teresa was from somewhere up North. Her family had made a stopover in Atlanta on their way to Florida during the land boom there in the 1920's. Somehow, they'd taken more than a little time to resume their journey. By the time they finally departed, Teresa had grown up and found a good job with a stenographic service in the Rhodes-Haverty Building. She'd also met her "true love." In time, she grew to love the former while the latter never panned out. But she felt at home, stayed in Atlanta, and flourished in her surroundings. She faithfully attended mass at the Shrine of the Immaculate Conception down on Hunter Street. Recently, Miss Dixie had announced that Teresa would be helping her develop some Italian cuisine for the boardinghouse to "mix it up a little," as the landlady had phrased it.

Miss Dixie stuck her head in the dining-room doorway. "Ya'll take a seat! Breakfast's ready to be served!" she announced, trying to get the meal under way. With this "call to order," the newspapers disappeared from the table to avoid the wrath of Miss Dixie. She had her rules after all. The two most recent arrivals seated themselves at the oversized dining table initially put in place years earlier by Dixie's father for his large family.

Shortly thereafter, the matron of the household came in with a platter of fried eggs, accompanied by Cliff, carefully balancing a plate stacked high with fried ham slices. Miss Dixie went to each boarder and provided them the number of eggs requested, if any, followed by a slab of ham, delicately browned to perfection by the lady of the house. With that achieved, Miss Dixie departed and reappeared with a large bowl of grits, ladling out a portion as generous as the individual requested. Cliff found his customary seat next to his father, while Miss Dixie returned with a platter of buttermilk biscuits and finished by informing everyone, as she did at virtually every breakfast, that there was more of everything in the kitchen if anyone wanted anything. "Just speak up! If you ain't at home, you oughta be!" she laughed, as she wiped her hands on her apron and took her rightful place at the opposite end of the table from her husband. Rhamy then returned thanks to the Good Lord for His bounty. Afterward, passing the pitchers of milk, water, and coffee, the platter of biscuits, a boat of redeye gravy, the salt, pepper, and butter, as requested around the table, the troop proceeded to eat. The Flemings' theory about the morning meal was simple. A hearty breakfast could stick with a person all day, possibly precluding the absolute need for lunch. The money saved on that alone was more than the little extra paid for a residence at the rooming house.

The meal had no more than begun when the telephone in the hall rang. The landlady excused herself and hurried off to answer it. Matt's first thought was that some heinous crime had been perpetrated somewhere in the city, and the *Atlanta Georgian* was calling to get him to respond. He paused and sat quietly, waiting for a call to the phone. Though she spoke in hushed tones, the time Miss Dixie stayed on the call made it apparent to the reporter that it had nothing to do with him or his job. At one point, Miss Dixie laid the phone's receiver down on the small telephone table and closed the large pocket doors that separated the dining room from the hallway. When she returned to the dining table, she was met by the gazes of all present. Such an early morning phone call was rare, though not unheard of at the boardinghouse.

Miss Dixie took the opportunity to satisfy the quizzical looks and to address some family business in the same explanation. "That was Ruth. The girls aren't feeling good and Floyd's on the road for several days. Since Ruth's just getting over that bad cold, I think it would help her if I could pick 'em up some time today and bring her and the kids over here for a couple of days." As she spoke, the landlady looked to each of her female boarders. "They can stay in the spare room on the third floor, if you ladies don't mind the extra folks for a short time." All gathered knew of the anxiety Miss Dixie felt whenever anyone caught cold or was otherwise sick, owing to the Fleming family loses during the 1918 pandemic. The entire Fleming household, boarders included, was, indeed, very much like family. Owing to her considerate nature, the consensus among the household was that any spare room in the house was Miss Dixie's to use as she saw fit. As the third-floor residents nodded their agreement with the plan, Mrs. Fleming smiled her gratitude and continued. "I can give Ruth a hand with the girls, and it'll give us a chance to visit, Rhamy. But I'll need to use the Plymouth today to go over to Mechanicsville to pick 'em up. And, while I'm out, I can go by and pay the light bill."

Rhamy was more keenly aware of his wife's apprehension about colds and flu than anyone else. "No problem, Sweetheart. I'll take the streetcar to work."

The meal resumed full throttle at this point. Amid the quiet conversations during breakfast, Mr. Fleming asked his son whether he'd cleared some unidentified "mess" in the barn, now used as a garage on occasion by the Flemings. After Cliff assured his dad that the job had been done that morning when he went out to gather eggs, Rhamy seemed satisfied, but assured his son that he'd check it.

Matt took that opening to broach an idea that had occurred to him earlier when Cliff had entered the kitchen. "Mr. and Mrs. Fleming, I was wondering whether you would mind if I took Cliff to the Crackers' season opener today. I've got two tickets that one of the sportswriters gave me, and my girl has to work. It's a three-thirty start so it won't interfere with his school too much, and my deadline for the evening edition will have come and gone." While the youngster suddenly sat upright with his attention riveted on Matt, Miss Dixie looked uncertain. Matt continued his entreaty, "Because they're talking about a huge crowd showing up, I thought I'd leave my car here, and we'd take the streetcar, if that's all right with you. That way, I won't have to worry about parking my car, and someone else can fight the traffic to and from the field."

The other conversations and the irregular clinking of knives and forks against plates ceased momentarily as everyone awaited the outcome of this turn of events. Cliff, who dearly loved the game of baseball, held back as long as he could during the ensuing hush, but finally burst forth, "Please, Momma? Daddy? Please?"

Rhamy broke into a smile and nodded, as did Miss Dixie. The matter was settled. Cliff let out a small whoop which was met by a stern look from his mother, who wouldn't tolerate such carryings-on at the table. The boy immediately mumbled an apology so as not to endanger his good fortune.

"I'll be back at one thirty to get you, Cliff, so we don't miss any of the opening day hoopla. You'll probably need to take a jacket. It's supposed to be sunny but might be a little chilly, especially if we're sitting in the shade."

"He'll be here and ready," Miss Dixie assured Matt.

"One other thing. Like I said, the game isn't scheduled to begin until three-thirty, but, because of the opening day festivities with Governor Talmadge and Mayor Key, Cliff and I may not make it back in time for supper. So, we'll probably stop and grab a sandwich or something somewhere on the way home, if that's all right. There're a few places between the ballpark and here to grab a bite. One I've eaten at before is near where Peachtree meets Ponce." Cliff beamed at this opportunity to eat at a restaurant, a rare treat for him in the current state of things in the world.

"Well, okay, but let me getcha some money before you leave."

"Not necessary but thank you, Ma'am. My treat. I'll be glad to have the company of someone who loves baseball as much as I do."

"Evelyn likes baseball, too!" interjected Diane quietly but earnestly, ever the protector of the love match she'd put in place.

"Yeah," Matt chuckled at Diane's remark. "I didn't mean to imply she didn't, Diane. All I'm saying is that Cliff is my first choice if Evie can't make it."

"Governor Talmadge and Mayor Key on the same podium," Rhamy threw his head back and laughed. "That'll be fun to watch, right there. Worth the price of admission all by itself. I think the governor still holds it against Key for bellyachin' against Prohibition and the blue laws. The mayor even called Prohibition a failure while he was in France in thirty-one. His stand cost him his Sunday school teacher's position, too. Talmadge was probably as happy as could be during the recall vote in thirty-two and most likely mad as a cat tryin' to bury crap on a marble floor when the votes of the Negro folks saved him from losin'."

"Rhamy! Don't be coarse!" Miss Dixie was quick to chastise such talk at her table. Cat crap, indeed! she thought. Not at my table! At the same time, she gave her son a disapproving look when he giggled at his daddy's comment.

"Well, it's true!" Rhamy was a man's man without being overbearingly so. But, while careful around and respectful of his wife, especially at the table and in the presence of the boarders, he would, on occasion, dare to provoke her scolding by speaking his mind. "Sorry, ladies," he quickly added, somewhat sheepishly, to the third-floor residents before finishing his thought. "But I think the governor's still steamed about the city council's legalization of near beer sales back in thirty-three, too!" After a sip from his coffee cup, he finished his thought. "That man has a long memory!"

During the ensuing conversations, Diane turned her attention to Matt. "Evelyn is really excited about seeing that Bing Crosby movie at the Paramount this weekend," she gushed.

"Yeah," Matt responded with all the deadpan he could gather. "I couldn't possibly be any more excited it about myself than I am." Diane smiled until it seemed to occur to her that Matt's declaration could be taken one of two ways. She gave him a questioning look, to which he merely responded with a wry grin.

Seated on either side of Miss Dixie, Teresa and Victoria had been in quiet conversation with the landlady throughout breakfast. Matt, ever the one to enjoy a good meal, hoped that they were deep into some culinary conspiracy.

At one point, Joshua reminded Miss Dixie that he would not be at supper the next night. Ever the nosy one when something different happened in the boardinghouse, Diane had to ask what was going on with her fellow boarder. The young man simply explained that he'd been invited to dine elsewhere tomorrow evening. Rhamy smiled knowingly. Passover Seder, he surmised.

When the meal concluded, Mr. Fleming expressed his gratitude to his wife with his customary mealtime "Much obliged, Ma'am." And, as usual, Miss Dixie responded with a coy, even girlish smile.

Cliff eagerly started clearing the table without coaxing from his parents. Diane watched quietly as he gathered the plates and eating utensils and made his way across the hall to the kitchen. Just above a whisper, she said, "Cliff certainly isn't risking any chance of losing that trip to the ballpark." Everyone tittered at this observation, knowing full well the truth of the statement. The household was, indeed, like one extended family.

After everyone left the dining table, Matt excused himself from a chat with Diane and took the opportunity to propose that Mr. Fleming let him drive the landlord to work. Rhamy initially declined with his thanks, but Matt persisted with the logic of the suggestion. "I know the abattoir is up near the stockyards off Marietta Street, right? So all I have to do is shoot right back down Marietta to the newspaper offices. No problem. Besides there was a serious automobile accident along that route yesterday, and I need to look at the scene before I write it up." After some back-and-forth, Matt finally persuaded the older man to accept the ride.

Minutes later, Matt strode down the first-floor hallway toward the massive front door with its oval cut-glass window. As he passed a door leading to the parlor, he noticed Victoria curled up on a chair with her March issue of *Modern Screen* magazine. No doubt, she was experiencing "the magic of the movies beyond the theatre," as someone had put it, while she waited for time to leave for her job. Joan Crawford graced the periodical's cover. He made a mental note to sneak a look at it if the opportunity presented itself. The image of Crawford's gams he'd seen several years ago as she tapped across the silver screen in *Dance, Fools, Dance* was still with him. Now there's a woman I wouldn't mind escorting across a hotel lobby to a waiting elevator, he reflected. His daydream was cut short by the stark realization that he wasn't *exactly* sure what he'd do even if he got Joan Crawford into a hotel room. On that uncertain note, he resumed his departure from the boardinghouse.

Outside, Matt leaned against his Ford Tudor parked in front the boardinghouse and smoked a cigarette, admiring the foundation azaleas beginning to bloom nicely. He decided he'd try to stop by Davison's and tell Evie of the change in his plans regarding taking Master Fleming to the game. When he made such a visit, a rare occurrence to be sure, he carefully pretended to be a legitimate customer so as not to jeopardize Evie's job. He was certain that he'd occasionally come under the wary eye of a floorwalker, a floor manager, or some such person of authority. His biggest challenge, at those times, was feigning interest in some merchandise offered while trying to have a quick, rather closed-mouth exchange with Evie.

Through the smoke of his Old Gold, Matt studied the brick boardinghouse he'd called home for some time. Miss Dixie's father, a onetime wealthy merchant, had built the home for his large family in 1891 and paid cash. According to Rhamy, the man's intent had been a debt-free home to last for generations, saying that, no matter what else happened, they would have a roof over their heads. Unfortunately, Miss Dixie's father had lost everything except the house in the "Panic of 1893." The family more or less fell apart as time passed and the siblings left home, died, or went off to war. By the middle of the 1920s, Dixie and Rhamy were married and had begun a family of their own in the home where they cared for her parents. The house was "inherited" by Dixie by default after her parents died in the late 1920s. With its oversized rooms, wide front porch, and balconies on each level above the porch, the house was a fine place to call home until Matt married and moved on. And the great food was a plus. Suddenly, Mr. Fleming scrambled out of the house and down the front steps toward the car at a gallop. "Sorry to keep you waitin', young fella. You sure you want to do this?"

"No problem. It's all settled. Hop in!" Once behind the wheel, Matt cranked his car, and the V-8 engine roared to life. Matt grinned. That sound of power from under the hood always gave him a rush of exhilaration.

"That motor sure sounds good, Matt! Our Plymouth is a couple of years newer than this Ford, but ours never sounds as eager to hit the road as this thing does."

Matt smiled more broadly and nodded. "I'll let you in on a little secret, Mr. Fleming. Remember, after Pretty Boy Floyd was killed in Ohio late last year, when I went up to Adairsville trying to dig up some story from locals who might have known him or his family when they lived in Bartow County? Well, on that trip, I had this baby doing over sixty miles an hour on one stretch of the Dixie Highway headed up there."

"You don't say? Well," Rhamy laughed in amazement, "I won't tell the cops if you won't!" Before Matt pulled away from the house, Mr. Fleming asked, "Which way are you goin'?"

"I figured to head over to Forsyth Street and from there down to Marietta Street and on to Brady."

"Sounds fine!" With that, the older man settled in.

Matt turned the car around and drove west on Houston the short distance to Peachtree Street where they stopped beside the ornate Candler

Building, sheathed in its snow-white Amicalola marble. He waited for traffic to give him a chance to proceed. Peachtree Street was already a center of activity at this early hour. Initially, they rode without either man speaking. As the young man crossed Peachtree Street, and started to make a left onto Forsyth Street at the Rhodes-Haverty Building, Rhamy nodded in its direction and looked up at the twenty-one story structure. "That's the building Teresa works in. Tallest building in Atlanta."

"Yes, I know." Matt said quietly as he negotiated the turn, avoiding a new Auburn Roadster whose driver felt he was above abiding by what rules of the road there were and what common sense otherwise dictated. "Look at this guy! He's got more to lose with his car than I do with mine!" Matt got his self-control back and waved the man on past his Ford before driving on.

When the tension of the moment had passed, Rhamy continued his thought. "I recollect when the Fourth National Bank Building was opened in January, 1905, and was promoted as the tallest building in town. That lasted a little over a year 'til old man Candler erected his office building. Taller by *one* story. Now the Rhodes-Haverty Building is tallest. But that won't last long. They just keep gettin' higher and higher. Don't know what this town's comin' to sometimes. Soon enough, we won't be able to see the sun."

Matt smiled sideways at his passenger's ruminations as he continued south on Forsyth Street, passing the Rialto Theater where bits of paper scuttling across the sidewalk in the slight morning breeze were the only reminders of the moviegoers from the night before. Arriving at Forsyth's intersection with Marietta Street, they stopped between the rather mundane-looking Palmer Building and the vacant lot where the old post office and customs house once stood facing Marietta Street and the majestic Henry Grady Monument. In its latter days, the old post office building had served as city hall until the new one was built at the corner of Washington and Mitchell Streets. The old building, which had been standing since 1878, had been demolished five years earlier. Everyone now waited to see what structure would replace it. As they sat, paused for an opening in the traffic, Rhamy and Matt could see men, possibly messengers, hurrying into the Western Union Building across the street. Finally, Matt turned onto Marietta Street and drove up the roadway's slight incline toward Cone Street.

As they passed the *Georgian-American* Building to their left, Matt reflected how the calm exterior belied the organized chaos he knew was going on inside as they prepared for another day's run of the presses. Rhamy turned halfway in the car seat toward Matt and sat with one arm over the seat. "I really appreciate your takin' Cliff to the game today, Matt. He loves baseball and doesn't get to go to a game very often, I'm afraid. I just can't always be there when I want to. Such is the life of a workin' man." Realizing how that might have sounded, he added, "Of course, I mean with a job with hours like mine, not yours." That still didn't come out right to Rhamy's way of thinking. "No offense meant, Matt." The landlord tried to recover from his self-proclaimed *faux pas*. "Do you need money for his ticket or food or anything?"

"No offense taken, Mr. Fleming. I understand what you meant. No problem about Cliff going to the game with me. Again, I'll appreciate the company. And no money needed. I'm not Rockefeller," Matt said with a wink, "but I'll manage."

At one point, the traffic on Marietta Street came to another halt. Matt lowered his window to enjoy the cool morning air. The two men sat in the Ford next to a stopped streetcar, loading and unloading passengers. Through the car's windows, they could see black men and women getting up from their seats for white passengers as they boarded and took the now-vacant spaces. Such was the "code" of the time. An imaginary line separated the "white half" in the front of a trolley from the "black half" in the rear. If the white half filled, the whites could just keep sitting farther and farther toward the rear. Blacks had to give up their seats and no black person could sit anywhere in front of a white person. Mr. Fleming sighed noisily, shook his head, and made clucking noises of disapproval.

"Wha'ja thinking?" Matt asked.

"Well, you know, Matt, that I'm no FDR progressive, no bleedin' heart. But I certainly don't agree with the Klan, either. Not by a long shot. You know that from our conversations. And I've got my biases and my faults. But I'll be damned if I agree with the attitude of Jim Crow laws. They're like a big shadow coverin' the land. Yeah, that's what they are, a big shadow. Why, I've seen a time or two when a streetcar would be packed in the back with coloreds and completely empty up front. I'd get on and there'd be some nasty white man or woman who'd get and go sit right middle-way of the damned streetcar. Just so no black person could sit in front of them in all those empty seats. Just for the hell of it. And it's not only here in the South either, Matt. One of the guys at work just came back from visiting relatives in Columbus, Ohio. On their way back, the family stopped at a restaurant in a town about thirty miles south of Columbus. Know what a sign in the restaurant's window said? 'We cater to white trade only.' Right in the window! Smack in the middle of Ohio!"

Matt listened quietly as the older man paused and shook his head before continuing. "Look, I ain't got no use for no-account folks who could be somethin' better if they tried but won't make the effort, be they black or white. But those colored people ain't on that trolley this time of the mornin' for a joyride. They're ridin' *to work*, maybe *from work*. And maybe dog tired. Seein' those colored women on there, I'm guessin' more than a few are domestic workers, like maids and such. So, they can come into our houses, cook and clean, make beds, take care of our kids, do pretty much everything, and then they can't *sit* by us. Negro folks work, at least for the most part, just like white folks, I reckon. They go to church, they eat, sleep, laugh, and cry. Same as us. And those same whites go home, read their Bibles, and sing a song to their kids, a song that includes the words 'red and yellow, black and white, they are precious in His sight.' Hypocrites! All of 'em!

"The idea that coloreds should be treated that-a-way 'cause of their skin color just don't make sense to me. Look, I'm a southerner and damned proud of it. I'm thinkin' that there's a lot to be proud of bein' a southerner. But the War Between the States is over. Let's move on. Speakin' of which, my granddaddy worked aboard a blockade-runner during," he showed a trace of a smile, "the 'War of Northern Aggression.' He was a seafarin' man all his life. He always said that a chain is only as strong as its weakest link. How long can this nation stay strong, be the best it can be, if we let a link in the chain, like the coloreds, remain weak 'cause we hold 'em down. That's all. Sorry about my language, but it's just beyond my ken."

Far more intelligent than his few years of formal education might indicate, Rhamy Fleming was a philosopher of sorts, a student of life and of human nature. Rhamy had a voracious appetite for knowledge and read constantly, a trait he was trying to pass on to his son. And like many people during their lives, he'd chosen an occupation he knew well and enjoyed, but not necessarily one with high social standing in the world. Social acceptance meant little to Rhamy Fleming. Others could take him or leave him, for all he cared. Just treat him fair, and he'd return the favor. His employment left him with the time and energy to watch and study the habits, nuances, dispositions, and traits of his fellow man as he went about his daily routine, interacting with others and "people watchin'," as he called it, when he occasionally made deliveries. Through the years, many people had learned too late the mistake of correlating Rhamy's acumen with his station in life. Despite Matt's young age of twenty-six years, he had recognized all this about Mr. Fleming early in their relationship. It had deepened his respect for the man.

Knowing Mr. Fleming as he did, Matt had expected something along the lines of his words. Rhamy Fleming *never* lacked the courage of his convictions. The older man had a keen wit and was not reluctant to voice his opinion about current events or wrongs as he saw them. When Senator Huey Long had visited Atlanta back in February to promote his share-the-wealth program "to save the nation from capitalism," as he put it, he wanted to use the Atlanta Municipal Auditorium, the largest capacity building in town, for his "show." Unfortunately for him, the hall had already been engaged by a wrestling promoter for a match between the "Masked Red Demon" of Chicago and Dory Roche of Scranton, Pennsylvania. Having read of the conflict between the two events, Rhamy was quick to observe, "One brand of hokum's as good as another."

Despite Mr. Fleming's reputation for frankness, Matt was somewhat stunned at his outburst, because few people would give voice to such thoughts for fear of the reaction. Maybe his landlord felt that comfortable around him, he supposed. Matt didn't reply. It wasn't that he didn't agree to some extent. He wasn't sure how he felt about some things. He was thinking about the older man's words when traffic jolted to a start.

For a long time neither man spoke, each absorbed in his thoughts. Traffic thinned when they reached the curve in Marietta Street after Latimer Street. As a large, long-haul tractor-trailer made a slow, wide turn from Simpson Street onto Marietta, headed north in front of them, they came to a halt. The rig's movement seemed to drag on interminably, primarily due to the southbound traffic failing to give it the room to maneuver. The truck's driver was compelled to back slightly to gain a better angle. Each time he backed up, the front driver in the southbound lane moved forward slightly, trying to squeeze past the rig. That move only compounded the problem. Somewhere beyond the intersection a car horn blared furiously. The truck had both streets pretty much blocked, so there was nowhere for Matt to go.

As he sat there and watched the debacle before him, Matt recalled the admonition from his city editor, Edward Barnes, on his first day as the police beat reporter for the *Georgian*. Mr. Barnes had learned that Matt hadn't grown up in Atlanta and, as a result, didn't know a great deal about the town's past beyond General Sherman's visit in 1864. "Get to know the city and its history as much as you can, young man, beyond Sherman's second visit." *Second visit?* Matt had pondered. Mr. Barnes continued and gave Matt three distinct reasons for learning as much of Atlanta's history as possible. "First, when you know a city's history, you'll better understand its present and its reaction to stories. Second, you need to know the streets because you can't chase a story if you can't find your way around. And, lastly, you may end up covering for someone one day and writing an article beyond the police blotters and that knowledge can mean the difference between a real headline grabber and just filler." In light of that advice, Matt had spent many of his subsequent free hours in the Carnegie Library studying the city's history and otherwise trying to learn the streets. The time had been well spent.

Sitting in his car, waiting for the truck to navigate the intersection, Matt recalled the history he'd learned about Simpson Street, named for Atlanta's first lawyer, Leonard C. Simpson. He'd died at the relatively young age of thirty-nine in 1860 and was buried in Oakland Cemetery, a bastion of Atlanta history in its own right. By the time Woodrow Wilson and his law-school classmate opened a law office at Marietta and Forsyth Streets in 1882, Atlanta practitioners of jurisprudence had mushroomed from the original Leonard Simpson to one hundred forty-three in a population of some thirty-seven thousand souls. As Rhamy Fleming was fond of saying, "Any town too small to support one lawyer is certainly big enough to support two."

Finally, common sense reared it weary head and the truck could complete its turn. The two men looked at each other and shook their heads. Matt could not imagine Atlanta traffic ever getting any worse. He chuckled, "You know, Mr. Fleming, a cop friend told me that if you want to discover the extent of human stupidity, try directing traffic."

As they cruised along Marietta Street, Rhamy quietly recalled the differences between the things he'd seen on his commute through this part of the city last year and now. What they called the Great Depression seemed to have bottomed out last year from all he had read and had seen. Although severely affected by the economic despair, the City of Atlanta seemed to have suffered less than had the rural areas of his state and less than its counterparts to the North and West of the country, owing in part, he supposed, to the fact that the area's strong industrial base that had only recently begun to form.

Despite that, as he commuted to work in 1934, when the national unemployment rate hovered at about twenty-one percent, he'd regularly seen men standing aimlessly in front of stores, some of which had been boarded up. Some men leaned against the buildings as if the structure was the only thing holding up them and their hopes. Their breaths had made gray clouds in the cold air of early winter. Others had been clustered in small pockets on street corners, smoking and commiserating. Occasionally, he would see a man sitting on the curb itself, in the depth of despair. These men had lost jobs, pride, and hope, not necessarily in that order. They felt diminished, less valuable, less a whole person if not working.

From his conversations with others, Rhamy had learned that these men would often leave home in the morning in the sole hope of being in the right spot at the right time when a job offer, even if only for one day, came along. Time seemed to wear that optimism down. Sometimes they simply departed their houses so they wouldn't have to face the hunger and hurt in the eyes of their wives and children. That fact was added to the reality that, if they weren't at home during mealtimes, whatever food *might* be in the house would go further toward feeding their family. Better the men, rather than their kids, miss a meal and suffer hunger pangs. As one hard-luck fellow, who'd come to the abattoir looking for work last year, told Rhamy, "Bacon ain't but ten cents a pound. But where you gonna get ten cents, mister?"

Although things were looking up in 1935, the national unemployment rate lingered somewhere above fifteen percent the last time Rhamy'd read or heard about it. And many of those fortunate enough to have jobs, found themselves supporting extended families whose breadwinners had lost theirs. Rhamy Fleming was grateful that his son-in-law Floyd had a decent-paying job with the railroad. The landlord pondered the situation. When men have sunk low enough and their kids' bellies are as empty as their hopes, they become easy marks for any crackpot with a good enough line of palaver, be they Nazi, communist, socialist, or fascist. The Order of Black Shirts had shown that fact in Atlanta in the spring of 1930. Thankfully, the movement hadn't lasted in the state's capital.

Mr. Fleming had felt a wave of despair for those men he'd seen last year and for their families. Yet, at the same time, he'd also felt gratitude for the good fortune he had in his life. The picture he saw as they drove now was far less bleak. But, nonetheless, life was still difficult for many of those trying to provide for their families. Huddles of gaunt, hopeless-looking men still stood here and there.

The two men lay some distance behind them without saying anything until Matt made the right turn onto Brady Avenue. After a short drive on Brady, Mr. Fleming nodded and said, "You can just pull over up there, Matt." As he was receiving the instructions, Matt, who had become aware of a very unpleasant odor assailing his nostrils, raised his window. "The wind from the stockyards must be just right," Mr. Fleming laughed. "It's an 'acquired taste', Matt." As directed, Matt eased his car off the road to the front of a long, low building bearing a sign indicating it to be their destination. A few men stood outside in small groups awaiting the start of their workday. As Rhamy Fleming hauled his deceptively muscular bulk from the car, he turned back to Matt and said, "Thanks again, Matt. I owe you one." After he started to close the car door, Rhamy paused, reopened it far enough to lean his head back inside. "Oh, and keep my boy in line this afternoon. He can be a handful at times."

"He'll be fine, Mr. Fleming. Don't worry about him. See you tonight."

Rhamy Fleming closed the car door and joined his coworkers. Matt turned the Ford around in front of the building and traveled back down Brady Avenue to Marietta Street.

## CHAPTER 2
# The Crime Beat

After turning onto Marietta Street toward the business district, Matt began to reflect on the world as it currently stood. Working for the newspaper brought him face to face with the day's news bulletins more than many people, he assumed. And some headlines caused him to question the priorities and thought processes of some people. He heaved an audible sigh.

Recent international news flashes made the world seem turned upside down at the moment. As the city prepared to celebrate the area's surviving Confederate veterans of the bloody Civil War in ten days and the memory of the "War To End All Wars" still burned in the hearts and minds of so many people, Hitler and his goose-stepping minions made headlines by threatening all of Europe. Not to be outdone by the mustached German, Benito Mussolini, leader of the elder brother of Nazism, Italian fascism, was ramping up for war against Haile Selassie in North Africa. April had begun with Hitler's and Mussolini's saber rattling, and the front pages had shown their rants and threats to have worsened as the calendar moved on. The pair seemed determined to march the world again to war. Ironically, newspaper advertisements offered readers "proverbial German hospitality" aboard the ships of the Hamburg-American

Line, while the Reich simultaneously clamped down on religious publications and beheaded alleged spies and other prisoners.

At the same time, seemingly desperate European leaders were holding talks in Stresa, a town on the banks of Lake Maggiore in Italy. There, representatives of France, Great Britain, and Italy were attempting to salvage a crumbling peace while also seeking to resist any future attempt by the Germans to change the Treaty of Versailles. Meanwhile, it was reported that an assassination attempt on Pierre Laval, the French foreign minister, and Premier Mussolini had been thwarted.

Recently, Matt recalled, a newspaper had displayed a nearly full-page spread of photographs of submarines, or underwater boats, as the piece had termed them. The article accompanying the photographs predicted them to be the scourge of the next war. He wondered whether General Billy Mitchell would take exception to that prophecy. Regardless, Lloyd George appeared to have been correct when he'd reputedly said during the last World War that "This war, like the next war, is a war to end war." Matt supposed that, despite which weapons would dominate the next war, the predominant headlines would proclaim the deaths of many thousands. He hoped that his country could avoid being sucked into the conflagration and that his death would not be among those being reported.

Matt smirked to himself that the only "good news" coming out of Germany these days was the announcement of Hermann Goering's wedding on the tenth of the month to the former actress Emma Johanna "Emmy" Köstlin. Good news if the union counted as such for anyone except the poor bride of the rather portly World War ace.

In headlines on the national front, while Europe threatened to explode, Americans fretted over Woolworth heiress Barbara Hutton's divorce from a self-styled Georgian prince named Alexis Mdivani. Matt shook his head at the thought of such misplaced anxiety. One of paper's newsroom nestors had suggested that possibly some locals didn't understand the meaning of the word "Georgian" as used in the article. Matt snickered as he recalled the moment when the room burst into laughter. Elsewhere, one Arthur Flegenheimer, alias Dutch Schultz, prepared for his tax evasion trial in upstate New York by declaring himself a much-wronged citizen who was, in reality, a public benefactor. To add to the misery of the continuing economic depression, Japanese textile production's upswing was resulting in the closing of U. S. mills, including some in Georgia. Finally, the country was still reeling from the deaths of over a dozen Williamsport, Maryland, high school students, returning from a chemistry lecture when their bus had been hit by a speeding train the previous Thursday night.

Locally, the month began with newspaper advertisements urging readers to "Wake up your liver bile!" That lovely thought appeared on the same day as the "uplifting" piece about the dancing twin sisters from Baltimore, Lillian and Violet, who had been detained by the local authorities when they arrived in Atlanta on Sunday. At the ripe old age of sixteen, the pair was scheduled to appear with a troupe at the Capitol Theater. Were their "talents" to be displayed in one of the theater's "intimate girl revues," perhaps? Matt mused. The exhibition had been with their parents' approval, as long as they sent some of their pay home to mama and papa. The irate parents called the Atlanta Police Department for their help because the girls had never been paid during their time on tour. As a result, no money had been coming to the home front. One of the *Georgian*'s "Underwood wags" declared it to be a classic story of the choice between the virtue of a loved-one and greed or the need for money. Regardless, their father had arrived in town shortly thereafter to cart them back home, without pay.

Meanwhile, Communists openly fomented unrest by distributing propaganda leaflets among neighboring Alabamians resulting in a headline declaring "Hand of Moscow Falls on Alabama," a nifty play on words of the Guy Lombardo song from the year before, "Stars Fell On

Alabama." Owing to its frequent use as a symbol by the Communists, Matt would have used the headline, "Red Stars Fell on Alabama." But, then, he reckoned, he had enough issues with his beat without trying to run someone else's. Finally, seventeen Atlanta police officers had been ordered to take physical examinations to determine their fitness for duty.

Yep, could the world be a more messed-up orb in April, 1935? Matt wondered as he slowly passed Cain Street where Marietta Street widened a bit. The intersection was the scene of the automobile accident he'd mentioned to Mr. Fleming, and Matt slowed and visually gathered the information he needed for his story.

Of course, Matt's sphere of news items revolved around local and regional crime stories. Oh, sure, he'd had a few crime stories that had made the front page in a small way, such as the submachine gun robbery of a grocer as he parked his car at his house back in January or the bombing of a building contractor's office the following month. Those were the crime beat stories he felt he was meant to write and not the traffic accidents and fires he was so often relegated to posting. Though he'd made the front page with the big January narrative about the overnight fire at the Georgia Railroad Freight Depot, more recently known as the Atlanta Joint Terminal Building, where he'd scooped his counterparts at the rival papers with some of his account, earning him a raise, it still wasn't the big crime story he craved. Other than the Muse's Store robbery in March and the subsequent capture of the three perpetrators in April, Matt had found nothing significant to write up. The funny thing was, as much as Matt craved a big crime spree, he felt some remorse knowing that such an event might well cause someone's injury or death. And he was having trouble getting past that guilt.

Crossing Peachtree Street to make his way down Decatur Street to police headquarters, Matt shook his head at the thought. He couldn't afford to feel too much regret about the misfortune of others when doing his job. As his city editor had put it when Matt had written the accounts of the events earlier in the month, "With all due respect to the dead, the suicide by carbon monoxide poisoning of a St. Louis paint salesman and a mysterious Alabama woman together in a car and the occasional bootleg liquor raid doesn't put ink in my pen." Whatever his boss had intended by the statement, Matt took it to mean that he had to find "meatier" stories for the paper. The problem for Matt was that the most salacious crime-related narratives seemed to keep coming across the Universal and the International News wire services. For example, how could he compete with the mid-January news flash of Ma Barker and her son Fred, both of whom had captured the country's attention for the last several years, being killed in a blazing shoot-out with Federal law-enforcement agents in Florida? Or vie with the Lindbergh kidnapping trial, which had kept the world riveted on the Hunterdon County Courthouse in Flemington, New Jersey, for thirty-two days in January and February? Or with the April first headline proclaiming that the U. S. Supreme Court had ordered a new trial for two of the Scottsboro Boys? Stories like these tended to titillate the readers far more than did the breaking up of a local illegal corn liquor ring. All Matt could do was tell what there was to report and "hope for the worst," as one of his fellow newsmen with the dubious moniker of "Brick" had told him.

---

Matt parked as close to the police station as he could and briskly walked the remaining distance. As he bounded up the steps and into the building, the desk officer glanced up from writing in his ledger and nodded. Matt returned the nod with a slight wave of his hand and moved past the front desk to the press room. The room was empty except for one of his competitors' newshounds in a disheveled suit, slumped over and asleep at a small desk. His stubbly mug suggested to Matt that something big was brewing and the man had been there for some time waiting for the story to break. Matt made a rather feeble attempt to rouse the man, but to no avail. Only his irregular snores gave any proof that life remained in the listless body of his opponent in the circulation wars. Grabbing the stack of overnight police reports, Matt quickly flipped through them, trying to find the source of the other man's "vigil." The only report of note was of three men who had staged an armed robbery at a filling station in Ringgold, Georgia, up near the Tennessee state line. They were now reportedly heading toward Atlanta. That had to be the story, Matt supposed. The rest of the reports were fairly routine, barely worthy of a small write-up. The only other incident report in the stack worth noting was that of an employee from the city tax collector's office being admitted to Grady Hospital for a gunshot wound to his ankle. The account said that he was wounded as he bent to slide a tax notice beneath a resident's door and his revolver slipped from its holster, fell to the floor, and discharged. Boy, Matt thought, I can hear the jokers at the paper now. And Mr. Fleming will have something to say, he was certain.

Reports in hand, Matt walked out to the desk officer. Extending the sheaf of papers, he asked the officer whether there were any more reports or any updates on the three robbers headed for Atlanta from North Georgia.

"Nah, that's it for the reports. And they think them three from Ringgold doubled back and headed to Chattanooga. At least that's the last we heard. The sheriff up there said he thinks they were picked up in Chattanooga, so he's goin' up there to have a look. As you can see, he got a pretty good description of two of 'em."

"Oh," Matt said, nodding toward the press room, "it just looked like Bud in there had been up all night waiting for some news item."

"Oh, he was up most of the night, all right." The older police officer paused to make a motion with his hand as if drinking from a bottle. "Came in here 'bout two or three hours ago. Staggered in there, passed out, an' ain't made a peep since. Don't wanna go home an' face the old battle-ax, I reckon. The cap'n said to just let 'em be. Too much paperwork if we lock 'em up. Besides, he ain't hurtin' nothin'. It ain't like the days when we kept a 'sleeper book,' ya know." Matt knew the officer to be referring to the days when many police departments kept a log of those down-on-their-luck men, and sometimes women, who would come into a station house and ask to sleep off a snoot full because they had nowhere else to go. The police logged them in and allowed them to sleep in a cell with no paperwork other than the entry in a small book. The system required much less effort and paperwork than sending a patrol wagon to haul someone away every time they were found lying drunk in the street.

Looking at the sparse material available to him for the next edition, Matt gave the officer his thanks and returned to the room occupied by his unconscious competitor. The man's snoring was louder now, with no indication of it diminishing anytime soon. As he made notes from the police documents, Matt looked over at the other man in the room and took little consolation in the fact that he may well scoop at least one writer from another paper.

Matt made his way back to his car and disgustedly tossed his fedora onto the front seat. He ran his fingers through his thick blond hair as he slid behind the wheel. He sat there for a minute, thinking that Barnes was not going to be happy if this is all he could muster for today's edition. Muttering to himself, Matt

*Matt Grimes' 1932 Ford Tudor*

stepped on the starter and pulled into Decatur Street's traffic. He turned onto Butler followed by a right turn to Hunter Street and made his way to the Fulton County Courthouse on Pryor Street.

His first stop at the courthouse was at Solicitor General Boykin's office on the third floor. John A. Boykin had been in office a long time and had endured some controversy, like allegations of being, at the very least, a Klan sympathizer. The man some considered the most feared man in the State of Georgia had also dealt with some difficult circumstances, including the murder of his chief investigator, Bert Donaldson, at the Georgian Terrace Hotel back in July, 1926. That had been before Matt's time at the paper. But, as far as Matt could tell, Boykin was a nononsense guy who took his responsibilities to the people, at least most of the people, seriously.

Once inside the prosecutor's office, Matt confirmed that the bills charging Joel Randall and his fellow arrestees with possession of burglary tools and explosives were to be presented to the Grand Jury that day. In addition, the day's calendar showed that bills charging the three men arrested for the Muse Clothing Store and Kress Store robberies with those crimes were scheduled. A robbery at Ben Hill was also pending against the trio. Finally, the solicitor's office confirmed that it was moving forward with disbarment proceedings against some local attorneys who had been convicted and sentenced for cheating and swindling. Things were already looking up, Matt thought, as he closed the solicitor's door behind him.

While on the third floor, Matt quickly stopped by the press room to see if anything else was going on that he could use. He gathered a few barely newsworthy morsels there and walked to the Fulton County Police Department office down the hall. He spoke briefly with a friend, an officer on the county's special squad involved with illegal liquor raids. Over time, they had developed something of a symbiotic relationship. The dedicated and ambitious policeman periodically gave Matt advance or inside information in hope of front-page write-ups or splashy headlines to promote the squad's work.

The police officer had been a key to the success of a raid earlier in the month. The squad, acting on "secret information," had visited the warehouse of a beer distributor where, they'd been told, a shipment of gin and whiskey had been received. Upon arrival, the squad couldn't find any trace of the liquor. While questioning employees of the warehouse, Matt's friend noticed that a piece of molding was missing from the edge of the linoleum floor covering. When the raiders pulled back the linoleum flooring, they discovered a four by five feet trap door. Beneath the door, the officers found a storeroom dug into the earth. The covert space contained eighty-six cases of assorted liquors.

Matt thought it was a great story and had given it a big play. Unfortunately, Mr. Barnes didn't see the liquor raids as significant news items. After cutting back on the write-up, he consigned it, as he did most other illegal liquor raids to secondary pages. He had occasionally reminded Matt of Al Capone's words that all he'd ever done was to supply a demand that was pretty popular. "Not a big deal," the editor would say, "particularly in light of the enactment of the 21st Amendment. Just because Georgia is refusing to repeal the prohibition on liquor doesn't make it a big story." Matt suspected that Mr. Barnes's heart was made a little sadder, his thirst slightly harder to quench with each successful raid. His city editor's approach to the write-ups had changed in March. Governor Talmadge signed a bill ending the state's Prohibition almost two years after Atlanta's city council had taken matters into their own hands. The council had passed a city ordinance for 'near beer' and wine. The decree took the raids from being a violation of the state's prohibition statute to being a violation of alcohol tax laws, as Matt understood things. But the city editor still didn't see the numerous raids as big news. Even so, Matt again promised the officer his best efforts to get the sought-after headlines and story placements. The *Georgian* correspondent finished his rounds at the Sheriff's office on first floor before checking by phone with a friend at the Federal Courthouse and driving to the newspaper offices on Marietta Street.

Back at the *Georgian* offices in a space just off the newsroom, Matt checked the wire services for any news that might have come in relating to his beat. A guilty plea had been entered in the kidnapping case of a prominent Minnesota banker, Edward Bremer, whose family had ties to the Schmidt brewing company. The abduction had been carried out by the Barker-Karpis gang, led in part by Doc Barker. With this turn of events, in addition to the deaths of his Ma and brother Fred, Doc's luck had soured. Another item caught Matt's eye as he read the print-offs further. The Bruno Hauptmann jurors had held a "reunion" dinner and square dance. For God's sake, he lamented, that story will probably make the front page before any of mine do.

When he'd finished scanning the wires, Matt sat at his desk and pounded on his old typewriter, composing the leads on the stories he'd gathered for the next edition. Pulling the last of the copy from his typewriter, the young journalist walked to the city editor's office and knocked on the door. Edward Barnes, a cigar clamped in his mouth beneath a thick-bridged nose in the center of his face, looked up from where he was bent over his desk. His editor often put Matt in mind of the cigar-chomping newspaper editor, played by Edward G. Robinson, in *Five Star Final*. Mr. Barnes had the same relatively short body shape, though Barnes was probably a spot taller, and the same ever-present stogie. The editor was on one of the candlestick telephones on his desk talking *at* someone, animatedly waving a hairy arm that extended from a rolled-up shirt sleeve. Through the glass enclosed office, from which he kept a careful eye on the comings and goings in the newsroom, Barnes saw his police beat reporter standing outside his door. The city editor waved his hand holding the phone's mouthpiece, indicating to the young man to come in. Matt opened the door, crossed the small office to his boss's desk, and waited. Barnes motioned him to a chair. "Okay, okay, give it a four column box," the older man growled into the telephone. "Use that picture of the crashed car we looked at. Headline over the photo and caption underneath. Fit the wire story in below the picture. Give it two columns. Make it look like something!" Barnes roughly replaced the receiver in its cradle and looked over his desk to Matt.

"Good morning, Mr. Barnes. I've got several items for the next edition. There's not a lot of meat here. Some, but not a lot. But it's all that's taken place overnight that we know of so far. Of course, they didn't discover the Muse robbery for several days, so there may be something else in the offing. But that doesn't do anything for today's edition."

"Morning, kiddo," the editor responded, his tenor tempered somewhat. He took the offered material from Matt, quickly read through it, and made notes with the blue pencil he always kept somewhere close by, usually behind one or the other ear. His hand holding the cigar beat a tattoo on the desk as he read. As his editor perused the material, Matt couldn't help reflecting on the situation in which he found himself. He liked the old man and was learning a lot about the job, but he felt so inadequate for the task sometimes. And underappreciated, too. And sometimes he thought all he did was run around town and peck at a typewriter. The editor is always Mr. Barnes to us younger reporters, he contemplated, but I'm just "kiddo" to him. He probably doesn't even recollect my name. The young man recalled reading that Babe Ruth always called people "kiddo" when he couldn't remember their names. Matt quietly moaned at this notion.

When Barnes returned his smoke to his mouth and scribbled marginal notes in what the reporter took to be a perturbed manner, Matt sat and further contemplated his situation. What am I supposed to do about my stories on the day's events? Matt grumbled to himself. Apologize for the lack of a juicy news item? Right now, the whole town's buzzing about three principal stories. First, there's a Methodist preacher advocating the repeal of Prohibition in violation of "church law," whatever that is. Then there's Talmadge's ranting about FDR's agricultural policies, specifically the processing tax on cotton. And last but not least, the city's abuzz about the opening of the Crackers' season. But those stories weren't doing him any good. They weren't his beat. As he sat there, Matt read again the placard on the wall behind Mr. Barnes desk. The editor called it a set of newspaper doctrines he'd picked up somewhere. "A newspaper has only four criteria: Publicity, Periodicity, Currency, and Universality."

Barnes removed the cigar from his mouth with all the affection of an old maid plucking a dead bud from her favorite plant. He pulled tobacco bits from the end of his tongue with his other hand. Flicking them haphazardly toward an ashtray, he looked up at Matt. "Okay. The probe of the fire department due to faulty hoses during Monday night's fire at the Warren Company on Fair Street is good stuff." The older man returned to reading the remaining leads.

After a few more minutes of making notes in the margins, he began handing the individual sheets from the stack of papers back to his correspondent as he ticked off the stories. "The rest of it sounds copacetic. Work up something good on the yegg squad charges before the Grand Jury, but not too lengthy. Just keep the public's interest. We don't want to wear out the readers on the subject before the trials come up. You still have an 'in' with that guy from the yegg squad, don't you?" The editor went on as Matt nodded. "Okay. Give the Randall bit enough of an article to run a photo with. You know, blah, blah, blah. Maybe we can twist a headline out of it. I think that there's one picture of the county cops looking over the contraband they seized from Randall's mob that we haven't printed yet. We'll use that. Just give the tax guy who accidentally shot himself a small treatment. You know, something sort of cynical. I think folks will love the irony in that one. Give a decent write-up to that Dekalb trial of the burglary gang. Make sure you work in the bit about the machine-gun battle at Snapfinger Creek with the gang before their capture. The readers'll devour it." Mr. Barnes sighed and shook his head as he continued, "The public hasn't lost its fascination with that Baby Face Nelson – Pretty Boy Floyd – John Dillinger gangster crap from last year yet." Again, the editor paused in reflection for a second. "They probably won't for a while, either. Not if Hollywood has its way."

"Write up something brief on the colored guy being sentenced for counterfeiting and about the drunken driver on Peachtree Street wrecking three vehicles and the other traffic mishaps. Put together a short piece about sentencing of the narcotic fugitive caught in Augusta after he'd escaped while awaiting trial in Federal court here. What's his name again?" Without waiting for an answer, which he often did, the editor moved on. "Compose something short on the transient from Florida losing his feet in the train accident at Union Station yesterday and the two Negroes sentenced for forging relief orders." Barnes paused for a breath and again looked up at his young journalist. "The stories aren't much, but they're a lot of 'em and we'll work 'em in."

As he spoke, the editor snapped the cigar from his mouth and examined the extinguished end of it as if a smoke had never gone out on him before. He dragged a fresh cigar from his shirt pocket, bit it, and put a match to it. Matt stood to leave. "By the way, here's a piece that isn't strictly in your ballpark, Matt, but I think you could give it a really good treatment. Show some cynicism. Fair but cynical, understand? Cynicism is a strong trait of any good journalist." Matt again nodded as his editor continued. "That's the ticket. I know you've got it in you." Barnes handed the young man a typed page of facts. The essence of the tale was about a local female chiropractor, who had been shot when a gun was accidentally dropped by a man building her an operating table. She sued him and was awarded one dollar. The man had to pay court costs. How many of these stories about accidental shootings by dropped guns can I do in one day? Matt wondered.

Matt hesitated to depart when he'd finished reading the last page he'd been given. "Sorry about the stories. That's all there was. It seems –"

"Oh, don't worry. We'll hold the extra edition for another day." The sarcasm bit Matt hard. The editor saw it in his face. In a more mellow tone, he continued, "Hey, it is what it is, Matt. Sometimes we simply have a slow news day. Or a busy day full of small stories. But it'll work for today. Tomorrow'll be better. Besides, between Talmadge, Mussolini, and the Georgia football player dying in that car wreck," the city editor said, looking down and carelessly shuffling through some papers on his desk, "there's no room on today's front page for a Negro counterfeiting fifty-cent pieces anyway." Matt thought that Barnes could be very crusty sometimes.

Matt hesitated again. "Seems like we're playing both sides against the middle on that fire department probe, Mr. Barnes."

The older man raised his eyes to his young employee and smiled slightly. He leaned back in his swivel chair and rocked gently, his fingers locked behind his head. "Do you recall, Matt, what I told when you first asked me for this job?" Matt felt that he'd been given so much information in such a short period of time back then that he had no idea what the editor was talking about. During his first month as a reporter on the newspaper, the novice was told so many things to absorb that he'd likened it to trying to drink water from a fire hose. Barnes was recalling his sage advice to the young man. "Sometimes your work here may require you to 'comfort the afflicted and afflict the comfortable.' It's just that simple. And remember, principles won't patch your britches, son."

Yeah. Crusty, all right, Matt reflected. "Yessir, Mr. Barnes. I understand." Matt thought he understood, anyway. Satisfied that the editor *did* know his name after all, Matt moved to his desk. As he sat, he wondered whether he'd ever fully get the hang of being a reporter. He looked around at the others busily working in the newsroom and studied them for a long moment. The babel of their chatter, some loud and strained, the clatter of their typewriters, and the noise of the wire service teletype bells ricocheted around the newsroom to him. Some were reporters to imitate and others were not his idea of what a member of the press should be. Okay but iffy. Matt smiled and waggled his head. Just like every profession, he guessed. He really wanted to be a top-notch journalist, but he wasn't certain whether it would ever come to him. Breaking his reverie, he lit a cigarette before he started writing his assigned articles.

The young man's thought process was interrupted when Mr. Barnes appeared a few minutes later and sat a hip on the corner of Matt's desk, swinging his lower leg to and fro. The editor's cigar dropped a large slough of ash on his desk. Barnes didn't seem to notice. "Say, Matt. I've given that story of yours about the fire department probe some thought. Like I said, it's good stuff. I've decided that it's front page material. Play up the unhappiness of the company president and his subordinate – what's his name? – and their demand for an inquiry about broken hoses. Also the company's claim that only one Fire Company initially responded. But, in fairness, make sure to work in the fact that – what was it, eight? – yeah, eight firemen had to be treated for injuries, et cetera, as a result. This is nothing more than a budget issue regarding money for new hoses and equipment. As I recall, the fire department had asked for $7,500.00 for new hoses and the finance committee gave them $2,500.00. Check those figures. But I think it rates a bigger-than-normal headline on page one. Too many people still around who remember the devastation of the so-called great fire in May, 1917. By the way, I hear that the fire department had to get hoses from a private company. If you don't know, check on that, too." The editor paused for a second, as if thinking about the piece, and gently pulled on an earlobe. The "earlobe pull" was known by everyone to indicate that Barnes was deep in thought. Just as quickly, he stopped the tug and concluded, "Give me a good article, son." The editor heaved himself off the desk and ambled back toward his office.

Matt's face split in an enormous grin at the opportunity to put a good story on page one. "Sure thing, boss. I'll check on the private company hose angle, too." Apparently, Mr. Barnes had gotten a haircut that morning at Mr. Herndon's barber shop. A black man, Alonzo Herndon, owned a barber shop a short distance north of Five Points on Peachtree Street. The establishment had been dubbed the "Crystal Palace" because of its amenities featuring porcelain, brass, and nickel fixtures and more than two dozen custom barber's chairs upholstered in dark green Spanish leather. Considered by many the swankiest barber shop in Atlanta and possibly in the entire South, it was frequented by only the best clientele. The patrons were exclusively white and predominantly wealthy, including Atlanta's businessmen, judges, doctors, lawyers, politicians, and ministers. Also to be included on that list were astute newspaper editors or veteran journalists, intending to pick up the latest off-the-record news tidbits being quietly bandied about among the customers. That is also to say, those newspaper people who could afford the price were customers there. Mr. Barnes could. Matt was relegated to his regular three-chair Pryor Street barbershop, where the art décor consisted of a gasoline station's calendar and the only connection to being Spanish the chairs had was their probable use in the Spanish Inquisition. The solitary brass present was an old, overused spittoon.

The city editor moved on, then stopped abruptly, turning back to face Matt. Placing his hands on his hips, Barnes called out, "Hey, I hear you're planning to go to the game today." Matt gave a quick nod, hoping that he wasn't about to hear the death knell of that idea. How would he tell Cliff? "Well, have fun. And check in with the city desk afterward."

"As usual, Mr. Barnes," Matt said, much relieved. He took one last drag from his smoke before crushing it out in the ashtray overflowing with cigarette butts on his desk.

Matt had each story well in mind as he set to work. However, he put additional effort into the fire department probe item since it was destined for the front page. When he finished fleshing out the stories at his typewriter, he snagged a copyboy who then walked the articles for the next edition to the copy editor's desk. The copy editor, a small and unimposing, bespectacled older guy named Clyatt Cowart, pushed aside the glue pot on his desk and ran through the usual check for format and style, his ubiquitous blue pencil in hand. Mr. Cowart's review was only the first of many steps Matt knew would occur before his stories hit the street in the next edition of the *Atlanta Georgian*.

---

After the short conversation at their initial meeting when Matt had applied for the open position of police beat reporter, Mr. Barnes opined that Matt only had an "*inkling* of what becoming a correspondent really meant." The young man recalled how the city editor had laughed at his intentional pun. Matt had chuckled, too, although his was more a nervous titter. He had really been sold on his chosen profession when Barnes walked him through the various functions and stages required to actually put a newspaper out to the public. From the various beat reporters, to the features, wire, copy, and city editors, then to the engraving and composing rooms and the stereotyping department and more, then ending with the press runs and the circulation department, the idea and process was something Matt had taken to immediately. He'd had a taste of the process during his short stint as a copyboy. That job was how he got his foot in the newspaper's door. He knew producing a newspaper was something of which he wanted to be a part.

---

As he waited for Mr. Cowart to finish his review of the fire department article, Matt's thoughts drifted back to the conflagration suffered by his hometown, Augusta, Georgia, in early 1916. He'd only been seven at the time, but the strong, gusty March winds that added greatly to the destruction were still vivid in his memory. The winds had been so strong, his momma told him later, that burned hymnals and prayer books from Augusta churches had been found across the Savannah River in Aiken County, South Carolina. The fire destroyed businesses and residences alike. His parents had provided shelter to a few of the some three thousand people left homeless by the blaze. The shock and heartache he'd seen in the faces of those who'd lost everything to the fire took the "adventure" out of having a house full of company for the little boy. The memory was one he'd not soon forget.

---

The young reporter was still sitting at his desk when Clyatt looked his way, smiled from under the dark-green eyeshade resting on his bony forehead, and gave him a thumb's up. Matt felt a sense of relief. Now on to Evie, Cliff, and the rest of the day, he celebrated to himself.

# CHAPTER 3

# Opening Day

After a quick lunch with Evie at the Woolworth's counter across the street from Davison's, Matt hustled down Ellis Street to Carnegie Way and his car in a parking lot there. Before heading back to the boardinghouse, the blond reporter had to make his afternoon rounds hurriedly so he could pick up Cliff at the appointed time. The various stops resulted in no new crime-beat stories to add to his morning's efforts. He checked in with the newspaper by telephone from his last stop. Matt was a few minutes late as he pulled up in front of 71 Houston Street. Cliff was waiting patiently on the front porch steps. As he approached the boy, reading a *New Fun* comic book, Matt smiled. The young journalist had heard something of the new publication. He was not sure exactly what the high school or college-aged pair of characters, Jigger and Ginger, was up to in the comic book. However, considering what he'd recently heard about the current campus shenanigans, he was pretty certain Miss Dixie would not approve her twelve-year-old son finding out. Matt avoided that topic altogether, asking instead about another of the publication's characters about whom he'd heard. "So what's Jack Woods up to now?"

Cliff looked up from under the bill of his Crackers baseball cap. "Aw, nothin' really excitin'. He's just fightin' some Mexican guy named

Miguel who works for some other Mexican guy named Nogales," he replied as he scooped up an edition of *Famous Funnies* lying beside him and jumped from the steps to greet Matt. With a look of impending gloom, Cliff rolled the comic books tightly and gazed at him. "We're still going to the game, ain't we?"

"I don't know any reason that we shouldn't. Do you?"

"No, Matt. I mean, Mr. Grimes. I'm ready! Momma said to tell you I've had lunch." The youngster slapped the rolled up comic books against his leg with excitement.

"But still a little hungry, right?" The boy smiled sheepishly. "Where's your jacket, Cliff?"

"It's over there," he responded, pointing to a windbreaker draped over the arm of a porch chair.

"Well, get it and let's go! Is your momma here?"

Cliff dropped the comic books in the chair and pulled on his jacket. "Nah, she went to pick up my sister and her two little terrors." Matt gave Cliff a look Miss Dixie would have been proud of. The young man was quick to respond and defend his comment. "Well, they are! Those two are always gettin' in my stuff when they're here. They're like Larceny Lu and Big Boy to my Dick Tracy!"

On occasion, Matt was struck by the maturity Cliff showed. Sometimes, he was like a midget in a twelve-year-old's clothes. "You wouldn't exaggerate would you, Cliff?" The boy merely frowned and pursed his lips in response. On other occasions, he was a typical twelve-year-old boy. "Never mind. C'mon, let's go!"

The guys walked the block and a half west to Peachtree Street with Cliff's eager pace leading the way. There, they caught a northbound streetcar near Loew's Grand Theater. The car was fairly crowded although Cliff found a seat in the last row of the fluid, imaginary line that separated the "white half" of the car from the "black half." Matt chose to stand beside his young charge rather than force the black woman seated just behind him to give up her seat. Rhamy's words from that morning kept ringing in his ears. The streetcar motorman marched back to where Matt stood and looked down at the older black woman seated there. Matt thought the man looked to be maybe a dozen years older than he was and about six inches shorter. The uniformed man held what the blond reporter thought to be a switch steering stick. Matt had seen these used to beat black passengers who violated racial "etiquette" by refusing to give up their seats when extra white passengers boarded the streetcars. In the past, he'd watched the occurrences without direct emotional involvement in them. Somehow, it was different in this moment.

Matt gazed at the man's menacing face and, then, for the first time, Matt looked at the woman. Really looked at her. She was a much older woman, petite to the point of appearing emaciated and frail. The woman peered back at the two men from hopeless-looking eyes, proud yet pathetic, set on a worn and weary black face. Then, she quickly turned her eyes to face the front of the car. The woman had an equally worn pocketbook and some sort of shopping bag in her lap. The switch stick, as it was commonly called, seemed to Matt to be far beyond what was necessary for even the short, wiry man who stood next to him to make any point to this small, unthreatening woman, despite her "offense."

"You gotta get up," the uniformed man growled, pointing to the sign in the front of the car. It read, "Colored seat from rear toward front. Whites seat from front toward rear."

"That's not necessary, sir," Matt said hesitantly, trying to recall whether motormen had near or outright police powers on the streetcars of Atlanta. They certainly had ready access to the police. Either way, all the streetcar man had to do was blow his whistle and a police officer would come running, ready to carry out his instructions. But he also recollected Rhamy's proclamation from earlier in the day.

"You tryin' to tell me my business, boy?" A cold smile played at the corners of his mouth.

"No, sir. What I'm saying is that I have a very bad back. It pains me something fierce when I sit down. I *need* to stand. I *have* to."

The streetcar man fixed his eyes intently on Matt's, studying his younger antagonist. A long moment passed. In that time, Cliff turned in his seat and looked up at Matt, confusion marking his face. His eyes widened in surprise at the situation. He'd never heard Matt say anything about a bad back. Meanwhile, the black woman sat stoically facing straight ahead. She had no say in the scene playing out before her. She was there to take direction, like it or not, at the whim of those around her. Finally, the motorman spoke harshly to no one in particular and, seemingly, to everyone. "All right, but she's gonna hafta get up at some point when somebody gets on."

Matt felt emboldened by the success of his stand. "Well, that'll be on somebody else then."

The motorman bowed up at Matt, as close to his face as the shorter man's height would allow. "And what does that mean, son?"

"It means that I have a bad back, and it hurts to sit down."

The streetcar man glared at Matt, and then glanced at the woman and Cliff, before returning his eyes to the young man standing next to him. Matt, for the first time during the confrontation, felt threatened. Not happy with the circumstances, the motorman, nonetheless, moved back to his position and got the car moving again. Others sitting nearby, both white and black, seemed to release a collective sigh in gratitude for the end of the little drama. Some of both groups looked between Matt and the woman with an assortment of thoughts and emotions shown on their faces. Matt worried briefly about how the whites in the crowd perceived him. Cliff continued to look up at his older friend with uncertainty in his eyes. Sensing that the boy was about to speak, Matt pressed a forefinger finger to his lips and winked. The black woman, who'd sensed the doubt in the Cliff's face, also looked up at Matt. Her expression was a blend of puzzlement and gratitude. Nothing more was said of the matter, however. The motorman was still giving Matt what his grandma would have called the "evil eye" when he and Cliff changed streetcars for the downhill run on Ponce de Leon Avenue.

The Ponce de Leon line's streetcar was packed with fans, all in a festive mood. The crowd was a noisy, rambunctious mob. Two older men were causing much of the noise in a friendly argument about the name of the ball field itself. They kept the packed car entertained debating across the aisle about the appropriateness of the name Ponce de Leon Park versus the more recent, though short-lived christening of it Spiller Field. The latter name was bestowed on it after Rell J. Spiller, who went from grocery clerk to wealthy concessionaire, entrepreneur, sports enthusiast, and club owner, rebuilt the grandstands with concrete and steel when the wooden ballpark burned in 1924. The stadium had reverted to its original name, Ponce de Leon Park, in 1933.

As the streetcar reached the bottom of the incline at Penn Avenue and began its rise toward Hunt Street, the two men kept up their friendly debate. While one of the men was a traditionalist and maintained that the old name was better and the ballpark's name should not be a monument to one man's ego, the other was just as adamant that the man who rebuilt it as a larger ball field with better seats than the old stadium benches should get credit for his investment.

After a minute or two of listening to the dispute on the car, Matt again pondered Rhamy's words about race relations from that morning and his upbringing and thoughts. Matt supposed he'd been brought up the way he thought many people were. His parents had their prejudices, make no mistake. They weren't Klan people by any stretch, but they had their biases. And they weren't shy about stating them, while maybe not seeing them as prejudices. But they also taught him things that weren't necessarily in line with their philosophies. They brought Matt up to treat others right and to take people as they came to him. Many times, Matt had heard people say this or that bad about a person, which might put him on guard about a man or woman he hadn't met yet. But, then when he'd meet them, they'd turn out to be fine people and not at all like they'd been described. So long as they didn't show Matt a different side, he was fine with them. At the same time, he might have had someone portray to him how wonderful a person was, and, then when he'd meet that person, he found them vile and nasty. So, Matt tended to take individuals as they showed themselves to him, how they treated him and acted around him. Their skin pigmentation didn't matter, because he'd known good and bad, both black and white.

Somehow, through it, Matt's background taught him that the Negro was somehow inferior to his race. Despite the attitude of his parents, the first funeral Matt ever remembered going to was for the black woman who'd raised his daddy while Matt's grandparents and the woman's husband and sons had worked their sharecropper patches. The young writer had his biases, too, like Rhamy, but he also had opinions that might not run the same as most of his fellow citizens. So, as Matt thought about it, he guessed one could say that he'd gotten mixed messages from his parents. Not *everything* his parents and their culture had taught him was wrong. Should he even care what the other white riders on that streetcar thought of him if he did what he considered right? Questions remained in Matt's mind. What is the answer and how do I apply it to my life?

Matt didn't have long to ponder the issue. As the streetcar approached Ponce de Leon Park, where the downward run bottomed out, the street crowd, moving in the same direction as the car, grew. And with them, the noise level also rose steadily. Matt smiled as he watched his young charge. Cliff's excitement was palpable, the incident with Matt's "backache" and the motorman long forgotten. Or so Matt supposed. As he gazed at the traffic congestion, Matt was very happy that he'd opted for the streetcar instead of driving. If this wasn't going to be a record crowd for the game, it'd be darned close to it, he thought. Once at the park,

Matt, Cliff, and most riders clamored off the streetcar. The sky was clear, the air cool and crisp. The day was almost perfect for a baseball game.

Matt and his young charge clicked through the turnstiles into the grandstands, where the rollicking mood was reaching even more of a crescendo. They found seats along the first-base line. While Cliff was impatient for the game to start, Matt watched the coming and goings on the field. Former Olympic diving champion, Georgia Coleman Gilson, and her husband appeared on the field. She was joined by a very shapely and attractive young woman wearing a Cracker sweater and a ball glove. The second woman, Matt learned, was Miss Louisa Robert, daughter of the Georgia Tech graduate, L. W. "Chip" Robert, who had recently been appointed Assistant Treasurer of the United States. Though her father had been a superior athlete while at Tech, Matt recalled, Louisa had also made a name for herself in the world of sports as a member of the 1932 United States Olympic swimming team.

Governor Talmadge, too, was on the field, bat in hand. After a long round of obligatory photographs among the participants, the coatless governor assumed a batter's position at home plate. Miss Robert took the mound to deliver the first pitch. In Matt's estimation, the woman seemed much more comfortable in her role than the governor did in his. That impression was reinforced when Miss Robert's first pitch thumped the left-handed-batting governor on the leg. Somewhere, Matt mused, FDR is laughing to himself. After a protest by Governor Talmadge, who claimed he'd not been ready for the throw, Miss Robert delivered another toss. This offering was hit back to the shapely pitcher, who, after momentarily bobbling the ball, made a throw to first base for the easy out as the crowd roared. Another snicker from the White House? Matt wondered.

This display had been preceded by much pomp and circumstance, which had included music from some bands, marching around the field with the ball teams in tow, the flag raising, the awarding of a very large cake to Mr. Earl Mann, former Ponce peanut vendor at twelve and current the vice president of the club. The festivities also involved the presentation of floral horseshoes to Claude Bond, the young Atlanta native making his Southern League umpiring debut, and to the beloved, longtime veteran ump Steamboat Johnson. Matt recalled that the man's famous moniker came about during his first visit to Atlanta in 1919, in the days before loudspeakers when the umpire had to announce the starting batteries for the teams. His deep and loud voice was likened by the *Georgian's* sports editor, Ed Danforth, to that of a Mississippi steamboat. Mr. Danforth had written that he'd be "Steamboat" Johnson to Atlantans from that point on. The nickname stuck. The yarn was a matter of pride for the many baseball fans at the paper and was retold often in some form. Its telling always delighted the beloved veteran sports editor.

Matt loved baseball and delighted in the whole spectacle. All in all, the pregame revelry was everything it'd been advertised to be. Although fairly short of Cliff's estimation of "almost a million people," the journalist was still amazed at the size of the crowd, even for a season-opening game.

Finally, to Cliff's great satisfaction and the crowd's approval, the Crackers took the field under the leadership of manager-third baseman Eddie Moore, the former four-letter athlete at St. Stanislaus College. Matt was suitably impressed with how spiffy they looked in their new white home uniforms with red numbers and red and black caps. The *Georgian* reporter saw that the pitching matchup, too, was an interesting footnote to the game. The Smokies' starting hurler was Clarence "Climax" Blethen, formerly of the Crackers, while the Atlanta team opened with Harry Kelley, who had long been a thorn in the Crackers' side as an opposing pitcher for other teams, most recently Memphis. When Blethen took the mound for the Smokies, a man behind Matt and Cliff shared a story about Blethen, which he swore to be the truth as he knew it. Supposedly, as the man told the anecdote, the forty-something-year-old Blethen had false teeth, and he carried them in his hip pocket during games. At some point during a game a few years earlier, Blethen had been compelled to slide into a base. When he did, the teeth somehow bit him in the butt, an injury that bothered him the rest of that game. The story made baseball lore. The tale brought a shout of laughter from all within earshot. The satisfaction derived by the nearby Cracker fans was compounded by the three runs the home team pushed across in the bottom of the first inning.

The game progressed very agreeably for Cliff, Matt, and the rest of the Atlanta fans: the right-handed Kelley pitched a great game; first baseman, Harry Taylor, was brilliant with his fielding exploits; and the big Hawaiian playing center field, Harry Oana, who Matt later learned was playing in his first opening-day game in his six years in league baseball, had four RBIs. One of Oana's hits was a towering home run in the seventh inning that landed among a cheering throng of black fans in the left-field stands. More than a few proud Crackers' fans began to file out even before the Smokies came to bat in their half of the eighth inning, but Cliff was determined to stay until the last pitch. And so they did. When the dust settled, the Crackers, with thirteen hits, were victorious in their home opener against Knoxville, nine to zero.

*Atlanta Crackers' Opening Day, 1935*

As Matt and his landlord's son were leaving their seats at the game's end, a minor incident put a damper on an otherwise great afternoon for Matt. When he moved into the aisle, Matt made room for Cliff to get into the walkway also. In doing so, Matt stepped back and onto the foot of the man behind him, causing the man to stumble slightly. When he turned around to apologize, Matt faced a short, large-eared, hawk-nosed man, who wore a superbly tailored three-piece suit topped by a distinctive tall-crown fedora. He also bore an unfriendly expression. The man's much larger companion reached around the shorter man and, with one of his huge hands, shoved Matt, snarling, "Watch it, buster!" For the second time that afternoon, Matt felt a personal threat coming from a complete stranger. His frustration at the situation rose. Although Matt was not a brawler, he wasn't accustomed to getting pushed around either. The big man looked the tall reporter over as if he were measuring him for a coffin.

Looking between the two men, Matt said firmly, "I was about to say that I'm sorry, mister. No need to get tough about it."

The smaller man fashioned a menacing smile, showing a glint of small white teeth, and interceded. He raised the back of his open hand to his large companion's chest as the intimidating man moved toward Matt. "It's all right, kid. No harm done," he said in a voice with a lot of silk in it. Turning to his friend, the man then quietly said, "Everything's okay, Walt. You've got enough on your plate already without gettin' into a scrap here. Let it go."

"Whatever you say, Eddie," his bear-of-a-man cohort drawled grudgingly. The man's intimidating face changed to a mirthless grin that showed a hint of danger.

With the words of the shorter man, the episode ended. Matt was both annoyed at the incident and relieved that it didn't go further. Who the hell were these guys, anyway? he fumed. Some days, it seemed the whole world was ready to fight at the drop of a hat for no reason. Matt blew it off, glancing at his strap watch, and now focused on getting his young charge fed and home. They departed the park with the rest of the happy horde.

---

A short time later, the pair climbed down from their streetcar at Peachtree Street and crossed to the west side of the roadway for the short walk south to Rector's Café. Cliff stopped his replay of the game long enough to ask Matt where they were going. The young journalist pointed a short distance down the sidewalk to a sign, which had the word "Rector's" arched above the vertical word "Café," jutting from the building. The boy was slowly reading the sign to himself when they entered the building. Despite having consumed what Matt thought was an incredible number of peanuts during the game, Cliff said he was hungry. Both opted for the daily special, and the entire meal was spent with the boy continuing his recount of the game.

Matt readily recognized that the young man, a lanky southpaw and, therefore, likely destined to spend much of his playing time at first base, was particularly captivated by the play of the Crackers' first baseman, Harry Taylor. He grinned at Cliff's exuberance as the boy recalled Taylor's ability to stretch for the ball when necessary. From watching a few of Cliff's sandlot games on a Saturday here and there, he knew Cliff to have more than a fair amount of talent in his own right. The young reporter decided that it was a good thing that their seats had been on the right-field side of the grandstands even if they'd been in the shade and a little chillier than he'd hoped. Matt glanced at his wristwatch and, because of his charge's rambling description of the game, realized that they were going to be later than he'd intended getting home. He eased the Cliff through the meal as best he could whenever the young man stopped his replay to take a breath or a bite.

---

Cliff and Matt walked through the boardinghouse's front door just after eight o'clock that evening. The warmth of the house was a welcomed relief from the constantly falling temperatures of the evening. The boy immediately set off to find his daddy and, no doubt, to provide another play-by-play of the game. As he latched the screen door and closed the entry door behind him, Matt heard the crooning of Bing Crosby on the boardinghouse's new Philco 45 F console radio coming from the parlor. Recently, Miss Dixie had replaced her old 1930 Crosley cathedral-style table radio with the new Philco console. The event was filled with all the excitement and fanfare of the launching of a new battleship. The Crosley, in turn, was carried across the hall to the Fleming family's smaller parlor. The secondary parlor was only used when Rhamy wanted to listen to some sporting event or a political speech of no interest to the rest of the household. Matt expected to join Mr. Fleming at that radio to listen to the Baer-Braddock fight coming up in June.

Yep, Matt thought, as Bing finished "I Wished on the Moon," eight o'clock on Tuesday evening and Bing Crosby on the Georgia Tech radio station. Like clockwork. Too bad that Russ Columbo had lost the "Battle of the Baritones." Of course, Matt reconsidered, too bad about Columbo's tragic, premature death, too. Before Matt even looked in the parlor's doors, he could set the room's scene in his mind. The third-floor residents of the household would all be seated as close to the radio as possible, nearly swooning. What was there about this Crosby guy? Matt mused on the thought. Sure, he had a nice voice, but his just wasn't a mug Matt thought girls would go as batty over as they did. He'd felt the same about Rudy Vallee and see how that went? So what do I know? Matt reflected. Who can figure women? Anyway, Melvyn would be lightheaded, too, but not at Bing's vocal renditions. He'd be clandestinely watching the object of his hidden ardor, Amanda, from across the room behind an evening edition other than the *Georgian*. Given the radio program being aired, Joshua would probably be in his room. Mr. Fleming would be in the far corner, reading a magazine or a book while Miss Dixie would probably be in the kitchen, still cleaning up after supper or planning the next meal. No one would be helping her. Because Miss Dixie believed she was the only one who could do the job the way she wanted it done, the landlady preferred to go it alone.

As he entered the parlor, the scene was what he'd imagined. The three younger female boarders had chairs pulled up reasonably close to the radio. Amanda, the oldest of the quartet, was on the nearby divan, a respectable distance for a "more mature woman," but within swooning distance nonetheless. Melvyn was at the parlor's card table, lurking behind the evening news. Cliff was excitedly moving around in front of his dad's chair in the far corner, explaining the unassisted double play made by the Crackers' first baseman in the eighth inning. Matt approached them as the youngster was finishing his replay of the game by telling his dad about the prizes the different players had won for their various feats. "And one guy got a watch for driving in the first run, and the second baseman got some clothes and stuff just for hitting the first two-bagger," he shared excitedly. "Boy, I could have a whole chifforobe full of clothes!"

Rhamy, who wanted to return to reading the magazine resting on his lap, tried to calm the boy while implanting some parental advice. "I have no doubt that you can play the game, son. But I reckon maybe you need to be a little less boastful about your skills. Remember that the best spokesman for that is your play on the field." As Cliff nodded his understanding and apologized, Rhamy told him to go see his momma. Cliff hurried through the dining room and across the hallway to the kitchen. His excitement had not waned.

Mr. Fleming looked up at Matt and grinned. "So, how was the day, Matt? Did he behave himself?"

"Oh, yeah, he was fine, Mr. Fleming. And I think he had a really good time."

Rhamy shot a fleeting look over his shoulder in the direction Cliff had rushed and chuckled. "Yeah, I believe you can say that again. He probably won't sleep tonight! Sounds like it was a great game. Anybody put a ball into the magnolia tree in center field?"

"It was a great game. And, no, sir. Only one homer was hit, and Oana sent that to left field. Sorry that we're so late getting home. The stop for supper took longer than I expected."

Rhamy grinned and nodded again in Cliff's direction. "Well, with the junior Red Barber in attendance, I can imagine it did. He'd rather play or talk baseball than eat, any day!" Again, Rhamy beamed, swelling with pride as he spoke of his son. "Oh, Miss Dixie wanted to see you when you got in. And thanks again, Matt." When Matt smiled and nodded, Mr. Fleming went back to reading an old copy of the now-defunct *Mystery League* magazine, bearing a damsel in distress inside the silhouette of a lion on the cover.

"Sure thing, Mr. Fleming." Because Bing was in the middle of "It's Easy to Remember," Matt gladly departed the room. The song was touted in the newspaper advertisements for *Mississippi* and reminded Matt of his date for the coming weekend. While I love spending time with Evie, I sure hate the idea of missing Harlow, Matt lamented, as he left the parlor and walked down the hall to the kitchen door. Miss Dixie and her daughter, Ruth, were sitting at the side table, shelling peas. Matt had almost forgotten that Ruth and the girls were coming to visit. "Hello, Ruth, Miss Dixie. Mr. Fleming said you wanted to see me."

Ruth smiled faintly. "Hello, Matt. How've you been?" She looked very tired.

"Fine as frog's hair, thanks. How are the girls? How are you feeling?"

"They're better, thank you. They're upstairs asleep, thank goodness. Well, they are if Cliff and Freckles didn't wake them loping up the stairs. And I'm fine, thanks."

Miss Dixie got to her feet and moved to a metal cake saver atop the stove. "Matt, I have a piece of orange cake left for you from supper. Are you interested?" She grinned, knowing the answer. "If, by chance you are, take a seat."

"You know I am!" Both the women smiled. Matt again recalled how pretty Ruth was despite her weary demeanor now. She probably favored her mother's youthful appearance, before the burdens of life had overtaken Miss Dixie. Matt took a chair at the kitchen table. "What about Cliff? Did he get any cake?"

Miss Dixie laughed as she returned to the table and put a fork and a plate with a generous slice of cake in front of Matt. As she walked to the refrigerator to get Matt a glass of milk, she spoke over her shoulder. "Lands sakes, yes! That boy's had his. He was like a hound dog with a pork chop. It was gone that fast."

Matt took his first bite of unexpected treat and beamed, savoring the delicious flavor. No Merita Cakes for Miss Dixie, he thought. Thank goodness!

When he'd finished the cake, Matt quickly washed his plate, fork and glass and set them in the drying rack by the sink. Despite Miss Dixie's past protests about Matt feeling obligated to clean up after himself, they'd reached an understanding. Matt had been brought up to do it and supposed his future wife would expect it. While his landlady made it clear that he didn't have to do so in her house, she was very grateful for the effort.

Before going upstairs, Matt made a quick telephone call to Evie. During their brief conversation, she sighed in a moaning sort of way she sometimes did. The sound of it stirred him. After a moment's silence, they stammered through a confirmation of their dinner-and-movie date for Saturday night and rung off the line with a promise to speak in the meantime.

As Matt disconnected from his call with Evie, he found he needed to draw a deep breath and compose himself before telephoning the paper. He looked around sheepishly as he dialed the number. The call was going through when Mr. Fleming brought Matt that afternoon's edition of the *Georgian*. In the excitement of the day, he'd almost forgotten his article. In truth, he hadn't forgotten. It simply hadn't come to mind yet. The older man smiled broadly, nodded, and gave Matt a solid pat on the back. The young boarder mouthed a thank-you to his landlord as Rhamy walked into the kitchen. Like Mr. Barnes had said, Matt's account of the fire department probe was on the front page and continued on the second page. The young journalist beamed with pride.

Matt reached the night desk man, who offered him his congratulations on a very good piece of writing in the fire department story. The young man swelled with pride again as he thanked his older coworker. To Matt's relief, nothing of note was going on at the moment. After explaining he could be reached at the boardinghouse for the rest of the night, Matt finished the call and climbed the stairs to his room, carrying the paper with him. He was ready for some sleep. Maybe Harlow, Crawford, or even Miss Lombard might come calling in his dreams tonight. That happy thought brought a grin to his face as he walked the second-floor hall to his bed. He was still thinking of the femme fatales when he eased into bed. In the middle of a smile, he fell asleep.

# CHAPTER 4

# Crime and Romance

The next morning seemed to come much earlier than usual for Matt. He'd had a fitful night's sleep, visited not by the starlets for which he'd hoped but by threatening figures wearing fedoras and dapper, three-piece suits and in motormen's uniforms. Shaking off the images, Matt quickly prepared for the day. Back in his room, he removed his suit pants from the straightback chair where he'd drowsily draped them the night before instead of hanging them in the wardrobe. Fully dressed now, he checked his appearance in the room's small mirror and opened his bedroom door. Mr. Fleming was leaving Cliff's room, across the hall from Matt's.

The landlord stopped and asked Matt, "Have you seen Hafta this morning?"

"No, sir, I didn't see or hear him, so I figured he was still asleep."

"Not a chance! He's still too excited from the seeing the Crackers' game with you yesterday. I thought I heard him moving around earlier, but now I can't find the rascal. And I know him too well to think he's already doin' his morning chores." Mr. Fleming paused in thought for a second, and then moved down the hall. "See you at breakfast."

Matt closed his door and followed Mr. Fleming down the stairs.

At the customary hour, the boardinghouse occupants were clustered around the breakfast table. Rhamy was later than usual taking his place at the head of the table. He was followed into the dining room by Cliff, who turned to toss his ball glove back into the hallway before sitting at the table. Matt chuckled to see the youngster bearing a baseball glove at this early hour. Mr. Fleming was right. The household dug in to the pancakes and bacon being served by Miss Dixie, and the conversation flowed. Rhamy was gently chiding Cliff for his early-morning "workout." "You just can't start bouncing a ball off the side of the barn and catching it at daybreak, son. I don't want the neighbors or the boarders complaining about the noise. You need to be considerate of others. Besides, wasn't it a tad chilly this morning for baseball?"

"Aw, I just *have* to practice! It wasn't *that* early. Or *that* cold. Baseball players have to be tough! And I wanna to be ready when the Crackers need a new first baseman!" Cliff's exuberance for the game had been notably increased by yesterday's outing. He was deadly earnest.

"I thought I heard a thumping noise coming from out back early this morning," Melvyn put in. He never missed an opportunity to be a wet blanket.

Rhamy smiled thinly and shifted his attention back to his son. "Well, I'm sure you'll have plenty of time for that, Cliff. From what you told me last night, it sounds like Taylor's gonna be at his position for awhile."

"Won't you mess up your baseball by throwing against a wall like that, Cliff?" Victoria asked.

"Nah, I was using a tennis ball. It's only practice anyhow." Cliff swirled the large chunk of pancake on his fork around in syrup before plunking it in his mouth.

Amused, as always, at the shenanigans of the child, Diane joined the exchange. "Wherever did you get a tennis ball, Cliff?"

"Oh, I traded for it with Raymond Grigsby."

Cliff's response caught Miss Dixie's attention. Fearing the disappearance of some relatively valuable household article, she arched an eyebrow and asked, "And what exactly did you trade, young man?"

Unaffected by the implications of the question, Cliff nonchalantly answered, "Just an ol' comic book and a lizard." As relief swept over his mother, the rest of those assembled snickered.

"Well, we're gonna play 'beno,' Cliff. Okay?" Mr. Fleming said firmly.

Cliff nodded his understanding. "Yessir."

"Beno?" one of the girls asked.

"Yes," Mr. Fleming responded, showing that winning grin of his. "There'll *be no* more of that early-morning practice." Again the there were chuckles around the table. Mr. Fleming's sense of humor and wordplay were a source of amusement to all.

"Matt, are you still looking for a new Easter suit?" Joshua inquired, making a bid to outfit his fellow boarder for the coming holiday. "I can get you a good suit with extra trousers, a new shirt and tie, and even a new felt hat in a pastel shade, if you want one, for a good price. Instead of extra suit trousers, you could get a pair of coordinating slacks, if you want."

The young writer was still trying to navigate that nether world between sleep and consciousness. He took long drink of coffee. His dance dates with Evie earlier in the month had put a dent in his wallet, but he did need a new suit, as his girlfriend kept reminding him. A pastel hat sounded a bit much, though, Matt considered before responding, "Oh yeah? How much would that set me back?"

"Depending on which suit you choose, starting at around forty to forty-five dollars."

"Ouch!" Matt winced.

"Keep in mind that Hirsch Brothers has a payment plan. You can make three payments of one-third each on the tenth of the next three months." The deal sounded better to Matt already. Without a doubt, Joshua was a salesman.

Melvyn threw in his two cents' worth. "Say, that sounds pretty reasonable to me. I might even come in to see you myself, Josh."

Joshua, who'd always made it very clear that he didn't care for the shortened version of his first name, ignored the piano salesman and came back to Matt. "If you get a chance, Matt, come by Whitehall Street and see me."

"I might do that, Joshua," Matt replied, emphasizing the man's first name. "Thanks." The young men exchanged smiles and nods.

"So, how's your back feel this morning, Matt?" Mr. Fleming inquired with a wry grin.

Initially, Matt was confused. "My back?"

"Did you hurt your back?" Miss Dixie and Diane spoke over one another, asking the same question.

Before Matt could respond, Mr. Fleming continued, "Yeah, Cliff told me about it this morning. He said that it was bothering you yesterday on the streetcar." Matt caught the older man's grin and wink as the others gazed at him in puzzlement.

A little embarrassed, Matt chuckled and gave a quick look to Cliff, who seemed oblivious of everything but sopping up as much butter and syrup as possible with his remaining pancake morsels. Matt returned to Mr. Fleming. "Oh, that. Yes, it's fine now. Thanks. It was only a momentary spasm." The older man said that he was glad to hear about it. Matt merely nodded in reply. A few seconds later, the two men traded knowing, lowered glances.

As the meal was concluding, Miss Dixie said she needed to get moving so she'd be ready when Ruth and the girls came downstairs. The landlady had decided to let them sleep as long as possible because none of them had gotten much rest lately. On cue, Cliff began clearing the table as the household disbanded.

A short time later, the newsman closed the screen door behind him and charged down the boardinghouse steps into the cool morning air. Atlanta was rapidly reaching that time of the year, Matt contemplated, when the mornings were chilly enough to call for a jacket. Unfortunately, a person would be carrying the coat around, not wearing if he could help it, in the warmth of the afternoon sun. Soon enough the cooler days would give way to the oppressive heat and humidity of an Atlanta summer.

Matt made his Wednesday morning rounds, but the pickings were slim. Aside from the follow-up stories about the continuing fire department probe and the "Snapfinger Creek gang" trial, there was little in the way of local crime for Matt's beat. Some wire stories, like the continuing kidnapping trial in Minnesota or the recapture of Raymond Hamilton, a condemned Texas outlaw who'd killed a prison guard when he'd escaped custody, were more appealing than anything the young local police beat reporter could offer. A road bandit here, a few automobile crashes there was all in the way of copy to hand to Mr. Barnes. The city editor looked over Matt's leads and halfheartedly threatened to send him to cover the big Atlanta Food Show opening the next day for lack of something better for him to do. "After all," he reminded Matt, "the fire department's band is playing there tomorrow evening and the police department's band will be there Saturday. Those guys are on your beat, right?"

Matt felt his face redden as he gave his boss a shoulder movement, a hint of a shrug. Obviously, he wouldn't refuse an assignment, but he didn't want to be condemned to covering "the latest method of serving cereal" at the food show either. "I'm doing the best I can, Mr. Barnes."

"I know, son. Just keep plugging. Your day will come," the older man said with a reassuring smile. He handed the leads back to his reporter. With that, Matt returned to his desk and, as the grizzled veteran correspondent Brick had once termed it, tried to make "chicken salad out of chicken crap."

It didn't seem all that important either way. Much of the next edition was coverage of the Crackers opener anyway. The local baseball coverage even overwhelmed a piece about Dizzy Dean, of Matt's beloved St. Louis Cardinals, being injured during a game on Tuesday. When he'd finished his stories, the young man left the building and walked out onto Marietta Street's busy scene under forbidding skies and the continuing cool temperature.

With the day wearing him down, Matt decided to take care of a personal item that he hoped might also make him feel a little better. He stopped by Hirsch Brothers on Whitehall Street. He met with Joshua, who walked him through the selection of a new suit. After talking it over, Joshua persuaded Matt that gabardine would be most appropriate for his line of work because it would probably wear better than the other options. Matt opted for the extra pair of trousers instead of the "harmonizing slacks" offered by the store. He also picked out a new dress shirt and a silk Ottoman tie to go with the navy-blue suit. However, he passed on the "feather-weight, pastel-colored felt hat" Joshua offered. After Matt signed up for Hirsch's three-month payment plan, the two young men shook hands in mutual appreciation. As Matt left the store, he pondered his decision. He wasn't conflicted about the suit he'd bought. With that, he was well satisfied. His anxiety lingered because he'd never "charged" anything, as the store described their "purchase plan." The thought of it made him a bit uneasy. Mixed emotions filled his mind and cut short any possible uplift he'd hoped for.

Matt's afternoon circuit was no more productive of newsworthy items than the morning effort had been. Eventually, he traveled back to Houston Street. The rain showers promised by George Mindling, the local weather sage, had moved into the area by the time Matt pulled his car to the curb in front of the boardinghouse. He dashed from the Ford and scampered up the steps to the front porch, where he lingered and lit a cigarette with a flourish. For the moment, the rain dripped softly from the house's eaves to the azaleas. The air was still chilly, but the combined effect of the rain, the cool air, and the cigarette was pleasant. Matt relaxed on the porch swing. From the other side of the closed living-room window next to the swing, he could hear the radio as Little Orphan Annie and Sandy made their way through another adventure. Matt heard at least one "Gee whiskers" come from the Philco, which backed up to the window. The young reporter pictured Cliff sprawled on the rug in front of the radio, rapt in the tale's plot, whatever it might be. The downpour increased slightly in its intensity as the temperature dropped. He needed to see Evie something fierce. She was always able to pick up his mood when he was down in the mouth. If this rain let up, he decided, he'd call her and invite her for a drive, maybe a Coke at The Varsity or somewhere. Soon, Matt heard Miss Dixie's call to supper. He tossed the butt of his cigarette over the porch rail into the azaleas and went inside.

The absence of Joshua at the table made room for Ruth, while her girls ate at the kitchen table. Sporadic peals of little-girl laughter crossing the hall to the dining room made Miss Dixie nervous. She fretted over the possibility of Freckles, ensconced under the table, bothering the girls while they tried to eat. Ruth assured her mother that the opposite was most likely the case and that the girls would be fine. Further, Ruth proposed that they let things be and she would clean up whatever mess resulted. As usual, the evening mealtime was a social occasion with one and all catching up with everyone else's lives.

After a superb meal of fried chicken, mashed potatoes, green peas, and cornbread, followed by chocolate pudding, Matt telephoned Evie. Because the rain had not let up, she suggested that he come to her house for a visit instead of them going for a drive somewhere. Matt accepted the invitation, but with hesitancy he couldn't explain, even to himself.

Matt was already feeling disheartened by his day. A visit to Evie's gorgeous family home in Ansley Park later that evening didn't brighten his spirits like he'd hoped. Evie's father, Wilmer, a senior executive with the telephone company, and her mother, Maryse, a nurse at Grady Hospital, always greeted him warmly and made him feel at home. Despite that and notwithstanding spending time with his girlfriend, the feelings of inadequacy that Matt harbored about being able to provide for Evie in a manner to which she was accustomed kept his spirits low. His girlfriend had often chided him about such thoughts. During the visit with Evie and her parents, they planned to meet and attend Easter Sunday church services together at the Nash family church. Evie's parents also invited the young reporter to join them for dinner at the Piedmont Hotel afterward.

The rain was merciless as Matt turned onto Houston Street and parked his car in front of the boardinghouse. Inside, Matt found a scene of domesticity. Mr. and Mrs. Fleming, Teresa, and Ruth sat in the round-backed chairs that circled the parlor card table, playing Parcheesi. Victoria sat nearby, leisurely turning the pages of a *Photoplay* magazine with the beguiling Myrna Loy on the cover. Guy Lombardo and his Royal Canadians filled the room with "Did You Ever See a Dream Walking?" from the radio. Cliff was sprawled on the floor with a comic book. Miss Dixie felt compelled to account to Matt for everyone by explaining that Amanda was upstairs, Joshua was still out, and Diane was on a date with "that man." Exhausted, Matt said goodnight to the group and excused himself. He dragged himself through his preparations for bed. The Sandman was beating the heck out of Matt. Sleep came quickly.

---

Matt awoke Thursday morning to Mr. Fleming's report that the Crackers had fallen to the Smokies in Knoxville the day before, nine to three. In reaction, much to everyone's amusement, Cliff spent breakfast grumbling about the lost chance for a Crackers' perfect season. Before the gathering dispersed, Miss Dixie announced that Ruth and the girls would be going home that afternoon. The three were well rested and feeling much better. Floyd was scheduled to return home from the road the next day, and Ruth wanted to be there to greet him.

Matt's circuits of the law-enforcement agencies and the courthouses that morning and for the rest of the week yielded few noteworthy stories of interest to his area of responsibility. Only one item rated a smile from the city editor. That Thursday morning at ten, the Atlanta Board of Firemasters launched an investigation of the Fair Street fire, which gave Matt a short item at the bottom of page one and follow-up articles thereafter. The city expected a pitched battle between the Warren Company representatives and Fire Chief Parker. And, as it turned out, they got it.

All the other stories on Matt's beat during the rest of the week amounted to what Mr. Barnes ungraciously called "filler." One intriguing, yet unresolved case was that of a woman, who had been missing from her Lee Street home for ten days after her bloody coat had been found on Fair Street. Another titillating matter involved a dispute in recorder's court over the respectable duration of a good-bye kiss between a husband and wife. Acknowledging that he was a bit old-fashioned, the judge had commented that, in his day and time, a four-minute kiss was a tad too long but dismissed the case anyway. A Superior Court judge granted a mistrial in a murder case when three defense witnesses were shy about responding to their court summonses. On the lighter side, two girls, mistaking a fire alarm box for a mailbox when trying to mail a letter, turned the handle on the firebox, thus setting off a false alarm. After two Atlanta fire companies responded, a fire department captain gave voice to the question of how a person who could write a letter could not read well enough to tell the difference between a fire alarm box and a letter box. Meanwhile, in Federal Court, another round of trials for liquor law violators was continuing.

A second Superior Court judge sentenced a Peachtree Street newsstand operator and an unemployed moving picture operator for the sale of lascivious literature and the showing of an obscene moving picture, respectively, in separate cases. Matt pointed out in his article that, after the entry of guilty pleas, the confiscated film, titled *The Gay Count*, was screened in the presence the court, the prosecutors, the defense counsel, and investigators. The participants were also shown "a quantity" of the seized literature and photographs. No one reported whether the rest of the court's daily calendar was thereafter "postponed." Of course, there were the ubiquitous traffic accidents and injuries in the week's fodder that made up the only other reportable material available. With stories like these to report, Matt felt his presence as a correspondent at the Atlanta Food Show was not beyond the realm of possibilities. He could almost smell the food and hear the bands as he approached Mr. Barnes each day.

For the moment, the world still seemed topsy-turvy as The League of Nations censured Germany for its rearming, a seventeen-year-old California girl gave birth to triplets while her husband was a guest of their county jail for one hundred eighty days, Bruno Richard Hauptmann's lawyers squabbled over defense funds, and Governor Talmadge continued his harangue against FDR and his New Deal as Georgians suffered through the continuing consequences of the Great Depression.

Despite its chaotic nature, the world of news did provide Matt and others a good laugh occasionally. Friday evening, as the boardinghouse gathered for supper, Melvyn mentioned that he'd heard on the radio that one hundred eighty-five men had started the running of the Boston Marathon earlier that day. "They're gonna have to either limit the number of people running in the thing or stop it altogether. You plainly can't manage that many people in a single race. It's not possible!" he exclaimed.

"Oh, I don't know about that," the normally restrained Joshua put in. "The Holy Scriptures tell us that more than 600,000 people raced the Pharaoh to the Red Sea, and they made it all right."

As Rhamy guffawed, the discussion now captured virtually the entire table's attention. Before the red-faced piano salesman could respond, Diane interjected, "Just wait until women begin entering the race, Melvyn. Then the number will be a lot higher than one hundred eighty-five."

"Don't be ridiculous, Diane. A marathon is something like twenty-six miles long. That distance is far too great for a woman to run. They're too fragile! It will *never* happen!" Melvyn insisted. Rhamy and Matt, both amused at this episode, caught the momentary look Melvyn gave Amanda in hope that he hadn't overstated his case against female runners. For her part, Amanda appeared to be a thousand miles away, oblivious of the conversation. A brief, poignant silence marked the moment. The plump piano player swallowed hard and, bearing a supercilious grin, went on undeterred, "I mean, after all, a woman has her proper place. And a manly sport is not it."

"Yeah, well, don't tell Babe Didrikson that!" Victoria had joined the fray. Teresa laughed aloud.

"Who's that?" Melvyn demanded.

"You'll find out, Melvyn. You'll find out soon enough!"

Outnumbered and outgunned, Melvyn Briggs meekly, quietly withdrew from the "field of battle," and supper ensued.

———

Saturday evening finally rolled around. Evie and Matt went to see *Mississippi* at the Paramount Theater amid the bustling activity along rainy Peachtree Street. Watching the downpour, which had been a constant the last several days, Matt wondered aloud whether the Crackers would ever play another home game. Evie joined in his amusement at the thought and added, "Cliff will certainly be upset if that happens. He may never get his chance at the first-base position." Matt had shared with his girlfriend the story of the youngster's dreams of glory on the Crackers' team.

After waiting in the line, which seemed to have moved at a glacial pace, the couple finally bought their tickets and found seats in the balcony. The balcony, where Negroes were forced to sit if they attended, was Evie's choice, nonetheless. From this spot she could better "people watch," one of her favorite pastimes. Before the feature film, a newsreel was shown, part of which touted the most recent advances of Roosevelt's New Deal programs. It also included a segment about a late winter sleet and hailstorm in Minnesota, and, of most interest to the young couple, contained a review of baseball's spring training, with the Cards' Dizzy Dean, the Tigers' Schoolboy Rowe, a few of the Giants' standouts, and the Babe in his new role with the Braves. A scattering of laughter stirred through the audience when, during the newsreel segment on the New Deal programs, a loud, disapproving "harrumph" was heard somewhere among the orchestra-level crowd. Matt jokingly speculated to Evie that Governor Talmadge was in the audience. The best part of the feature film, in Matt's opinion, was W. C. Fields as Commodore Jackson.

They followed the movie with a late supper at the Shanghai Inn, on the opposite side of Peachtree but within walking distance of the Paramount. Matt's girlfriend always enjoyed going there or to the nearby Wisteria Gardens for a meal. Over a dish of the "house specialty," chop suey with egg rolls, the couple talked about their strong feelings for and their commitment to each other. Evie casually mentioned having children together. She stopped short. The two gave each other meaningful looks as their faces reddened faintly. They quietly, bashfully ate their chop suey.

Afterward, as Matt drove Evie home, she broached the idea of taking a day trip to someplace called Lake Winnepesaukah in Rossville, Georgia, up near the Tennessee state line. She explained that it was an amusement park owned and operated by a family her daddy knew from years past.

The pair agreed to make the day trip, picnic basket in hand, sometime soon before it became unbearably hot.

———

Matt was unfamiliar with the town of Rossville or that part of the state. He'd been born on a farm near Augusta during the "Flood of 1908," throughout which, as his parents later told him, people were getting around downtown by paddling flat-bottomed boats along Broad Street, the city's main thoroughfare. Matt smiled to himself as he recalled his momma telling him how the 1908 flood brought on a flurry of levee construction on the Savannah River, giving the locals a feeling of security until the next deluge a few years later. Following his graduation from the Academy of Richmond County's last class before the school moved to its new campus on Baker Avenue, he enrolled in the University of Georgia. There, he played a little football under Coach Woodruff, including the highly successful 1927 season, a year marred only by a final-game loss to those much-despised Yellow Jackets of Georgia Tech. And now, Evie, whose entire family followed Tech religiously, periodically dragged him to their home games at Grant Field. She'd become a huge fan of the Jackets when her older brother had attended the school.

Funny how things in life worked out sometimes, he reflected. Matt had never ventured much outside Richmond County before making his trek to Athens, and then later to Atlanta. He'd arrived in the state's capital with his degree in journalism from the University of Georgia's Grady School of Journalism to seek his "fame and fortune" on the staff of the *Georgian*. The irony of graduating from a school named for the legendary Atlanta journalist and University of Georgia alum, Henry Grady, who'd been a formidable editor for the *Constitution*, was not lost on Matt. He thought he'd learned a lot about his home state during his time at UGA and while at the *Georgian*, but, occasionally, realized that he still had much to discover.

---

After driving through unrelenting rain, their date ended on the Nash home's front porch. Saying goodnight was becoming more difficult. Matt stalled. Evie was reluctant to go inside despite the late hour. Finally, the night ended with a long embrace and a passionate kiss at the door. Yearnings. Evie stepped inside, but before closing the door, she leaned her chin back toward Matt and whispered a tease, purring, "Now go back to your boardinghouse room and wish we were married, Matthew Grimes." Mouthing a kiss from a big smirk, she closed the door. As she disappeared behind the door, Matt reached for her playfully. He smiled and felt his face flush simultaneously. His drive home along streets washed clean by the recent rains was a long one.

---

The next morning, Matt, dressed in his new suit, made his morning rounds early in order to meet the Nash family at the appointed time. He found no significant local fodder for his typewriter. A few wire service crime stories were the only headline grabbers. Matt held a growing feeling of glumness at the lack of any newsworthy items. He wanted a cigarette, but opted for gum instead. He withdrew a stick of gum from his coat pocket, unwrapped it, and slid it into his mouth. His jaw moved easily as he chewed the gum. It wasn't the same as a smoke, but he was meeting the Nash family in a short time and this would have to do. He was trying to quit smoking, thus far unsuccessfully, although he had cut back. Evie was encouraging the effort. Her boyfriend never smoked in front of her or her parents. It explained the ever-present pack of Wrigley Doublemint gum to be found somewhere in one of his pockets.

After the Easter services and a fine meal in the grand dining room of the Piedmont Hotel, Evie and Matt walked around Piedmont Park briefly before he drove her home. At the house, Matt declined Mrs. Nash's invitation to come in for a visit, explaining that he needed to make his afternoon visits to check on any "dastardly deeds" of note for the newspaper. When he did make his circuit, the young correspondent found nothing to cause the slightest excitement.

---

Back at the boardinghouse, Matt found Cliff sitting on the front steps, reading the Sunday comics section, a familiar red box of Sun-Maid raisins and a big bottle of Ko-Nut Kola within reach. That boy can pack away some groceries, Matt mused as he approached the porch. He knew for a fact that Miss Dixie had prepared a huge spread for the midday Easter meal. He'd smelled the ham already in the oven when he'd left that morning. Freckles lay nearby on the porch, longingly eying the raisin container. As he climbed the steps, Matt peered over his shoulder at the youngster and asked, "What's going on with Buck Rogers, Cliff?"

"I dunno. Buddy and Alura are in Mormor in some kinda tower and walkin' through walls made of some kinda light. It's science stuff, Matt," he shrugged. After absentmindedly using the boarder's first name, Cliff ducked his head slightly and slowly looked around, expecting a reprimand from his mother. Neither seeing nor hearing her, the boy returned to the funnies and continued, "I don't really understand all of it. I'm only in the sixth grade, for Pete's sake!"

"Well, what about Joe Palooka? What's he up to?"

"Aw, the big goof was walkin' with Knobby in a fog in London, and he fell down a manhole!" Cliff's eyes never left the page, and he only shook his head.

Matt laughed but took the hint. *The kid is too busy for small talk.* So he knelt long enough to scratch behind Freckle's ears and murmur her name. As he rose, Matt noticed, for the first time, that Diane was sitting on the swing at the end of the porch, smoking the remnant of a cigarette. Smoking was forbidden inside the rooming house. He strolled over and sat on the swing beside her. Music from the parlor radio drifted through the open window. Diane tossed her extinguished butt past Matt and over the rail. Matt watched it arc into the foliage as he pulled a partially crumpled pack of Old Gold's from his coat pocket and jostled a cigarette up through its opening. He held the pack out to her, and Diane pulled the offering out, smiling gratefully. Apparently lost in thought, she nonchalantly put the cigarette between her lips almost seductively. Matt shook off the image and retrieved a second smoke. After tapping the end of it on the arm of the swing, he lit both, guarding the match flame with cupped hands. He snapped the match toward the azaleas and watched it follow the path of Diane's discarded cigarette. Matt took a deep drag and held the smoke in his lungs for a long minute before releasing it. Diane was watching him as he exhaled. She knew the background of the young man trying to quit and snickered as she leaned in close their faces were practically touching. Giving him a playful push, she said softly, "Still haven't kicked the coffin nails yet, eh?"

"Nah. Still trying." He paused for another pull on his smoke. "I thought you'd be somewhere with Dave this afternoon."

Her face darkened, her eyebrows drawing together in a scowl. "No. He *said* he had some business or something he *had* to do. Said he'd call later. Maybe. Sometimes…" She didn't finish the thought.

"I don't know the guy, Diane. I'd barely recognize him on the street. But I'd bet you could do better for yourself, if you wanted to."

"You're right, Matt, you don't know him, dammit!" she snarled in a whisper. Matt's face reddened in embarrassment. Taking a breath, she softened her tone. "Sorry. Just don't preach, Matt, please. I think I'm in love with the big lug. So please don't judge." Frustrated with the situation, she shook her head, tossed her half-smoked cigarette, and made motions as if getting up to leave.

As she started to rise, Matt put a hand on her arm. When she relented, sat back, and took a deep breath, he fixed his eyes intently on hers. In them he saw sharp glimmers of pain and confusion. "Don't go, Diane. I'm sorry. I was outta line, and I'll keep my yap shut. It's none of my beeswax. I only want you to be as happy as I've been with Evie since you brought us together." She jerked her head, looking closely at him. Quickly turning the idea over in her mind, she made a face of sorts. Matt read her thoughts through that face and went on, "And no, I don't talk to Evie about you and Dave. I figure, if you want her to know *anything*, you'll tell her yourself. Okay?" He bumped her with his shoulder and grinned. She blushed but simply smirked in return. Diane accepted another smoke Matt offered. She bent toward his lighted match, inhaled, and threw her head back.

Over Diane's shoulder, Matt saw barely discernible movement in the parlor beyond the window. Abruptly, the radio's music stopped and piano music filled the room. The pair on the swing looked at each other and shared a thought: Melvyn's in the parlor with Amanda. Diane and Matt rocked back and forth together in momentary laughter before settling back to an amused calm with periodic titters. Cliff gave the pair a questioning sideways glance before returning to his Sunday funnies. As the piano music continued, they finished their smokes in silence.

---

The Monday-morning run yielded virtually nothing in the way of local crime beat occurrences. Again, wire service stories took center stage, or, in this case, front page. The first such account told of a bank teller running amok in the Chicago area and killing two of his three offspring, ages twenty and fourteen, before being disarmed by a wounded son. A Georgia connection to the story was revealed when it was discovered that the twenty-year-old daughter had graduated from Brenau in nearby Gainesville. Another out-of-state item dealt with the charred bones of a missing Maryland woman being found in the home of a Pennsylvania doctor who had been treating her. The only other noteworthy report was a Wirephoto from the Associated Press of a man who'd tried to rob a bus driver in Cleveland, Ohio, and had suffered the outrage of over a dozen of his fellow passengers for his efforts. The photograph showed police trying to help the mutilated, humiliated specimen to his feet. Closer to home, a Rome, Georgia, mother of three died after being struck on the head and robbed as she was returning from Easter shopping on Saturday. Matt groaned aloud about the state of the world as he read the story at the teletype. What little he had to report would get short shrift on a day when pieces like these would dominate the headlines in all three local papers.

Matt typed what few story leads he had and went to the Ed Barnes's office.

"Is this all you got for me, kiddo?" The anxiety the young man had felt about his city editor's reaction to his effort overtook him as he looked across at the older man. Barnes's furrowed brow crumpled further. He let the copy he'd been given for the evening edition fall to his already-cluttered desk. The editor put his hand to his forehead and gingerly drew his index and middle finger across it. He sighed and reread the copy before him.

Matt shifted his weight from one foot to the other while he waited and tried to think of something to say. But before any response could be formulated, Barnes continued, "You mean to tell me that nowhere in the city of Atlanta, in the great state of Georgia, is there anything more newsworthy from the police blotter than two pedestrians being struck by a car on Marietta Street?" As the young man started to speak, the editor preempted his reply, exclaiming, "Oh, yeah, that's right! I almost forgot your blurb about the guy from Cabbagetown arrested for beating his wife and her boyfriend!"

When he felt it was finally his turn, Matt spoke, "Mr. Barnes, I know that it's not much, but I can't commit the crimes, and then report them, too. Just earlier this month, Boykin reported that the number of pending murder cases in Fulton County was at its lowest, ten I recall he said, in many years. He also said that the number of other offenders being held in jail was down to a little more than three hundred fifteen versus the average of more than four hundred normally incarcerated. Remember, sir? Look, I know your motto is 'if it bleeds, it leads.' But that's it." Matt splayed his hands over the desk. "That's all there is. Sure, it's not the Harsh-Gallogly killings, but that's all there was for last night and this morning." He'd not been at the newspaper back in the twenties when George Harsh and Richard Gallogly, the two rich, young "thrill killers," as the papers labeled them at the time in comparing them to the famous Leopold and Loeb case from a few years earlier, had gone on their spree. Even so, Matt had heard enough about the pair, one of whom was related to the owner of the *Atlanta Journal*. At the time of the crimes' reporting, the *Journal* had not mentioned Gallogly's connection to its owner. "Just a slow news day, I guess. Maybe we'll get lucky tonight and someone will go on a killing spree." As he concluded, Matt smiled, but only for the second it took for him to see his boss's reaction to his flippant remark.

Mr. Barnes quickly cut his eyes up at the young correspondent without moving his head. Matt could feel his face flush. The editor did not like sarcasm save for its appearance in one of the newspaper's editorials directed at a politician or unless he specifically aimed at it in a particular news item. The young man quickly, silently nodded, trying to look apologetic in his hope that it would suffice for contriteness. The city editor liked the kid. Matt had spunk and initiative, was tough, and learned fast. He'd made good, fast friends in the various police agencies. Reliable sources were always a plus. Matthew Grimes merely needed more confidence. Some days on the police beat were slow. Barnes knew that, and he walked a tightrope between pushing Matt to do better and not discouraging the young man. "Close the door, Matt, and sit down. Let's talk for a minute." The editor waved Matt's leads at him. "Besides, you don't have *too much* work to get these ready for press." As the big reporter's face reddened, Barnes laughed, "I'm only kidding, son. Relax for a minute. Sit down." Matt closed the office door and dropped onto a chair.

"Matt, let me give you a little history lesson so you know I understand what you're dealing with." The older man leaned forward on his elbows and steepled his fingers. "When you came here and started as a copyboy, you had your sights set on being a police beat reporter. You told me that was your goal, your dream. Truth is, son, if you haven't learned it already, everybody here starts on the police blotter. Everybody. It's my policy. If they cut it on that, eventually they move on to something else. Something they really want." Matt looked around at the bustling crowd in the newsroom, and then back at his boss. "Of course, if somebody's hired for a particular feature, like Mildred Seydell was for the society page, they don't start on the police beat. But, generally, they do."

"Brick?"

"Yeah, even Brick." The city editor laughed, "But when Brick was reporting the beat, the town was still called Marthasville. So when he or the others give you any grief, it's because they've been there." Barnes held up his hand. "And, before you ask, I began the same way. That was a long time ago, of course, but yeah." The editor decided to let the young man chew on that a second before continuing, "And, not to sound like an old fart, it was a lot more difficult in many ways back then. The paper was located over on East Alabama Street at the time. Fewer telephones. Harder to get around town then." Barnes reflected for a second and beamed. "Oh, brother, I had a full head of steam when I started. I remember the first time I called the paper with murder stories. Three of them on the same night. I was really excited. The guy on the night desk phone sounded excited, too. 'Really?' I recall he asked me. 'Give me the details! Where'd they occur?' When I told him the addresses, he stopped me. 'Wait! Are these all niggers?' I told him I didn't know for certain who the people were yet and asked what difference it made since they were murders. I was idealistic about what being a newspaper reporter meant, you see. He told me in no uncertain terms that, for future reference, when there's anything along those streets or in that section of town, don't call the paper. 'Don't bother us,' he said. 'It's not news.'" Barnes went silent for a reminiscent moment. "Not news!" the editor slammed his fleshy fist on the desk. The crash reverberated through the newsroom. Conversations halted momentarily as uncertain looks were cast toward Barnes's office, and, then, they resumed. The abrupt, angry action stunned Matt. "Two women and a man, three human beings, are murdered and it's not news! By God!" Barnes paused, calmed himself, and took a deep breath. "I guess what I'm saying, Matt, is that things have changed some in many ways, but I know it's still tough some days. And you'll probably see many more changes if you stick with it. If you want to be an ace reporter, you have to act like one, son. Just stay the course and keep working hard. You're doing fine."

The city editor's smile stole back as he held out the pages of leads typed by the young man. "Okay, get out of here, write 'em up, and give 'em to the copyboy." Back to business, Matt thought. He tried to pluck his pages from Barnes's hand, but the editor retained his grip and added an admonition, "And, Matt, you're only as good as your last story." Matt finished the last half of Barnes's sentence in unison with him. The editor had drummed that into Matt since his first day, and he'd heard him tell others a hundred times. Barnes gave Matt a slight grin and released his grip. So the young newsman decided to depart on that happy note. As Matt turned, Mr. Barnes imparted one more bit of wisdom. "And don't forget, Matt, that your big piece from yesterday is lining the bottom of a birdcage today." The young man nodded as his boss held the encouraging smile. "Close the door behind you, please, Matt."

Matt stopped and stood outside the editor's office door, taking a deep breath. He believed that Barnes truly understood his dilemma. He moved through the maze of desks with the clacking of typewriters bouncing around the city room. Brick met the young journalist at his desk and plopped his pear-shaped form on one of its corners. He gazed down at the young man through a perpetually hung-over expression. The old man jabbed a cigar into his mouth and leaned down toward Matt. "Not much to report today, eh, kid? Tough break." His breath was brutal. Bad whiskey and cheap cigars. Brick stopped to light the smoke.

Thank God, Matt thought. Hopefully, it will cover some of the offensive tang.

The older reporter continued after setting fire to the stogie, "Maybe one of Candler's baboons will escape from his menagerie and terrorize the neighbors again. Now, *there's* a possible crime story." Brick stumbled off the desk and shuffled away, laughing loudly.

Matt looked up from his typewriter at the departing figure. He made certain his voice was loud enough for everyone else to hear, as he called out, "Hey, Brick, I just read on the wire services that Mae West has admitted to having been married to you at one time!" The remark stopped all the other correspondents in the middle of their sentences. They took the bait and hurriedly made their way to Brick to heckle him or to give him their congratulations. They were a relentless band when it came to manhandling each other. Brick could be heard laughing and telling the throng that West would get no "heart balm" from him. In reality, the wires that morning revealed that the buxom, blonde film siren had denied another marriage rumor, this one to a Frank Wallace, making it her eighth reported previous marriage in the last three months. The guys were really giving Brick a hard time. Matt grinned as he inserted a sheet of paper into his old Remington and aligned the page.

---

Tuesday's rounds did little to lift the young correspondent's spirits. Although there were more news items for his beat, they were a collection of sad tales. One account involved the death of a policeman who succumbed to burns he'd suffered in a fiery, on-duty motorcycle accident the afternoon before. Other separate traffic mishaps left a woman and a child in critical condition. Meanwhile, a child was accidently run over and killed by his father in another incident. A black man lost his legs right below the knees in Inman Yards as he was struck by a train while crossing a track. He told police that he'd only ridden the rods into town right before the accident occurred. In another item, the Fulton County police department's crusade against carnival gambling had led to a raid on one of the traveling shows. In a follow-up story, the Atlanta Fire Department was exonerated of any negligence charges related to the Warren Company fire. Before his day ended, Matt dutifully composed the articles under the watchful eye and guidance of Mr. Barnes.

---

After an evening meal of Miss Dixie's meat loaf, mashed potatoes, and homegrown green beans followed by thick slices of apple pie a la mode, everyone settled into the parlor for a quiet evening with the radio providing background music. At eight o'clock, Bing Crosby's show came on. God help me, thought Matt, as he tried to concentrate on a short story in a back issue of *Black Mask* magazine. The writer was one new to Matt named Raymond Chandler. He liked the guy's style. He stopped reading for a second and looked to the Philco from his position on the end of the sofa farthest from Bing's crooning. If I'd gotten to the radio before Amanda, he contemplated, we'd be listening to Ben Bernie's Blue Ribbon Orchestra now. Amanda sat at the other end of the divan, looking radiant and quietly turning the pages of a *Saturday Evening Post* with circus bareback riders on the cover. Melvyn had taken up a position in the corner chair usually occupied by the landlord this time of the evening. He'd found the perfect spot from which to gaze upon Amanda's lovely face. The piano salesman was simultaneously ogling Amanda while giving Matt the evil eye for sitting so close to her in a seat he might have taken up himself. Teresa sat at the card table, waiting for her landlady with paper and pencil. The two were going to look at some recipes for Italian meals they'd discussed at supper. Not surprisingly, Joshua was in his room. Victoria had not appeared in the parlor yet. Diane had recovered from her morose demeanor of Sunday afternoon as she danced her way through the door earlier for a date with Dave.

Mr. Fleming came to the opened pocket doors that separated the dining room from the parlor. He saw Melvyn sitting in the corner chair. He stood silent for a long minute. For his part, Melvyn either didn't see his landlord, being intently focused elsewhere at the moment, or simply chose to ignore him. The affable Rhamy smiled and sat in the chair across a small side table from Melvyn.

During the airing of *Camel Caravan*, Deane Janis was torching her way through "Remember My Forgotten Man." When she was at the point in the song of complaining about her guy being put behind a plow, the phone rang in the hall. Miss Dixie pushed her chair back from the table with a "Dear me! Who could that be?" Her husband shot to his feet from his chair and told her he would answer the call.

Matt looked up from his magazine in anticipation. For some reason, the words attributed to Mark Twain came to mind: "The telephone is an infernal device whereby any damn fool with a nickel can ruin your whole day."

Mr. Fleming soon returned to the parlor. "Matt, it's the newspaper for you. And the guy on the other end seems pretty excited." Matt leapt to his feet and hastily made his way to the phone.

# CHAPTER 5

# The Morningside Murder

At the phone table, Matt snatched up the receiver as he inhaled deeply. Now, he was excited. "This is Matt Grimes," he blurted into the phone.

"Matt! Richardson on the night desk here!" The man was speaking so rapidly, so breathlessly, Matt could scarcely grasp what he was saying. "You need to get to Pelham Road, up in the Morningside area in a hurry! There's been a shooting, a murder, we think, in the seventeen-hundred block of Pelham Road!"

The reporter scribbled some information on a notepad from the table. "Do you have a cross street?" Matt wasn't very familiar with that part of town. There wasn't a lot of criminal activity in that area, much less murders.

The nightside man on the city desk held the partially covered phone away from his mouth and yelled at someone else in the room. After a distant murmur, Richardson yelled, "Rock Springs Road, did you say?" Then he returned to the phone and Matt. Richardson had calmed some meanwhile. "Okay, okay, we think it's somewhere around the intersection of Pelham Road and Wildwood near Rock Springs Road in the Morningside neighborhood."

"Morningside?" Matt pondered aloud.

After a moment's silence, Mr. Richardson said, "Yeah. I know you know the way there, Matt, but go over it with me quickly." Matt was perplexed, but before he could respond, the night desk man went on, "That's right, Matt. From the Five Points area, take Peachtree up to either Thirteenth or Fourteenth Street where you make a right turn. That's right. Go over to the park and – what? Hold on, Matt." Someone else was speaking to Richardson from the background. It sounded as if chaos reigned at the other end of the line. Matt could picture the man on the other end of the telephone, his pipe clinched between his teeth, puffing smoke as he talked. Mr. Richardson was a good guy, Matt thought in a rush of relief. The reporter didn't know who might be overhearing Mr. Richardson on the other end, but he was grateful to the night desk man for his understanding and his surreptitious help. Matt was writing the directions as the man spoke. "Okay! I got it!" the night desk man called to someone. "Okay, Matt, that's right. At the park, you'll turn left onto Piedmont and go north 'til you reach Springs Road where you turn right. You're correct. Springs Road'll run you right into a multiple-street intersection, and one of those roads is Pelham." Richardson paused, and Matt scribbled notes. "Yeah, I'm sure you're right. There'll probably be lots of cop cars and activity in the area, so you shouldn't have any trouble finding it." He lowered his voice and, close to the phone, asked, "Got it?" Then, in a normal tone, "We're sending Rogers to meet you there as your camera man," referring to a staff photographer. Before he rung off, Richardson snorted, "Get there pronto and make old man Hearst proud, son!"

Matt finished his scribbling and said, "Yeah, I have it. Thank you very much, Mr. Richardson! I'll call you with whatever I get as soon as I can." He put the phone back on its prongs absentmindedly as he looked at his notes. Suddenly, his brain clicked into action. Time was of the essence, so there'd be no time to call Evie. The young man ran up the stairs to collect his hat and coat, along with a notepad and pencils. On his way to the front door, he let the Flemings know what was going on and told Miss Dixie that he may not be back in time for breakfast. She handed him a thermos of hot coffee she'd prepared in case, as she put it, the night was a long one.

---

Once in his car, Matt checked his flashlight to make certain it was still working, and then stepped on the starter. He pulled away from the curb and headed toward the Morningside neighborhood. The drive up Peachtree Street and along Piedmont Avenue, each virtually barren of traffic then, was a breeze. Matt took advantage of the situation to push his speed as he cruised Peachtree. On the way north, he reflected on something he'd told Evie when they began dating. He recalled telling her that a police beat reporter never knows when a call might come, day or night, which meant no regular hours for him. When he turned onto Springs Road, the traffic picture changed. A tangle of cars, police and civilian, could be seen down the road. Matt pulled to the curb a short distance from the intersection with Pelham that Mr. Richardson had mentioned. Putting his press card in his fedora's hatband and picking up his flashlight and notepad, he climbed out of the Ford and walked briskly toward the hub of activity. At least the rain, which had inundated the area for the past week or so, was gone, Matt reflected. As he approached, a uniformed officer stopped him until he pointed to the press card.

The cop shone a flashlight up at Matt's hat and dropped his hand. "Oh, okay. But stay out of the driveway and the yard. They're still investigatin'."

"Was it a shooting or a murder?"

"I'm told that a guy was shot to death."

"Is the body still here? I don't see an ambulance."

"Nah, it was gone before we got here."

"Got a name for me?"

"Yeah, the name's Reynolds. R-e-y-n-o-l-d-s," he beamed broadly.

Matt made a quick note. "So, what was the dead guy's, uh, Reynolds's, first name?"

The officer laughed sheepishly, "Oh I thought you meant my name. I dunno the dead guy's name." He hiked a thumb toward all the activity. "You'll have to ask up the line there."

"Thanks, uh, Officer Reynolds." Matt walked away, shaking his head, hoping that the people in charge of the investigation had a little more on the ball. Or maybe my question was obscure, Matt speculated. Shrugging off the issue, he quickened his pace.

Where Wildwood met Pelham, he found the apparent scene of the crime, an imposing two-story brick home on a corner, landscaped lot that sloped downhill to the street in front and downward to the driveway on one side. Steps and a walkway led from the driveway up the slope to the front door. In what light there was, it appeared that fabric awnings covered all the home's windows across the front of the house. A light could be seen burning in virtually every room across the front of the home. A big sedan, possibly a Graham, was parked in the driveway behind another car of indistinguishable make. The second car sat in a garage, which opened beneath a large portion of the residence built above. Though a light burned where the steps met the driveway, the bulk of what illumination there was came from police cars pointed at the scene. Matt also saw several flashlights in use as police officers meandered around the property, presumably searching the grounds for any clues. Several men in suits, probably detectives, stood in huddled conversation next to the sedan in the driveway. They were using flashlights, periodically, to peer inside the sedan's open passenger window. The automobile getting all the attention was difficult to identify precisely with only the rear end visible in reduced light. Whatever it was, it was out of Matt's league. Other detectives and uniformed officers milled about, presumably conducting other aspects of an investigation.

Officer Reynolds had been correct in his admonition. The police were keeping anyone other than law-enforcement personnel away from the yard and the driveway. Matt couldn't find an official who would speak to him at the moment. He saw that his counterparts from the *Journal* and the *Constitution* were dealing with the same problem, standing around as mere gawkers at this point. While Matt stood in the street at the bottom of the driveway watching the proceedings, the *Georgian's* staff photographer, camera in hand, approached him unseen.

"Hey, Matt! Ja just git here?"

Startled by the unexpected greeting, Matt jumped slightly at the man's words. He turned to see the dimly lit lopsided grin and heavy eyelids of the tall, thin *Georgian* photographer, Harlan Rogers. Rogers was from somewhere in the Deep South. Exactly where, Grimes was uncertain. Rogers was painfully shy and kept to himself much of the time. Matt assumed that, based on his mannerisms and dress, Harlan's childhood home must have been far more rural and isolated than Richmond County had been when he'd grown up there. The reporter supposed that he came from an area about which Matt's grandpa would have said, "It was so deep in the woods that they had to pipe the sunshine in and the moonshine out." Initially, no one at the *Georgian* really understood how Harlan, who they thought had probably never seen a camera before arriving in Atlanta, could be so adept at its use.

As it turned out, they were wrong about the young man's previous familiarity with photographic equipment. During a conversation over coffee with Rogers after the Terminal Building fire back in January, Matt had learned the secret of the younger man's knowledge of photography. Harlan told the *Georgian* reporter of an uncle who, following a brief period of training in Rochester, New York, had been assigned to the photographic section of the AEF's Air Service in the last stages of the Great War. His involvement, Harlan had told Matt, may have been for only a short period, but the uncle caught the photography bug bad and brought it home to his nephew after the war. Harlan had learned a great deal from his uncle, before the older man headed west "to capture the world through a lens."

Although Rogers was smart as a whip when it came to common sense, he was "just plain country," as Matt's grandma would have said. In Matt's estimation, there was nothing wrong with being "country." They were his roots, too. In the relatively cosmopolitan Atlanta of 1935, though, it stood out. Harlan's attire normally showed it. Tonight was no exception. There was enough light for Matt to see that he was wearing a suit coat over a flannel shirt buttoned to the neck, but without a tie, and work pants ending at a pair of well-scuffed brogans. The ensemble was topped with a cloth cap pulled low over his eyes. Despite his lack of sartorial splendor, Rogers had a keen sense for photography. And that was all anyone at the paper, including Matt, cared about. Matt had gained much respect for Harlan's ability and work ethic during the January fire. A sort of bond of trust had evolved between the two during that event. The reporter responded to Harlan's question, "Yeah, I've only been here a few minutes. Have you been here long? Did you get any pictures yet? Or is it too dark?" As he spoke, Matt returned his attention to the activity in the driveway,

Rogers also watched the people around the sedan as he spoke. "Just got here a minute or two ago myself. Yeah, too dark for anythin'. And they won't let me git close enough to git anythin' good, even if wasn't too dark. But a detective said that one of 'em would be here in the mornin' to let us get some pictures. Sounds like they ain't haulin' the car right away."

"The car? Why move the car?"

"Well, I heared that guy over there say the dead guy was shot while he was asittin' in that car."

"What guy said that? Where?" Matt followed the photographer's outstretched arm as Harlan pointed toward two men standing on the grassy area between the driveway and the side road. They were barely visible, beyond their cigarette tips randomly glowing in the dark.

"Swell! Thanks, Harlan. I'm going to see what I can learn. Hang around in case anything worth your talent pops up, okay? I'm going to try to buttonhole somebody who knows something."

The photographer nodded enthusiastically and fidgeted with his Graflex camera. "Yeah! Sure, Matt!"

Matt moved around the edge of the lighted area, working his way to where the two men stood talking quietly in the dark. As he approached the pair dressed in suits, he tripped over something hidden in the dim light and stumbled into one of the men.

"What the hell?" the man snarled aloud, as he turned and grabbed the reporter. He shoved Matt hard, nearly causing him to fall. At the sound of the commotion, nearby conversations stopped. Matt tried to right himself and shot the beam of the flashlight in the man's face to better see him and to make an apology. The man slapped the flashlight hard and pushed the journalist away again, growling, "Get that damned flash outta my eyes, boy!"

Turning the light to show the press card in his hat band, Matt apologized. "Sorry, friend. Matt Grimes from the *Atlanta Georgian*. I was trying to get some information about what goes on here."

"Well, first of all, I ain't your friend, ace. And next, I ain't talkin' to no newshound!" The flashlight's brief glare had shown the brawny man to have wide eyes and a broad brow above a pockmarked face. He stormed off. "See ya later, Jimbo," he grunted over his shoulder as he marched off in high dudgeon.

"You don't have to be a jerk about it, bub!" Matt called behind him angrily. He was tiring of all the "tough guys" he was encountering recently and decided to bow his neck.

The guy stopped momentarily and made a move as if to turn back to where Matt stood. He looked around at the crowd of men standing in the area while they watched to see his next move. The powerfully built man shook his head, laughed derisively, and walked on.

Even in the anonymity of the prevailing darkness, Matt was embarrassed by his awkward movements. But he was also pissed at the guy's attitude. He briefly used his flashlight to look for the obstacle that had caused his stumble, and then abandoned the notion. As others' conversations renewed, Matt turned his attention to the man still standing there. "I really am sorry, mister. Just trying to do my job. Who was that jackass anyway?"

"Don't worry about him... Matt, was it?" The man jerked his head in the departing guy's direction. "That fella you called a jackass and a jerk is *Detective* Arthur Rutherford. He can be touchy sometimes. Okay," the man paused and sighed, "he's a pain in the ass most of the time. Right now, he's pissed 'cause Chief Poole detailed this case to Detectives Denny and Engelbert." He laughed grimly as he glanced toward the retreating figure. "And they call me hard to get along with." The lighted tip of his cigarette bounced up and down as he spoke in the faint light.

"I don't care if he's J. Edgar! He doesn't have to be such a hard-ass when a guy's trying to apologize for an accident!" Matt paused, took a deep breath, and then asked, "Is there someone here giving out official press information?"

The man smiled at the fortitude and moxie the young man showed. In the halo provided by what light there was, Matt saw the man hold out a beefy hand. "I'm Detective Greerson, Matt. Jim Greerson." Lowering his voice slightly, he went on, "I'm not the official press person, but what the hell. Who knows, maybe the more info we get out to the public, the better the chance of getting some line on the killer? Besides, you caught me in a good mood. I don't know much, but I'll be glad to share with you what I do know. Only don't attribute it to me personally. Got it?"

As the journalist suspected, the two men were plainclothes detectives. He realized that it was too dark to write legibly at this point, so he'd have to rely on his memory until he could make notes. "Yeah, I've got it. Strictly an anonymous source. I'm Matthew Grimes of the *Georgian*. Glad to meet you, detective. What do the police know so far? Who's the victim and where is he? I understand that he was not here when the police arrived. Is that right?"

"Okay, hotshot, let me answer one question at a time," he said, matter-of-factly. "But so I don't have to answer 'em twice, what say we walk over to where the light's better and you can write this down?" Matt nodded his silent gratitude. The pair walked to a nearby police sedan where the reporter removed his notepad and pencil from an inside coat pocket. Propping a foot up on a running board, the journalist laid the notebook on his elevated thigh to use the lights of a vehicle behind them to write. When Matt was ready, Detective Greerson leaned in close against the car, glanced around, and spoke in a low tone, "The dead guy's name was Guyol. Eddie Guyol. And I heard that he was taken to St Joseph's Infirmary. But I don't know if he was in a meat wagon or not. He was gone by the time we got here. And he's dead. DOA. Shot once, it looks like. Anyway, they've recovered a single .45 caliber slug in the car from a through-and-through shot to the head."

"Is that the Eddie Guyol of the numbers racket? The 'bug'?"

"You catch on fast, sport. How many Eddie Guyols do you suppose there are in the Atlanta directory, anyway?"

"Yeah, right," Matt chuckled at the question he'd posed. He knew the name, of course, through his job but just couldn't quite put a face with it. "So was it a robbery? Are there any witnesses? Any suspects?"

Realizing he was asking back-to-back questions in his excitement again, he finished with a laugh and a contrite, "Sorry, detective."

A faint smile crossed the officer's face. "From what I understand, his wife, Myrtle, was with him when he was shot, but nobody's talked to her yet, that I know of. She's at St. Joseph's but unhurt, from what I understand. Some people were in the house at the time, but they say they didn't see anything. And no, no suspects." The big cop looked toward the men standing at the car in the driveway. Matt followed his gaze. The policeman went on, "I mean Guyol had a reputation as a square shooter, fair, always paid his debts. So who knows exactly why he was shot at this point? Looks like it might have been a stickup attempt. But, it could be connected to the lottery, or to some debt nobody knows about, or retribution for something he did or somebody he'd hurt or wronged somehow. You know he's been loosely connected to some deaths in the past. Or maybe some ambitious son of a bitch is trying to grab Guyol's organization. Hell, maybe it's a holdover grudge from his liquor racket in years past. No, no suspects outright, but how many mugs in this town would profit from or be happy with his death?"

"You're right. Who knows?" Grimes decided he needed to call the paper right away and give them what he had so far. Locating a telephone suddenly became his highest priority. Hopefully, he could do so without having to leave Pelham Road, a strictly residential neighborhood. He stood upright and looked around. As he did, he noticed for the first time that Detective Greerson, while heavier and far more muscular than he, was slightly shorter. He had a hard-knuckled look about him. A strong jaw sat below a wide mouth that bent equally as easily into a broad smile or an angry grimace. Playing so much football and sizing up opponents had always caused Matt to notice such things about people around him. That experience, combined with his still-developing journalist's eyes and nose for details, made it a force of habit, he guessed.

When Detective Greerson saw the reporter looking around somewhat frantically, he inquired, "What's up, Matt? You all right?"

"Oh, yeah," he said absently. "I need to find a phone PDQ to call in to the paper." Then, he saw a couple, dressed in formal evening clothes, standing by a lamppost in a front yard across the street and at an angle from the crime scene. "Can you excuse me, detective, and let me get back with you a little later?"

"Sure, kid. You gotta earn a nickel."

"See you in a few." Matt hustled to where the man and woman stood gaping. He introduced himself and showed them his press card. Before he could ask to use their telephone, they quietly bombarded him with questions about the incident at the Guyols' home across the street. Their attire, her with a sequined evening gown and matching wrap and him with a superbly tailored tux, indicated they'd only now returned from some gala event. Their haughty attitude pointed to a reluctance to approach anyone and ask tiresome questions. Matt brushed off their queries and asked to use their phone. They turned and looked at each other guardedly. When he recognized reluctance on their parts, the newshound struck a deal with them: they could listen to his call to the paper and that would answer many, if not all their questions about the police presence. They jumped at the opportunity to be "in the know" without having to appear proletarian.

In the cool night air, Matt followed the couple to the front door of what gave the impression of another magnificent home on Pelham Road. From the grand porch lights, the young reporter saw a brick exterior with a touch of Tudor styling on the second floor above the entry door. However, the presence of Tudor on the exterior did not prepare the young man for what he'd find inside.

Once beyond the foyer, the reporter was led into in a large, brightly lighted room. From there, he was shown across a large Mandarin rug, which covered the hardwood floor, past oversized furniture, an abundance of teakwood, red lacquer, and gold-framed photographs and artwork to a deep chair beside an elaborate, colorful side table. The table held an ornate lamp adorned by a fringed shade bearing the likenesses of various Oriental figures. Also on the table was a wooden box of distinctive Far Eastern design. If Evie likes the Shanghai Inn and the Wisteria Garden restaurants, wait until I tell her about this place, Matt mused to himself. He sat in the chair, uncertain whether the pair would ever show him to a telephone. The lady walked over and, smiling proudly, opened the box to reveal a gold-colored Catalin mono-phone telephone. The big reporter tried very hard to act suitably impressed. He smiled briefly at them and nodded his thanks.

Matt lifted the instrument off its cradle and dialed the night desk number. As it rang, the young reporter imagined the headline for the article he would write. Richardson answered on the third ring. "Mr. Richardson, Matt Grimes here."

"Hey, Matt! Whaddya got for me, kid?"

"It *was* a murder. The man killed was Eddie Guyol."

"What? Eddie Guyol? Are you sure?"

"Yeah, it was Eddie Guyol, all right. But nobody can come up with a clear, certain motive for the killing yet. Could be a robbery or a vendetta or maybe something else. Don't know at this point."

"Oh, brother, this is big, Matt! What else do you have?" Matt filled Richardson in on the rest of the information he'd learn thus far and the best angle he took from it. He did so to the accompaniment of restrained "oohs" and "aahs" from his bug-eyed hosts, who would occasionally stare at one another in shock. "Okay, Matt, I'm switching you to rewrite. I'm gonna put the best rewrite man I have here on it. Give him what you have. And stay on the story! Call us if we need to send somebody else to the police stations to handle the routine tomorrow morning. I want you to stay on this story. But, when you've gotten everything you can, get back here and write the piece for the final. Did Rogers show up? And did he get anything for us?"

"Yeah, he's here. It's pretty dark right now, but I'm sure he'll have something in time for the early edition."

"Okay, great! Hold on. I'm switching you to rewrite."

After a few seconds, another man, the rewrite guy, was on the line. Matt dictated the lead paragraph and gave him the other information currently available about the killing. He finished with a flurry by saying that footprints and a bullet were the only clues so far in the slaying of Eddie Guyol, the Atlanta numbers racket kingpin. "Sounds like a headline to me, Matt! I'll mention that to the copy editor. Good work! I'll pad the thing if you can't get here in time to write it up for the next edition. Call back with any updates, okay?"

"Sure thing! Thanks! I'll be back in touch!" The rewrite man rang off. Matt put the phone back without haste, looking into the startled faces of the home's residents. He then carefully closed he box with an intentionally elaborate movement. "Well, thank you very much, folks. I truly appreciate your help." Matt rose from the chair. Neither of the inhabitants stirred from their stunned disbelief, only mumbling what a nice man their neighbor had been. Matt jammed his hat back on his head and said, "Thanks again. I'll show myself out."

Back out on Pelham Road, little seemed to have changed in Matt's absence. Several police cars had departed, although there were still enough of them clogging the roadway to give a fair amount of light to the area. And fewer officers seemed to be loitering about. Initially, Matt didn't see Harlan Rogers anywhere in the area. Concerned, he walked toward the Guyol driveway and stood, searching for his photographer.

"Wha'ja lose, Matt?"

Startled, the writer spun and found Rogers sitting on the running board of a squad car, camera at the ready. Matt regained his composure and asked, "Anything new to report, Harlan?"

"Nah. But I'm stayin' here 'til the cock crows, if I hafta, to git a picture of that car and driveway and anythin' else that might show up."

Matt patted his companion's shoulder as he spied Detective Greerson a short distance down the street, talking with the reporter's old pal, Detective Rutherford. Rutherford was backing away from Greerson with his lower arms extended from his sides in a shrug. Greerson was saying something Grimes couldn't quite make out. Without taking his eyes off the pair, Matt slapped Harlan on a shoulder and said absently, "Good deal, Harlan. Stay on top of it. I talked with Mr. Richardson at the paper. He's counting on you." The reporter started walking toward his "anonymous source." At the same time, Rutherford turned and marched quickly away from Greerson and toward a nearby car, swinging a Borsalino hat against a thigh as he moved. Greerson appeared to drop his hands in disgust. As Grimes and Rutherford passed each other at a distance, the detective saw the newsie, frowned, and gave off a loud, contemptuous snort.

"Horse's ass!" Greerson muttered under his breath as Grimes approached. The blond reporter was still stunned at the detective's openly expressed opinion of a fellow officer. Greerson, guessing the young man's thoughts, looked at him and said in a flat, toneless voice, "It's all right, kid. He thinks the same thing about me, too." They watched Rutherford climb into a car and drive away.

"So, detective, anything new? Does anybody know what Mrs. Guyol had to say? And how can I find out? I need to get back to the paper and write this up." Matt looked to the detective whose eyes were still following the departing Rutherford.

"Yeah, a couple of things have turned up," Greerson began absently, "including Mrs. Guyol's statement." He turned to Matt as a notion came into his head. "*Yeah*, one thing in particular I need to check on. And you could help maybe. Do you have a car here?"

"Sure. I drove up. But –"

"Here's my problem. I was stuck having to ride up here with Rutherford. Now, he's been sent somewhere by the chief and, he says, he was told to go alone. I think he's just trying to weasel his way onto the case without me. He's sort of a publicity hound." The detective's voice reflected his exasperation. "We don't get a lot of big cases like this, and it could put a mug on the map, if you know what I mean. Anyway, so, now I don't have a crate to get around in. I'll tell you what. If you'll give me a lift, I'll fill you in on what we know up to the minute. The place I need to go is on the way back to your newspaper anyway. It's on Peachtree, south of here."

Matt quickly scanned the area and decided he'd done about all he could do there. He supposed he wouldn't necessarily learn any more at the scene, and Greerson could give him some inside scoop. Besides, Rogers's dogged determination and innate ability would ensure he'd get what a photographer needed for the paper. "Sure. Where do you need to go?"

"Let's hop in your crate, and I'll tell you on the way." As they walked, the detective muttered, "I need a cuppa java. Maybe we can find a place."

Grimes led the Greerson to his car and they clambered in. As Matt pressed the starter, he looked at the detective. "Did I hear you say that you wanted a cup of coffee, Detective Greerson?"

"Yeah, but it's not that important. And call me Jim, please."

"Sure. Well, if you want some coffee, Jim, there's a thermos somewhere by your feet. I think it'll probably still be hot. The coffee's black, if you take it that way. Just pull out the cork and use the top for a cup. My landlady gave it to me as I headed out the door tonight. She usually does. It'll be good. Anyway, I don't want any right now. Help yourself." Matt turned the car around, slammed it into gear, and sped off.

The grateful detective found the container in the dark and poured himself a cup. He inhaled its heady steam. "It's still good and hot. Thanks, Matt. It's been a long day."

"Say, before we get too far down the road, maybe you'd better tell me where I need to take you."

"Ever heard of the White Lantern restaurant? And I use the term 'restaurant' loosely. It's more of a sandwich and hamburger joint."

Matt searched his memory as he stopped at Piedmont Avenue. "Yeah, well, I know the name, but never ate there." Before making the turn onto Piedmont, the young reporter paused. He speared his mouth with a cigarette and lit it. His nerves were working overtime and he needed its calming effect.

"You haven't missed much. It's a restaurant, all right, but it's turned into a clubhouse for minor league ne'er-do-wells. By the way, go to Twelfth Street and make a right there. The joint's on Peachtree between Twelfth and Eleventh Streets."

"I don't get the connection with the White Lantern, detective..., uh, Jim."

"Well, while you were calling the newspaper, one of the guys came to the scene from taking a preliminary statement from Myrtle Guyol at St. Joseph's. She's kind of hysterical right now, so it's sort of jumbled, but he was able to get *some* information, muddled though it may be. Turns out that she may not have called for an ambulance *or* the police after her husband was shot."

"What? You've got to be kidding me! Did she call *anybody* for help?"

"Well, it's not clear, but Mrs. Guyol claims that she tried to get an ambulance from Grady Hospital at first. And, she says that, when there was some 'delay' involved with that, she had their maid call the White Lantern to get hold of Walter Cutcliff, Eddie's business associate. Eddie and Cutcliff work... uh, worked the bug together in their association called the Home Company. It's the biggest of the four Atlanta outfits involved in the numbers racket."

"Yeah, I've heard the names. Hey," Matt flinched, "wait a minute! Isn't Cutcliff the guy arrested after a high-speed chase where a car he was in wrecked while running from the law about two weeks ago? And they found a couple of gunny sacks of lottery tickets in the car, right? Yeah, I did a short piece on it."

"Yeah, that's him. Cutcliff's known for driving around town faster than hell, always trying to outrun the police. Anyway, he hustled to Pelham Road when he got the call. They loaded Eddie into the back seat of his Hudson, and Cutcliff and Myrtle drove him to St. Joseph's. Eddie was DOA there. Meanwhile, somebody at Grady confirmed that they were called about a shooting but were only told it was on Rock Springs Road. When they asked the caller for an address, the phone went dead. Whether that call was from Mrs. Guyol or her household, who knows?"

"That *is* odd. Don't you think? Huh." Matt contemplated the idea for a second before continuing, "Anyway, what did she say about the shooting?"

The detective took another sip of coffee. "Mrs. Guyol says they were on their way out after dinner. Not sure where to. The shooter, who she says was short and about thirty, came out of the bushes by the driveway and shoved a gun through her open passenger-side window. She says she'd never seen the man before. He said something to Eddie about having it coming to him and fired. The slug apparently killed Guyol instantly. The Guyols thought it was a robbery when the guy first appeared with the gun. So they ditched valuables onto the floorboard of the car. Money and jewelry were found in the car. And get this. Eddie had over two thousand dollars on him when he was shot."

"Zowie! Some night out!" Matt paused as he approached Twelfth Street. "But, hey, if Eddie didn't recognize the killer either, sounds like it was a robbery." After a pause, he said, "Oh, wait, I guess it could still have been a hired hatchet man maybe."

"But that takes us right back to hired by whom? Hired by somebody looking to move up or take over his piece of the bug here in town, hired by somebody with a grudge from Eddie's bootlegging days or some other revenge angle? What?"

"Yep. It does. Nothing but questions."

"Yeah. Questions that won't be answered by Mrs. Guyol for a while anyway, even if she can answer 'em. Her doctor and her lawyer have shut that flow for now. But questions I hope to get some answers for at the White Lantern. Hey, Matt, on Twelfth Street, turn left when you get to Peachtree, and then slow down. You can let me out anywhere along there."

The reporter turned onto Twelfth Street, pulled to the side before its intersection with Atkinson Avenue, and stopped. He turned in his seat slightly to face Jim. "Look, Detective Greerson, I don't know exactly what you're going to find in this place, but I'd like to go along with you."

"Matt —"

"Hey, I'm no debutante. I played football against some pretty rough characters when I was at Georgia and can take care of myself. I take full responsibility for my actions. And this can only add to the story I have to tell my readers." Matt chuckled, "After all, I *did* give you a ride. C'mon, detective. Tit for tat."

"UGA, huh?" the detective grinned without opening his lips. "Well, we'll have to talk about that later." Greerson sat in the dim light and considered the proposal. He was uneasy with the idea. Taking a civilian into a situation like this could be foolhardy. He didn't expect any gunplay, only conversation of sorts. The kid had grit and didn't seem to be a pushover. And two men in the joint, he figured, instead of going it alone, would certainly help his play. What the hell, he thought, I haven't strictly followed the rules for a while now, anyway. "Okay, look. This place is where a lot of the lottery operators congregate. Generally, they're not a violent bunch, but, as I think tonight's events show, that can have exceptions. I'm gonna go in there and brace a few mugs. You know, see what I can learn. And that's if there's anyone still there after tonight's shooting. Sometimes, these jamokes can be like cockroaches. When the lights come on, they tend to scatter. If you go in there with me, you *will* do everything I say! And you *won't* do anything without me! Is that understood? Just act like you own the joint. I'll feel responsible for you. And I'm not all that comfortable with that."

"Okay!" Matt nodded vigorously and quickly turned back to the steering wheel.

Detective Greerson reached out and grabbed his arm with a hard grip. "Wait, Matt. There's a funeral home, Blanchard Brothers, just around the corner on the same side of Peachtree as the White Lantern. Pull into their parking area. We'll walk from there."

Matt swallowed hard and, looking askance at his passenger, laughed grimly. "Funeral home? Is that what you consider a pep talk, Jim?" Both laughed as the Ford pulled back into the street.

After a time, the tall reporter parked and fell in beside Detective Greerson, standing at the passenger door of the Ford and checking his Colt OP service revolver. "I don't suppose you have one of these, do you? Know anything about guns?"

"Yes, I know guns and no, I don't have one. Do I need one?" Matt whispered excitedly. He realized that his forehead was beading with sweat despite the cool night air.

"Hopefully, no. But you may be getting ready to enter a shadowy world that's unfamiliar to you, Matt, except through maybe a couple of movies or a book or two. In the next several minutes, you're gonna meet some of the biggest wits, half-wits, and nitwits in this town. So stay close to me. Got your notepad handy?" Matt nodded and patted the left side of his suit coat, indicating the inside pocket, where he always kept it. "Good. Let's go. And stay close to me." Greerson returned the revolver to the shoulder holster inside his coat under his left arm.

"I got it, Jim. Stay close."

The pair walked to the eatery's entrance. Reaching for the door, Detective Greerson paused and looked sidewise at his companion. Matt, anticipating his next words, tried to swallow again and said, "Yeah, I know. Stay close." His mouth and throat felt very dry. His voice was uneven because of it.

Jim Greerson grinned and quickly pushed his way into the building with Grimes close on his heels. Most men in the room were a collection of thickset palookas. A few slimmer men stood and sat among them. At the pair's entrance, all conversation and movement froze like Captain Scott in Antarctica. The formidable bulk of many of the men gave the place the feeling that it was more crowded than it actually was. A gray pall of smoke drifted through the restaurant. At the sight of the detective, some men sat, some got to their feet, but all moved slowly, cautiously. Everyone kept his eyes on Greerson. Several of them held their hands up slightly in a gesture of surrender. A heavy silence fell over the room. A mug hurriedly took his hand off a square bottle of scotch that sat on one of the tables. The counter, running along the wall to one side of the eatery, and the other tables held a varied assortment of bottles of alcoholic libation, menus, ashtrays, and playing cards. Matt had the impression that grease-soaked air had changed the colors of the walls and the linoleum over time.

Greerson kicked the door closed behind him. He held his hands out, palms down in a soothing motion. "Now everybody stay calm. I think you know who I am, and, contrary to popular opinion, I think you're all smart enough to figure out why I'm here. So we'll play nice and nobody'll get hurt."

A man in a filthy apron was located behind the counter. As he stood between it and the "No Spitting" and "Cash Only" signs on the wall above a griddle behind him, he started to raise a ruckus about the detective's presence, but Greerson quickly cut him off, never taking his eyes off the patrons. "Shut your squawkin', mac! If you'd like, I can shake this greasy spoon and your customers down, but good. I'm sure I can find enough contraband to give Boykin reason to padlock the door to this dump! Permanently!" The guy clammed up.

Quickly, but in a smooth motion, a large man with a distinctive cube-shaped head moved from his chair and approached the front door where Greerson and Grimes stood. He wore a baggy gray suit and had a big bulbous nose and a receding hairline that peeked from beneath a snap-brim hat cocked back on his head. That head sat on an extremely thick neck. The strapping man intentionally walked into the restraining hand Jim held up. He tried to keep moving forward as he pressed, to no avail, against the detective. When the "contest" went Greerson's way, the man bellowed, "Outta the way, flatfoot! You got no right to keep us here!"

"I'm conducting a murder investigation, Gutowski." Jim Greerson's voice was flat and toneless. "Now be a good boy and go back and sit down."

The guy he'd called Gutowski made an angry, guttural sound at the detective and reached his right hand toward his left shoulder. Greerson made a polished, complicated movement ending with his Colt in his working hand. The baggy-suited man initially hesitated, and then showed the detective a tight smirk, moving his hand farther under his left lapel. In an abrupt, decisive motion, Detective Greerson laid the barrel of the Colt alongside Gutowski's head, with enough force to buckle the big man's knees. His back arched, and then went loose. Gutowski's lid flew to the floor behind him. His eyes showed white as he dropped to the linoleum and his hat disappeared beneath him. The air sounded with a gasp from some of the room's occupants. Others merely snorted disdainfully.

The sudden action by Greerson, lacking any apparent anger, startled Matt. The *Georgian* newsman didn't recover from his shock until he heard the severe voice of his companion evenly, firmly saying his name. "Matt, get the gun from inside this punk's coat." The detective nudged Gutowski with his shoe and held his gun at his side as he scanned the room. Nobody moved. "Jeez! Some folks just have to do things the hard way," Jim sighed, shaking his head. Before Grimes could comply,

Greerson quietly added, "Wait a second, Matt." His voice rose to the rest of the men in the eatery. "Now before my partner does that, let's all take our guns out very carefully from wherever they are and lay them on the floor at *your* feet where I can see them. Easy. Use the thumb and forefinger of your left hand. For you mugs who don't know what a forefinger is or which hand is which, just watch what somebody else does and follow suit. No monkey business." The men complied gingerly. In a matter of seconds, the floor was littered with handguns of various calibers. "Okay, Matt, go ahead."

Matt kept his eyes moving around the room as he crouched beside the semiconscious man. Gutowski's breathing consisted of stertorous noises. As he squatted, the blond reporter got an unintended whiff of the fallen man, who smelled of prehistoric cigarette smoke, sweat, and Dentyne. Inside Gutowski's coat, Matt located a big black .45 automatic. Right before he straightened, the young man was startled again by Detective Greerson yelling, "Don't move!" Matt jumped up with the gun pointed generally in the hoods' direction. Through the bruisers in the crowd, he saw the object of Jim's attention against the far wall of the restaurant. A jockey-sized man with a thin nose and a weak, ineffectual chin had been slowly easing his way along the wall toward a door at the rear of the room. Now, he stood bug-eyed, shaking beneath his skin as his Adam's apple bobbled above his collar. When Matt looked back at the detective, he was motioning to the misguided fellow with the barrel of his gun. "You heels stay put! There won't be any back-window moves here tonight, boys. Anybody who tries it'll be sorrier than Gutowski there."

In a low voice, Greerson said, "Clear the gun, Matt." The detective glanced at the hesitant young man next to him. "Just clear it," he said more firmly, though in a low tone. Matt slipped the magazine out and carefully ejected the shell from the chamber.

"Now, keep the magazine and the round and give the gat back to Gutowski." Matt slipped both items into one of his coat's side pockets.

He took the meaning in Jim's broad grin and dropped the heavy weapon hard onto the whimpering man's soft belly. The action resulted in a loud groan.

The policeman scowled at the crowd. "I want everybody to put his hands on a table, where you sit, where you stand. Make sure I can see 'em. Move 'em and you can share floor space with this jerk. Or worse." He gave the supine hood a swift kick to the ribs, producing a half-conscious howl. Glancing down at Gutowski, the detective snarled, "That's right. Just lie there and moan." He turned slightly toward the guy behind the counter. "That goes for you, too, *chef.* Hands where I can see 'em." The man quickly complied by laying his hands on the counter. Jerking his head toward Matt, Jim said, "Now, my partner here is going to come around to each of you. I want you to give him your name and address. That is, your *real* name and your *real* address. Don't get cute. And I want to know what time you got here tonight or if you left at any time for any reason. Like I said, don't get cute with my partner. He only *looks* like a debutante. He's a mean son of a bitch. Meaner than me. He has a happy trigger finger and an even happier blackjack. Now, one more thing." He paused long enough to shoot a sideways glance at the counterman. "You! You got any guns back there?" The man shook his head forcefully. "You got any bags in this joint?" The man gave Greerson an empty stare and the detective raised his volume, "You know, Einstein, bags, paper sacks like people carry your sandwiches out in!"

The counterman's face stayed blank. "What's a Einstein?"

The detective was getting a little peeved at this point. "For Pete's sake! You need to read something more than racing forms and the menus in this greasy spoon, mister! Answer the question! Do you have paper bags?"

"Uh, oh yeah." The man carefully, but quickly reached beneath the counter and laid a stack of bags on it.

"Now, my partner is gonna come around and collect all the .45 caliber gats you bums were holding." He glanced at and spoke low to Matt, listening intently. "Matt, empty the ammo out of *all* the guns other than the .45 calibers you collect and put those rounds in a separate bag." He returned his eyes to the other men and raised his voice again. "When he gets your *correct* name and your *correct* address, he's gonna label a bag with your name and put your .45 in it. Got it? And while he's getting your information, I want to talk to some of you. You!" Greerson called out one of the men standing nearby. "Come here!" he shouted, motioning with his gun barrel.

Matt stepped forward and reached into the left side of his coat for his notepad, creating jittery flinches in several onlookers. The correspondent enjoyed a brief smile of satisfaction at the effect. He picked up the bags from the counter and approached the closest table, making sure nothing and no one was between him and his law-enforcement companion. What followed was the reporter gathering the names and addresses, various calibers of ammunition, and four .45 caliber handguns from an interesting array of hard characters in one of the most remarkable half hours of his life. As he did, he became less timid about the situation. Sporadic commotions arose at the end of the room where Detective Greerson was questioning the thugs, but Matt never caught the drift of the hubbubs.

By the time Matt had finished gathering the data from everyone else, Gutowski had come out of his fog and had made his unsteady way to a table. The big goon's crumpled hat and handgun sat on the table in front of him. He was wearing a rather large weal on the side of his noggin when the reporter sat at the table to collect his full name and address and his automatic. Matt bagged the gun first. The big goon glanced at his hat and, then, looked hard-eyed at the young man. Gutowski twitched his head in Greerson's direction. "Run up an alley, copper! Both of ya grit cops can kiss my ass!" he exclaimed, groggily. "I ain't tellin' ya shit! Ya get me? So what're ya gonna do about it, peckerwood?"

"How about we just run your ass in, put you in the Tower, and lose your paperwork for a while?" Matt had heard of such ploys but wasn't sure how they were pulled off.

"My mouthpiece'll have me out before you can change your drawers. 'Course, maybe *you* never change 'em, punk. Maybe your grit mama —"

Matt flicked a large open hand out and slapped Gutowski hard, very hard, across the welt that decorated the side of his head. The sound of the slap ricocheted around the eatery. The big man made a slight move toward Matt but then stopped short and threw a beefy hand over his injury instead. Through it, he refused to release the scream that surged right behind his teeth, lips, and puffed-out cheeks, but his eyes, showing sharp flashes of pain, watered. The reporter had shocked himself by his instinctive reaction to the slight, but he felt some satisfaction at the same time. He returned the hood's glare and saw a drop of sweat run down the side of Gutowski's nose as beads formed on his wide upper lip. Bravado can only carry a hooligan so far, Matt surmised. To add to the mug's discomfort, the young writer gave him a wide grin. Several gathered goons shifted in their chairs, but said nothing.

Grimes quickly looked around in the detective's direction. Nothing. Greerson either didn't notice or didn't care. "Your shyster's going to have to find you first, jackass. I'll move your happy ass around so much, the chairs won't even have time to get warm from one place to the next," Matt growled between gritted teeth. The young man knew he was talking through his hat, but he was enjoying the game by this time. In the end, Gutowski, still holding a protective mitt over the weal, had a change of heart and spilled his information.

When he'd finished, Matt sidled over and leaned sideways against the end of the counter, positioned so the hoods were still in view. He put the bagged firearms and ammunition down on the floor beside him. The man behind the counter stood frozen in place. "How about a Coke?" When the man hesitated then flashed a nasty leer as he moved toward a dispenser, the young reporter thought the better of it. No sense in drinking somebody's warm spit, he decided. "Never mind, mister." Matt nodded to the counterman's previous spot. "As you were." When the man returned to his position and slowly, grudgingly placed his hands back atop the counter, Matt retrieved the bags, turned, walked to the door, and waited. He could feel the eyes of the men on him. Suddenly, under the glares of these hardened thugs, the journalist became a bit less comfortable with the game he'd been playing. Nevertheless, he held his smug grin.

Soon, the detective joined his young cohort at the front door. He turned to face the assembly of goons. "Okay, boys, thank you for your cooperation. This place is now closed for the night." The men sat or stood in place, hesitating, uncertain. "Get out!" Still, the men only looked at each other, but no one stirred. Greerson drew his weapon and held it at his side. "I said to get out now! Every mother's son of you! Out! You," he yelled, indicating the man at the counter, "that means you, too! Get out, all of you! Hit the pavement! Lock this rathole up!" The men collected their weapons and started moving toward the door at a fair clip. Defiant to the last, Gutowski was the last goon out the door, sneering as he departed. Greerson and Grimes stayed until the counterman had turned out the lights and locked the doors.

# CHAPTER 6

# A Needless Killing

As the detective and the young *Georgian* journalist walked along Peachtree Street toward the funeral parlor and Grimes's jalopy, the younger man kept glancing around into the low-lighted areas nearby. Greerson stopped walking and chuckled, "You looking for somebody?"

Matt turned and faced the cop. "Aren't you at least a little concerned out here on the street after that session with those gorillas?"

The older man dug a package of cigarettes out of a pocket and offered one to his companion. The young man set the bags down on the sidewalk and tapped his cigarette on a thumbnail. They set fire to the smokes. Greerson inhaled deeply. "Nah. They're gonna feel enough heat for a while with the repercussions from Guyol's murder without bringing more unwanted attention by messing with two detectives."

Matt picked up the bags and leaned in toward Greerson. "You mean a detective and a reporter pretending to be a cop."

"Either way. By the way, how many .45s did you get? And did you get their information?"

"I collected five guns, including Gutowski's. And, yeah, I got their information." Matt handed the bags to Jim, who deposited them on the sidewalk while they smoked and talked.

"Any trouble?"

"Nah. A piece of cake."

"I'm not sure Gutowski would agree with that assessment."

Matt felt his face redden slightly. He was glad the light was low. "Yeah. Well, sorry."

"Why? Did he freely give you the stuff you needed or was he giving you a hard time?"

"Well, he was a bit hesitant at first. But he got the idea after a while."

Detective Greerson chuckled. "Sounded and looked like he wasn't the only one who caught on to the play. Don't worry about it. You did a good job. Everything's copacetic. I've had long history of run-ins with Gutowski. Thanks to one of those encounters, he did a stretch down in Milledgeville a while back. No, there's no love lost there. The mug's out of Chicago or Cleveland or Buffalo, somewhere up on the Great Lakes. I understand he came down here after pulling a five-year jolt somewhere up there. Anyway, Gutowski thinks he's some kind a badass here among the hicks. In a degrading way, he calls southerners 'grits' and 'peckerwoods.'"

"Yeah, I noticed."

"Anyway, like most of 'em, he only *thinks* he's a hard case. He *can* be nasty mean when he thinks he's got the advantage. But that bluff can be called. Anyway, for a while in there, I was thinking that maybe you'd missed your calling of being a cop."

"Uh-uh. Not me, Jim. Thanks anyway. I'll stick to reporting the police beat, not working it." He paused, took a drag from his cigarette, and followed up with a chortle, "But, damn, that was fun!" Surveying the street, he went on, "Funny thing, though. Most of those jokers said they lived in some hotels along Mitchell Street. You know the ones where most guests register under the names Jones or Smith and you don't have to answer questions at the front desk."

"No doubt. That area has been on the skids since the twenties." Greerson turned to sweep the street with a glance. "What with cars becoming more common, viaducts being built, and Union Station's construction, Terminal Station and that area along Mitchell have definitely declined. The area's lousy with crime and its slimy element now. And Smith's Restaurant over on Mitchell has become something of a hangout for the joy girls." The detective dropped his cigarette and crushed it with his shoe. He reached down for the bagged guns. "C'mon. We'd better get going. That is, 'we,' unless you've had enough excitement for one night."

Matt flipped his cigarette toward the street and watched it end its long arc with a spark on the pavement. "Oh, hell no! Not nearly enough fun for one night! Especially not if it adds to my story! Where to now?"

"C'mon. I'll tell you in your flivver."

"By the way, what're you going to do with those guns I collected?"

"I'll turn 'em in and see if the boss wants to check 'em here or to send 'em off to the FBI for testing to compare with the round that killed Guyol. They're doing some interesting stuff in their new lab. We'll see."

"And the ammunition? I got .32, .38, and .25 caliber rounds."

"What I can't use myself, I'll hand out to guys at the police department."

When they were in Matt's car, he laughed, "Hey, before I forget, I want to ask you something, Jim. When you wanted a cup of coffee, why didn't you get a cup at the White Lantern?" The young journalist was feeling a little euphoric at the moment.

The detective set the bags on the floorboard at his feet. "I didn't think I'd be welcomed enough to rate any service. At least any kinda service I thought I'd be happy with. Probably the same reason you didn't get that Coke." They shared a laugh.

"So back to business. Did you learn anything in there? What's up?" Matt asked.

"Well, that sort doesn't have much to say when talking to the police. But one of the guy's in there wanted to meet with me later and talk. He knew he couldn't talk in front of everybody in the restaurant. I'm not certain what he has to say, but I think he might be worth listening to."

"Which one?"

"His name is Charlie Newsome. He was the one who probably seemed most like a former prizefighter. Quite a character."

The car was too dark to scan his notes, but the newsman recalled the man in question without them. He recollected the man's handsome, but battered face with its thick and spread nose, which had been broken but well set, the scars at the cheekbones, the white disfigurement above one eye, and his large hands, clean but course. When he'd absently reached out to shake Matt's hand before their conversation, the reporter had seen that one knuckle had been broken badly. "Oh, him! Brother, he spent a few rounds in the ring, didn't he? He's got a bit of scar tissue on that kisser. And that cauliflower ear. It's as thick as a cubed steak. Jeez!" Matt started the Tudor and switched topics. "Where to, Jim?"

"He said he'd meet us in front of the Tip-Top Billiard Room. We'll pick him up there. Know where it is?"

"On Pryor, right?"

"Yeah. That's it."

Pulling out onto southbound Peachtree Street, Matt asked, "So what's this guy Newsome's history? Do you know?"

"Yeah, I know a little or a lot about most of 'em. I'm told that Charlie hailed from somewhere in the North Georgia mountains. He came from dirt-poor people, so he worked for a timber harvesting outfit almost from the time he could first walk. The job was grueling, but the hard work made him strong as an ox. Anyway, he somehow got hooked up with a boxing promoter passing through the state. The guy took Charlie up North, straight to New York from what I understand. This joker put a pair of gloves on Charlie, trained him some in the manly art of pugilism, and shoved him into a ring under the moniker of 'Nitro Newsome.' " The officer paused to reminisce for a minute. "I actually saw a fight poster promoting him in some match when I was at Camp Mills in New York just before shipping out in '17."

"Brother, he's got the size for it!"

"Yeah, well, Charlie did all right for a while, but his heart was never in it from what I hear. Never was mean enough. No killer instinct. The yarn goes that, after about nineteen years in the ring, he was tired, washed up, and he quit."

"Wow! Nineteen years is a helluva long time to take a pounding in a sport you don't like."

"Well, his daddy'd died in the meantime, and Charlie felt like he owed it to his widowed momma to keep sending her money. She still lived somewhere in the Georgia hills from what I understand. He never married, because, as he told me once when I had to run him in on a battery beef," and here Greerson lowered his voice and mimicked an over-the-hill boxer, " 'Dames is bad for da legs!' " When he finished, he returned his voice to its normal pitch again and went on. "Anyway, he was pretty messed up in the head by the time he quit. He was what the less kind would call a punch-drunk stumblebum. He couldn't hold a regular job, even if there'd been any to be had. So Charlie drifted back here to Atlanta. He couldn't find any legit work to suit his 'talents' here either. So, at first, he was on the bum. Then, he went on the dole, you know, on relief."

The detective chuckled. "And this is where the myth and the facts of the tale may collide. If you believe the account that made the rounds, the first time Charlie went to apply for assistance, he filled out the paperwork, and then went into some lady's office with it to be approved or something. She was sitting behind a desk and looked across at him. He only sat there, kinda foggy like. She held her hand out for his paperwork and said, 'Mr. Newsome, can you show me your form?' The legend goes that Charlie jumped up and shadowboxed for about a minute before she could make him stop and explain that what she really wanted was to see his application." The men shared a hearty laugh before Greerson finished. "Whether it's the true story, he eventually got involved with Atlanta's criminal element as their muscle. But, again, his heart wasn't in it. So he ended up merely doing odd jobs for 'em. Oh, once in a while, they'd show his sizeable bulk to somebody just for the intimidation factor, but nothing more. Mostly, driving mugs around and running errands."

Matt turned left from Peachtree Street onto Hunter Street at the lighted window displays of High's Department Store, and then onto northbound Pryor. "He seemed pretty harmless to me, despite his size. You sure seem to know a lot about him."

"Yeah, he's a big palooka at this point, a good guy really. Some of what I know about Charlie, he told me when I pinched him that one time. Pretty affable guy. He sat in the stationhouse and yapped. Some of it came from other people, and, as I said, some from stories making the rounds, true or not. But he has something he wants to say to me. And I probably need to listen."

The Ford pulled to the curb near a fireplug before they'd reached Kenny's Alley south of Alabama Street. They didn't see Newsome. They waited and smoked in silence as Tuesday night bled into Wednesday morning. A few people strolled along the sidewalk, possibly leaving from the few restaurants in the area or maybe even the sheriff's office south of where the pair sat.

After a brief period, Matt and Jim saw the silhouette of a man, bent over slightly, who stumbled out of the alley up the street. He had his hands in front of him, holding his stomach. He swayed a bit before collapsing against a building there and slumping to the sidewalk. Another drunk, they thought initially. "Looks like somebody got hold of some bad 'shine," Matt voiced softly. They each held that impression until a couple approached the downed man. The female passerby screamed and jumped back from the fallen figure as her male companion stepped between the two and pushed her away. The big cop reacted instinctively, grabbing the flashlight from on the seat between them and heaving himself out of the car toward the commotion. He tossed his cigarette as he ran. Matt quickly followed his lead.

When they reached the scene, Detective Greerson shone the spot on the man and his worst fears were realized. Charlie Newsome sat against the building with his hands, covered in blood, still holding his abdomen. The red liquid dribbled steadily between his fingers. Bodily fluids pooled where he sat. His face was a welter of blood and bruises. One eye was swelling toward closed. Pinkish froth seethed on his teeth between his parted lips. From under a worn jeff cap, helpless eyes looked up at the detective and the young reporter, who squatted beside the collapsed figure. The amount of blood kept Greerson from knowing whether the big man had been shot or stabbed. Though he'd not heard the reverberation of a gunshot, the pug looked to have been gut shot. A quick search of the alley by the detective, with the flashlight and gun in hand, revealed nothing except a blood trail. When he returned and knelt beside Newsome, Greerson could see the hopelessness of the situation. He'd seen this kind of wound before, far away and long ago.

"Somebody's worked him over pretty good with their fists," Matt whispered.

"Uh-uh," Detective Greerson disagreed in a whisper, shining the flashlight's beam on several long, straight bruises and abrasions on the battered man's face. "They pistol whipped him. Whoever did this knew that fists alone wouldn't have much of effect on a mug this tough."

When Newsome tried to move, Matt and Jim restrained him. "Stay still, Charlie!" Jim admonished. "Matt, go call headquarters! *Quick!* The pool hall!" As the young man began running down the sidewalk, Greerson yelled after him, "And tell them to get an ambulance here *now!*" The detective brought his head back around toward Charlie. "Take it easy, big guy. You'll be fine. Just breathe slowly."

Someone spoke from behind him. "Are you shittin' me? That guy's gonna die right here!" the male half of the couple yelled over Jim's shoulder.

Charlie's eyes enlarged at the man's words before squeezing shut in a grimace of pain. Enraged, Greerson sprang up to the man's face. "Shut the hell up, dumb ass! Get the hell away from here!" When the man hesitated and bowed up, Jim looked at the woman. "I'm a police officer, dammit! You'd better get him the hell outta here, lady, before I lock both of you up as material witnesses!" The woman pulled her recalcitrant companion away through the gathering crowd and yelled at him to shut his "fat mouth."

Meanwhile, Matt found a pay phone in the Tip-Top and quickly fished a coin from his pocket. He called police headquarters. As the phone rang, he adjusted the mouthpiece. The idea that the department was only about three blocks away ran through his mind. Billiard balls clicked and spun under a thick haze of cigarette and cigar smoke in the room behind him. When the station answered, he hurriedly explained the situation. That quick, help was on its way. In his nervous excitement, Matt needed three tries before he successfully replaced the receiver on its hook. By the time he returned to the wounded man's location, two beat cops had arrived on scene. One remained while the other raced to a call box to confirm the incident with headquarters. When Matt moved to kneel beside Jim, the uniformed officer tried to stop him. "He's with me, officer," Greerson said impatiently. Knowing the detective by sight, the officer grudgingly complied.

They couldn't keep the wounded man from trying to speak. Greerson leaned in close to Charlie as he weakly, breathlessly whispered, "Got to go see, Mrs. Dunbar... Pershing Point... 'partments... got to see her. My girl... papers... love her..."

The crowd moved closer and their chaotic chatter increased. Finally, Matt had had enough. He looked at the uniformed officer and yelled, "Get these people back, dammit! Give him some air!"

The officer squared his shoulders to the young man and looked down at him menacingly. "Say, fella –"

From his kneeling position, Jim Greerson punched the policeman's leg hard and, frowning, nodded to him when he looked down to meet his gaze. The officer grudgingly followed Grimes's demand and moved the crowd a good distance away. Sirens sounded faintly on the night air in the distance, closing in.

The two men could do nothing to stopping the bleeding. The detective moved his mouth close to the wounded man's ear and asked, "Who did this to you, Charlie? Who was it?"

The tires of an ambulance and a police car squealed as they rounded the corner down the street at the same time. Charlie's mouth twisted open to speak. His eyes enlarged and strained as if trying to see a distant object through fog. Suddenly, Charlie Newsome's face convulsed and his entire body shuddered before going limp. Jim reached out and held a finger against the side of the ex-prizefighter's s neck, feeling for a pulse. There was none. He was gone.

"Damn!" Detective Greerson rumbled hoarsely under his breath. Matt heard it as a statement of anger, sadness, and frustration.

In that dark moment, Matt was struck with an idea. As the two men rose from Charlie's body, the reporter gently took Greerson's lapel in hand and pulled him closer. He whispered, "What do you think about not saying Charlie's dead and having the ambulance guys treat him as a badly injured person."

"What? What the hell?" The police officer's response was louder than Matt had expected.

Maybe it was a crazy idea, but the young man persisted in quiet tones. "Have the ambulance leave with its siren blaring. If the people who did this are anywhere nearby, they may think that they didn't finish the job. They may panic and make mistakes." While Jim Greerson mulled the idea over, Grimes plunged forward with his thoughts. "Look, they're going to take him to Grady anyway, right? A doctor there has to pronounce him dead, right? So what harm comes from running back to Grady with the siren going like he's still alive. It's late. Not a lot of traffic. Maybe we shake things up a little. We can't bring him back, but maybe, just maybe, he can still help us."

The detective smiled weakly and quietly responded, "'Us?' You've taken to those plural pronouns pretty quickly, Matt." He shook his head, but replied in a low tone, "I doubt seriously if the bastards who did this are still anywhere around." The big cop rubbed his jaw for a second, admiring the younger man's ingenuity. "Oh, what the hell. Can't do any harm. I'll go talk to the ambulance people."

Shortly, Greerson returned with two men from the ambulance carrying their stretcher. As they worked, the detective spoke in a louder than necessary voice. "Gently, guys. Take it easy with him. He's hurt bad." Matt noticed that one of the ambulance men looked at the other, smirked, and rolled his eyes, while complying with the agreed-to instructions. The detective had one of the uniformed officers get the names and addresses of those in the crowd. Soon, the ambulance crew had Charlie Newsome bundled up and in the back of their vehicle. It left in a cloud of dust with its siren wailing. Greerson again spoke with the first two uniforms to have arrived, told them what he'd seen, gave them Charlie's name, and worked out an agreement about his part of the report to be filed at headquarters.

As the crowd dispersed and the street returned to some degree of calm, Matt patted his coat, searching for a cigarette. Jim did the same. Both men came up empty. As they lingered on the sidewalk, Matt tried to read the detective's face in the dim light. "Now what?"

"Well, it's getting pretty late, but I feel the need to follow up on what Charlie was able to tell me before he died."

"I heard him say something, but I couldn't make it out because of the crowd noise."

Greerson voice was soft. "He said that I needed to go visit his girl, a woman named Dunbar, who lives at the Pershing Point Apartments. Charlie said that she was his girl and he loved her. He mumbled something about papers, too." Jim paused and winced. "God, I hate the idea of giving bad news like this to somebody."

"Are we going tonight?"

"Yeah, it's late, but, if there's something *she* can tell us and whoever did this knows it, she could be in danger. I don't know what Charlie may have told his killer before he was murdered. I need to see her now. But you –"

"I'm included in this, right? You wouldn't drop me now, would you?"

"Look, Matt. Here's the deal. I've already involved you in this crap too much. I need to check in at headquarters and see if I can find out where the hell Rutherford is. He's the one who should be chasing down leads with me."

"Yeah, but that's just it! I'm *already* in! If you can't find him, can I tag along? I *think* I've earned it," Matt pointed out in his plea. "Same rules. I'll do everything you tell me to do and won't do or say anything without your say-so. Oh, and I'll stay close." Matt finished with a grin.

"Okay. If Rutherford's at the station house and ready to roll, that's it. If not, we go together. But we've used your car enough. We'll pick up mine at headquarters and use it if we go together."

"Deal." The journalist kept his fingers crossed that his luck would hold. In the time it would take to drive the two or three blocks to police headquarters, he'd never get the answers to the dozen or so questions he had.

The two men returned to Grimes's car and piled in. As the Ford's V-8 roared to life, Greerson said something that struck the reporter as strange. "I don't feel very much of anything anymore, but I really hated to see Charlie go out like that." His voice was cold and unpleasant. To Matt, it seemed the detective was somewhere far away at the moment. He drove on toward Butler Street.

When Matt parked, he turned toward his older companion and threw his arm on the back of the seat. "I'm going to come in and see if there's anything new to report, and then call the night desk with what I have. I'll be in the press room. Let me know what's going on, okay?"

Jim agreed and they made their way to the headquarters building. While Greerson disappeared into the bowels of the structure, Grimes went to the press room to call the night desk. The room was empty, as Matt would have expected for this time of night. Anybody working the Guyol murder would be out on Pelham Road or at St Joseph's. When he sat at a table, Matt glanced at his watch. He saw that it was just before one in the morning and far too late to call Evie. He realized that he'd have to catch up with her later that day. Then, he called the night desk man at the *Georgian* and filled him in on the story that he had to that point. Before being transferred to rewrite, Matt assured Mr. Richardson he was would stay on it for the rest of the night. He repeated the lead and the rest of the narrative's details to the rewrite man with a promise that he'd be in early enough to write up the complete item for the first edition. The only problem arose when he discussed the death of Charlie Newsome, because he couldn't directly or with certainty tie it to either the death of Eddie Guyol or the numbers racket. He had to admit that it could have been a horrible coincidental murder. It *could* have been, but he doubted it.

Hanging up the phone, Matt pushed himself from the chair and patted his pockets in search of a cigarette. Then he recalled that both he and Greerson had failed in the same effort back on Pryor Street. Slowly, he realized that he'd smoked more in the last four hours or so than he had in the last couple of weeks. Matt decided he needed to slow that pace. As he stood there searching for a piece of chewing gum, he realized that Detective Greerson was standing in the doorway, grinning. Jim had been in the room long enough to see Matt's fruitless search for a smoke. He tossed a new pack of cigarettes across the room to the reporter. "I bummed 'em off one of the other detectives. Keep 'em." Matt grinned and began to break the pack open. Even though they were Chesterfields and not his regular brand, he would be glad for a cigarette, any cigarette. He'd start cutting back again… later.

Greerson followed the cigarette pack from the door to where his young companion was unwrapping the smokes. As he walked across the well-lighted room, Matt noticed, for the first time, a barely discernible limp in the detective's gait. "Well, you're in luck, I guess. I can't find Rutherford anywhere." Matt smiled at the news as Jim continued, "Chief Poole doesn't know where he is either. My guess is he's chasing something somewhere he considers a hot lead on the Guyol murder. Or, if he's given up on worming his way into the Guyol case, he's shacked up with a broad and a bottle somewhere."

Matt considered the idea. "Maybe he's onto something big, Jim. You think?"

"Rutherford hasn't had a good idea since sleeve garters became popular. Whatever else he may or may not be, Artie's a good cop. But not everybody's cut out to be a good detective. Just between you and me, Matt, there are men in this police department, not naming names, of course, who couldn't find rice in Chinatown, unless they *really wanted* to look for it. They're in the department because they have 'invisible' friends in high places."

The reporter's mouth drew up in a silent "oh" as he nodded his understanding. That the Atlanta Police Department had, for some time, been permeated with members of or supporters of the Ku Klux Klan, the "Invisible Empire," was a well-known supposition. Nothing more needed to be said.

"Let me reiterate one thing about that last statement. Rutherford's a good cop, just not a great detective. Of course, that's only my opinion. But I don't have 'invisible' friends. In fact, I don't have *any* friends. Certainly, no 'political' friends. My daddy always told me to keep skunks, bankers, and politicians at a distance. I'm here because I'm just enough of a don't-give-a-shit asshole to get results."

"I don't see that in you, Jim. Not at all."

"Oh, it's there, kid," he sighed, as he gazed vacantly past Matt toward one of the windows and the blackness beyond. "Ask around. Just keep watching."

Matt was stunned when he looked at Greerson's face. To the newsman, the detective looked as if his mind were a thousand miles away. Nonetheless, the young *Georgian* correspondent swallowed hard and moved on. "So what's the plan, Jim?"

The detective seemed to return from wherever he'd been in that moment. "Let's head up to Pershing Point Apartments. I hate to roust some jane outta bed at this time of night, but it may be for her own good. And it may lead the investigation somewhere. But from here on, we need to have an understanding."

"Okay..." Matt drawled, uncertain of what was coming next.

"It has to be understood that you can't print anything that we're purposely holding back from the public, something that only the killer might know, for example, and that would let us know we've got the right person when we get 'em. When the time comes, you can have first crack at the information. Does that make sense?"

"Yeah, sure. But, so far, there's nothing like that that you've told me, right?"

"Right. *So far.*" Jim scanned the room. "Well. If you're ready, let's go."

Leaving the building, the detective agreed to drop Matt's car off at his boardinghouse on the way to Pershing Point. He followed the young reporter to the Houston Street house in his car. During the drive, Matt discovered that he still held Gutowski's magazine and bullet in his coat pocket. He dropped them on the passenger-side floorboard for now. As Matt parked near the house, he saw a figure sitting in the faint glow of its front porch light. He gave Greerson a quick wave, indicating he needed a second, and ran up the steps. Rhamy Fleming sat on the swing, gently moving back and forth. The landlord had a cigar going. He rose as the young man approached him. Rhamy smiled a greeting.

"Mr. Fleming, what are you doing up and out here at this hour?" Matt's voice was scarcely more than a whisper.

"I just couldn't sleep, Matt. We heard about the murder on the radio. Are you all right?" Before the young man could respond, Rhamy jutted his chin toward Greerson's throbbing Hudson 8 Coupe and asked, "Who's that?"

Matt quickly explained, "I'm fine. I'm working on the murder story now. And that's an Atlanta detective. We're headed to see someone now who may know something about it." He patted his landlord on the shoulder. "You need to get some rest, my friend. Miss Dixie will tan my hide if I'm responsible for you being too tired to work. Besides, you're gonna scare the daylights out of the milkman if he comes upon you sitting out here. I'll see you later today." They shared a smile, and the young man trotted down the steps to the car idling at the curb.

As Matt scrambled onto the car seat, the detective drove away from the curb. "Who was that?"

The young man looked back at the boardinghouse fondly. "That was my landlord. He was only concerned about me and what was going on. It's kind of like living at home with the parents sometimes. He's good people. He and his wife both are good folks." As they turned onto Peachtree Street, Matt asked, "So, are you married or what?"

In the flickering light, Matt could see that Jim's face hardened suddenly as he shifted uncomfortably in his seat. After a couple of seconds, he responded with a hard edge in his voice. "No." Owing to the tone of the detective's response, Grimes let the subject drift and settled in for the ride. Time lay on the air between the two men.

When Greerson finally spoke, he filled Matt in on the additional dope about the Guyol murder he'd picked up while he was at the police station. The journalist made notes in the available light as they drove north.

In due course, Detective Greerson parked around the corner from the nine-story, three-year-old Pershing Point Apartment building, located within the "V" formed where Peachtree Street and West Peachtree Street met. The area had been Goldsboro Park, Matt recalled, until late 1918, when the city honored General Pershing by changing the name to Pershing Point. It also occurred to Matt that they weren't that far from the Nash residence in Ansley Park.

"Okay, Matt, Charlie's girlfriend's name is Dunbar. My intent is to approach her gently to see what she knows and why it was so important to Charlie for me to come see her."

The two men left the car and entered the building. Greerson found a Dunbar listed as living in apartment five-fourteen. Taking the self-service elevator to a lurching stop at the fifth floor, they quickly located the apartment. The detective glanced at his wristwatch, breathed deeply, and pressed his thumb hard against the door buzzer. It droned somewhere inside the apartment. When no response came forth quickly enough to satisfy the big cop's concern, he rapped hard on the door. After a second heavy knock, they could hear movement from within. A tiny female voice came through the door. "Yes? What is it?"

"Ma'am, I need to talk to you. I know it's late but it's important."

"Who are you?"

Greerson looked a little embarrassed by his oversight of not identifying himself from the beginning. "I'm Detective Greerson with the Atlanta Police Department. May I speak to you, please?"

"Do you have identification?"

Greerson dug out his bronze shield and identification card and held them up to the door. "If you crack the door open, you can see my badge, ma'am."

The door opened slowly. A single, wary eye peered from behind it. The policeman moved his badge down to the eye's level and held it there. After a long minute, the woman pulled the door open and turned back into the room with slow, shuffling steps. The men swept off their hats and followed her into a well-kept and nicely decorated room. She stopped by the back of a sofa and faced her two visitors. "I'm sorry gentlemen, but a body cain't be too careful nowadays." Her voice was light and pleasant but held over the remnants of sleep interrupted. From the light of a floor lamp that burned in the corner, the men garnered their first good look at the woman. Both were initially stunned. The woman was much older and far different from what they'd expected. Short and sturdy, she wore a flannel bathrobe of indiscernible color and indistinguishable pattern. The top of the cinched bathrobe's front was clutched tightly to her throat by an aged but strong hand. A row of curlers protruded from the gray hair that framed her face. But what staggered both men most was her apparent age: she appeared at least two decades older than Charlie. "What can I be adoin' far ya?" she asked, stifling a yawn.

The police officer awkwardly glanced down at his hat as he held it out in front of him. When he looked back up into the woman's eyes, he said, "Well, ma'am, we're sorry to bother you at this late hour, but it's very important. I... uh, I think we need to see your daughter. Is she here?"

"Well, young man, I ain't got no daughter." She crossed her arms and bowed slightly. "Now, can ya'll please tell me what this here's about?"

"Are you Mrs. Dunbar? There's no younger Mrs. Dunbar here?"

"Well, I'm sure as fire there's a younger Mrs. Dunbar somewhere in the world, young fella. But I'm the onliest one that lives here."

"Well, you see, ma'am, Charlie Newsome sent us here to see a Mrs. Dunbar."

"Oh, Charlie. My dear, sweet Charlie. Why didn't ya say so? Let me go in and put on somethin' a bit more fittin'. I ain't used to greetin' folks like this," she laughed waving her hand across her body, indicating her attire. Before either man could say anything, the shambling figure disappeared into an adjoining room. "Ya'll take a seat! I'll be right back!" she called over her shoulder as she closed the door behind her.

The men sat on the sofa and waited. The only sound in the room was the ticking of a clock on a nearby table. Then, Jim drummed his fingers impatiently on a side table and heaved an audible sigh. After a second or so, Matt whispered, "Is it me or does she seem a tad old, even for Charlie?"

"Yeah, I'd say so. But, like my grandma used to say, 'There's a lid for every pot.' Maybe he just liked older women. *Really* older women."

"Zowie! I don't get it. But I've heard Brick say that older women are great. He says that they don't tell and they're grateful as hell."

Greerson winced and asked, "That's harsh. Who on earth is Brick?"

"Just one of the guys I work with."

"Remind me to avoid shaking his hand if you ever introduce us."

The door opened and Mrs. Dunbar rejoined the men. She was wearing a shapeless print housedress and flats. The curlers had given way to faintly coiled, unruly tresses. Before sitting in a chair facing the divan, she asked, "Now why would my son send you to see me at this hour?"

"Son?" both men exclaimed in unison. They looked at each other in shock.

The old lady took a turn at being surprised. Her face went blank. After a moment, she spoke. "Yes, my son! Charlie Newsome is my boy. Didn't he tell ya'll I was his maw?"

Suddenly, Jim Greerson couldn't bring himself to tell the old lady of her son's death. Leave that to some other poor, dumb son of a bitch from the department. "Well, no ma'am. We didn't speak for very long, you see. He simply mentioned your name and this apartment building. And he said we needed to see you. Called you his girl and said he loved you."

"Well, a momma always wants to be her boy's 'girl' and always wants his love, but Charlie was probably talkin' 'bout Vivian. She's his girlfriend."

"Okay, Mrs. Dunbar. Help me out here, please. Your name is Dunbar, not Newsome. And I understood you lived up north of here."

"Oh, that. Well, ya see, whilst Charlie was up North boxin', Caleb, that was his paw, died. Charlie sent me money when he could, but I needed somethin' a little more, well, dependable, ya might say. Then I met Mr. Dunbar, a widow man, at a church social back home. We was both lonely, ya see. We got on good, so we got married after a spell. Then after about two years of bein' hitched, dang if he didn't up and git kilt in a mill accident. 'Bout that time, Charlie come back home. Once he got steady work, he brung me down here from Gilmer County and got me this here place." Mrs. Dunbar paused long enough to scan the room slowly. "It's nice, but it ain't home, if ya know what I'm asayin'. I miss the folks and the mountains."

"So, did... do you see Charlie very much, Mrs. Dunbar?" Greerson glanced sideways along his eyes in Grimes's direction. His look was uneasy. "Do you know what kind of work he was... he's been doing?"

"Oh, yes, Charlie comes by and visits for a spell ever so often. He's a good boy. And, no, I don't know what he does nowadays, but he must be pretty important to be makin' the money he does. And his boss really likes and trusts him, too."

"I'm sure you're right, ma'am, but what makes you say that? That part about the trust, I mean."

"Why, them men had an important meetin' right here in this very room. Some kinda plannin' session. Right here. Couldn't even trust their own folks enough to have it in their own offices."

"A planning meeting?"

"Well, that's what Charlie called it. I don't know the nature of it, 'cause Charlie said the men needed privacy and he sent me to a movie at that theater on Peachtree Street, I think it is. Oh, I git so turned 'round in this town. Ya know the one I mean?" Greerson didn't know for certain, but he nodded so she'd continue. "Anyways, it's the one that's red on the outside and has the red and green tile fountain right in the lobby! Inside the buildin'! Land sakes! I never saw nothin' like it! Seein' it was better'n watchin' the movie, I tell ya. Somethin' about some kinda lancers with that Cooper fella. It was –"

"Oh, she's talking about the Tenth Street Theater," Matt interjected.

"Yeah, I know. I recognized it when she mentioned the color and the fountain." Greerson spoke to Grimes but never took his eyes off Charlie's mother. "Excuse me, ma'am, but getting back to this meeting they had here –"

"Oh, well, like I said, I don't know nothin' about it, 'ceptin' that Charlie was all upset by the time I got back here. He was asittin' at that table right over there all in a fuss, a smokin', and a drinkin' coffee and a writin' stuff on some papers."

"What kind of stuff, Ma'am?"

"I ain't rightly sure, mister." Her face reddened slightly. "Ya see, I don't read or write so good, myself. Just read a little bit and print. But Charlie was a writin' like a house afire."

"Do you know what he did with the papers?"

"Well, when he lit outta here later, he put whatever he had in a envelope and took 'em with him. But I'm not for sure where to. The papers seemed kinda important to Charlie, so I'd be guessin' they went either to his boss or to Vivian's place for safe keepin'."

"Hey, Jim, I think *The Lives of a Bengal Lancer* is still showing there. My girl and I saw it about a week or so ago."

"Yeah? Say, Mrs. Dunbar, when did they have this meeting here anyway?"

"Well, it was this past Sunday." She smiled sweetly. "Sunday afternoon after church, of course."

Matt sat quietly making notes on his pad as Jim mulled over what Mrs. Dunbar had told them. His thought process was interrupted when the old lady added, "I told all of this to t'other detective. Of course, he wasn't very nice about askin'."

Again, the two men were taken aback and quickly glanced at each other. Artie Rutherford's name came first to Greerson's mind, but he questioned how Rutherford had learned of or could have known about the woman and had gotten there so fast. "What other detective, Mrs. Dunbar?"

Mrs. Dunbar's face scrunched as she tried to recall a name. "Oh, I just cain't recollect his name. A foreign-soundin' name, it was. I'm sure y'all know him. He was a big man with a gruff voice. Not meanin' to be unkind about it, but he had a nose big enough that you could hide stuff in it. Kinda a nasty nature, too. Pushed his way in here." Her voice was filled with indignation. "He was so contrary that I almost didn't tell him 'bout Vivian. He never would show me his badge like you. Charlie always told me to ask for their identifyin' stuff if anybody ever come acallin' here."

A moment of icy panic clutched at Greerson's heart. His face darkened suddenly and the muscles in his jaw protruded. Trying not to show alarm, he quietly asked, "Was his name Gutowski?" Matt jerked his head in the detective's direction. Wide-eyed dread played across the tall reporter's face.

"That sounds 'bout right. But I ain't very good with names, detective."

Calmly, the man asked, "Mrs. Dunbar, what's Vivian's last name? Do you know where Vivian lives or where we might be able to locate her? It's very important that I see her as soon as possible. Tonight, if possible."

She stood slowly, brushing the front of her housedress, and said, "Let me git my book." She scrunched her face in frustration, blushed slightly, and added, "I don't recollect her last name, detective. Maybe it's in my book. Charlie give me a book of pages so's I could or he could write such down for me. My mem'ry ain't what it used to be." With that, she bustled off toward the room where she'd earlier changed clothes. The two men looked at each other without saying a word. The uneasiness in Jim's eyes said it all. When she returned and dropped onto the chair, the old lady continued, "Here 'tis. They have a little house on, uh, Altoona Place." The word "Altoona" came forth slowly as if more memorized than read. "Yellow, Charlie said it was. Altoona's somewheres in Atlanta, but I ain't got a notion of where. Charlie could tell you exactly where 'tis."

"That's okay, Mrs. Dunbar. I know exactly where it is," Greerson said dully, absently, as he leaned and reached his hand out to the lady. "Can my partner copy that information, please, ma'am?" She bent forward toward the men and handed the book directly to Matt. "Get the phone number, too, Matt, if there is one."

"No last name, Jim," Matt said softly. The reporter duly recorded the address and phone number, a Walnut exchange, on his notepad before returning the book to Mrs. Dunbar.

Matt looked at Jim pointedly with expectation, as if the latter had failed to do or say something. Ignoring the stare, the detective stood, so his companion did the same. "Well, thank you Mrs. Dunbar. Again, we're very sorry to bother you at this hour, but it was very important."

The men retreated to the door, followed by Mrs. Dunbar. "Oh, heavens, detective, that's all right. Folks my age don't seem to git or need as much sleep as youngun's like you. Oh, my goodness, I just realized that I never offered you gentlemen any coffee or anythin'."

The young reporter nervously spun his fedora on his hand as the detective said, "Thanks anyway, Mrs. Dunbar, but we've troubled you enough."

"If you see him, give my Charlie my love, won't you?"

Matt tried to swallowed, but his mouth was dry, his nerves on edge. Greerson muttered a soft, "Sure thing, ma'am." She closed the door behind them.

As they walked down the hall toward the elevator, Matt turned to his companion in disbelief. His face mirrored the depth of his frustration and confusion. "I don't understand, Jim. Why didn't you tell –?"

The detective squared up to his companion and held up one of his broad palms. "Look, Matt. I don't like people very much and I don't give a shit about most things, but I plainly couldn't tell that old lady that her son was probably murdered by some vile son of a bitch lowlife." He paused, sighed heavily, and shook his head. "I've done dozens of death notifications in my time. But this one? Uh-uh. Just couldn't do it. It'll keep 'til the department or somebody else gets around to it. She's apparently safe from Gutowski or whoever's behind this play. If not, we'd've found a corpse. But that may not be true for Charlie's girlfriend. We need to find her and quick! And, hopefully, that'll get us to those papers." He paused momentarily in contemplation. "They may mean something or may not. But we need to find Vivian." Glancing at his wristwatch, he turned and continued briskly toward the elevator. "Besides, telling Mrs. Dunbar about Charlie and the comforting of her that'd have been needed would have delayed us. We need to move to find Vivian now!"

Matt kept stride with him, reading from his notes. "The house is in the two-hundred block of Altoona Place, wherever that is."

"You're gonna find out very soon, sparky," Jim said thinly.

Leaving the elevator on the ground floor, Jim moved quickly to a pay phone in the lobby. Matt intuitively handed him his notepad with Vivian's telephone number. Greerson dropped his nickel, dialed, and waited. The reporter closely watched the face of his companion. Following about a dozen rings with no answer, the detective gave the younger man an anxious expression. "I don't like this! Let's go!"

# CHAPTER 7

# The Missing Papers

After making their way down Peachtree Street, Greerson steered the car across Cain Street past the Red Rock Building and the bus station. Beyond the normal activity in and around the terminal, the buildings appeared dark and lifeless. In the eerie quiet of that early morning, they wound their way in a generally southwesterly direction before finishing on Greensferry Avenue, which then became Westview Drive. Neither man spoke as they drove. Greerson was planning his next move based on one of several contingencies. Matt was still trying to read his companion and understand his thought process back at the Pershing Point Apartments. Before long, Greerson turned left onto Altoona Place and stopped. The lane was bare of street lighting.

Matt looked to Jim. "How the hell are we gonna find the house in this darkness?"

"There's a flash somewhere by your seat. Grab it and scan the houses on your side of the street 'til we find a number. Then we'll just feel our way."

"Scan the houses with a flashlight at what, two in the morning? What happens if somebody decides to take a potshot at us?"

"Simple, Matt. I'll shoot back," Greerson replied carelessly, his voice deadpan, as he scanned the neighborhood.

Matt moved around in his seat and dug for the light. "That's easy for you to say, Jim. It's *my* side they'll be shooting at. And if you're firing back, I'm likely caught in a cross fire," he laughed nervously. But Detective Greerson was having none of it. He was focused like a bulldog on finding Vivian. Once Matt found the flashlight, he swept it across the front of the house adjacent to Westview Drive. No numbers were visible on or around the structure. "Nothing," he told Jim.

The driver eased the car down the slight incline of the street to the next house, which, like the first, appeared in the faint light to be an unpretentious bungalow. The detective stopped the car and, resting his left arm on the steering wheel, leaned toward his passenger, straining to find a clue to the street number. The flashlight revealed a wall-mounted letter box, emblazoned with hand-painted digits, next to the front door. "Okay, Jim, this is the even-numbered side of the street. So Charlie's place will be on your side."

As the pair faced forward, they saw lights showing through the windows of a home several places down the street on the left. Jim shifted the car into gear, easing his way, veering to the left, and killing the headlights as they moved. He braked the car to a stop in the front of the modest bungalow. He cut the Hudson's motor. "Is that house white, yellow, or light gray?" he asked. "I can't tell." Matt handed him the flashlight, which, in turn, revealed a light-yellow exterior and a numbered mailbox next to the front door, which was centered on the front of the house and was covered by a small gable. The numbers matched Matt's notes. Lights shone to the outside through the four tall, narrow cottage-style windows, two on either side of the front door's stoop. No movement could be seen in the house. He turned to Matt. "You said before that you know guns and know how to use 'em. Was that true or just spur of the minute bullshit?"

"I grew up on a farm near Augusta. We had rifles and hunted a lot. And my dad had a handgun he carried when he took cash to pay off the tenant farmers when the cotton came in. I went with him most days. He was pretty much an expert with guns and insisted that I learn how to use them. I did, I have, and I can."

"Well, the situation has moved to a new level." The big cop reached behind him. "Here. Take this." Matt could see in the soft light thrown from the house that Jim was extending a revolver to him. When the reporter's face reflected surprise, the detective gave him an insistent nod. "Look, I'd rather you have a gun and not need it than need it and not have it. Tuck it away before we go inside and leave it there unless things turn to shit. Otherwise, it's the same rules as before. Don't do anything without my say-so."

"Got it, Jim." As he spoke, Matt hefted the gun, held it barrel down to the floorboard, and examined it. In the dim light it appeared to be a Smith & Wesson large frame, .38 special. The gun felt good in his hand. He quickly broke open the cylinder and verified that it held six live rounds. Snapping the cylinder back in place, he looked up to see Greerson, watching him carefully and smiling. The bulky detective was recalling his youth on a truck farm in a county west of the city.

"Okay?" the detective asked. Matt smiled sideways at him and nodded.

They quietly eased out of the Hudson and pushed their doors nearly shut. The pair slowly walked across the tall weeds covering the front yard to the rutted driveway that ran down the left side of the house toward the back. As he walked, Greerson, whose eyes had adjusted to the low light level, hurriedly checked the driveway. The light coming through windows on the side of the house helped. No cars were visible. Momentarily, they stood at a front corner of the bungalow and, then, turned to move across its front. When they reached a window, the older man gestured for Matt to stay put. The detective placed himself flat against the house's exterior beneath a window. He eased his face to the opening to steal a quick look inside. When he pulled back, he shook his head. Matt understood this to indicate that he'd seen nothing, no one.

Jim checked the second window. Nothing. While the young journalist stayed in place, Greerson moved around the small stoop to a window on the other side. Meanwhile, Matt searched the neighborhood through the darkness for any signs of life. He half expected to be the target of an irate neighbor's buckshot at any second. He watched Jim as he repeated his moves at the third and fourth windows. After a quick look, the officer moved to the small porch and signaled Matt to join him.

Before he knocked on the door, Greerson whispered, "There's a woman in a back room packing a suitcase in a big-ass hurry. I could see her through the shade and an open door on the other side of a hallway. She looks like she's getting ready to pull the big flit. Couldn't see anybody else." He positioned Matt to the side of the door and took up the same position on the side by the doorknob before he rapped his knuckles hard on the door's surface. Silence. Then, furtive movement. The lights coming through the two windows closest to the driveway were extinguished. It caught the pair on the front stoop by surprise. Then, stillness again. Detective Greerson pounded the door a second time. Nothing. An uneasy silence seemed to have enveloped the bungalow. Jim had experienced this kind of utter, deadly stillness during the war after an artillery barrage ended.

The detective placed his hand on Matt's chest, making sure he stayed in place for the moment. After that, he reached for the doorknob haltingly. When he found it unlocked, Jim turned the knob and pushed the door open slowly. He yelled through the opened door, "Detective Greerson! Atlanta Police Department! Anybody in the house, come out with your hands up! Now!" Again, his shouts met the hush of a graveyard. His gun at the ready, Jim Greerson moved quickly through the door and to his left into the room, slamming his body flat against the front wall. The only illumination in the room streamed faintly from lights down the hall through a doorway connecting to that passage. "Detective Greerson! Atlanta Police Department! Come out with your hands up! Now!" As he yelled, Jim's free hand swept the wall, searching desperately for a light switch. He located one in short order and lit the room with one motion.

Greerson found himself in a living room, empty except for cheap pieces of furniture that appeared to be from a secondhand store. To the left of center on the back wall of the living room an arched opening connected to a small dining room-kitchen combination. The room was dark. The doorway to the hall was on the side wall in the back right corner of the living room. The illumination from the room Jim was in bathed the stoop where Matt waited. "Hello! I know you're in here! I saw you through the window!" Greerson still received no response to his shout.

The detective tried to size up the situation quickly. Maintaining his guard, Jim spoke over his right shoulder and quietly told Matt to stay in place until he checked out the house. With that, Greerson crept toward the arched doorway. As he moved, he glanced sideways through the door leading to the hall. The fleeting look revealed no signs of life. Past the arched doorway, he found a light switch for the space. The dining area held a small round pine table and four straightback chairs of the same wood. The kitchen consisted of nothing but the basic appliances, a messy counter, and a sink half-full of dirty dishes. He stood very still for a minute and listened intently. No discernible sounds could be heard from further inside the house. The kitchen had a door leading to the backyard. The door was closed. Next, he carefully moved to an opening that connected the kitchen area with the hallway leading to the rest of the bungalow.

Greerson slowly edged his head up to the kitchen doorjamb and into the unlit hallway far enough for his right eye to determine the passage was still empty. The quick glance also revealed that there were four doors down the passage. All of them were open. Rectangular shafts of light lay across the hall floor from the front room closest to him and from each of the two openings at the far end of the hallway, one to the front and one to the rear of the house. The fartherest two doorways were across the way from each other at a slight angle. The officer stepped into the corridor and flattened himself against a wall. Leading with his raised revolver and moving sideways, he found that the first hallway door opened to a small bathroom on the back of the house. He quickly found a light switch and checked the space, which was in disarray but empty. The detective took a deep breath. He could feel sweat forming on his forehead, causing the inside band of his fedora to stick there. The door directly across from the bathroom was to a small front bedroom, lighted by an overhead fixture. The room was empty other than a secondhand bureau standing against the far wall. The big cop made his way along the hallway to the next door that led to another small bedroom, also on the front of the bungalow. A ceiling light illuminated the space. The musty-smelling room, held little except a few boxes, a small cast-off table, and a straightback wooden chair. This was the room through whose window he'd spied the woman in what turned out to be a large back bedroom.

Greerson turned and moved quickly into the back bedroom, his Colt leading the way, expecting trouble. No one was there. The same type of second-hand-store furniture, as he'd found in the living room, filled the room. A woman's hat lay on the bed next to an open, partially filled suitcase. An assortment of clothing was carelessly tossed about on the bed. Several drawers of a dresser were opened to some extent with clothes draped from their fronts and sides, as if hurriedly rummaged through. The bureau's top was a jumble of various items. The detective made a fluid sweep from the bedroom doorway to the distant corner, clearing the wardrobe as he went. The chifforobe held nothing of interest. Finally, he carefully raised the flounced edge of the bed covering and checked beneath the bed. Nothing.

Greerson holstered his gun and walked the hallway back toward the living room. As he moved around, he pulled off his hat and mopped his forehead and the hatband with a handkerchief before planting the fedora back on his head. "Matt, it's okay to come in now," he called out while he looked at some papers lying on the dining table. "The place is empty. The frail I saw through the window must've taken it on the lam out the back when we banged on the door."

With no response and no Matt after what seemed a very long time, the detective turned and started toward the front door. Matt slowly moved from the darkness of the front porch into the glow cast by the living-room lights like an evolving photograph in a darkroom developing tray. The young reporter held a look of stunned apprehension. Jim stopped short. As Matt shuffled in with his opened hands held at shoulder level, the reason for his expression appeared close behind him. The woman Greerson had seen through the window, followed the reporter, holding the working end of a revolver just behind his left ear. Her blue eyes showed large and frightened, but determined. She was half a dozen inches shorter than Grimes and had to peer around him to see Jim. When she was in the room, she kicked one leg back to shut the door behind her. The slamming door caused Matt to recoil hard, but the woman never lost her grip on his coat collar. Her hand with the tight hold on the big reporter also clutched his handgun.

Before Jim could react, she screamed, "Don't move, asshole, or this jerk has his brains decorating the walls of this dump!"

In an even, relaxed voice, Greerson said, "Look, I'm Detective Jim Greerson of the Atlanta Police Department. We're only trying to find a woman named Vivian."

"Yeah?" she shrieked so loud that her body shook. "That's what the last son of a bitch said, too! Just a cop, lookin' for somethin', he says! I ain't buyin' it just on your say-so, bub!"

"Okay, wait!" Jim blurted and held his hands out in a soothing motion. Matt saw the same move by the detective for the second time that night. Though, this time he watched through panicked eyes. In a calmer voice, Jim went on, "Let me show you my badge." The woman tensed visibly. "Easy, lady. Take it easy. Don't do anything we'll all regret. I'm gonna move slow, all right?" With that, he gently lifted his coat with a forefinger and thumb to reveal his holstered gun, saying, "I'm showing you my gun, so you know where it is." Releasing his coat lapel, he continued. "That's because I need to reach in my side coat pocket to get my badge. Okay? It's in this pocket," he finished, using a slight hand movement to signify the right side of his coat.

"Be careful, mister, or I swear I'll kill this guy! And then I'll try for you, too! I'm better with this gun than you think!" She swallowed hard. Her eyes darted from the cop to her captive and back again.

Greerson nodded slowly. "I believe you, lady. Really I do."

"Use your left hand and two fingers to do any reachin'!"

"Okay," he replied slowly. He reached his left hand across his torso into his coat's side pocket. Removing his badge and identification card, he held them up and extended them for her to see.

"Stop!" she spat at him. Her outburst startled both men.

Greerson was at a loss. "What? What did I do, lady?"

"Nothin', bub! Nothing yet! I just can't read that shit from here!" About six feet separated the two. "Hand 'em to this fella. Careful! And you," she indicated her hostage with a sharp yank on his coat, "take 'em and hold 'em up by your shoulder where I can see 'em. And no funny business. I've had enough bullshit for one night! I'm tired and I'm mad as hell! So move easy." She jerked her hold on Grimes again. "Keep your head and you may live through the night." Her voice reflected a grim determination Greerson had heard in others before. Despite the circumstances, he grudgingly gave her credit for her smarts. The woman had immediately recognized that he was right-handed and demanded he use his left hand. Plus, she had quickly devised a way to read his identification without moving or losing the upper hand in this little standoff. She was not one to be taken lightly, the detective surmised.

Cautiously, Jim leaned forward and placed the items in Matt's outstretched hand. The blond reporter, certain his heart could be seen beating through his shirt and coat, made sure they were right side up, and then carefully eased them into the position the woman had demanded. The revolver never left the side of his head. The women looked at the badge and card a protracted minute before relaxing. To Matt, it was a minute that seemed as long and uncomfortable as a proctologist's middle finger. When she dropped Matt's gun from her other hand to the floor, the *Georgian* reporter flinched again slightly.

She collapsed onto the living room's sagging couch, crying. As she buckled, she dropped her gun onto the cushion beside her. Matt tossed his identification back to Greerson, who darted for the woman's handgun and scooped it and Matt's revolver up, dropping the latter into his side pocket. For his part, Grimes slumped on a nearby chair and shakily dug for a cigarette. When he'd managed to get the end of it to the match's flame, he took his deepest pull ever as the smoke rushed into his lungs. He waved the match out and tossed it to the floor. At this point, he didn't care about propriety. The quiet relief of all three exhausted people filled the room. They sucked the air.

"Gimme one of those, will ya, sport?" the woman on the sofa said matter-of-factly as she held her hand out. She acted as if nothing had happened between them in the last several minutes. Matt's first inclination was to ram the whole pack down her damned throat. But the idea quickly passed, and he moved to her side on the divan. Tears still streaked her face. He shook one out of the pack for her.

Matt dug a folder of matches from his pocket, but, before he could strike a match for the woman, Jim spoke. "I could sure as hell use one of those gaspers myself." The young man handed him a cigarette and struck a match. Both people leaned into it carefully as he lit their smokes for them. As he watched the female intently through a pale gray tendril of smoke curling toward the ceiling, the detective stood over her and emptied the five .38 caliber rounds from her revolver. The old nickel-plated, top break gun had been manufactured by Iver Johnson's Arms & Cycle Works out of Boston. He lifted the gun slightly in her direction. "This is an oldie," he observed. She didn't stir. He looked at the reporter and made an all but imperceptible nod of his head toward the chair the young man had formerly occupied. Matt huffed but shifted back to the chair. Jim sat beside the woman. "Is there anybody else here?" She shook her head wearily. "Can I take it that you're Vivian?"

The woman shuddered and tilted her head back as if to stem more tears. Then, she slumped forward and nodded her response as she pressed her long fingers against her temples. From this vantage point, Matt got his first real look at her. Vivian looked to be about thirty, but she may have been slightly older. She was pretty, though her skin was without makeup. She was tall, lissome, and wore a button-down-the-front, maize-colored pique skirt. Her more than ample bosom filled a matching short-sleeved blouse. Ironically, while she wore gold-tone jet filigree button earrings, she was without shoes at the moment. A large mouse was forming under her left eye. It matched the sizeable mark on the angle of her jaw below it. One corner of her mouth was smeared with dried blood. An abrasion adorned one side of her neck, and bruises were taking shape on both her upper arms. She'd been manhandled, hard and very recently. All in all, Vivian came across as a sloe-eyed, hard-bitten girl who, just now, looked scared and woozy. As he watched her, she pulled a clump of her shoulder-length, mouse-colored hair behind a sizeable ear, one of her salient physical features. The effect snapped Matt back from his reverie. He momentarily fingered a cigarette burn in an arm of the chair.

Suddenly, with all the windows shut, the air in the room seemed heavy, oppressive. The young journalist had never felt so drained, not even during his football days at Georgia. "Vivian, do you mind if I make us some coffee? That is, if there's any in the house."

Vivian kept her eyes closed and nodded. "Coffee's in the upper cabinet beside the back door. Pot's on the stove." Matt moved to the kitchen.

Jim asked, "Is that how you snuck out and circled back around on us? The back door?" When she didn't answer right away, Detective Greerson reached over and nudged her arm. She moved with a start and pulled away from his touch. "Well?"

Vivian opened her eyes and looked at him. Her face showed an equal measure of toughness and vulnerability. "Yeah," she gasped. "I wasn't sure who you were, no matter what you said." They could hear Matt rattling around in the kitchen. Vivian looked away from the detective and in that direction. She nonchalantly glanced at the tip of her cigarette.

"You said that somebody else had been here, Vivian. A cop? Was that tonight?"

The lithe woman fiddled with a faded doily on the sofa arm beside her. "Yeah, tonight. And no, not a cop. Just a crud pretending to be a cop. The big slob said he was a detective just like you did. Only one problem. I'd seen him hanging around the wrong places at the wrong time for him to be a cop. Even a wrong one. And, at the time, he was acting like he was the muscle of the operation. He just didn't *know* I'd seen him. I knew what he really did for a livin'. Numbers. Probably some other shit, too, but the bug for sure."

Greerson nodded toward her injuries. "Did he do this to you?"

She went on exactly as if the detective hadn't asked the question. "If I coulda got my hands on that gun, I'd a killed the bastard."

Detective Greerson pressed. "Do you need to go to the hospital, Vivian?"

"Nah. I'm just sore in places. Maybe some bruised ribs. My boyfriend knows about bruised ribs. And yeah, the big creep pretending to be a cop did this to me."

"Where'd you get the gun, Vivian?"

"My boyfriend, Charlie, gave it to me. Said I might need it for protection. I wish I coulda got to it earlier tonight."

"Charlie Newsome?"

Vivian got a faraway look in her eyes, and a slight smile crossed her lips as if an undertaker had prepared her for a viewing. "Yeah, Charlie Newsome." The grin broadened. "Charlie's my honey. He's the only guy I've ever really loved, who really loved me back. And not just to use me, either. He's different, not like the rest of 'em, not a skirt chaser. We're gonna get outta here and get married. Get a chicken farm up in the mountains." She looked at Greerson. "You know Charlie?"

The detective hesitated before replying, "Yeah, I know Charlie. He's a good, decent man. I like him." Jim realized that his young companion was standing in the arched doorway, glaring at him in an accusatory manner. He was drying a coffee cup with a dish towel. The tall reporter waggled his head, turned, and disappeared back into the kitchen. Greerson tried to brush off the guilt imparted by the look. Returning to Vivian, he said, "Tell me more about your visitor. What did he look like? What was he doing here? Did he say?"

Her smile edged away. "He was a big galoot with a big face and an even bigger nose. I tell ya, if I just coulda got that gun, I'd of blown that big beezer off his face." She paused momentarily, as if recalling the events and the person. "Yankee accent. I don't know his name. He said he was lookin' for papers Charlie wanted to turn over to the cops, and that I needed to give 'em to him. When I wouldn't cough 'em up, he started in on me." She grinned without parting her lips and, then, touched her jaw tenderly. Wincing slightly in pain, she went on, "I was a tougher dame than he was used to pushing around. I could tell that. It was killin' him." She beamed, as if reliving her triumph. "He learned that people may call a woman a 'frail' nowadays, but the word 'frail' doesn't apply to all of us." Greerson smirked, believing that statement.

"He wanted to do more to me, but I think he was afraid he might need to come back to get what he wanted. He didn't want to kill the goose that was hidin' the golden egg. Cretins like him are about as common as a run in a pair of twenty-five-cent stockings." She paused, frowning thoughtfully, and turned to Jim. "I don't want Charlie to know about the beatin'. Okay?" She took a deep, quivering breath. "I'm gonna tell him I was in a car wreck with one of my girlfriends tonight. Maybe he'll buy it. But I just don't want him going after that creep. And I don't wanna delay us gettin' outta here to that chicken farm. We're both sick to our back teeth of the whole business."

"Do you know what papers this goon was talking about, Vivian?"

"Yeah. I don't know what's on the papers, but I know what papers he was talkin' about. Charlie brought 'em home with him this past Sunday. He was all excited about 'em. We hid 'em. Right here. I told the big slob who was here tonight that Charlie had 'em somewhere else, but I didn't know where. Maybe in a safe-deposit box, maybe with a mouthpiece, I told him."

Greerson leaned toward her and quietly said, "I think I know what Charlie has on that paper that's so important to these people. It could hurt a lot of them, including the bum who did this to you. Would you be willing to let me have them?"

Vivian leapt from the sofa in a surprisingly graceful move. The effect was spoiled when, initially, she reached to the sofa arm to steady herself. She bent over and stubbed out her cigarette in a large glass ashtray on the small coffee table. The ashtray, made to look like alabaster, had a chip in the corner and was overflowing with cigarette butts, most with deep-red lipstick. The effort mussed her hair. When she straightened again, Vivian tossed her head back to get stray strands off her face. She stared hard down at the detective. "Charlie said those papers are our ticket outta here. So long as we have 'em hidden where they can't find 'em, they won't touch us. *Really* touch us."

"Vivian, do you really think you have them hidden where they can't find them? You know this big lummox will probably come back. And next time he may bring some pals. Give you the works *and* this house a better going-over. You don't think he can make you cough up those papers? Smart up, Vivian! Get wise to yourself! Tonight, he probably figured he was working against the clock a little bit. Maybe figured I was right behind him on his trail. Next time..."

"I dunno. Let me think, will ya? If Charlie gets here before you leave, maybe he can decide. I don't know where he could be at this hour." Her voice trailed off as she glanced at the front windows, before she walked toward the kitchen. On her way, she swung to her left and twisted a knob on the table model radio in the room. She half turned her head and called over her shoulder, "I feel like some music." The radio hummed faintly to life and light glowed behind the dial. Vivian joined Matt at the kitchen counter.

"Coffee'll be ready in a minute, Vivian," Matt grinned. The woman gave him a smirk that registered somewhere between "really?" and "are you kidding me?" as she reached into a lower cabinet and retrieved a bottle of Canadian Club. After a minute or so, a tune from some far off station played softly in other room. Vivian picked up a glass from the counter and eyeballed it. Not satisfied, she blew into it. A second look into the bottom of the glass apparently gave it her "Good Housekeeping Seal of Approval." She raised the glass to Matt with a questioning look. He smiled and shook his head. The young man decided that, as tired as he was, booze would finish him for the night. Vivian picked a second glass and repeated the process to her satisfaction. Then she located a pack of cigarettes in a drawer. With the cigarettes, the bottle, and the two glasses in hand, she returned to the living room.

Greerson beamed when he saw what she was carrying. She returned the smile and set the items down next to the ashtray on the coffee table. "Will you do the honors, detective, or are you 'on duty'?"

Jim reached for the bottle as Matt returned with two steaming cups of coffee. He sat one on the table near Jim. The reporter took his cup and plopped in the same chair, watching the scene before him. Meanwhile, Jim poured a little whiskey into the glasses. Vivian, having finished lighting a cigarette, picked up her glass and raised it in a toast. "Here's to chicken farms!" Their glasses touched, and they downed their drinks. "Now, let me show you what a real drink looks like, detective." The woman then poured herself a portion of whiskey that Matt decided would have made him howl at the moon. She gulped it down nonchalantly and used the back of her hand to wipe her mouth.

Greerson smirked, while pouring some whiskey into his coffee. "Well, I'm more 'on duty' than that, Vivian."

She turned and laughed when she saw the expression on Matt's face. The young man stared blankly, thinking of the news about Charlie Newsome that would have to befall her sometime soon. She misunderstood his air and shot an irritated look his way. "Whatsa matter, college boy? Yeah, you, college boy! It shows all over ya! What? Don'cha ya think somebody like Charlie could love a dame like me?"

The young reporter sat with his mouth opened slightly, surprised by her outburst. Before he could say anything, the detective looked at him, swallowed hard, and interceded. He shifted on the seat toward the woman beside him. "Wait, Vivian, it's not what you think." She turned to Jim, unknowing, uncertain what to expect. "He isn't thinking any such thing. He just knows that we have to tell you something that's not gonna be easy. For any of us." The smoke in the closed room suddenly seemed heavy and choking. Abruptly, she felt a fright that even good liquor couldn't dull. She bit her lower lip and dropped her cigarette carelessly into her whiskey glass.

"Tell me. What is it? Is it... is it Charlie?"

The detective held Vivian's forearms in his hands. He looked down at his hands for a long minute, uncertain how to begin. He cleared his throat. Then he gave the woman a soft up-from-under look and told her the whole story, though in muted tones. His narrative, of course, included the fact that Charlie had tried to meet with him earlier, probably to tell him about the papers and to get them to him. As he spoke, Vivian's eyes rounded into delft saucers. She tried more than once to pull from his grip. A white line showed around her mouth. Her lips began to quiver, and her face suddenly took on the appearance of a prelude to a scream.

Toward the end of his telling, Vivian's watery eyes drifted away and she gazed vacantly. Her mouth twisted in heartache, and tears streamed down her cheeks. Finally, wrenching away from Greerson's hold, she sprung from the couch and screamed, "No! It ain't true! Not Charlie! Not now! It's gotta be a mistake!" Vivian spent the next minute or so with her arms crossed, clutching her elbows, and looking miserable. She moved away and cried uncontrollably, stumbling around the room in a trancelike shuffle, moaning a sorrowful "no" every so often. At one point, she knocked over a small set of shelves holding knickknacks and gewgaws. The woman didn't seem to notice.

During this time, Jim and Matt periodically glanced at each other in helpless desperation, but neither stirred. Finally, the detective moved from the sofa and walked to the woman, who, by that time, was cowering low in a corner of the room, crying miserably. Vivian pushed herself up the wall and twisted to fall into his arms as he approached her. He held her and let her cry hard on his chest. She held him in tight desperation. Greerson pushed her out to arms length and growled low, "Charlie didn't deserve this! *You* don't deserve this! I'm gonna find the son of a bitch that did this and make him pay, Vivian!" He paused and looked deeply into her eyes. "I promise."

She fell back against his chest. "Kill him for me, detective. Kill whoever did this," she said nastily without raising her head. Matt saw the set of Greerson's jaw and didn't envy whoever was on the detective's mind then. In the short time he'd known the police officer, Matt considered him no man of nuance, as he'd shown in one minute with Gutowski, ruthless, and the next with Vivian, compassionate.

The reporter, unable to help, not knowing what to say, sat quietly, smoked, and drank his coffee as the aftermath of the tragedy played out before him. Better left to a policeman who's been here before, he thought. After a time, Jim again held the woman out from his body and looked at her keenly. "Vivian." He shook her gently when she didn't respond. "Vivian, I need your help now." She opened her eyes and looked at him dully. "Vivian, you have to give me those papers that Charlie hid."

Anger rapidly flashed in her eyes. "You bastard!"

"Listen –"

"That's all you care about! Those lousy papers! You son of a bitch!" she shrieked, as she pulled hard away from his grip. "Get outta here! Both of you get outta my house!" Vivian whirled and cringed and started crying again.

Greerson reached and grabbed Vivian once more, shaking her. "Listen to me, dammit! Do you hear yourself? One minute, you're asking me to kill the guy who murdered Charlie! The next minute, you won't give me the *one thing* that will lead me to the people behind his death. The *one thing* that might help bring the whole rotten thing crashing down! Those papers may be the key!" As she struggled against him, Jim pulled her close again, holding her tight and letting her cry.

After what seemed to Matt an interminable duration, she stopped crying, pulled back, and looked up into Greerson's eyes fixedly. "All right. Just promise to make this right." She wasn't sure it mattered anymore, but she said it. Her voice held the dead weariness of despair.

"I promise, Vivian." Greerson's voice was cold and brittle.

The woman broke the embrace and walked down the hall, followed by Greerson. She was still weeping softly. Matt quickly joined them. Vivian turned in to the first front bedroom down the corridor and moved to the bureau. The men stood just inside the room and watched. She jerked open a drawer and reached to its underside where she removed an envelope that had been secured to it by masking tape. Turning back to the men, she slammed the drawer shut and leaned her hips against the dresser. The woman looked at the envelope for a minute before she slowly extended it to the police officer. He walked unhurriedly to her and accepted the offering. When he took it, Vivian burst into tears again and ran from the room.

The two men looked at one another, once more seemingly helpless in the circumstances. They found her on that sagging sofa, her face plunged into a throw pillow, crying quietly. Greerson tried to decide whether it was the clutter on the bed that made her choose this spot or it was the painful memories of that intimate place with Charlie that drove her from the bed. No telling, he thought. The two men quietly watched Vivian for a long while, each lost in his feelings, both exhausted.

The girl sobbed quietly. The radio continued to play softly from behind its dimly lighted panel. A car drove past. An eerie, cacophonous mating message, cicadas maybe, sounded past the windows. And the girl continued to mourn. For Charlie. For herself.

———

Atlanta Detective Jim Greerson and *Georgian* reporter Matt Grimes sat at the small dining-room table in the yellow bungalow on Altoona Place, drinking coffee, smoking cigarettes, and watching the form sleeping on the living-room couch. Earlier, as Vivian finally cried herself to sleep, Matt had pulled a blanket from the bed down the hall and laid it atop her slumbering figure. Meanwhile, Jim had extinguished the radio. Vivian had a fitful sleep, at best. From some documents lying around the house, they determined that her name was Vivian Gilbert. While she slumbered, the men quietly discussed various things. Matt used the interval to ask the detective the questions he had on his mind about the night's events thus far. The men had also decided that Vivian needed to get away from Atlanta. They'd agreed to get her to wherever she wanted to go, within reason. The envelope containing Charlie's papers sat unopened on the table between them. Jim would wait until he got back to headquarters to peruse them. He'd assured Matt that he would get first crack at whatever information they held. The young man had earned that much in the detective's estimation. The long day and longer night were beginning to take their toll on the two.

Matt looked hard at his companion. "I have to ask you something, Detective Greerson." He'd used the man's title purposely. "Did you really mean the promise you made to her tonight? You know, to kill whoever murdered Charlie." Greerson didn't reply right away. He drew a long breath, let it out silently, and looked pensively into his coffee cup. Matt persisted. "I mean, I don't know you very well. We've crammed a lot of crap into the last eight or so hours, but you don't strike me as a cold-blooded killer. Tough, yeah, but... not a killer."

After a time, Greerson said softly, "Let's just leave it at the fact that there's a first time for everything, kid." His tone was without emotion. The detective's blunt, cold response stunned Matt. Neither man spoke for a long time. Finally, Jim broke the stony silence. "Say, I thought you said your dad taught you to hunt. What happened to that experience when you were out on that stoop?" Jim chuckled as he asked.

"Yeah, I know how to hunt, but I've never had critters stalk *me* before." Matt took another sip of coffee. "Besides, she came up behind me as quiet as a church mouse peeing on cotton. She is one cagey, tough girl." He looked at her sprawled shape with some admiration mixed with sympathy.

"Yeah, but she's got a vulnerable side, too. We sure saw that tonight. Then who doesn't?" The reporter nodded his agreement as the detective continued, "Speaking of pissing, you did a good job maintaining bladder control when she had that gun to your head. I've known a lot of tough thugs who wouldn't've held up to that as well." When Matt looked at Jim, searching his face for sarcasm, Greerson reassured him with a backslap. "Honestly, my friend." When Greerson uttered that last word, he shocked himself. The word was not one he used often or readily.

The young man smiled his appreciation at the comment, but felt compelled to add something. "Well, Jim, to be honest with you, it wasn't my *bladder* I was worried about controlling, if you get my drift." Both men laughed.

The sound of their laughter roused the sleeping woman. She rolled beneath the coverlet and looked at the two men. Suddenly, the events of the night seemed to come back to her, and she looked haggard. "Charlie," she moaned softly. The men expected the waterworks to start again, but she only lay quietly for a short while, before asking, "What time is it?"

Matt looked at his wristwatch. "It's just after five a.m. How do you feel?"

"How the hell do you think I feel?" Her tone wasn't nasty, only mordant. Vivian swung her legs around and sat up, adjusting her skirt before putting her face in her hands. Occasionally, her shoulders would shake, but she made no sound. The two men traded glances. She gave forth with a strangled sob, and then sat without moving for a minute or so. Vivian was trying to hold herself together from inside. "I'm sorry..." she said through her fingers. Abruptly, she looked up. "Say, what the hell's your name anyway? I got Jim's but never heard yours."

"It's Matthew Grimes. Want some breakfast? Uh... Vivian, is there any food in the house?"

"Some, I guess, but I don't know what —"

"Look," Jim interrupted, "I don't want to break up this tea party, but, we think you need to get away from Atlanta, Vivian. Things could get a little rough for you here. Where were you going when you were packing last night?"

"To the mountains with ..." Her voice trailed off. After a moment, she sighed, "Charlie was the first man who ever saw somethin' better in me than what I was."

Before a crying jag began again, Matt jumped in. "Listen, Vivian," he said sharply, "Detective Greerson's right. Do you have someplace you could go where you have friends or family?"

"I got folks in Kentucky. Lexington. They'd take me in 'til I got on my feet. Is that really necessary?"

This time it was Greerson's turn to push the idea of her leaving. "What do *you* think, doll face? Do you *remember* last night's visitor? Do you *really* want to be here when he comes back with his friends? And he'll come back. Either to get the papers he didn't find last night or to take it out on you for letting somebody else get his hands on them."

She took that in, nodding. It didn't take her long to decide after she rose slowly from the sofa. Her movements reflected the pain and soreness her body felt. The mouse under her eye had "matured." The eye was swollen, as was her jaw. "Well, at least the rent's paid 'til the end of this month, so nobody'll notice the place being empty for a while. And this furniture is just secondhand stuff that we got at a furniture place over on Mitchell Street. Charlie," she stammered momentarily, "paid cash for it. Said we'd get better when we resettled on the farm." Vivian stood with a stoic expression for a minute, looking around at what she and Charlie had called home. Then, she moved toward the hallway. "I'll finish packing." She stopped and looked down at her dress. "This dress looks awful. It's all wrinkled from sleepin' in it. Do I have time to change?" She looked mournfully at the two men.

Greerson moved from the chair and stubbed out his cigarette. "Take the time if you need it, Vivian. We'll get you something to eat at the bus station or somewhere around there." After she went down the hall, he looked at Matt. "I think a bus ticket to Lexington will run about five or six bucks. We can manage that between us, can't we, partner?"

"Yeah," Matt smiled, "it's for a worthy cause." He gave the detective the seven dollars he had in his pocket. He explained that it was all he was carrying, but, hopefully, it would cover his share of Vivian's breakfast and her bus ticket. Greerson tried to give some of it back to the younger man, but Matt wouldn't hear of it. "I can get a small draw at the newspaper for expenses."

---

An hour later found the three ready to leave the bungalow on Altoona Place. Without having to rush and with what she termed "protection" from the scum of the rackets, Vivian packed all the things she wanted. She'd filled three pieces of luggage and an old duffle bag left from Charlie's boxing days. So she was less depressed than she might otherwise have been. The rumble seat area was overflowing with her belongings. Matt teased that, with the amount of baggage she was toting, she might need a bus all to herself. As he had closed the door to the bungalow, Detective Greerson looked around the living room and recalled the rest of the house. Not much to show for the forty-two or so years Charlie Newsome spent on earth, he contemplated. Vivian lingered at the street, staring mournfully at the small house. Her swimming eyes filled with pain as if she were saying good-bye to a lost loved-one. Matt Grimes thought he understood her feelings. Jim Greerson knew her pain.

Daylight was beginning to break as the three squeezed into the Hudson. Jim started the car and wrangled it back toward Westview Drive. The short drive revealed the neighborhood to be one of nondescript, modest bungalows, more than a few showing small signs of neglect.

After they turned onto Westview, Matt quietly asked whether Jim would mind dropping him off at the newspaper so he could write the article for the early edition. Earlier, Matt had toyed with idea of telephoning the night desk from the Altoona Place bungalow. Although there was a lot to talk about with Mr. Richardson, Grimes didn't have much more newsworthy items at this point. The reporter finally ditched the notion of a phone call that might be overheard by Vivian. He didn't want to upset her further. However, he needed to get his account of the events submitted. The young correspondent spoke around the woman who sat between them. "I hate to bail out on you before we get her on a bus, but I need to get this in by my deadline. I can't go back to the boardinghouse first. My bed'll be too much of an attraction. If I lay my head down at this point, I might never get up again." Matt insisted that he be dropped off at the corner where Magnolia crossed Marietta Street. That way, he explained, the detective could get Vivian to the bus station quicker and the three-block walk to the *Georgian-American* Building would wake him up some and give him time to think the story over before he had to sit down at a typewriter. Jim readily agreed with a promise that they'd get back together later so he could fill Matt in on what Charlie's papers had to say. The reporter jotted down the telephone numbers to his desk at the paper and to the boardinghouse and gave them to Jim.

The woman had listened intently to their conversation. "Hey! What gives?" Vivian demanded. "Ain't you a gumshoe, too?"

The young *Georgian* reporter admitted his true occupation. He assured her that, when Charlie's story was printed, his reputation would come out okay. Satisfied, Vivian settled in and began quietly humming "Blue Moon" low in her throat. When Matt looked at her and smiled, she paused long enough to explain, "It was... our song. Charlie and me." She whimpered slightly and returned to humming the tune. He watched her awhile longer. Jim would periodically glance over and look at Matt as he watched Vivian.

A short distance before the Magnolia Street and Marietta Street intersection, Greerson pulled the Hudson to the curb. Matt lifted his feet off the floorboards and piled out of the car. Turning to Vivian, he gave her a quick hug and wished her well. She sobbed a good-bye and her thanks. Her thank-you held a tinge of bitter irony. The reporter returned the revolver Greerson had given him some hours before. Jim took the gun but immediately held it back out to Matt. "You may need this again."

"I'll get it from you when I see you next. Don't forget to call me." The detective agreed and Matt closed the door. With that, the car pulled away toward the bus station on Cain Street.

Matt briefly watched as the maroon Hudson with its black fenders jostled its way through the early-morning traffic. Then, he turned and moved southeast on Marietta Street. The young man was very tired and took his time getting to the newspaper offices. The hour of his deadline was nowhere near tolling yet. Taking in both sides of the street, it was a ten-minute walk past Beaudry's new, where Matt had bought his Ford, and used car lots, a grocery store, a hotel, lunchrooms, tobacco merchants, real-estate offices, tailor shops, gasoline service stations, garages, parking lots, the Federal Reserve Bank, and two buildings, the One-O-One Building and the Glenn Building. In the latter two, you could do everything from get a haircut to finance a car. Three blocks farther to the east was the vibrant business district of Five Points, Atlanta's "Great White Way," and the surrounding area. The convergence of Peachtree, Decatur, and Marietta Streets and Edgewood Avenue was the heart of Atlanta, he reflected. As tired as he was, Matt felt an unexpected and strange sense of euphoria about the moment, regarding this place. It seemed to him that a man could enjoy a full life without ever leaving the ten-square-block area.

The phone on his desk was ringing as he stepped into the city room. He dashed for it and found Evie on the other end of the line. He glanced at his watch, which showed it was just after seven thirty.

"Matthew Grimes, where have you been?" she demanded. "Diane called me and said she didn't think you'd been home all night. What's going on?"

"Good morning to you, too, Babe. I went out last night on that Eddie Guyol murder you're going to read about in today's papers. While I was there, I got connected with a detective who's working an angle on it, and we spent the night chasing down leads and people. In the excitement, I simply never had a chance to call you. I'm sorry. Listen, I'll tell you all about it when we see each other, which I hope is soon. And why is Diane sticking her big nose into –"

"Don't you go blaming Diane! She likes you and cares about us! So don't you dare say anything to her! It was her caring, not being nosey, Matthew Grimes! I was worried!"

"Well, there's nothing to worry about. I only now walked into the office." Grimes saw Mr. Barnes watching him closely from his perch in the city editor's office. "Look, I have to go. I have a lot of work to do in a short time. And, Evie . . ."

"Yes?"

"Please stop using my name like that. I feel like I'm back at Richmond Academy getting yelled at by a teacher." They laughed.

"Okay, sweetie. Call me."

"After I get some sleep."

"Okay."

As Matt dropped the earpiece on its hook, he saw his city editor rise from behind his desk. The young reporter moved quickly to the man's office. On his way, he walked past Brick who was typing, reading, and, then, laughing at what he was writing. When he approached the door, Barnes sat back in his swivel chair and waved him inside. He motioned Matt to a chair.

A dead cigar twitched in the corner of Barnes's mouth. "Good morning, Matt. Do you mind telling me where you've been all night? Rogers said," the editor raised a cautioning hand, "and I *browbeat* it out of your friend, mind you, that you left the murder scene relatively early last night with some guy."

"Well, yeah, Mr. Barnes. I got all I could from Pelham Road, so in exchange for a ride, a detective working on the case let me go with him while he looked for answers. So I spent the night with the detective."

Mr. Barnes threw his head back and laughed, red faced. "I don't think I'd put it just that way if you tell Brick about your night. You'll never hear the last of that!" Matt smiled and the editor reverted to a more serious tone. "Have you got anything good for the next edition?"

"Yessir. That's why I came in early. The murdered man's name was Eddie Guyol. He headed one of the numbers organizations here in Atlanta."

As Matt spoke, Barnes, known for smoking a stogie down to where not enough was left for even a hobo to bother picking it up, tried to relight his cigar remnant. He nearly burned his nose in the effort. The editor recovered and gave the match an angry toss at nothing in particular. Matt succeeded in pretending not to notice and in restraining giddy laughter born of exhaustion. The editor returned his attention to his newsman. "So I heard. I've got an old photograph of him somewhere." The older man rifled the clutter on his desk. "We'll run it with the story. When Rogers called in, he said he got a good shot of the car in the driveway, with a cop standing by it about where they figure the killer stood. We'll run that, too. You ready to write it up?"

"Yessir! I'm going to need someone to cover the morning rounds for me. And, if possible, the afternoon one, also. I haven't had a wink of sleep since night before last."

Before Matt finished his last sentence, Barnes was on the phone. "Yeah, Barnes here! Is Rooney in the building?" After a response from the other end, he said, "Well, what about that other guy? What's his name? Yeah, yeah, the Wallace kid!" Another pause was followed by, "Well, look I don't care if you have to send the delicate, but shrewd Miss Seydell! Get somebody to cover the police beat rounds this morning and this afternoon!" He smiled and winked at his reporter. "Grimes is getting ready to write his biggest story ever for the front page!" He replaced the phone with gusto. When he looked up at Matt, he was frowning thoughtfully and rubbing his chin. "Okay, this isn't Eddie Guyol's first time in the papers. Go back to, uh, the fall of 1928 or 1927, I think it was. I recall it 'cause the damned fool almost got one of my favorite nightspots closed! Mrs. LaFavor will probably know. Check with her. She'll have a bunch of background for you. So go get it, kiddo! This is front-page, banner-headline stuff!" he waved his stubby cigar in dismissal. Matt slid off the chair to leave. "Oh, here's Guyol's photo. Get it back to me with your lead. And say, by the way, Matt, you look like hell."

The journalist merely smiled weakly and took the picture. But he was too tired even to give it a glance at the moment. Fatigue was catching up with him but quickly. He dropped the picture on his desk as he headed toward Mrs. LaFavor's area in the bowels of the building.

Margaret LaFavor held sway over the newspaper's morgue, that dusty receptacle of a space where old newspaper articles and other historically significant documents were kept. She was a very old, bespectacled, walking encyclopedia of newspaper history. Some held to the rumor that she'd carried water to the Confederate soldiers defending the city when Sherman came to town in '64. Others said it was a barefaced lie; she'd hauled ammunition. Whatever the truth of that matter, she'd reportedly outlived four husbands. Every so often, someone would mention within Brick's hearing that she now had her eye on him as number five. It sent shivers down whatever spine he had left.

When Matt walked into her "territory," Margaret was there at the counter, as was the ever-present Lucky Strike dangling from her lips. Cigarette smoke trailed upward from the ashtray at her elbow as well. In his early days at the newspaper, he'd been told that Mrs. LaFavor had been a "victim" of Lucky Strike's promotion in the late 20's when the brand was touted as a route to thinness for women. One typical ad had said, "Reach for a Lucky instead of a sweet." Notwithstanding that Margaret was already as thin as an Andersonville inmate, she bought into the idea wholeheartedly and increased her cigarette intake to seven packs a day. And her countenance showed the abuse. Margaret's crop of thinning red hair sat atop a face as wrinkled as an eight-month-old jack-o-lantern and with about the same tint. In addition, her raspy voice was about two octaves below Bing's. Brick said she carried her voice in her socks.

Matt explained his situation to Mrs. LaFavor. She told him she'd heard about the killing on the radio that morning. "Oh, I remember Eddie Guyol, all right. Wait just a minute," she drawled around a cigarette, as she shuffled away from the counter. From somewhere behind shelves, she called out, "Oh, yeah, I recollect the incident you're talkin' about. It was in October of 1927." She returned with a sheaf of papers. "Yes, here it is. October twenty-first of '27. Some kind of rhubarb at a fashionable nightclub on the north side of town, it was. A place called the... Peachtree Gardens. Papers called it a riot. *Riot!*" she laughed. "The cops arrested Guyol and four *women*. Must've been pretty tough dames to be caught up in a riot in a nightclub! Anyway, Boykin charged him with assault with intent to murder, as I recall. Yeah, here it is." She laid a newspaper article on the counter and spun it to face Matt, pointing with a knobby, nicotine-stained finger. A gray tip of ash fell off the end of her current smoke. "He beat the manager of the joint with a blackjack during the rumpus."

Margaret leaned back from the counter and took a long drag on her cigarette. She puffed smoke with each word as she continued, "Eddie hailed from New Orleans. He came to Atlanta at some point and started as a tire salesman. That wasn't a good enough job for him, moneywise, though. He had bigger ambitions. Eddie liked racehorses, but not necessarily playing the ponies. He owned some bangtails. Liked to run 'em back in New Orleans and down in Florida, so's I heard. Anyway, selling tires didn't support the lifestyle he had in mind for himself. So, when Prohibition was passed, the story goes that he went into bootlegging. He made money there. Then, when Prohibition was repealed, he moved into the numbers, and some other stuff, I hear. I've heard he was into loan-sharking, too. He and his buddy Cutcliff were."

The reporter jotted down some notes, thanked Mrs. LaFavor, and made his way back to his typewriter. On the way, he remembered that he needed to ask Mr. Barnes for some cash. He also had a growing need for a cup of joe, so he swung by the office coffeepot. The coffee was much stronger than he normally liked it, but he decided it was what he needed at the moment.

Arriving at his desk, Matt plopped into his chair and drank some hot liquid. He needed a minute before he undertook the assignment. Taking another gulp of the hot, black liquid, the young man set the cup down and leaned forward with his elbows on the desk, holding his face in his hands. As he tried to clear his head, Matt looked at his desk through his splayed fingers. In that second, he had his first glimpse at the photograph of Eddie Guyol his editor had given him. Matt dropped his hands in astonishment. The guy in the picture was the same smaller man he'd had the brief run-in with at the end of the Crackers game a week earlier. It wasn't a face you'd forget after even a brief encounter, he concluded. In the photo, the man was wearing the same distinctive tall-crown fedora and a similar three-piece suit. The young man studied the picture for a few minutes, trying to reconstruct the event in his mind. And now that he knew his partner in crime was a man named Walter Cutcliff, Matt couldn't stop from wondering whether Guyol's companion at the ball game, who he'd called "Walt," had been Cutcliff. Not that it mattered, but the coincidence struck Matt. It gave him some measure of renewed energy. Or maybe it was the coffee.

The exhausted reporter hovered over his Remington and pounded out his lead on the Pelham Road murder. Matt was well ahead of his deadline at this early hour. So, using his notes and his recollection, he also wrote up everything he'd learned on Pelham Road and what Detective Greerson had told him about the investigation to that point while it was still fresh in his mind. He omitted the episode at the White Lantern for now. It added nothing to the story at this point, and Barnes might not approve what he'd see as recklessness on his journalist's part. Matt wrote up a separate piece on the murder of Charlie Newsome and its possible connection to the Guyol killing.

For the moment, he also skipped any reference to Charlie's papers. There would be time enough for that, he reflected, when he learned exactly what was in them, what Greerson thought they meant, if anything, and who they might implicate, if anyone. In the back of Matt's mind was also the desire to make certain that Vivian was clear of the state before anything about them hit the streets. When he'd finished typing the copy, he believed that it was the best thing he'd ever written. He made his way to the city editor's office.

Inside Barnes's office, the editor read over the lead and the two full articles the correspondent had written about last night's events. His blue china pencil occasionally danced on the pages here and there. "This looks fine, Matt. Great job! On the subject of the Guyol murder, we'll run Rogers's crime-scene photo in a four-column spread at the top of the front page under a big, bold headline. A short cover line over the picture and the caption underneath. Your piece will be alongside it. We'll put the story on the right side of the front page next to the photo." Barnes held the notion that the stories on the right side of the page always garnered more reader attention for various reasons. His primary theory was that, as a reader scanned the page, it was the last thing they'd see before turning to the next page. "We'll replay it in the later editions with pictures and more text. We may wait until then to use that photo of Guyol. Keep their interest. By the way, you know the *Constitution* is saying that there were two shots fired into Guyol's car. Your piece says only one shot."

"Well, I have inside information that Myrtle Guyol told the police there was only one shot. In addition, the cops recovered only one .45 caliber bullet inside the car on the rear seat. The bullet that hit Eddie was a through-and-through shot. And the empty shell casing was found on the seat where Myrtle had been sitting. Clearly, it was an automatic pistol. So somebody over there has some bad info. I stand by what I wrote."

Barnes smiled at the young man's fortitude on the point. "Inside information? Is that your 'anonymous source'?"

The journalist drowsily nodded. "Yessir." He was quickly running down like a clock that someone had forgotten to wind.

"Are you sure about some of these other facts like who Myrtle Guyol called after the shooting, by whom and how Guyol was taken to the hospital, what Myrtle said about the shooting and the shooter?"

"Yessir, as much as anybody who wasn't there for the actual events can be."

"And the people inside the home at the time?"

"They say they didn't see anything."

Suddenly, someone started pounding on the editor's office door, calling his name. "Yeah? What is it?" Barnes called out impatiently. The man at the door explained that some local politician wanted him on the phone. At that point, Grimes noticed that the noise level in the city room had increased considerably since he'd arrived. Barnes sighed heavily and rolled his eyes. "Get a number and tell whoever the hell it is that I'll call them back!" He returned to his young reporter. "Now, what about that phone call Grady Hospital reported receiving?"

"Well, that's a puzzling point. If it was from the Guyol home, why would they say the shooting was on Rock Springs Road? And then, when they were asked for an address, why would they just hang up? It doesn't add up. Strikes me as more likely a call from a neighbor who heard a shot and who wasn't exactly sure where it came from. Then why not call the police?"

"Any idea what the angle for the killing was?"

"Could have been any number of motives. The police are looking at several of them. Although, as I said in there," Matt responded, pointing to his article, "robbery seems unlikely for several reasons. Nothing, neither the sizeable amount of money nor the jewelry, was taken. And then, there's Myrtle's statement that the killer told Eddie he had it coming to him. It doesn't sound like something a robber would say. After all, Guyol was into bootlegging before, and then was loosely tied to the murder of a guy killed in his Piedmont Avenue apartment a couple of years ago. The cops also want to talk to Myrtle's ex-husband. So the possibilities of grudges abound in this case. Maybe somebody's trying to take over Guyol's racket."

"Okay. Keep plugging away on the story, Matt. Stay on it. We'll probably put out an extra edition. Now, about this killing of the ex-prizefighter, Charlie Newsome. While I'm impressed with your firsthand account of Newsome's last minutes when you happened on him right before he died," the editor paused for a second and shot a curious look at his employee, "how do you connect it to the Guyol murder beyond mere coincidence? Sure, he may have been involved with the Eddie's numbers outfit, the Home Company, but that doesn't necessarily mean they're linked. What else do you have?"

Matt felt himself blush. "Well, first, the detective I was with last night feels very strongly that they're connected."

Barnes's eyebrows rose. "Is that your 'anonymous source' again?"

"Yessir. He spoke strictly on a condition of anonymity. He feels that Newsome was getting ready to spill the beans on some things about Guyol's murder and was killed to stop him from doing just that." Matt was worn down, too tired to argue forcibly. In addition, he thought that there were things better left unsaid to Barnes now. As a result, his statement of the case for the link was made without too much conviction

Barnes frowned thoughtfully and tugged on his earlobe. "Okay. Well, for now, we're gonna run it as only another unfortunate murder, not a think piece. No personal opinion, discussion, or analysis. Just the bare facts. Observe and report. If you get more of a connection later, we'll look at it. All right?"

"Sure, Mr. Barnes. There's one other thing." Matt explained that he had spent some money during the night to get more information for the story. The city editor agreed to get him some cash to compensate for his efforts. Barnes made a quick phone call and had twenty dollars waiting for him from petty cash. When his reporter made clear that he'd only spent seven dollars, the editor insisted that Matt may need more money before the story was done and what he'd garnered thus far was well worth the extra cash. The correspondent was grateful and too tired to argue.

"Go home, kid, and get some rest." Mr. Barnes returned the copy to Matt and walked him to his office door. "Great job, Matt! Really!"

After getting his stories past the copy editor and collecting the twenty dollars, Matt grabbed a streetcar on Marietta Street and, building at the edge of exhaustion, made his weary way back to his boardinghouse. Miss Dixie greeted him at the door just past ten thirty. "Oh, my Lord, Matt! You look plumb tuckered out. Rhamy told me about seeing you last night. Are you hungry?" Without waiting for a response, she plunged ahead, "Let me get you a sandwich and a glass of milk. Maybe a piece of cake?"

"I could eat," the young man smiled at the woman's maternal instincts toward her roomers. "But I need a bath and some sleep, though." He felt as if he were moving around in a thick fog.

"Well, you go on upstairs and get a bath, and I'll bring you somethin' to eat in your room after."

"Thank you," he said softly before trudging up the stairs. Matt passed on his normal morning shower routine of covering his large body with thick suds in hot water, followed by a rinse in dead-cold water. The rinse water always helped him wake up, but he wanted no such help right now. He felt he could barely stand through the shower. Back in his room, he put on his pajamas. The last thing Matt could recall was sitting on the side of his bed before giving himself to sleep's undertow.

---

Matt slowly opened his eyes to find Miss Dixie standing over him, gently shaking him back to consciousness. He only heard the last part of what his landlady was saying. ". . . so sorry, Matt, but there's a man on the phone for you. He says he's a detective and needs to speak to you. Says it's very important."

As groggy as Matt's mind was, it snapped into gear at her words. "Yes, ma'am." He sat up and propped himself against the headboard for balance. "I'll get dressed and be right down."

"Just put on your bathrobe, Matt. Nobody's here but us, and this man seems in a hurry."

"Okay, if you're sure, Miss Dixie. What time is it?" The young man could see the daylight through the windows.

She nodded vigorously. "I *am* sure. And it's a little after two o'clock." She said as she left the room, closing Matt's bedroom door behind her.

A minute later, Grimes blearily picked up the receiver in the downstairs hallway. From where he stood in the hall, Matt could see Miss Dixie ironing clothes in the kitchen. Laundry day, the young man thought right before he spoke, "Yes. Detective Greerson?"

"Well, how's the boy?" Greerson greeted the *Georgian* reporter. The detective sounded as if he hadn't missed a wink of sleep in the last decade. As Matt started to respond, Jim continued, "Hey, are you still game for more follow-up on Charlie's story?"

"Well, I'm vertical at this point and that's all I'm sure of. But, of course, I'm up for anything!" Greerson's question and energy helped Grimes's wake-up process move along. "And I've got too much invested in this to stop now! What's going on?"

"I can explain it better when I see you. Are you dressed? Your landlady said you were asleep."

"I need to get dressed. But that won't take long."

"Well get dressed and scrape your face if you need to. We're going calling on some *special* people this afternoon. How about I pick you up on the Pryor Street side of the Candler Building? That's close to where you live, right? Say, in about an hour? Snap it up, kiddo!"

"Sounds good. See you there." Matt replaced the receiver. He could hear Miss Dixie moving around in the kitchen. He stuck his head in the door. As usual, his landlady was fussing with preparation of the boardinghouse's next meal between stints at the iron. "Thank you, Miss Dixie. I'm headed out again. I don't know if I'll be back in time for supper."

"Matt," she turned and wipe her hands on her apron, "what about somethin' to eat? I made you a sandwich earlier, but when I brought it up, you were draped across your bed snoring like a bear." She laughed, "That girlfriend of yours is going to have to get used to that snoring if you two get married." She nodded her head toward the monitor-top refrigerator. "The sandwich is in the icebox."

"I appreciate it Miss Dixie, but I really need to hurry to meet this detective." Matt grinned and added, "Besides, I'll bet there's a young man who'll come through the door from school any minute who can lay waste to that sandwich."

"Land sakes, you know he can! But you need *somethin'*, Matt," she pleaded.

"I'll be fine for now. Thanks. I need to run."

"Okay, Matt!" she called behind him as he climbed the stairs. "Lawd only knows what you've gotten yourself into, but just be careful!" She laughed, shook her head, and moved back to her stove.

# CHAPTER 8

# A Reluctant Lawyer

Forty minutes later, Matt was moving along the block and a half on Houston Street that separated the boardinghouse from the Candler Building. The rain, which had besieged the city earlier in the month, had still not returned. But the young man had heard on the radio, as he passed the rooming house parlor, that it was expected to move back into the vicinity that night. The air was thick with the "feel" and the smell of rain, either remnants of what had recently departed or the threat of what was headed their way. For now, however, the skies were only partly cloudy and the temperature hovered around seventy degrees. An afternoon like this, Matt thought as he walked, made life simple if you didn't have too much on your mind. Unfortunately, he did. His brain was a jumble of different thoughts and concerns. He was eager to hear from Detective Greerson about Vivian's departure, of what the latest developments in the Guyol case might be, and, of course, what, if anything, Charlie's papers might have revealed. Also, Matt was torn between wanting to call Evie that evening and wanting to follow the detective anywhere the evidence might lead, anyplace he might be allowed to go along. He hoped for answers to some of these questions, at least, when he met with Jim Greerson.

On reaching the Candler Building, he waited on the sidewalk beneath the intricate carvings at the Pryor Street entrance. After a few minutes of standing, Matt started feeling fatigue overtaking him again. So he filled the time trying to guess the names people represented on the carved panels between the first and second floors of the ornate building. He understood them to be famous people from the fields of the liberal arts and sciences. Because each person was reported to have been carved with symbols of the tools they may have used in their occupation, the correspondent felt it would be easy enough to decide who each bust symbolized. Anything, he thought, to keep from nodding off in the afternoon warmth. People leaving the building and passersby gave him quizzical looks as he stood staring at the carvings. Matt laughed to himself as he imagined that most citizens departing the building were still doped from their visit to one of the many dentists occupying the structure, and, therefore, couldn't think straight anyway.

The *Georgian* correspondent was making some headway with his self-imposed challenge when he heard his name being called from the street. "Hey, Grimes!" Matt turned his head. Jim Greerson was calling through the open window of his now-familiar Hudson. "What the heck are you doing?" As the reporter turned

*Detective Greerson's 1931 Hudson 8*

around to respond, the police officer waved him off and yelled, "Just wait there! I'll be right back!" The detective drove to the corner of Pryor and Houston and turned right onto Houston, causing Matt to wonder where Jim could be going. He was still too tired to come to snap conclusions. Then it occurred to him. Jim was driving to Galanty's parking lot only a short distance down Houston and on the same side of the street as the boardinghouse. Sure enough, after a time, Greerson came trotting down the sidewalk toward him. They shook hands. The younger man liked the big cop but was still trying to figure what made his companion tick. "Well, what *are* you doing?"

"I was looking at the carvings on the building and trying figure out who they are?"

"Oh, are they supposed to be particular people?"

"Yeah. Look. That's the easiest one. Shakespeare. See the Greek theater mask?" He pointed to several figures as he rattled off names. "Wagner, Raphael, Michelangelo, –"

"Honus Wagner?" he laughed. "Is that supposed to be Honus Wagner?"

Greerson was still chuckling when Matt complained, "Oh, you're a real comedian! Oh, yeah! A comedian all right! That's 'Wagner' like with a 'V'." The young man pointed to several other busts. "Seriously, there are three that I can't figure out, though."

Greerson started backing his way down the sidewalk toward Houston Street. "Maybe they're Moe, Larry, and Curly. C'mon!"

"Who?"

"The Three Stooges." Matt stared after Jim blankly. "The Three Stooges! Don't you ever go to the movies?"

"That's about all I *ever* do! But I don't get it." Matt followed Jim's lead toward Houston Street while tossing a glance over his shoulder at the three unknowns.

"They're those three guys who're always doing stupid stuff and beating up on each other in the short features they show at the movies."

Grimes caught Greerson just as the detective turned around and began walking forward. "Oh. Oh, *those* jerks. I know who you mean now. Yeah, my girl thinks they're hilarious. I think they're kind of stupid."

"Well, never mind, we need to move. But, first, I'm famished. Have you eaten lately?" The detective quickened his pace.

"Well, no."

"Well, come on then! I'm hungry!"

The pair briskly walked the short block on Houston to Peachtree Street where they crossed and made their way past the inviting aromas coming from Schulte's cigar store to the Tasty Toasty Sandwich Shop. Before they walked into the lunch counter, someone shouted Jim Greerson's name from the street. He stopped, turned, and called back to a conductor, all smiles and waving animatedly at the detective from a stopped streetcar. Jim yelled a friendly greeting and touched his hat.

"Who's that, Jim?"

Greerson chuckled. "He's a guy from my hometown over in Carroll County. His name's Parrish. We went to the same school over there, Mount Zion Seminary, although he was several years behind me. He's was always a helluva baseball player. At one point, Parrish played ball in a city league here. Maybe he still does. I just don't see him as much as I used to." Matt was watching his companion's face intently. He'd not seen the police officer that happy in the short time he'd known him. The morose cloak that seemed to shroud him evaporated momentarily. The young man thought that Jim's mind was somewhere back in a happier time, a more contented place. In that moment, Greerson seemed to look at the streetcar without seeing it. Just as quickly, the detective gave a hint of a head shake and looked at the reporter. Matt's face blanched as if he'd been caught peeking through a knothole into a girls' dressing room at a summer camp. He quickly looked away and toward the sandwich shop. The pall had returned it seemed. Neither man said anything.

The two men strolled into the eatery. The lunchtime crowd had long since departed, so they could sit down at the far end of the counter to a quiet daily sandwich special and talk.

"So how'd it go with Vivian? Did she get on a bus?"

"Yeah. As a matter of fact, I was able to get some breakfast into her and get her a ticket to Lexington with the seven bucks you gave me. Her bus left about an hour after we got to the station. I gave her a sawbuck to tide her over until she reaches family up there."

"How was she... you know, emotionally?"

"She was still pretty shaken about Charlie. He must've treated her like a queen. She really loved him. No question about that. At one point, while we were sitting and waiting for her bus to leave, it dawned on her that she wanted to be here for his funeral. It took all I could do to convince her that her life would be in danger if she stayed. And Charlie wouldn't have wanted that." After a pause, he added, "I promised her I'd get him buried at Oakland Cemetery. She was suitably impressed because of the prestige the place has. I didn't tell her about the Potter's Field they have there. Whaddya think?"

Matt smiled. "Well, we can do that much for them anyway. I'll work on it through the newspaper." He sat in silence for a moment, thinking about the previous evening's events. "What's the latest news of the Guyol murder investigation?" As he spoke, their lunch plates and Cokes were set on the counter in front of them.

"Well, Chief Poole's added detectives to the investigation. Remember I told you last night that he'd assigned the case to Engelbert and Denny." Matt nodded as he reached for his notepad and pencil. "Well, he's added the four detectives from the lottery squad. That dugout's getting a bit crowded." Jim bit into his sandwich.

"The lottery squad. That's Davis, Woodruff, McNaughton, and... who's the other one?"

"Hildebrand."

"Oh, yeah, Hildebrand." Matt paused and smiled. "But no Rutherford?"

"No. No Rutherford. And Artie's plenty sore about it. Left on vacation this morning. So, because you've shown me you can handle yourself, so long as some broad isn't sneaking up behind you, I figured you could go along with me for now."

Matt blushed. "Oh, yeah? Well, she had that kind of guts and she was pretty good at it is all I can say!" Both men laughed. "It won't happen again, though!"

"Anyway, they've all but abandoned the robbery angle for the murder. They're looking at the possibility of a grudge as the motive. I'm not convinced and won't be until I see what Charlie's papers say."

"You mean the envelope didn't contain Charlie's papers? C'mon, give!"

"When I opened the envelope that Vivian gave us last night, it turned out to be a letter to some lawyer, instructing him to turn over the papers to the holder of the letter."

"What?"

"You could say Charlie played it smart. He put the papers in the hands of a mouthpiece to hold for him so's nobody could lay his hands on them directly. But we need to get to that shyster as quickly as possible. His office is in the Kiser Building down on Pryor Street."

Matt was chewing his bite of sandwich thoughtfully. He shifted the food into a cheek on one side of his mouth and muttered, "Ironic, huh?" He looked at Greerson and continued, "That the key to the thing might be located so close to where Charlie died."

The detective nodded grimly. "True enough, Matt."

"This lawyer's in the Kiser Building? God, I didn't think anybody still had offices in that place." Matt recalled reading or hearing the rumor that the old building, built in the late 1800s, which had more recently stood forlorn and mostly empty, was scheduled for demolition soon. The old structure was often referred to as the "Law Building," primarily owing to those words being emblazoned above its main entrance, but also, in part, because of the predominant occupation of most of its tenants. "Is he the *special* people you said we're going to see?" As Jim nodded, Matt went on, "If he's got an office in the Kiser Building, he's not *that* special!" He paused to sip his Coke. "Well, when do we go?"

"As soon as we finish eating. By the way, Cutcliff is offering a five-hundred-dollar reward for the capture of Eddie's killer." Matt made another note.

Later, as the men left the sandwich shop and walked back up Peachtree Street toward Greerson's car, a bulky, muscular man stepped from the cigar store, watching the pair intently.

---

After a short drive, Detective Greerson parked his Hudson on Pryor Street in front of the Kiser Building, which exuded an aura of failed ambition. He turned in the seat and held out a Smith & Wesson .38 special to the young man. "Remember this?" Matt nodded. "Okay, I've got this to go with it," Greerson added, putting the revolver in a dark-grained leather underarm holster and extending them to his companion. "Same rules as always, right?"

"Right." Matt took the gun and checked it for ammo, before removing his coat and pulling the rig on. After putting the holstered gun under his left arm, he eased into his coat and rolled out of the car.

As they crossed the sidewalk and passed under the inscription above the front door, Jim said, "The lawyer's name is William Sleiz. He's on the second floor." The detective pronounced the name as 'sleaze.' Moving across the lobby, he motioned with his hand. "Let's take the stairs."

Bounding up the stairs, Matt observed, "That's an unfortunate name for a lawyer, isn't it?" Greerson merely smirked.

Emerging from the stairwell, they found themselves in a dimly lighted, shabby hall. After a short walk around the second-floor corridor, they located the attorney's office. The top half of the office door was a translucent glass panel. The occupant's name, "William R. Sleiz," was painted in badly faded gold letters forming an arch across the glass at eye level. The requisite "Attorney at Law" had been fashioned in a horizontal line below his name. The room number was beneath that. The paint used for the title and room number was as washed out as that used for the man's name, as dreary as the building itself. The transom above the door was open, but none of the sounds that one might expect from a busy office were coming from it.

Greerson glanced at his companion, turned the clear glass knob, and eased the door open. Inside, they found a small outer office, empty but for the necessary secretarial trappings. An empty hat and coat tree occupied one corner. A thick layer of dust coated the desk, typewriter cover, telephone, and a nearby filing cabinet. The same was true for a visitor's chair and a side table, resting on the top of which was a *Saturday Evening Post* from August, 1933. The girl on the cover, clad in an orange bathing suit, was also blanketed with dust. A milk glass bowl light was suspended from the ceiling. Only one of the two lightbulbs in it was working.

The solid oak door to the inner office was ajar. No discernible sounds could be heard from that quarter either. The two visitors glanced at each other as the detective crossed the exterior office and gave the second door a slight push with his fingertips. The pair entered the lawyer's carpeted domain, which had been decorated with cheap, dark paneling in an obvious effort to give the space a more refined, sophisticated look. It failed. Adding to that letdown was an apparent contest for the room's ambience between stale cigars and old floral arrangements. The cigars were winning. Bookcases lined one wall and were filled to some extent with law publications, mementos, and curios intended to give their owner an air of knowledge and importance. They succeeded no better than did the paneling. An oscillating fan in a corner of the room made a faint, soothing murmur.

Books and papers covered a modest-sized desk, with enough room left over for a man's foot. The appendage's owner was flopped back carelessly in a swivel desk chair and faced away from his visitors. The two men could not see his face. Sporadic sputtering told the pair that the resident was dozing. Greerson cleared his throat with enough noise to give the lawyer an opportunity to save face. No response was forthcoming. He then stepped to the desk and picked up a large book. Lifting it to shoulder level, he let it drop. The resulting resounding crash jolted the lawyer and caused him to slide further down in his chair. He kept himself from falling to the floor only by grabbing the chair's arms. The book that had rested on his lap until that moment fell pell-mell with another crack.

The man stumbled to his feet hurriedly and made a clumsy effort to gain some measure of composure. The short, stocky, middle-aged man tried surreptitiously to dab drool from the corners of his mouth with his handkerchief. It didn't go unnoticed. "Yes, gentleman? I didn't hear you approach. I apologize," he drawled in an exaggerated syrupy voice that probably had the desired affect when projected on the common masses in a jury box as he declared his client's side of things. The detective recognized this lawyerly tone from his time spent in courtrooms as a witness. In the present surroundings, it seemed a bit overplayed. "Because you were not announced, I assume my secretary is still at luncheon. What can I do to help you?" His full-fledged jowls rippled robustly as he spoke. When he stopped speaking, he smiled broadly. To Matt, he brought to mind an aged, overfed Spanky McFarland from the "Our Gang" comedy shorts at the movies.

Greerson turned his head and smirked knowingly at Grimes and, then returned his attention to Attorney Sleiz. He gave him back his smile. "I'm here to pick up some documents left with you by Charlie Newsome." He handed the envelope he'd received from Vivian to the lawyer. Initially, the counselor's expression was uncomprehending. The name meant nothing to him.

The detective released an exasperated sigh. "Charlie Newsome. The former boxer? Came here earlier this week?"

"Ah, yes, Mr. Newsome." As he spoke, Mr. Sleiz removed the letter from the envelope, unfolded it, and read carefully. His perusal took a bit longer than would reasonably be expected. Both men watched the lawyer's eyes, behind which the wheels of legal interference turned mightily. When he finally peered over the document, he haughtily asked, "And who might you be, sir?"

"Does it matter?" Greerson's patience, if ever on display, was not in evidence at the moment. He could see through this lawyer like a new pane of glass. "The letter says that whoever has it will be given the papers Charlie Newsome deposited with you," he put it to the lawyer.

Sleiz leaned forward, his hands on the desk, and his eyes got small and tight. His face reddened and the undulation of his cheeks increased as he bowed up and demanded again, "Who might you be, sir?"

The detective heaved another heavy deep breath. He pushed his hat back on his head of black hair, thinning slightly and yielding to a widow's peak. "Well, I might be Ty Cobb, but I'm not. It doesn't matter who I am. The letter you're holding clearly states that the papers Charlie Newsome gave you are to be given to its bearer. That's me, counselor. I want the documents." His tone was scarcely more than a whisper but was packed with angry determination.

Sleiz was feeling the heat. His face turned a darker shade of red as he tried hard to swallow. "Well, now see here! I have to protect my client's interest in this matter! He –"

"Your client is dead, counselor," Jim interrupted, this time in a in a flat, toneless voice.

The lawyer reflected a mild degree of shock at that turn of events. His bushy eyebrows furrowed as he pondered the circumstances for a minute. "He is?" Greerson nodded grimly. Sleiz shot a glance at Matt, also nodding. "Well, that complicates the situation most appreciably."

"It doesn't change a damned thing, Attorney Sleiz. And don't play stupid. It gets me sore."

The stocky man bowed up yet again and crowed, "I beg your pardon, sir, but the name is pronounced Sleiz with a long 'i', not a long 'e.' The name is of German extraction."

The beefy detective placed his fists on the desk, knuckles down, and leaned over them toward Sleiz. "At this point in the conversation, I like my pronunciation better."

The air then seemed to come out of the attorney. His face went ashen and he dropped back into his former swivel "bed." "But I really do need to know who is making the demand for the documents in question, sir."

Greerson straightened and flipped out his shield. "I'm Detective Jim Greerson, Atlanta Police Department, and I'm investigating Charlie Newsome's murder. I want those papers!"

"Murder!" Sleiz's response was an exclamation, not a question. After a pause, he said, "Well, what if –"

The detective's patience had been played out by the uncooperative Mr. Sleiz. "What if I bounce your ass around this office until you decide to play ball?" Jim looked at Sleiz but spoke to his companion. "Matt, I may need you to go out into the hall for a few minutes."

"See here, Detective Greerson! Is that a threat against my person?"

"Take it anyway you like, but I'm not leaving here without those papers! Or you in custody for obstruction of justice! Or both!" In one angry motion, Jim made an impatient gesture and swept the desk clear of its clutter with his hand.

The indignant lawyer got to his feet and moved his eyes to Matt. "You heard that, young man! He threatened me!" As Sleiz looked his way, the blond reporter quickly turned to the bookshelf near the door and ran a finger over the volumes there. "You heard this man threaten me, sir!"

Matt left his finger in place on a legal volume and turned his torso slightly toward Sleiz. He looked at the man sideways along his brown eyes and calmly said, "I'm sorry. Did you say something to me? I wasn't paying attention. I was looking for a copy of the *Marbury versus Madison* decision. Do you have it?" With that, he nonchalantly returned to examining the shelved books.

For his part, Sleiz immediately saw the futility of his approach and relented. He licked his lips and returned his gaze to the big cop. "All right, I have the papers right here." The attorney sat back onto his desk chair and, pulling a cluster of keys from a pocket, unlocked a lower desk drawer. From the drawer, he removed a small strong box, which he unlocked with another key from the same collection. He searched through the contents until he came to the envelope Detective Greerson sought. He pushed the envelope slowly across the desk and lifted his hand off it even slower. "Here it is." The detective examined the envelope and saw that the handwriting on the outside was the same as that with which the letter was written, that of Charlie Newsome. He then tore open the envelope only to make certain the same handwriting was contained on the documents inside as well. The crestfallen attorney tried to regain some dignity for his station. "I do need you to sign something showing that you received the documents."

"Glad to. Now that wasn't all that hard, was it?"

The attorney merely blushed and harrumphed in response as he wrote two receipts for the detective's signature. Greerson signed, and the attorney handed his copy to him.

The attorney chose to continue the charade of high-handed congeniality, as he rose and started to move around the desk. "I bid you good day, gentlemen."

"Don't bother, counselor. We'll show ourselves out. Good-bye."

As they passed through the anteroom, Greerson made a loose motion with his hand toward the magazine on the side table and laughed. "I'll bet that *Post* was published about the same time Sleiz had his last paying client, aside from Charlie Newsome, in here."

Jim and Matt departed the lawyer's office and moved down the corridor toward the stairs. As they rounded a corner, a door quietly opened behind them. The large man from the cigar store came out into the hall and walked slowly and quietly in the same direction. Greerson took notice and had a sudden uneasiness. He looked directly at his companion and said, "Well, I guess we'll go back to the station house and take a look-see at what we have."

Matt started to speak. The detective stopped walking and gave the guy behind them a sharp, sidelong look. The man turned quickly to a door on his left. He rapped hard but carelessly on the door's shiny reddish panel and glanced askance at the men down the corridor. He wore a nondescript brown suit. A gray fedora cast his face into shadow. He returned his attention to the door, shot an indifferent glimpse toward the ceiling above it, and knocked hard again. The effort was unconvincing. Greerson reversed course suddenly and charged across the intervening space between them. It took the man, who froze, by surprise. The detective reached the stranger before he could react. Greerson's slight limp, which Grimes had noticed earlier, was not in evidence as he moved. Jim's quick rush ended with the big stranger being slammed hard, face first into the solid oak door where he stood. Matt was shocked in place by Greerson's surprising move. The subject of Greerson's attack clutched at air as his hefty bulk slid to the floor. He'd been hit hard enough to empty his lungs. Blood spurted from his broken nose and oozed from a split lip. The blow took the starch out of him. The detective's powerful arms flipped the limp figure onto his back. Then, Jim straddled him. The man's hands moved around in abrupt, confused, helpless motions, neither offensive nor defensive.

Matt's attention was momentarily diverted to a door behind him where a man's head appeared unexpectedly partway into the corridor and vanished behind the slamming door more quickly. The tall reporter then turned his attention back to the clash down the hall.

Jim cocked his arm with its meaty fist. Before he could strike a blow, he saw it was not needed. Unnecessary or not, he brought his huge knuckles hard on the man's kisser. Matt saw and heard Greerson's crushing punch land. He likened the sound to a board striking a watermelon. As Matt stood where he'd been when the scene evolved, the police officer roughly grabbed the fallen man by the lapels of his suit coat and lifted his upper body from the filthy tile floor. He removed a large handgun from inside the man's coat and slid it down the hallway in his companion's direction. The *Georgian* reporter sidestepped the gun as it skimmed past him. It came to rest a few feet beyond.

A door opened and a man stepped into the corridor on the far side of Greerson and the downed man from Matt. He stared briefly and started to say something. "This a friend of yours, mister?" the detective looked up and yelled at the newcomer. After shaking his head vigorously, the guy disappeared back into the office space and closed the door as if he were afraid he might break it.

Greerson bent close to the man beneath him. "Listen, asshole! Can you hear me?" he demanded. His voice was loud and hard. The man tried to speak but only spewed blood droplets into the air. He made only a sibilant sound and finished by merely nodding weakly. "Okay then! I don't know for sure who you're workin' for, but I've got a pretty good idea! You go back and tell him to grow a pair and come for me himself! If I see you like this again, I'm gonna put you in a damned wheelchair! Permanent like! You got that, Mac?" Again, the man, gurgling blood, nodded feebly. Jim smashed the guy's head and upper torso back to the tiled floor hard. He kept a firm grip on the man.

Meanwhile, Matt had moved toward the two figures and stood next to his friend in stunned disbelief at the events that had unfolded. He'd felt no urgency to move. Jim was in no danger and certainly didn't need his help with the guy. The reporter was a mere spectator. There was simply nothing he could or needed to do. "What gives, Jim?"

"This goon has been following us, watching us since before we ate. He was probably sent to get this," Greerson answered, releasing his left hand from the man to pat his coat where he'd put the envelope. "Or maybe he was only sent to track it. I only suspected that was his play until he knocked on that door. Then I knew for sure."

"But how did you know?" Matt was still at a loss.

The detective jerked his head toward writing on the wall beside the door, which looked like every other door on the hall. In small, faded lettering, it read "Janitor's Closet." Matt read it and chuckled grimly. Greerson addressed the man on the floor. "Next time, you need to know the building you're in better, you stupid son of a bitch!"

Detective Greerson got to his feet. "Let's go." As they moved down the hall, Jim bent and scooped up the man's gun. He removed the magazine and the chambered round and handed them to his companion.

Matt dropped them into his coat pocket and chuckled. "Another .45 caliber magazine. Everybody keeps giving me these things. I'm getting quite a collection."

Greerson grinned. "You need to get the gun to complete the set, Matt." The detective started to slide the gun back down the passageway to its owner, but a notion came to him, and he stopped. He looked at the gun. The .45 automatic was identical to the one that Gutowski had been carrying the night before. Greerson knew that meant that the magazine and ammunition from that gun would fit this one. "Do you still have Gutowski's magazine?"

Matt had all but forgotten that it was still lying on the floorboard of his Ford. "Well, yeah. I do."

Jim held the gun out toward the young man. "Know how to use this thing?"

"Sure."

"Then take it." He handed the young man the big black automatic. "Both magazines will fit it. And, then, I can take back my .38. I'd recommend you get a shoulder harness for it. It's a little bulky to carry around in a pocket or your waistband. Maybe I can scrape one up for you."

Matt looked back at the man still lying supine on the floor behind them. "But –"

"No 'buts.' He doesn't need this roscoe anymore." Matt accepted the firearm.

The pair turned and continued to the stairwell. As they walked, several people emerged from behind closed doors to gawk at the pair and the rumpled man they left on the floor behind them. Matt put the loose round into the magazine and the magazine back in the handgun. He decided against chambering a round, though. Then, he tucked the gun into his waistband for now. When asked, the detective told Grimes that he'd never seen the guy he dealt with in the hall and wouldn't say who he thought had sent him. Greerson seemed totally unfazed by the events of the last half hour. He was still a puzzle to the young correspondent. Back on Pryor Street, as they climbed into the Hudson, the detective looked at Matt and asked, "Say, what was that Mayberry versus Madison stuff back in Sleiz's office?" Greerson still pronounced it "sleaze."

"It's *Marbury versus Madison*." Matt shrugged. "And don't ask me about it. It's some famous case I've heard bandied about by lawyers trying to sound more intelligent than the rest of us. I only recall the name because I dated a girl for a while when I was at Georgia whose last name was Marbury. And the town of Madison is about halfway between Atlanta and Augusta."

Jim was trying to wipe blood spatter from his coat sleeve with a handkerchief. "What made you think to say that?" he asked absently.

Matt removed the large handgun from his waistband and laid it on the floorboard. He laughed, "Damned if I know. It just popped out."

The two men sat in the car for a minute as Greerson mapped their next move. He voiced the opinion that there would be too many questions about Charlie's papers and far too many prying eyes at the police station to go there to read them. The men decided to go to the boardinghouse instead. If the documents held any evidentiary value about

# SHORTENING SHADOWS

either Guyol's or Charlie's murder, the detective would turn them in and explain what he knew of them.

———

Just past four fifteen in the afternoon, Jim parked his Hudson a short distance down from 71 Houston Street. The car's motor hiccoughed as it died. Before he got out of the car, Matt removed his coat and the holstered .38 revolver the detective had lent him. Jim put them on the floorboard and covered them with a blanket from the rumble seat area. The two men walked to the boardinghouse and bounded up the front steps. As they entered the hallway, Matt saw Cliff sprawled on the floor of the parlor listening to the final innings of a baseball game on the radio. Freckles was stretched out next to him like a lion in the sun. She raised her head as the two men entered, but returned to slumber at the sight of a familiar face. Matt and Jim strolled down the hall to the kitchen where the boarder knew he would probably find Miss Dixie fussing over one thing or another. She was sitting at the kitchen table, with her back to the door, chopping garlic cloves, when they entered the room. Across from her sat Adolphus, eating a plate of ham and eggs. He was busy sopping egg yolk with a piece of bread.

"Hello, Miss Dixie." Matt introduced his friend when his landlady turned in her chair. "Miss Dixie, this is Detective Jim Greerson of the Atlanta Police Department. Jim, this is my landlady and surrogate momma, Mrs. Dixie Fleming." Mrs. Fleming giggled at her roomer's remark.

Jim extended his hand to the woman, who said, "Just call me Miss Dixie. Everybody does."

"I'm very pleased to meet you, ma'am. Matt tells me he's found a good home here with good people." The landlady beamed happily. After they'd shaken hands, Jim edged around the table, looked at Adolphus, and asked, "And who is this healthy specimen?" Miss Dixie's eyes twinkled as she smiled, pleased at the man's gesture.

The move surprised Matt, who still could not read his companion, but who, nonetheless, continued the introductions. "Jim, this is Adolphus Teagler. He helps Miss Dixie with work and repairs around the house every so often." The black man looked up in alarm at the mention of his name. His large unblinking eyes fixed on the hefty white man standing before him. He dropped his fork on his plate and stood slowly. Adolphus, though older than the other two men, was still a substantial man in his own right. "It's okay, Adolphus. I just wanted to introduce you to my friend, Detective Jim Greerson." Relief played across the black man's broad, moon face when Jim held out his hand. The big black man wiped his hand on his plaid flannel shirt. The two men shook hands solemnly. In one moment, several Jim Crow laws, which Rhamy Fleming despised so much, had been brushed aside without fanfare.

"Adolphus fixed a couple of things around here today," the landlady said. "I worked him hard." The black man beamed broadly at her. "I don't know what I'd do without him. Go on now," she insisted to the man, "and finish your meal." Adolphus returned to his place at the table and slowly resumed eating. She turned to Matt. "Would you and Jim like some iced tea? I was just fixin' to make some for supper anyway."

Greerson spoke up. "Well, yes, ma'am. If it's no trouble, I'd be much obliged." The woman showed a wide smile at his words, and Matt thought he detected a girlish blush as she turned and bustled across the kitchen to her stove.

"Miss Dixie, is it all right if Jim and I sit at the dining-room table for a few minutes to look over some papers?"

"Sure, Matt. You two help yourselves. I'll brew up some tea and bring it in to you."

Jim turned and followed Matt across the hall into the dining room. "Grab a chair and I'll be right back, Jim." Matt lowered his voice to a whisper. "I need to ditch this thing," The young man held his coat open, revealing the automatic handgun in his waistband. Before going up the stairs, he closed the large pocket doors that separated the dining room from the parlor. The radio's baseball game was still in progress. In his room, Matt removed the gun's magazine, checked to make certain the chamber was cleared, and put the gun under an extra blanket in the bottom of his chifforobe. He hid the magazine in a sock. Making a mental note to get the other magazine out of his car, he hurried back downstairs.

Jim was sitting at the huge oak dining table with two glasses of iced tea and several pieces of paper spread before him. His hat was in a chair next to him. The pocket doors connecting to the parlor were open, and Cliff hovered over the table from the other chair next to the detective. The boy was kneeling in the chair's seat and leaning on his sharp elbows, planted firmly on the table, with his chin cupped in his hands. He gazed intently, yet uncomprehendingly at the papers. Matt stopped short. "Hey, Cliff, we need to do some work. How about running along, please?" Cliff didn't respond and didn't stir.

"Clifford Emanuel Fleming!" Miss Dixie called from the kitchen. Cliff's momma to the rescue, Matt thought. "Come here this instant!" Before the boy could gather himself and move, the landlady appeared at the dining-room door with Adolphus on her heels. "I need you to go help Adolphus restack that firewood out by the barn. He was just now fixin' to attend to it. It's his last chore of the day."

A mumbled "Yes'm" preceded a miserable twelve-year-old, who made his way with the black man and Freckles through the kitchen, into the pantry, and out the back door. Miss Dixie beamed at the two men and returned to her kitchen.

"Thank you, Miss Dixie." Matt took the chair vacated by Cliff and asked, "So what do we have?"

Greerson chortled, "Again with the plural pronouns, eh, Matt?" The reporter smiled as the detective went on, "Well it appears that some of the boys decided to have a private meeting about the numbers rackets in town and who was gonna run what. From Charlie's notes, it seems that they chose to use his momma's apartment for privacy and security. Charlie was there *because* it was his momma's place and also to provide the security. The best I can gather from his scribbling is that they were there to plan bumping somebody off. For whatever reason, they were pretty cagey in what they said. So they didn't mention any names outright. They only referred to a person they called 'Boss.' But, aside from Charlie, nobody else is missing or has turned up dead except Eddie. On top of their caginess, it kind of looks like Charlie only caught bits and pieces of the conversations. They probably treated him like always: run get this, fetch me a drink, and get me a sandwich. If I had to guess, I'd say he spent a fair amount of time in the kitchen and not around the table with the boys. He tried, though. God love him, he tried."

"So who was there? Does he say? Anybody you recognize?"

"Well, that's where it gets sticky again. Charlie only uses initials for the mugs there. I don't think he counted on being knocked off and not being around to explain his notes," Jim said sarcastically. "Knowing Charlie, he may have written this all down because of his difficulty remembering some things. Too many years of headshots, if you know what I mean." Greerson paused to take a drink as the young man nodded briefly. "I can pretty well guess who three sets of these initials stand for, but that's all it'd be, guesswork. And three pairs of the initials could stand for one of a couple of goons. Two sets of initials, I have no idea." Matt leaned over the table. "Like here," Jim said pointing to an entry on a page. "That 'W.C.' could be Walt Cutcliff."

"Sure that makes sense!" Matt blurted and sipped his iced tea.

"Sure. But it could also be Willie Carter, a major player in The Metropolitan, another of the numbers outfits in Atlanta. Willie's on a par with, say, where Gutowski is in the Home Company, Eddie and Walt's setup. And, if it's Willie, that could mean someone from another outfit was trying to grab Eddie's racket. And a few people in Eddie's crew were ready to go along, probably for a price. If it's Walt, it probably means he was tired of playing second fiddle to Guyol and wanted the 'throne' for himself. Maybe even for Myrtle. It's not unheard of for the widows to take over a numbers racket when the husband is bumped off. Either way, Walt gets his."

"Any other initials you recognize?"

"Well, my guess is that this 'C.G.' is my old pal Carl Gutowski." The detective's forehead furrowed. "That bastard." As he finished speaking, the muscles in his jaw stood out like a steel beam. The timbre of his voice revealed a subdued, but unmistakable anger. Suddenly, Greerson remembered where he was and glanced quickly toward the kitchen. Thankfully, his language brought no reaction from the lady in that quarter.

Matt let it drift and scanned the scrawling on the pages. He saw initials that caught his attention. "Do you know who this 'D. W.' is?"

"Could be a couple of people I know of. But, with the others present, my guess would be Dave Waters."

"Dave Waters, huh?"

"Yeah, you know him? Some people call him 'Dave the Dude' because of the fancy car he drives and the red carnation he wears in his lapel."

The skin on Matt's neck prickled. He lowered his voice so it wouldn't carry through the house. "A Brewster?"

Because Matt almost whispered his question, Jim looked around and spoke in a hushed tone, too. "Yeah, that's right? So you *do* know him?"

"Nah, I just think I've seen him around. That's all." Matt considered the matter for a few seconds. Then he waved his arms above the table and returned to a normal conversational level. "So, what is the bottom line with all this, Jim?"

"I think it's that Charlie got killed for what somebody *thought* he'd written down and maybe what he could add to his notes by way of testimony, and not what he'd actually committed to paper. But the truth is, as good-hearted as Charlie was, he wouldn't have made a very good witness with him being slightly addled and all. What a waste of a decent guy. Decent folks don't matter to some scum. Gutowski is gonna get his," he said evenly.

"Yeah, I guess." Matt was at a loss for anything else to say.

"I'll take these papers back to headquarters, turn them over to Chief Poole, and tell him what I know about them." Again, Matt nodded his understanding. "Of course, your name won't come up. That wouldn't do either of us any good."

"Does that mean we part company here?"

Greerson thought for a minute before answering. "Not necessarily. I like you, kid. And, to be honest about it, that's saying something for me. Hell, I'm not sure I've ever had a friend!"

"Well, what was that man named Parrish?"

The detective ignored Matt's question. "If anything comes up that I think might interest you, I'll call you. That is, unless it involves gunplay." He smiled sideways at his friend.

Matt chuckled, but kept his voice at a whisper. "Why let that stop you? I'm armed now."

"Oh, that's right! And that reminds me that I need to get you a shoulder holster. I'll take care of that for you." Jim glanced at his wristwatch and expressed the need to get back to headquarters to see Chief Poole. He started gathering the papers back into the envelope.

About that time, Miss Dixie appeared at the doorway, wiping her hands on her apron. "Excuse me, but would you like to stay for supper, detective? One of my boarders," she looked at Matt, "Diane, has a date tonight with *that man* and won't be here." Matt flinched at her words and glanced at Jim. "We eat at six-thirty sharp, if you're interested. We'd be glad to have you. We're having slumgullion tonight." When she saw uncertainty on the men's faces, the landlady explained further. "It's a recipe one of my girls gave me. I think the name is used for meat stews, but this is an Italian version of the dish. It has ground beef, garlic, onions, tomato sauce, and pasta. Teresa, one of our boarders, says it's delicious. You're welcomed to stay."

"Thank you very much, Mrs. Fleming, but I need to get some things done at the police station and won't be able to."

"Maybe some other time, then," Miss Dixie said, smiling and nodding, before she returned to her kitchen.

The two men walked to the front porch where they parted with a promise to keep in touch. As the detective was walking to his car, Miss Dixie joined Matt on the porch. Jim turned and waved to them. "He seems like very nice young man, Matt. Do you know if he's married?"

"He said he wasn't, Miss Dixie. But it wasn't what he said as much as the way he said it." She turned and gave her boarder a puzzled look. "Like there was a lot of hurt, maybe anger in the thought of it. I don't know." The young man laughed, as the maroon Hudson drove past, moving toward downtown, and the pair waved from the front door. "You wouldn't be trying to do some matchmaking, now, would you, Miss Dixie?"

"Oh, fiddlesticks, Matthew Grimes!" The woman looked around the yard and up to the darkening sky, blushing slightly, and walked back inside. "Looks like rain again," she moaned. Matt caught the screen door before it closed and followed her into the hallway.

Matt walked through the house and out to the back stoop. He sat on the steps and watched Adolphus and Cliff for a short time as they finished stacking the split firewood. Adolphus, a onetime timber caller for the railroad, sang a gospel hymn in his deep, rich voice as they worked. When they were done, Cliff and his dog quickly scampered around the side of the house. Matt surmised that he wanted to avoid the watchful eye of his momma. Adolphus ambled to where the boarder was sitting. The older man looked tired. Matt patted the step beside him. When the black man shot an uncertain look to the back door, the young man assured him, "It's okay. Have a seat, Adolphus. Unless you need to go."

"Naw, suh. I's could use a spell asittin'. Been a lawng day." Adolphus adjusted his stained bib overalls and sat gingerly on the step.

"Miss Dixie work you too hard?"

"Oh, naw, suh! She alluz be rat good to me. Pays me good *en* feeds me." He paused long enough to exhale noisily. "Times like dese, tis hard 'nough fo' a body to git work. Harder still fo' somebody like me," he said slowly, looking at Matt intently with moist eyes. In those eyes, Matt saw the same pathetic yet proud gaze that he'd seen on the streetcar the week before. He thought he understood, but, in reality, he knew he could only *try* to comprehend what the man felt.

"Well, I know how much you mean to Miss Dixie, too. I don't think she could manage this place without you, Adolphus."

About that time, Miss Dixie appeared at the back door with two big glasses of iced tea. The woman scanned the backyard and barn area. "Looks like another good job, Adolphus. Thank you *so* much." She handed the glasses to the two men sitting there. "Mr. Fleming works hard, and I appreciate your taking some of the load off him when he gets home." She made another search of the backyard. "Just where is that rascal son of mine? Into some devilment, no doubt!" Both men hunkered down in silence and traded knowing glances. The black man's eyes shined with mirth. "I swan when I find that boy…" Her voice faded as she reentered the back door, the screen door slamming behind her.

"I sho 'nough don' wanna be that young'un w'en she finds him," Adolphus laughed. They sat quietly for a while. Then, the men listened as a large truck slowly made its way down Houston Street in front of the house. The car horn, apparently belonging to an impatient motorist, blared nearby. The big black man shook his head. "Times is achangin' sho 'nuf. Lawdy, I can 'member when a body could lay down in the middle of Houston Street all the livelong day en not hafta worry 'bout nothin' comin' 'long to rile him. Nowadays, a dawg cain't even cross the road in safety." Matt laughed at the visual image.

They talked baseball, a thing both loved, for a time. Adolphus spoke with pride about the Black Crackers and how much he enjoyed going to their games when he could afford it and could get there. At one point, in a cautious voice filled with subdued pride, he also spoke of the fact that, when white folks went to a Black Crackers game, they were told they could sit anywhere they wanted, while blacks attending a Crackers game were relegated to the left-field bleachers. Matt understood that the older black man wasn't being confrontational in his comment, merely stating a fact of life as it stood.

The pair leaned back on their elbows on the step above where they sat, and quietly watched as clouds scudded across the foreboding sky. After a time, the two men finished their tea. Adolphus declined Matt's offer of a ride home, saying that his daughter was picking him up on her way home from work. They parted company with a handshake.

---

That evening, during the hearty meal of slumgullion, a delicious variation in the boardinghouse's supper routine, Miss Dixie brought up that a "very handsome" Detective Greerson had come by to visit Matt that afternoon. When her young boarder gave his landlady a big, knowing smile, she scrunched her face at him. The mention caught the attention of both Teresa and Victoria. Rhamy's interest was aroused also, and Matt had to promise to fill him in on the situation. Murder seemed the primary topic of conversation around the table that evening. Afterward, the household gathered around the Philco for their evening's entertainment. First up was *Burns and Allen*. Gracie was still looking for her "lost brother." Mr. Rhamy always insisted that she *had* to be a genius to sound so convincingly idiotic. That program was followed by the droll wit of Fred Allen and his variety show, *Town Hall Tonight*. The night rounded out with music from Guy Lombardo and his Royal Canadians. About halfway through the musical program, Matt was overtaken by somnolence and toddled off to bed. As he gave himself to sleep's soothing seduction, he was thinking of Diane and her boyfriend. If Dave was at that meeting at Mrs. Dunbar's apartment on Sunday afternoon, Matt wondered, is that why he was unavailable to see Diane that day? And was the date they had Tuesday evening, the night of Eddie Guyol's murder, set to establish an alibi for him? He felt bad for Diane. She was a good kid.

---

Thursday's morning rounds gave Matt plenty of newsworthy items about which to write. Overnight, the three men charged with the robbery of the George Muse Clothing Company store back in March, with break-ins at a local Kress store and the Trammell Scott Sporting Good Company and other capers, had escaped the city jail. The circumstances surrounding the daring escapade made the yarn even more appealing in the young reporter's view. Further investigation revealed that the sounds of the prisoners' sawing their way through the bars of the "escape-proof" facility were masked by the Police Departments Brass Band's practice nearby and by fellow prisoners singing ribald songs at the top of their lungs. After cutting their way clear of the cells, the trio had used bed linens to lower themselves onto an adjacent roof and hence to freedom. The embarrassment of the escape, which led to immediate finger pointing followed by calls for a thorough investigation of the matter, was compounded when an alderman made two sarcastic suggestions. First, he proposed that each cell be provided with a coil of manila rope to save wear and tear on the bed linens. Second, he recommended that the jail, centrally located as it was, be used for an auditorium and the Shrine Mosque, adjacent to the

Fox Theater, be used as a lockup because it would probably hold prisoners as well as the jail was shown to be doing.

Just that quickly, Matthew Grimes, crime reporter, had moved from the verge of being reduced to covering the Atlanta Food Show to being the busiest man at the *Atlanta Georgian* newspaper. He had an article on the front page under a banner headline for the second time in as many days. Eddie Guyol's murder also provided a few follow-up stories. Moreover, he was the center of the city room's attention as he regaled those present with the story of the jailbreak. His recollection of a news item from 1934 added to the tale. In November of that year, a new addition to the police station, which included an up-to-date jail, opened to much fanfare. The grand opening's celebration was short-lived and all present had to cool their heels for more than two hours when, in the midst of the prisoner transfer to their new abode, it was discovered that no one had the keys to unlock the facility. Other humiliating circumstances were involved with the opening of the new building back then, but Matt's yarn focused on the jail at this point. Eventually, the keys were located in Dekalb County. Brick led the newsroom laughter at the young man's recollection. The older reporter made a vague gesture with the fingers of a hand, proclaiming that he knew all along that the jail was "cursed." The story carried through the rest of the week.

---

The police beat reporter and the detective had not crossed paths since Wednesday. About midmorning on Friday, Detective Greerson called Grimes at the newspaper. They met for lunch later at the Brass Rail Restaurant on Peachtree Street, where they had the chicken pot pie lunch special. After a bit of pleasantries, Matt tried to talk about baseball and his beloved Crackers, still battling to stay at .500. Jim showed some animus against the subject and quickly changed the topic to recent events.

Although Matt was taken aback at Greerson's abruptness, he was eager to pick up whatever morsels of news the officer might bear.

The cop brought the *Georgian* correspondent up to date on the Guyol murder investigation. He explained that, although there were still those arguing the stickup possibility, the police department was moving forward with their theory of a grudge killing of some sort. The supposition was that an outside hatchet man had been brought in to do the deed. The search was on for him. So, he told his companion, nobody was interested in checking the guns the reporter had collected that night. That answered a question Matt had about returning Gutowski's magazine to the police for the tests. Jim swore, making it clear that the higher ups in the department and the detectives assigned to the case had completely discounted the information that he and Matt had gleaned the night of and the day after the Guyol killing. And they saw the murder of Charlie Newsome as no more than a mere coincidence. Jim added his opinion that the fact Newsome was not around to detail the meeting and explain his notes only helped them leap to their conclusions with a clear conscience.

"What does it mean now that Eddie Guyol's gone?" the detective asked rhetorically. Then, he answered his own question. "Someone else will just move in to take his place. The racket won't miss a beat." Greerson chuckled and, as if to prove the contention, pointed out that the number that hit the day following Guyol's murder was three-eight-one. Overall, Greerson was exasperated. Matt was disappointed. The reporter realized that, unless something big broke on the Guyol case, the story would slowly die.

Jim and Matt briefly discussed Charlie Newsome's funeral, slated for that afternoon at three o'clock in Oakland Cemetery. He thanked Matt for making the arrangements through the newspaper to get Charlie buried in the Potter's Field there. Greerson told his young companion that he was going to pick up Mrs. Dunbar and take her to the memorial service that afternoon. The detective explained that he'd gone by and visited Mrs. Dunbar the Thursday morning after Charlie's death and told her of the funeral arrangements then in the works. She'd already been notified of Charlie's death by the department, but he'd wanted to check on her. Mrs. Dunbar had been packing to move back to Gilmer County. She'd told Greerson that she had relatives there and that's where she'd feel more at home, especially with Charlie gone. When Jim made the offer, Matt declined to ride with them, saying he'd meet them at Oakland.

When Matt asked about the Muse robbers' escape on Wednesday night, the detective merely grimaced and shook his head. "I predict that some heads will role on that one. If not get lopped off, they'll at least get a good smack! Yeah, there's a red-faced search on for that trio."

Matt chuckled, "Yeah, no departure from an Atlanta jail has grabbed that much ink since Capone left the Federal pen here for Alcatraz last year."

By the end of the meal, Jim's mood has seemed to have mellowed. He chuckled and haphazardly apologized for his abruptness when the topic of baseball was broached. "Not a happy subject for me," was all he would say. Matt still could not gauge his new friend's disposition. He let it drift. Before they separated, Greerson handed Grimes a paper bag. In low tones, he told the young man it was an underarm holster for the .45 caliber handgun he now possessed and asked that he not open the bag until he was elsewhere. The young reporter thanked him and made another mental note to remove Gutowski's magazine from his Ford's floorboard. He kept forgetting it was there.

---

Beneath overcast skies with warm temperatures, three people and a nondescript clergyman buried Charlie Newsome in Potter's Field at Oakland Cemetery on April 26th at three p.m. Mrs. Dunbar wept softly during the short service. As they walked away from the plot, Charlie's mother, still sobbing, leaned on the *Georgian* reporter for support. Matt heard Jim mutter under his breath, "Not much to show for the forty-two years Charlie spent on earth." The young man could only grimly nod his agreement. The older lady didn't seem to take

*Oakland Cemetery's Hunter Street Gate*

notice of Greerson's words. Or maybe she simply knew the reflection to be true, requiring no comment.

As they were leaving the graveyard, Matt discovered the headstone of Leonard Simpson, the man he'd been reminded of only ten days earlier. Mrs. Dunbar shifted to the detective for support as they walked on ahead of Matt, who stopped briefly to read the epitaph inscribed beneath the Masonic symbol carved on the gravestone. There, he contemplated, lies still another man who'd died before his time. Despondency overtook the young journalist. Matt again recalled the hours spent in the library studying the history of his new hometown. He caught Jim and Mrs. Dunbar as the detective was helping her into his Hudson parked on Hunter Street. The young man expressed his condolences to Charlie's momma, wished her well, and said good-bye. Matt was swept up by melancholia as he watched them drive away. That sadness couldn't be overcome even when he, ever the huge baseball fan, realized he was standing at the spot on Hunter Street next to Oakland Cemetery, where the first organized baseball game had been played in Atlanta in the dark days after the Civil War. Later, the time it took to return to 71 Houston Street was as long as Matt could ever remember a drive taking.

# SHORTENING SHADOWS

Saturday night finally made its appearance. Matt and Evie had a date to go to a movie, followed by a late supper somewhere. Because they'd seen Evie's movie pick last weekend, she gave her beau the choice this time around. He scanned the papers and saw nothing that really grabbed him. Of course, the Harlow movie he'd really wanted to see, *Reckless*, had moved on from the Paramount and was nowhere to be found, while Bing Crosby and *Mississippi* still clung to life at Loew's Grand. There wasn't a single Harlow or Lombard movie showing in Atlanta. He did find a small nugget in an Ann Sheridan movie, titled *Car 99*, showing at the Capitol Theater. Matt wasn't sure of the storyline of the movie he was considering, but he'd noticed Sheridan when he'd endured *Mississippi*, in which she'd had a small role as a schoolgirl. He'd also seen her in minor roles in a few other movies. She was worth watching, in his estimation.

As Matt was leaving the boardinghouse, he saw Cliff sitting at the kitchen table, trying to color a comic strip from the evening's paper for some Myles Salt contest he'd heard the boy talking about earlier. Those in the household, who were remaining in for the evening, were taking up positions in the parlor for a night of radio entertainment. Rhamy Fleming sat in his usual corner chair, engrossed in a copy of *A Handful of Dust*. Miss Dixie sat in the chair across the side table from her husband, leafing through a stack of magazines. Diane, of course, was out with "Dave the Dude." Victoria was off somewhere.

Teresa was at the card table, writing a letter, but she looked up when Matt stuck his head into the room. She teasingly chided that he was going to miss the new Lucky Strike radio program at seven o'clock, *The Hit Parade*. He'd heard Victoria and Teresa talking about the new program which had debuted last week. Matt laughingly admitted that it sounded better than the usual Saturday-night-at-seven fare, *Roxy and His New Gang*, a musical variety program hosted by the former Pennsylvania baseball league player, Samuel "Roxy" Rothafel. If the program was as good as the girls made it out to be, he had a notion that *Hit Parade* could be around for a while.

The image of Lucky Strike's dark-green and red package also brought Mrs. LaFavor to mind, and Matt laughed aloud as he waved his good-bye.

The young man collected his girlfriend, who was coming down with a cold, for their date in his gray Tudor. In the time it took for Matt to close Evie's car door and walk around to the driver's side, she had stepped on and picked up the magazine from Gutowski's .45. In the excitement of the week, he'd forgotten it was lying on the car's floorboard. When he climbed into the driver's side, Evie brandished the magazine under his nose and demanded an explanation. When he tried to explain its presence and reluctantly admitted that he now owned a gun, a serious tiff ensued.

Evie was not happy about Matt's crime-scene participation, which was so involved the detective was routinely handing him such things. She was trying to understand the things his job entailed, but it bothered her a great deal. The girl vividly recalled reading several years earlier about a *Chicago Tribune* reporter being shot to death gangland-style in broad daylight during rush hour in front of dozens of witnesses. Although Atlanta certainly wasn't 1930 Chicago by any stretch of the imagination, the incident showed that people in Matt's line of work were not immune to the repercussions of the criminal activity on which they reported.

Matt knew Evie was used to being around guns. Mr. Nash had carried one daily when he traipsed around the regional forests looking for telephone poles while dealing with the occasional snake, bear, or moonshiner early in his career with the phone company. As far as Matt understood, her father still owned several. For his part, the young journalist was determined to maintain his uncertain connection with the police officer while he could and through whatever stories it might bring. While he was certainly no hero and did not expect to take any unnecessary risks, he would continue to follow Detective Greerson as close as he could. Notwithstanding the cop's being somewhat standoffish, Matt liked something about the man's seen-it-all demeanor. He thought he was a sharp police officer and a good source of information.

He grinned as he realized the three changes being around Jim had made in him: he smoked more, carried a gun, and seemed looser with his language than he normally was. Matt recognized that Jim Greerson and his dealing with him was a very touchy subject for Evie.

An uneasy truce between the two young lovers followed, but the evening did not improve with the movie. The flick dealt with a guy, who joins the Michigan State Police at his girlfriend's urging, and the risks and dangers his occupation puts on him. During some scenes involving gunplay, Matt could feel Evie giving him hard sideways looks. Words were not necessary. The date ended with a subdued meal at the Varsity, where rowdy Tech fans were celebrating sweeping a baseball doubleheader from Clemson College earlier in the day.

---

Despite the absence of rain, Sunday passed in dreary fashion. Evie's cold was much worse, and Matt didn't have a chance to see her. The couple did spend considerable time on the phone with each other Sunday afternoon. So much so, that, after a while, Matt felt compelled to ring off the boardinghouse telephone to let others use it. He walked down to the pay phone at Allen's filling station on the corner of Houston and Courtland Streets. Matt had to wait for a drifter to bang on the side of the telephone and finger the coin return before he could give Evie a ring back. Even with the girl feeling much worse than she had the night before, the couple covered many topics as they talked over the next several hours. Before they hung up, Evie, anticipating not seeing her boyfriend for a few days because of her cold, made Matt promise not to get into any mischief with his new friend, the detective. Matt laughingly promised to do his best.

Over the weekend, Matt's crime stories continued to grab some front-page headlines, though not as big as the Guyol murder or the jail break. In one article, a man had been shot and killed shortly past midnight Saturday morning in the hallway of a Parkway Drive apartment building. The investigation revealed that the dead man, a former star boxer, was merely visiting the residents of the apartment and had answered the door for them when someone knocked. He had been murdered in a case of mistaken identity. The killer was a man infatuated with the wife of the couple who lived there. According to her statement, she had refused to run away to New York with the murderer, who thought he was killing her husband. The killer's identity was known and a nationwide manhunt for the would-be lothario was on.

In addition, the aftermath of the city jail escape came down on some employees. Police Chief Sturdivant announced that it included a suspension for at least one turnkey, the transfer of some jailers to other duties, and changes in the lockup's policies relating to patrols of the jail, among other things. The three escapees responsible for the shake-up had not been located, although they were reported to be traveling with three women and had spent Thursday at a hotel in Columbus, Georgia.

The wire services provided the banner-headline story of a Hollywood fashion designer murdered by his chauffeur-secretary, who also critically wounded a second man. The alleged killer committed suicide shortly after the shootings. The tale revealed a connection between the designer and Aimee Semple McPherson and, of particular interest to the young reporter, Jean Harlow. The whole story had the hint of scandalous details lying just beneath the surface. A California sheriff's office captain only added to the titillation when he was quoted as saying, "They were strange men who led strange lives."

In a news item not related to Matt's bailiwick, for the first time since the World War, daylight saving time became effective in Atlanta at one o'clock that Sunday morning. Most of the time change passed without difficulty. Of course, there were those citizens who didn't understand the program or forgot to change their clocks. Then, there were many reports of white families being roused from their sleep early Sunday morning by their black maids and cooks who appeared for work an hour early because they didn't understand the time change. Hilarity ensued. At least, the reports were sidesplitting to the cynical wags in the *Georgian* newsroom.

# CHAPTER 9

# The Unwelcomed Visit

When he arrived at the newsroom from his Monday-morning circuit, Grimes found a message that Detective Greerson had called and asked that he call him as soon as possible. He wrote up his leads, such as they were, and pushed them through the review process before returning to his desk to phone the detective. When he came on the line, Greerson sounded upbeat. "Well, how's the boy?"

"I'm good, Jim. How're you getting along?"

"Not bad for a heathen! Say, how's about getting together for some grub? Make it a little later than normal. I've got something I have to handle first." He lowered his voice and, close to the phone under what sounded like a cupped hand, whispered, "I've got some things to tell you that might make interesting copy for your readers." He returned to a normal tone. "Whaddya say, kid?"

As he was listening, Matt had pulled a cigarette from a pack and was rolling it back and forth on his desk gently under his fingers. When he heard Jim's taunt about interesting copy, he stopped and swept the cigarette across his desk with the back of his hand. "Can't you tell me over the phone? I still have time to get it in this afternoon's editions. But I *am* on a deadline," he pointed out.

Again in a low voice, Greerson replied, "Some of it's on the q. t., Matt. So it can't go in the paper just yet. Probably tomorrow. You'll still scoop everybody. Trust me."

Matt's eyebrows furrowed. If he had a source like Greerson, who was to say that his competitors at the *Constitution* and the *Journal*, longer in the tooth than he, didn't also? And they might print something on speculation if only to try to scoop everybody else. "Are you sure you can't give it to me now?" When he had listened to dead air for a few seconds, he relented. "All right, Jim. You win, you sorry rascal. What time and where do you want to meet?"

"Atta boy! Can you meet me at the station house in about three hours? As I said, I've got something I have to do first. We can grab something at one of the places around headquarters. A lot of the guys here eat at 'em." He laughed, "That is, unless you're afraid of food poisoning."

Matt chortled. "Hey, slick, if you can take it, I can take it!" He slowly replaced the receiver on its hook and thought about his detective friend. From what he'd seen, Grimes considered Detective Greerson a pretty tough and stalwart fellow. The young man hoped he sounded bolder than he felt when it came to ptomaine. In the back of his mind was the notion that any hash house, operating near a police station and frequented by officers, should have enough sense to maintain a good, healthy place to eat. Matt was a touch frustrated at the circumstances of the supposed news stories, but he trusted Greerson. That was the bottom line. So he waited.

---

Shortly before one thirty that afternoon, Matt started for the door to make his way to police department headquarters. Brick stopped him a few steps short of the exit and solemnly solicited a cash contribution for a birthday present for old man Hearst. He explained that this was William Randolph Hearst's birthday, and the guys in the newsroom were chipping in together to get the newspaper's owner one of those revolving doormats that *Time Magazine* had mentioned back in January. Brick added that it was for the 'castle' Mr. Hearst was building in California. Matt, taken aback at the solicitation, muttered, "What the hell?" and looked around at the city room occupants in stunned bewilderment. The room erupted in laughter. Matt shook his head in amusement and moved toward the door. As he made his way to Marietta Street, Matt experienced what he understood the French to call "staircase wit." Too late, he thought of a retort to Brick's gag. He realized that he should have replied that it was also Duke Ellington's birthday and asked what were they getting for him? It wouldn't have been much of a riposte, but it was all he could think of. He waggled his head and chuckled. Some kind of shenanigans was always going on in the newsroom, he mused, usually centered on Brick.

Ten minutes later, he tucked the Ford into the curb on Piedmont Avenue around the corner from the police station. Next to his Ford sat a much older vehicle, parked by a fireplug. The young journalist took a second to look at a car rarely seen those days. He chuckled as he decided that it seemed to be something from the early years of the Roosevelt administration – *Theodore* Roosevelt's administration! The car in question was an old White Star touring car, dating from sometime during the first decade of the century. Matt recalled reading that the White Star Automobile Company had manufactured automobiles in Atlanta briefly, until they filed for bankruptcy after several years. The car was a dusty, hard-bitten relic that apparently functioned fine. After a time, Matt turned and hustled to the police station on Butler Street.

When the reporter entered the building, the desk officer was occupied. But it was not the usual human flotsam and jetsam Matt had seen there many times before. A watery-eyed, older man in threadbare bib overalls and a faded, long-sleeved, collarless chambray shirt stood before the officer's desk. His clothes had age on them, but they were freshly laundered. Above his shirt a sun-weathered neck revealed a hard life spent in the fields. The old gentleman was barely able to maintain his composure. A woman of comparable age stood nearby in a faded calico, floor-length dress and sunbonnet, dabbing her eyes with a lace-trimmed hankie as she waited. Her demeanor mirrored the heartache and humiliation the man bore. Both her dress and his shirt appeared to be homemade. The old farmer spoke in low tones that betrayed equal measures of embarrassment and sorrow as he scuffed at the floor with the toe of a battered brogan. As he talked, his hands fretted nervously with a tattered gray hat he held behind him. The hat showed the sweat stain of twenty or so years of planting seasons. The man softly explained that he and his wife were seeking any possible help from the desk officer to find their daughter who'd come to the "big city" and had gotten "lost." Periodically, he wiped his face and eyes with an old bandanna. It, too, looked to be fresh from the washtub and ironing board. Matt stopped short and watched the scene for a moment. He imagined it was a scene that played out hundreds of times a year in cities across the Depression-ravaged country. And they rarely resulted in happy conclusions.

The police officer, visibly uncomfortable with his role in this picture, glanced at the Matt and nodded a greeting. The young man took the opportunity to hold up his press card and quietly call out Detective Greerson's name. In response, the officer nodded toward a nearby door before returning his attention to the old couple and their anguish.

Passing through the doorway, Matt walked down a short hallway to the Detectives' Division. He almost collided with longtime Chief of Detectives Lamar Poole as the policeman was leaving the office space.

# THE UNWELCOMED VISIT

Chief Poole was a husky, business-minded man apparently in a hurry to get somewhere, but he took the time to direct the big reporter to Detective Greerson. Matt found his friend with his necktie loosened, both feet up on an opened desk drawer, and his hair, what there was of it, in an unruly mess. He looked as if he'd recently left a brawl. When the blond newsman laughed quietly at the sight, he realized the other men in the room had stopped talking and were giving him steely glares. A bit self-consciously, the young man nodded around. One of the men he saw was his buddy from the yegg squad. They acknowledged one another with a slightly deeper nod.

Then, Matt spied his old pal, Detective Arthur Rutherford, sitting across the room, eyeing him warily. At this short distance and in the full light of day, Matt had a good look at the man. His pockmarked mien bore a swarthiness the young man had not detected in the dark that night on Pelham Road. Rutherford was a big, barrel-bodied man, muscular turned saggy. He had extremely shaggy eyebrows, remarkable for someone as young as he appeared to be. The detective pulled a cigarette from his thick lips with even thicker fingers. When he shot the young reporter a thin smirk that worked toward intimidation, his upper lip curled back. His teeth were many and prominent. All things considered, Matt surmised, Rutherford's face was as inviting as a flat tire. In the detective's menacing gaze, Matt drew himself up to his fullest extent and returned the stare. Greerson furtively shifted his eyes between Grimes and Rutherford. After a few seconds, Rutherford made an effort to look mildly amused. Matt kept his hard-eyed stare at the detective. Eventually, the beefy detective's face shifted to a sharp scowl, and he looked down at the desk where he sat. He angrily rubbed out his cigarette in an ashtray. Detective Greerson beamed at this outcome. Looking at Matt, he concluded again that this kid had moxie and sand.

Matt held the deadpan gaze in Rutherford's direction for a few more seconds, before smiling and turning to Jim. He leaned over Greerson's desk and mumbled under his breath, "That was easy."

The detective sat up and met him about halfway across the desk. He jerked his head in Rutherford's direction and whispered, "Well, don't go runnin' away with yourself over it, kid. That Judge Crater act he pulled last week has landed him on the chief's shit list. Right now Artie's walking on eggshells. So don't go thinking he's a pushover or something."

Matt maintained Jim's conspiratorial tone, "I thought you said he was on vacation."

"That was the official party line. I toed it. 'Nough said."

Matt straightened and laughed quietly, "Understood. Well, now it's my turn to say that you look like hell. What've you been up to?"

Greerson ran his fingers through his thinning hair, slowly shifting in the chair. "Well, we had to go visit a lug about a robbery and shooting. Seems he didn't want to join us on our return trip to the police station. So I had to persuade him." Matt sat in a straight-back chair beside Greerson's desk. As Jim swiveled to face Matt, the younger man noticed, for the first time, that he had a dark bruise over his left cheekbone and an abrasion at his temple on the same side.

Matt stole a glance around the room and snickered, "Well, where is he? Is he at the jail already?" The question brought ripples of laughter from the other detectives working nearby.

"No. As a matter of fact, he's at Grady Hospital right now. He'll be here soon enough, though."

Matt's eyebrows raised in uncertainty. He'd seen how Greerson operated. He was very tough but, at the same time, seemed fair in his actions with and reactions to people. Jim had been friendly enough with him, he reflected. And Gutowski, he thought, had asked for the treatment he'd received at the detective's hands. The thug had even provoked him to a rough response. The man in the hallway of the Kiser Building apparently had nefarious intentions, which, only through experience and observation, Greerson had perceived and on which he'd acted. Matt couldn't fault Jim there either. Finally, Matt asked, "What'd this guy do?"

"He robbed a medium-sized grocery store down Valdosta way and shot the owner. Killed him." As Matt nodded his understanding, Greerson went on, "Worse yet, he shot the man's wife, who was working in the store with him at the time, *and* then shot their child who was also present."

"The bastard," Matt mumbled.

"The woman died, but not before telling the sheriff down there who'd done it. Turns out, he was a regular customer. Their kid, now an orphan, pulled through, by the way. Afterward, the punk hightailed it up to Tyrone, Georgia, just south of here, to hide out with relatives. We got a teletype to be on the lookout for him. When we contacted the authorities in Tyrone, they asked if we could lend them a hand in his capture. Apparently, his relatives there are connected with some important muckety-mucks in the county, and the Tyrone authorities wanted it handled straightforwardly. We were glad to help. Unfortunately, he gave up without too much of a fight."

"What do you mean 'unfortunately'?"

"Well, after reading what he'd done, some of the boys wanted him to try some gunplay when we got to him. Instead, he decided to use fisticuffs." The detective chuckled, "So, we may add assault and resisting to his charges, *when* he gets out of the hospital." The last part of the comment brought more cackles from a few others in the room. Greerson stood slowly, stiffly. He gingerly strapped on his shoulder holster, which had been hanging over the back of his chair, and pulled on his coat. He shook off the pangs, grabbed his hat and jammed it on his head. As he did, the reporter noticed scrapes on the knuckles of the detective's right hand. "Enough shoptalk. If you want, I'll give you more details on the arrest while we walk. Ready to eat?"

"Let's go!"

Detective Greerson related all the pertinent information about the Tyrone arrest they'd made as they walked to Maloof's Restaurant at the corner of Decatur and Butler Streets. When they grabbed a table in the restaurant, Matt noticed for the third time they'd eaten together that Jim always chose a chair facing the door. He assumed it was an occupational tendency. They were waited on by a tall, lethargic creature with a wedge-shaped face that reflected utter boredom. The man's Adam's apple moved vaguely in his lean throat as he took their orders. He nosily hung around their table until Jim Greerson removed his gun from its holster and casually laid it on the table between them. Suddenly, their waiter found something to occupy his time elsewhere, and his long lank body flitted away.

Before their meals arrived, the pair traded small talk, which eventually wound its way around to their college days. Although Jim was not much on small talk about himself or his life, Matt wormed out of him that he'd worked a year after high school to earn the money to attended Georgia Tech. Jim explained that he was at Tech, studying engineering, for a while before the start of the Great War. When war broke out, he and some of his buddies, caught up in the wartime fervor, left Tech and volunteered for the army. That was as far as Detective Greerson would go in discussing the war. He did, however, say that he'd attended the school for a short time following his return from Europe. When pushed about his war experiences, Jim quickly switched topics to the Georgia Tech – Georgia rivalry, the friendly banter about which was interrupted by the arrival of their food. Matt smiled faintly when he realized that this was what the detective had meant when they were in his Ford that night on Twelfth Street and he'd said they'd have to talk later about Matt's time at the University of Georgia.

The meal wasn't up to Miss Dixie's standards, Matt thought, but it wasn't the swill that Jim had hinted it might be either. As they ate, the detective gave the reporter some follow-up information on the Charlie Newsome case. "We're nowhere close to finding the evidence to make an arrest, but I know who did it. And so do you. So, there's nothing we can do officially, but I plan to pay my friend Gutowski a little visit when he resurfaces." Matt started to speak, but Greerson plunged forward, "He's been layin' low since Charlie's murder. But he'll show his mug at some point again soon, and I'll be there to greet him."

When Greerson took a sip of his coffee, Matt blurted, "Why are you looking for Gutowski? That is, without solid evidence against him for Charlie's killing?"

"Listen, kid. It's a cold, cruel world, filled with harsh realities that don't fit neatly into some people's idea of fairness or justice. You know and I know who killed Charlie. Besides, he went after that little old lady. She was lucky. Exactly why, I don't know. Then he roughed up Vivian. He might have done more to her if we hadn't been on his tail and if he didn't think he could come back later and get what he was after. Lucky for her, she got out of town. He's got to pay for some things one way or another. Catching bad guys is what I do, Matt. And I think I'm decent at it. But I can't fix families, whether it's Charlie's or anybody else's. All I can do is try to bring them a little bit of justice, but that's no fix. No fix at all. But that's all I've got to offer." He paused and stared away, at nothing in particular, before returning his gaze at the reporter. "Hear me, sport. This is just a job to me. I don't have any ideals about it. Not anymore."

Grimes let the topic drift. He thought that some subjects shouldn't be explored. As his grandma would have said, "I'm not lifting the lid off that pot." He merely nodded.

"In case you hadn't heard, the Guyol murder investigation is at a standstill for now. And, by the way, Vivian called me and she's settled in with relatives in Kentucky. Got a job waiting tables in some nice hotel's restaurant up there." Matt glanced at Jim with a look of mild surprise.

Jim grinned and explained, "I told her to call me and reverse the charges when she got to Lexington. Sounds as though she'll be fine. But, when she asked about Charlie's funeral and I told her about it, she did get weepy. I don't think Charlie's death has totally sunk in yet," he signed. "Oh, and Mrs. Dunbar left town." Greerson paused long enough to light a cigarette and blow smoke toward the ceiling. "Did you hear that the Muse robbers were caught?"

Matt was shocked. He'd heard nothing and hadn't seen anything on the wire services that morning about their capture. "No! That's news to me! When? Where?"

"They were arrested last night in a restaurant in Tampa, Florida. But now the fun begins. Tampa wants to keep 'em and try 'em for two armed robberies they committed there. They could get life in prison for those, and we might never see 'em back here. Boykin wants 'em for trial for the Muse and Kress burglaries, and the one at the Charles Suber Store in Ben Hill. Of course, he's fit to be tied about it, because he's got new charges going to the grand jury for a slew of other crimes. I hear he's gonna make the argument that the Feds could take legal priority over Florida and bring 'em back here because the Suber Store was also a post office. Anyway, now the fun begins."

"That's great news! I need to get this to the paper!" he said excitedly, standing from the table. He glanced at his wristwatch, paused, and fell back to his chair. "Well, too late for today's editions anyway." He jabbed a cigarette into his mouth, ripped a match from a folder, and set the butt afire. A quizzical look swiftly came to Matt's face. "But I wonder why Tampa? I mean, they escaped four days ago and only got to Tampa? They could have been halfway across the country by now. Or to Mexico or Canada."

"Well, this is plainly pure conjecture on my part, Matt, but I could make a guess." The reporter leaned across the table expectantly. "From what I understand, Tampa has a pretty well-organized criminal element.

And that organization has a good connection with Cuba. Put it together and the three hooligans may have been there trying to get out of the country. And, let's face it, Cuba's a pretty swell place to be holed up if you've got some cash. And, based on the jobs they've pulled, they probably did."

"Wow! That's an interesting angle."

"Well, as I said, it's only guesswork on my part. Oh, and one other thing. One of our men says they've got an idea about how those birds could cut their way out of the jail."

"Yeah, well, that's been a mystery since it happened, hasn't it? What's the story?"

"Listen, it's not for publication yet, but they suspect that a trustee, who'd been working in the cell block where the three were housed, was offered a few bucks, maybe a fin or a sawbuck, to get the three guys some hacksaw blades. That's the rumor anyway. The trustee in question was working off a fine he couldn't pay. So doubtless he needed the money. As you probably know, the registered trustees get one day a week off from their confinement. He –"

"No! I didn't know that!"

"Yeah, well, they do. Apparently, this trustee got the blades when he had a day off and smuggled 'em into the jail somehow, probably in his clothes." The big cop snickered, releasing a lungful of smoke, and shook his head. "Because the trustees are searched when they come back to the lockup from their day off, somebody else's head may be on the block if the saw blades were in his clothes and were missed during the search. And, of course, *now* they're gonna put tool-proof bars in the cells. I'll let you know when the story becomes official and you can use it."

"That'd be great, Jim! I'd really appreciate it if you can fill in the blanks of by whom and how much was paid, et cetera. I'm going to write it up with that information left out until you call me." Matt paused and said earnestly, "And, by the way, I really do appreciate the job you do." As Greerson smiled his gratitude for the younger man's words, Matt felt a tinge of guilt. He wasn't sure whether some things this officer did rated his admiration. Respect and like the man as a man, yes he did. The young man's attitude toward some of the big cop's actions might be another matter. Matt was conflicted. His uncertainty lingered like a ground fog at a cemetery.

Later, when the two men stepped back outside onto Decatur Street, they were discussing the idea of staying in close contact. From the corner of his eye, Matt saw the White Star touring car approaching. It sputtered up to a stop in front of them at the corner of Decatur and Butler Streets. The old man in overalls, who'd been talking to the desk officer in the police station, was behind the wheel. Beside him sat the old lady. The man's head hung heavy. The woman was crying. The reporter could hear her strangled sobs above the coughing of the car's motor as they briefly idled at the stop. If the detective noticed, he showed no sign of it. Yet again, the world's cruelty struck the young journalist in that moment.

Matt made his afternoon rounds and rushed back to the newspaper to check the wire services for stories about the Muse robbers being captured in Florida. The stories were there. Between them and the additional information Jim had given, the journalist wrote the leads and the article about their capture and the bureaucratic battle between the Tampa authorities and those in Atlanta regarding the disposition of their cases against the trio. Mr. Barnes and Matt verbally danced around the question of whether to include the possible Cuba-related reason the robbers had gone to Tampa. After pointing out that the young man didn't have sufficient facts or a "solid source" to back up his supposition, the city editor reminded his reporter that his copy must contain facts, not speculation or conjecture. Barnes vetoed that part of the article. Matt was forced to agree that the deduction was only guesswork and conceded the point. The young man recognized that it didn't matter anyway. The story would not rate much attention on a day when a strike at the Callaway

Textile Mills in nearby LaGrange, Georgia, dominated the headlines in all three local papers. The strike had produced the eviction by National Guardsmen of workers from mill-owned houses. The evictions brought about brawls between strikers and the guardsmen, resulting in injuries to a number of people and the arrest of nearly two dozen workers.

---

The boardinghouse meal that evening was eventful. The entire household was gathered at supper for the first time in several days. Miss Dixie was uncharacteristically restrained when she announced that she'd made friends with a woman, who was "not from around here" and who had recently started running a rooming house nearby. The new arrival was unfamiliar with regional dishes, but had brought a different culinary background with her to Atlanta. As a result, the two ladies had agreed to swap recipes. Miss Dixie stated her intention to add variety to the meals even beyond that given by Teresa's help. In that vein, the landlady served a hearty supper of corned-beef hash, cole slaw, and home fries. Much to Mrs. Fleming's subdued satisfaction, the affair was a delicious success.

The only blemish on the meal was a large shiner that Master Fleming brought to the table. The black eye was accompanied by a few abrasions on his face and neck, highlighted by traces of mercurochrome. When the boarders tried to tease the young man about his black eye and how it happened, his eyes filled with tears and he uncharacteristically refused to respond. It quickly became obvious that the subject was a serious one to the Fleming family. The topic was just as quickly dropped. While Cliff seemed very unhappy about the matter, Mr. and Mrs. Fleming appeared particularly upset about the situation, whatever it was. Uncharacteristically, both merely picked at their food. Their faces were strangely drawn and forlorn.

After supper, the group of roomers adjourned to the parlor as usual. This evening, the difference in their normal routine was the fairly somber mood that had enveloped them. Miss Dixie, as customary, occupied herself in her kitchen but, this time, with Cliff at her side. Rhamy went upstairs briefly and, then, came back downstairs and walked out to the front porch without saying a word. He made Freckles, who'd followed him down the hallway, stay in the house. This behavior, out of the routine for his landlord, caught Matt's eye. After a short time, the young man quietly excused himself from the other boarders and their expectation of when Fibber McGee's closet would crash. He sauntered out the front door, careful to keep the family canine inside. The older man was sitting in one of the wicker chairs at the opposite end of porch from the swing. His position gave him a view of Houston Street toward Peachtree Street. He was staring intently in that direction when Matt sat in the chair next to him. The landlord's normally loose, good-natured mouth was turned down harshly at the corners. He bore a tight, worried face.

Matt sat in silence for a brief time before speaking hesitantly. "Mr. Fleming, can you tell me what the trouble is?" The landlord remained rigid, watchful. His eyes held a peculiar expression. The young reporter had never seen Mr. Fleming like this. Very concerned, he plunged ahead, "I can tell something is seriously wrong, Mr. Fleming. Can I do anything to help? Please, talk to me."

Gradually, Rhamy Fleming's eyes saddened and watered. He slowly brought his head around toward Matt and looked at him woodenly. "Some older boys beat Cliff up after school today." As he spoke in a low voice, he slowly resumed his surveillance of the street. He stared past his boarder at the road as he spoke gravely. "They told him it was because we have a Jew and a Catholic living under our roof. And we give meals to a black man in our kitchen. Called the boy a Jew-lover, a nigger-lover, and a papist. Hell, he doesn't even know what a papist is! He didn't... he doesn't understand. He's just a boy!" Matt detected the older man suppressing a sob in a moment of stillness. "Do you think he knows or cares about somebody's religion? He's been raised to judge a person by how they act, not where they worship or what color their skin is, dammit! He's hurt and he's confused!" His voice was gruff with emotion.

Matt was stunned and felt helpless, but kept his voice at a conspiratorial whisper. "I can't believe this! Can I do anything, Mr. Fleming?"

"No, Matt, I don't think so. The last thing the punks said to him was that some of their daddies would be by here tonight. That's what I'm waiting for now." As he finished speaking, Rhamy reached a hand to a wad of cloth sitting on the table beside him. In the fading light, it had gone unnoticed by Matt until that moment. The young man saw what he believed to be the grip of a handgun extending from the cloth in which it was wrapped.

Stunned further, Matt whispered, "Is... is that a gun, Mr. Fleming?"

"It is," he replied solemnly. "It's a .45 automatic. Bought it off a friend who had it in the war. He taught me how to use and how to shoot with it. Other than that, I've never had it out of my bedroom until tonight. Never needed to. But, by God, I'll protect my family and my home. And I'll be damned if some fool's gonna tell me who can live under *my* roof or who can break bread at *my* table!" His voice rose slightly in angry determination as he finished, so much so he shot a fleeting look around self-consciously. Rhamy lowered his voice again, "I never go lookin' for trouble, but I'll meet it head-on if and when it comes, Matt." With a groan, he muttered, "Damned cowards."

"Why not call the police?"

Rhamy's voice took a disdainful tone. "Call the *Atlanta Police Department* about a possible *Klan* threat? Huh!" His voice softened but lost none of its resolve, "Look, I respect the work the police do, but I also know the stories about where their sympathies lay for the most part, Matt." The rumor was the worst-kept secret in Fulton County.

"I know one cop who doesn't cotton to those sympathies, Mr. Fleming."

Rhamy merely shook his head in a manner that showed he was resigned to face this without intervention from the authorities. "No time."

Matt realized that there probably *wasn't* time to get Jim Greerson to the boardinghouse, even if he could reach him on the phone. He had no idea where the detective lived. These thoughts passed through his mind as he paused before saying, "I'll be right back, Mr. Fleming." The young man hurried to his room and retrieved his handgun, inserting a full magazine. Now's the time, he told himself. He racked the slide to chamber a round, which automatically cocked the hammer. Then, Matt very carefully released the hammer with his thumb between it and the firing pin. He returned the safety to the "on" position. No time to adjust the shoulder holster and use it now, he contemplated. He tucked the gun into his waistband of his trousers at the small of his back, pulled on his suit coat to cover it, and quickly returned to the front porch. When he sat in the chair next to Rhamy, the gun proved too bulky to remain comfortably where it was. The young boarder recalled Detective Greerson's warning about trying to maneuver with a gun that size in a waistband. Reluctantly, Matt got up, removed the gun, and laid it on his lap when he sat again.

Rhamy Fleming's face reflected mild surprise at seeing the automatic. "What are you doing, Matt?"

"Mr. Fleming, this is *my* home, too. Teresa and Joshua are my friends and a lot like family to me. Adolphus is a good man, too. I'll be damned if I'll let you face this alone, whatever it is!" His voice was quiet but fiercely determined. "Sorry for my language."

In the twilight, Matt thought he saw Rhamy's eyes glistening again. He reached out and briefly gripped the older man's forearm firmly. Then he leaned back in the chair. The young man desperately wanted a cigarette for his nerves but decided to fight the urge. The two men sat together in the stillness of the fading daylight and waited.

After a short time, two vehicles slowly made their way in the gathering dusk toward 71 Houston Street, gradually pulling to the curb there. Rhamy and Matt, holding their handguns behind them as they moved, were already making their way down the front steps and out the sidewalk leading to the street by the time the vehicles braked to a stop at the curb. The lead vehicle, whose motor was left running, was an older, dark-colored Durant that had seen better days. The other was a newer Ford pickup truck. Its engine was not turned off either. Each vehicle held two people. Rhamy had expected there to be more men. He cautiously scanned the street in both directions.

*The Visitor's 1928 Durant*

Mr. Fleming moved toward the driver's door of the lead car. Matt, still holding his gun behind him with the safety now in the "fire" position, walked toward its rear so he could watch the truck's occupants. As Rhamy approached the Durant, the driver, a lean man with a wide, flat face and small eyes, produced a flashlight and shot its beam in the landlord's face. "You Rhamy Fleming?"

The landlord stood with one foot on the car's running board, defiantly staring through the open window at the men. By the glare of the flashlight, Rhamy saw that the men were strangers to his eyes. "I am. And who might you be?"

"Names ain't important, mister. We jus' come to deliver a message," he drawled. "We jus' —"

"I didn't think you'd have the balls to identify yourselves! I'm surprised you're not wearin' hoods, you chicken-shit cowards! Not that I give a damn what any of you has to say, but just what is your 'message'?" Rhamy's voice was rough and bitter, but never raised. His daddy had often repeated to him a favored farmer's saying: Words that soak into your ears are whispered, not yelled. As Rhamy spoke to the two men in the Durant, Matt eyed the two beefy, hard-looking men in the truck and wondered what he'd gotten himself into. Regardless, he was determined to stand steadfast for his friend and landlord.

Rhamy's resolute language seemed to take the two men by surprise. In addition, the Durant's passenger, apparently feeling threatened by Rhamy's words, produced a revolver, which he laid in his lap with an awkward flourish. He smiled menacingly, showing uneven yellow teeth in the flashlight's halo. When the smirk appeared on his dull face, his thick hair, combed back without a part, pulled back on his head. By the light of the flashlight, Rhamy also saw that he had arms the size of Yule logs. They extended beneath a dirty short-sleeved shirt worn under bib overalls. Tufts of coarse black hair grew on his upper arms and showed from under the shirt sleeves. The driver continued, "We heared that y'all are ahousin' some undesirable folks and invitin' other undesirables to eat in your house. Ain't fittin' for a Christian white man. Ain't fittin' aytall. We reckon y'all need to put a stop to it or we'll attend to helpin' you decide to stop."

"Listen here, you offal... you... you lowlife jackasses! Don't dare to use the word 'Christian' when you come here with that attitude in your hearts. I don't know and don't rightly give a damn who 'we' is! This is *my* house! And I decide who lives here and who eats here! If you don't like it, you can kiss my lily-white ass! So don't come around here threatenin' me! Or my family!" At this, the passenger fondled the gun on his lap. Rhamy quickly jerked his head in the man's direction. "Hold it right there, mister! Don't you move another muscle!" The man froze momentarily. As he spoke, Rhamy produced his .45 and laid it down on its side on the driver's window ledge, making sure it was pointed at the passenger. His finger was on the trigger. He continued, "Looky here, fella. That looks to be a double action revolver you've got there. Now, you can only shoot at one of us at a time and *maybe* hit the one you're shootin' at. Maybe," he drew the word out. "But by the time you shoot, pull back the hammer, and fire again, one of us is gonna make you dead!" The man slowly looked back around through the Durant's windows to where Matt stood.

The young newsman, having heard his landlord's words, brought his gun around from his backside and held it so it was visible in the glare of the truck's headlights to all the visitors. In doing so, he never took his eyes off the truck's strapping occupants. Initially, neither of them moved. Then, the Durant's passenger swallowed hard as sweat beaded on his forehead. The hand on the gun didn't budge, but with his other hand, he slowly retrieved a filthy handkerchief, and then wiped his face with it. Rather bug-eyed by this point, he timidly removed his hand from the revolver, instead, resting his arm on the passenger-side door with his elbow stuck through the open window. Rhamy watched his every move intently, guardedly. "Let me say one more thing before you 'gentlemen' take your leave. If my son comes home from school just one more time with even the slightest hint of trouble from any of your kids or their friends about this, I swear to God that I will hunt you down and kill you! All of you! If you think I'm kiddin' or won't do it, just try me! You've never seen anything as angry, as determined, or as fierce as I can be when my family is threatened! Do you get me?"

The driver tried to save face. "Well, thar's more of us than what ya see here, cuz. We –"

"First, I *ain't* your cousin! And second, you'd better bring a whole hell of lot more people next time, *if* you come back. 'Cause I'll be waitin' and I won't be alone! And at least some of the people with me'll be cops, too! Right cops! Not your kind! Now get the hell out of here! And if you're smarter than you look, you won't show your faces around here again!" Rhamy slowly withdrew his automatic from the window, lifted his foot from the car's running board, and stepped back from the door, holding his gun at the ready. Matt took a similar position where he stood. The two motor vehicles shifted into gear and drove away slowly. Matt walked to where Mr. Fleming maintained his position. The landlord and his young boarder remained in the yard and watched their departure. The vehicles drove down Houston a short distance and turned around, traveling back toward Peachtree Street. The two men stood their ground at the street as the Durant and the pickup truck passed them at a slower-than-normal speed. The occupants of the car looked straight ahead as they passed. The men in the pickup stole glances at the two men in front of the boardinghouse. The two vehicles disappeared into the nighttime and the clutter that was Peachtree Street.

It wasn't until Rhamy and Matt turned to go back inside that they realized that the rest of the boarders were standing at the screen door, watching intently. Freckles stood among them, wagging her tail enthusiastically. Rhamy stopped and put a restraining hand on Matt's arm. Turning to face the young man, he said, "Matt, I want to tell you how much I'm in your debt for what you did here tonight. I don't know that I could ever repay you."

"No need, Mr. Fleming. Like I said, this is my home, too. And you and those people standing in that doorway are like family to me." Matt chuckled, "Even Melvyn."

Rhamy smiled, but his voice was serious. "Please, not a word about the subject of this incident to anyone. Please."

Matt nodded energetically and chuckled again, "Who'd believe it anyway?"

In the light coming from the house, Mr. Fleming showed a dull smile as he eyed the front door. "You may be right." The older man's face glistened with sweat. Matt wondered whether it were the warm evening air or the tense situation that had caused it. The younger man knew why his forehead gleamed. The pair resumed their slow walk back to the porch. As they started to enter the dim glare of the porch's light, Rhamy nodded his head toward the door. "Please put your gun back in your waistband so they don't see it. And let's let this episode die a natural death. Okay?" Rhamy whispered from the side of his mouth. Matt was nodding again. "By the way, I didn't know you had a gun. Where'd you get it? I take it you know how to use it."

Matt stopped and turned back toward the street again to avoid the gun's detection by the household. He removed the magazine and gently cleared his gun's chamber, catching the round in his hand. Double-checking the safety, he slipped it inside his back waistband under his coat as he turned toward the house. "My friend the detective, the one who Miss Dixie met the other day, gave it to me. And, yes, I know how to use it. I grew up around guns. Besides, I'm pretty sure Detective Greerson wouldn't have given it to me otherwise. Is it a problem for me to have it in the house? I keep it well hidden and unloaded, but I can get to it in a hurry if need be."

"Uh-uh, Matt, it's not a problem at all. In fact, it was a godsend tonight." He fondly slapped his boarder on the back as they mounted the steps to the porch. Rhamy surreptitiously walked over and wrapped his gun with the cloth before going inside.

The gawking group moved away from the front door and back into the parlor when the two men casually sauntered into the house without saying a word. Diane, always the curious one when something unusual happened at the boardinghouse, hustled Matt into the dining room to ask what was going on. "Who were those men? What happened out there? It looked so serious!"

Matt spied Mr. Fleming watching from the hallway behind Diane. The reporter smiled weakly and said, "Nothing. Those guys got the wrong house. That's all." He left Diane standing openmouthed and passed his landlord with a wink. Rhamy went into the kitchen to speak with Miss Dixie as the young man climbed the stairs to the second floor and his room. Matt had had enough excitement for one day. He'd forgotten wanting a cigarette for his nerves.

# SHORTENING SHADOWS

A few minutes later, there was a light knock on Matt's door as he was preparing for bed. He walked to the door and opened it, peering from behind it to the hallway. Mr. Fleming was there. "Can I come in for a second, Matt?"

"Sure, Mr. Fleming! Come on in!" The boarder, standing in his undershorts, reached for his trousers draped over the room's straightback chair.

The landlord quietly closed the door behind him. "You don't need to bother with those, Matt, unless you want to." He laughed, "This isn't a formal visit. I'll only be a second." Rhamy held out a muscular hand. "I just wanted to say thank you again. There's no tellin' what kind of trouble your being there tonight might have saved me. Hopefully, it's over."

Matt took the man's hand and shook it firmly. "I'm glad I could help, Mr. Fleming. Anytime."

Rhamy casually stepped to the window that looked out of Matt's room to the front of the house. He scanned the street beyond the second-floor balcony, and then turned back to his boarder. "You know you can call me by my first name, Matt."

"Thanks anyway, Mr. Fleming, but I've got too much southern upbringing to change now. Plus it'll keep all the boarders on the same level this way, if you know what I mean."

Mr. Fleming broke into a broad grin. "I understand." Then his face took on a more solemn demeanor. "You know, Matt, I jokingly, at least, sort of jokingly tell folks that I'm the *nominal* head of this household. That is, at least on paper, I say. What with the house having belonged to Miss Dixie's parents and now with her running it like she does with our 'extended family' living here, she's really the true head of the household. Oh, I know it and I don't mind it. I'm not riddled with that foolish manly pride stuff people talk about nowadays. I work hard and, I think, hold up my end. But every so often, something happens, an opportunity comes along to make a guy feel like a man, like the protector of his family and his home. Fightin' the odds, you know? Gives him a reason to hold his head up. Tonight was one of those times." He sidled to the door as he spoke and made a slight, vague motion with his hands before opening it. His eyes grew moist. "And I want to say thank you for your support in that, young man." The older man quietly disappeared into the hallway behind the closing door.

As it was closing, Matt said softly, "Anytime, Mr. Fleming."

The subject of that day's events, that evening's visitors, was never again broached. Neither the men who'd come to the boardinghouse that night nor any of their "compatriots" ever made another appearance at 71 Houston Street, as far as anyone in the household ever knew. Cliff rebounded from the experience as the resilience of youth allows. He was, however, still inclined to get into brawls once in a blue moon and come home with bruises and abrasions. But the focus of those clashes was usually a disagreement about a called strike or a base runner's being safe or out in some sandlot baseball game somewhere in the greater vicinity of the boardinghouse.

## CHAPTER 10

# Death in the Afternoon

The more important Atlanta police blotter narratives of the week that followed "the visit" involved an eclectic mix of stories and crimes. The wounding of a Federal Alcohol Tax Agent, shot during a seizure of forty gallons of moonshine over near Conyers, grabbed front-page headlines on the first of May. Virtually the entire front page was usurped on the second of May by the shooting deaths of a locksmith and his female bookkeeper at his shop on Alabama Street. The locksmith's son, who said his father "had it coming," was arrested for the murders. On the same day, the newspapers announced that an Atlanta Police Department patrolman, who had fatally shot a black man during a scuffle the previous Saturday night, was being held on charges related to the incident. Also of note were the robbery of a Memorial Drive grocer and a report that "Old Sparky" had recorded one hundred and twenty-four executions in the eleven years it had resided in the Georgia Penitentiary at Milledgeville.

On the lighter side of the police reports was the story of the "accidental capture" of a bootlegger. He'd been found with two hundred and four gallons of corn hooch in his car when, during a chance encounter, he recognized a county police officer. The officer was on his way to work in civilian clothes. When the perpetrator started acting suspicious, the officer stopped him and found the contraband stored in one-gallon cans in the car.

On Tuesday, when Matt had scheduled a noon rendezvous with his girl, he had to attend an unexpected city council finance committee meeting. The gathering dealt with the police department's request for appropriations with which to purchase cars. The department wanted the vehicles to chase the numbers racket, which had gained more notoriety and focus since the Guyol murder. The prolonged meeting was starting to look as if it might bump up against his lunch date when several committeemen saved the day. They simply asked why the police could not "chase the bug on foot." Before the police committee chairman could formulate an answer, the group adjourned so its members could attend the Crackers' afternoon ball game. The young *Georgian* reporter dutifully jotted down notes, asked a few questions, and quickly left in time to keep his lunch date.

Evie and Matt ate lunch at the Brass Rail restaurant on Peachtree Street. As they lingered over an extra cup of coffee, she invited her beau to a ball game between the Davison-Paxon and J. P. Allen stores to be held that Thursday at the Bass Junior High School field on Euclid Avenue. The game was to be followed by a bite to eat with "the Davison's crowd" at the new Pig'n Whistle up on Peachtree Road. Matt gladly accepted the invitation. The blond reporter felt it best not to mention the visitors to the boardinghouse the night before. Evie was worked up enough, in his estimation, about his activities with Jim Greerson without making things worse with that story. Later that week, under very warm skies, the Davison's team won the ball game seven to six.

# SHORTENING SHADOWS

The following weekend passed without significant local crime stories to report. As the crime rate seemingly dropped, the mercury rose. The weather sages forecast a threat of showers moving into the area by the end of the week. Atlanta's annual cycle of hot and humid weather was on the horizon. Matt's Monday-morning rounds of the law-enforcement agencies' overnight reports yielded little in the way of newsworthy items. The young reporter's day, a washout so far, didn't grow any brighter when he slumped at his desk to look over the *Georgian's* latest edition. National and world headlines made him wonder why anyone would feel optimistic about human beings or their future. A war between Italy and Ethiopia seemed imminent as the planet's continued diplomatic clumsiness seemed destined to bring about another world conflict. What a wonderful world, the big blond reporter thought sarcastically.

Matt, still surprisingly full from Miss Dixie's ample breakfast, passed on the offer when Brick and some other *Georgian* reporters invited him to join them for lunch at the Dinner Bell Cafeteria across the street. He knew he needed to spend some out-of-the-building time with them to build some camaraderie and maybe to learn a thing or two about the job, but today wasn't the day. The young correspondent was in too much of a funk at the moment. Ever the movie fan, he spent a fair amount of the next hour reading follow-up newswire stories about a car crash involving actor Jackie Coogan. The accident had occurred late Saturday when the car Coogan was in plunged over a roadside embankment in the mountains east of San Diego, California. The crash injured the actor and resulted in the deaths of four other men, including Coogan's father. Looking at a photograph of the bed-ridden Coogan from the wire service, Matt contemplated how much the actor had changed from the youngster who'd been in the Chaplin film, *The Kid*, some fourteen years earlier.

Finally, the clock wound around to time for his afternoon circuit. Matt hauled himself out of his chair and headed out. He walked out into the bronze early-afternoon light and moved to his car parked nearby.

Clouds were building to the west. More rain, he thought. None of Matt's stops for news items bore noteworthy fruit. He saved the Atlanta Police Department for his last stop in hope of seeing Detective Greerson and getting the latest updates on the several stories to which the detective was privy.

After checking the press room and coming up empty for any meaningful news fodder, Matt walked back to the front desk. As he stepped to the front area, a uniformed officer was holding a man by the arm and discussing his charges with the desk officer. Grimes was waiting to get the duty officer's attention when the door leading to the Detectives' Division opened, framing the imposing Detective Artie Rutherford. He was pulling on the coat to a suit that needed pressing badly. As he moved into the area from the doorway, he saw the suspect being held by the officer. "Say, Coggins, where'd you catch this chiseler?" The surprised officer asked Rutherford if he knew his prisoner. "Oh, yeah, we're old buddies, ain't we Sweeny?" came a sarcastic response from the brawny detective, trying to smooth his suit coat without success.

"Sweeny?" yelled the uniformed officer, as he jerked the man's arm. "You said your name was Olsen!"

Rutherford guffawed, shaking his head. "He's just a small-time grifter I've picked up before on occasion." The detainee merely hung his head. At that point, Rutherford spied Matt standing near the front desk and sauntered to him. "Say, fella, aren't you supposed to be somewhere writin' Burma Shave signs?" The disdain in his voice was palpable.

"Ah, it's the 'always-cheerful' Detective Rutherford," Matt responded, smiling thinly. "Say, are you breaking in a new personality or are you always a jackass?"

Rutherford moved his face close to Matt's. "You gotta a problem with me, punk?"

"Why, no, detective!" Matt stood firm. "The very sound of your voice sweetens the air and fills any room with bright light." He changed his tone from sarcasm to deadpan. "But you *do* seem to have a problem with me for some reason that I can't fathom."

"Why you little puke, I oughta –"

"Ease up, partner," Detective Greerson's strong, smooth voice came to Rutherford over his chunky shoulder. "No sense in starting with nastiness, Artie." As he stepped around Rutherford, he stood so both men were in view and chuckled, "You'll have to forgive Artie, Matt. He never quite got the idea of that honey versus vinegar approach to life." Rutherford grunted and looked away. Jim smiled at the *Georgian* reporter and asked, "So, how's the boy, Matt?"

"I'm great, Detective Greerson." Matt felt compelled by some unwritten, unspoken code of decorum to use the detective's formal title in the station house in front of his fellow detective. "I was coming to see you to learn if there were any updates on the Guyol or Newsome murders. What's up with you?"

"Aside from what we last talked about, nothing new on either case. We're headed over toward Grant Park on a murder call." Rubbing his chin, Greerson asked, "Say, you want to go along?"

"What?" Rutherford protested loudly, rolling his eyes behind heavy lids. At the outburst, the conversation between the desk officer and the uniformed patrolman stopped momentarily as they looked toward the three men.

"Relax, partner." He jerked his head toward Matt. "As a newshound, he's gonna show up at the scene anyway. We're just keeping one less car from jamming the landscape. Besides, Artie, I've spent time with the guy. He's jake with me." Rutherford opened his mouth to protest. Greerson cut him off by adding, "Plus, and you know I hate to pull rank, I'm lead investigator on this one."

Although slightly hesitant only due to Rutherford's attitude, Matt eagerly accepted the invitation to ride along. "Sure! I'd appreciate it, detective!"

Detective Rutherford, obviously irritated at Matt's presence, jammed his hat on as he moved across to the doors. Greerson and Grimes followed. The angry detective pushed through the doors, moved down the steps, and plodded splay-footed a short distance along the sidewalk on Butler Street. Greerson, with Grimes at his side, turned on the sidewalk in the opposite direction. Matt, a wry smile tracing his lips, glanced back at the other detective as Jim gave a short, shrill whistle over his shoulder. Rutherford had already seen his mistake and was moving back toward the pair. He quickly fell in beside his partner as the senior detective led them to his Hudson. A few doors from the headquarters building, a scruffy-looking character in a worn whipcord jacket and a slouch hat, peeled himself off the brick wall forming the front of a bondsman's office. He followed the trio at a discreet distance. The move caught Matt's eye at once, but he said nothing. While the man trailed them, the young journalist shot sporadic sideway glances at Greerson, who seemed oblivious of the man's existence.

Abruptly, Jim stopped and quietly said, "Wait here a minute. I'll be right back." He turned and walked to the man who'd been following them. Rutherford made a sour face. Matt steeled himself for what he thought was to follow. As the detective approached the guy, both men stepped into the embrasure of a building. But, unlike the incident in the hallway of the Kiser Building, this encounter was quiet and apparently amiable as far as Matt could tell. Greerson spoke in hushed tones for a minute or so with the stranger whose uncertain face constantly searched the street. The detective handed the man something from his pocket and returned to Grimes and Rutherford. The guy remained frozen in the doorway, looking around sharply, as the three men continued to the car. After a quick, shifty-eyed scan of the vicinity, the disheveled man scurried across the street and narrowly missed being struck by a passing DeSoto Airflow.

"What'd he have, Jimbo?" Rutherford muttered, giving a look of scorn to Matt as he spoke.

"Just a line on Gutowski's whereabouts. I'll check it out later." Greerson saw a questioning look in the reporter's eyes. "He's a bindle punk I use periodically to get word of what's happening on the street. Sometimes I use him to get word out that I want spread on the street among the lowlifes."

Matt's curiosity got the better of him. "What about Gutowski? Where is he?"

"As I said, I'll check it out later." Detective Greerson's voice had an edge to it. They finished the walk in silence.

Matt was relegated to the Hudson's rumble seat for the ride to a street just west of Grant Park, located on the city's southeast side. During the trip, the young crime beat reporter clutched his hat to his head and thanked his lucky stars that the rain had held off and the temperature had dropped from earlier in the week. Through the back window, he could see the two men inside the car talking to each other but couldn't make out what they were saying. Rutherford was obviously unhappy about something. Matt could easily guess what that "something" was. The discontented detective spoke animatedly, shook his head, and jerked his left thumb repeatedly in Matt's direction. Whatever he was saying, his partner was having none of it. Greerson would merely turn to his fellow detective and give him a smirk, further aggravating Rutherford. After a time, the Hudson pulled to the side of Cherokee Place, several blocks from where it ended at the park named for a Civil War officer, but not, Matt mused, the one the newcomers to Atlanta often assumed.

As they bailed out of the car and started walking in the park's direction, Detective Greerson explained the nature of the call to his young friend. "The call was about a patrol officer's discovery of a girl's body in some thick bushes down here. The reporting officer said that she looked to be in her early twenties, but he wasn't sure because the shrubbery she's in is so thick, and he didn't want to move the body before we could look at it."

As they approached a small crowd of gawkers gathered on the street, an older uniformed patrolman came up to Greerson. The detective knew the man. "You're not gonna like this, detective," he said as he fell into stride with the big detective.

Greerson stopped abruptly and turned to the patrol cop. "Whaddya mean, Owens? What's going on?"

"Well, the young patrol officer over there called in the murder of a white girl. But I think it's a high yella nig –" The officer, looking directly at Greerson as he spoke, saw the detective's face darken suddenly and the muscles in his jaw stand out in anger. The uniformed cop froze momentarily, swallowed hard, and changed course. "She's a colored girl, I think, detective. Very light skinned, though." The detective's reputation for intolerance of certain words preceded him.

Detective Greerson leaned into the officer and made a subtle hand gesture toward Detective Rutherford, who had walked some farther along the street before stopping and waiting for his fellow investigator. Artie was looking toward the crime scene. The senior detective quietly said, "Listen, Owens, for future reference, don't get me confused with some whole other person. Okay?" Matt could only watch the events unfold before him, again a mere spectator of the life and times of Detective Jim Greerson.

The uniformed officer took a half step backward and ginned sheepishly. Trying to regain his fading composure, he stammered, "Yeah, yeah, sure, detective, sure. Sorry. Nothin' meant by it."

Detective Greerson stepped around the officer and continued toward the scene. "So what else can you tell me, Owens? Has the meat wagon been called?" he tossed over his shoulder as if nothing troublesome had happened between him and the officer.

The shorter Owens caught and fell in beside the detective, trying to keep stride with him. "Yeah, the morgue's been called. Looks like her head was bashed in and her throat was cut from ear to ear, as best I can tell. Blood everywhere. Kinda hard to tell too much what with the thick bushes and all. No witnesses. At least none that we found so far anyway. We'll keep lookin'. Oh, and we looked around for 'bout a block but can't find anythin' that might be the weapon that was used for either the bashin' or the slicin'."

"Good job. Thanks." Greerson increased his stride toward the death scene. Moving through the throng of onlookers, Greerson barked orders to the several uniformed officers present. "Get this crowd back! Nobody approaches this area unless I okay it!"

Matt watched as Rutherford assumed the role of an observer, standing away from the crime scene, holding a lighted cigarette inside a cupped hand. His body language made it obvious he felt, for whatever reason, that the effort was a waste of time. Meanwhile, his partner turned to address the mass of spectators, composed of both black and white people. When Greerson faced the throng, he noticed a husky black man approaching the crowd at a calm but brisk pace. The detective gave him a serious up and down. What caught his eye first was the clean, nicely tailored suit the clean-cut man was wearing. Not an earthshaking thing, Jim noted, but the Negro's appearance makes him stand out in this part of town. Maybe a preacher, Jim speculated. The man had a very dark complexion. The new arrival was powerfully built and appeared to be several years younger than the detective, who made a mental note of his observations. The black man stopped right outside the crowd and quietly watched.

"Anybody here know this woman?" As he spoke, he looked into the faces of those gathered.

An older black man, with a limp left arm and a distinct scar across his forehead, took a slight step forward. "I seed her around hyar sometimes, suh," he said haltingly, "but I don't knows her name."

"Thank you." The detective gently stepped toward the man. "What's your name, sir?" Jim Greerson asked.

The old man's eyes crawled sideways hesitantly, as he scanned the crowd before answering. "Me? Well, suh, my name be Darius. Uh, Darius Daniels. But ev'body jus' calls me Stitch."

The big cop gave the man a friendly smile. "Darius, huh? Like Dari'us, the Old Testament king?"

The old man returned a wide snaggletooth grin back at Greerson. "Yassuh, dat's right! Darius! My mammy say I be a king one day. Cep'n it di'nt tuhn owt dat way fuh me."

"Well, Mr. Daniels, every man's a king in his way, in his life," the detective responded while looking around and patting the man's shoulder. The old man returned a brief, tired smile, uncertain about and unaccustomed to such attention. Rutherford abruptly turned his back on his partner, walked to the opposite side of the street, and bent over supposedly to study something lying on the ground there. Detective Greerson gave an all but imperceptible shrug, followed by a motion to one of the uniformed officers. "Officer, talk to Mr. Daniels here some and see if you can learn anything else about this girl. He may know something he doesn't realize can help us." The black man smiled and nodded his appreciation to Greerson before moving to join the police officer beyond the crowd.

As Matt watched this situation involving the big cop and the old black fellow, he was again struck by enigmatic Detective Jim Greerson: mean but fair, a man of gelid reserve yet given to passions at times, gentle and vicious by turns. Matthew Grimes saw no evidence that the detective held any religious beliefs, yet he knew obscure segments of the Bible. In equal measure, the reporter was captivated watching the investigator at work but uncertain as to exactly who and what he was.

Detective Greerson turned his attention to the crime scene and the body. He stood a short distance back from the bushes where the body lay and studied the implications of what he saw. The girl's body was barely visible through a clump of vegetation, a mixture of witch hazels, nettles, and a stray hydrangea or two, all of which were being rapidly overtaken by honeysuckle. From what could be seen, the blood, a lot of it, was evident around the body, however. Flies could be heard swarming the corpse and the coagulated blood. A coppery odor permeated the air. Greerson made a negligent gesture with the fingers of his left hand, indicating an area between the street and the corpse and spoke aloud as he mentally walked through the scene. "She was dragged into the bushes from this point. Only a spot or two of blood out here by the street." Matt could see the distinctive scrape marks in the dirt Greerson was pointing out, despite the few footprints that had been plodded across them. "No sign of a struggle or a scuffle, though, so she was probably hit in the head at the street first to render her unconscious." Matt was taking quick, terse notes of what he observed and heard.

To approach the body from a roundabout direction rather than straight from the street, thereby disturbing the drag marks or any other clues, a determined Greerson walked several yards down the roadway and began slowly bulling his way through the thick undergrowth and bushes, crushing them and pushing them aside to the point of destroying a few to make room for a closer examination of the girl.

Reaching her location, the detective saw that at least part of the uniformed officer's assessment had been correct. The girl's head had been crushed by some heavy, blunt object and her throat slit. She was a slender, light-skinned Negro female, appearing to be in her early twenties, possibly younger. Jim found that death throe contortions often made it difficult for him to guess a deceased's age correctly. Though severe, Greerson estimated that the blow to her head had merely incapacitated her. The throat cutting had caused her to bleed out and die. Owing to only a trivial amount of blood anywhere but where she lay, Greerson also deduced that her throat had been slit where she was found. A large brownish pool had soaked into the ground beneath and around her head and upper torso. What had not soaked into the ground had coagulated on the clayish soil. Her face, neck, and dingy white blouse were caked with dried blood. From the state of the congealed blood, Greerson surmised that it had stopped flowing some time ago, probably sometime last night. As expected, her skin was cold to the touch. The big cop swatted at the numerous flies buzzing the girl's body.

Greerson noted that the girl's clothes seemed in proper order, eliminating, at least from outward appearances, that she'd been sexually assaulted. Relating to her clothing, however, one thing struck him as odd. She had no shoes over the blue stockings covering her feet. A quick glance around failed to reveal any footwear. He rubbed a thumbnail on his jaw in contemplation. The big detective considered it unlikely that the girl had ventured out onto the streets without shoes to cover the stockings on her feet. "Did any of you guys find her shoes anywhere?" he called to the uniformed officers from his position kneeling by the body, swatting again at the abundant, persistent flies.

Rutherford cursed under his breath, but loud enough for Matt to hear him. The reporter turned and gaped at the detective, who made a disagreeable face. "Damned if he ain't makin' this out to be a real investigation into a legitimate murder," Rutherford muttered. He returned Matt's steely stare.

The uniformed officers glanced at one another, looked back at Greerson, and shook their heads. "No, detective! We didn't see any shoes while we were lookin' for a weapon!" Officer Owens called out. "I think we'd've found 'em then!" Matt noted the fact on his pad.

As he looked in the uniformed officers' direction, Greerson shot a glance at the burly, well-dressed black man that he'd seen approaching the scene earlier. The man remained among the pack of gathered people, quietly observing. Suddenly, he seemed to become aware of the detective's notice. The man quietly detached himself from the crowd and moved away from the area. Greerson straightened and followed the man with his eyes. The object of the big detective's attention walked briskly but unhurriedly toward a dark-blue Hupmobile sedan parked next to a fireplug just around a vacant corner. The car pulled away from the curb and picked up speed as it disappeared on Martin Street. Another mental note. Detective Greerson returned his attention to the subject of his investigation. He decided that there was nothing else he could glean from the scene or the victim as she lay in it. He studied the area through which he guessed she'd been dragged from the street to where she lay. No other clues revealed themselves to his sharp eyes.

Greerson emerged from the bushes to the street and glanced back to where the dead girl lay. Officer Owens approached him. "I talked to the Daniels boy, detective. He's got nothin' more on the girl that can help us. He doesn't work a reg'lar job 'cause of his bum arm. He just kinda roams around this part of town lookin' to pick up a buck here or there doin' odd jobs. He says he'd just see her now and again. Doesn't know any more about her than that. No name for her. I got his address for your report. The morgue folks are here, too."

"Thanks." Jim looked up from his notes to see Rutherford ambling in his direction. He looked at his fellow detective, but spoke to Officer Owens. "Let the morgue people know they can take the body, but I want it held 'til I can get there to look at it closer. I don't know that it will help any, but I want to examine the body closer than I can here." Owens nodded, turned, and moved away.

Detective Rutherford stopped next to Greerson and released an audible sigh. "We wasted about enough time on this shit, Jim?"

Greerson squared up with the man. "Look, Artie, this is my murder case. You were all-fired eager to come along when you thought the victim was a white girl." Rutherford bowed up and started to speak but refrained when Greerson raised a meaty palm. "The fact that she's a Negro doesn't change my attitude toward the investigation. If you're unhappy about being here, you can either wait 'til I'm finished and ride back with me, catch a streetcar or hail a taxi back to the station house, or start walking in that direction. I'll pick you up on my way back *if* I see you walking. Suit yourself. Whatever you choose to do, Artie, it suits me right down to the ground!" Greerson was giving the other detective a cold stare.

Rutherford turned rigid but said nothing. He drew his lips back against his teeth, and then puffed them out again. Walking back to the other side of the street, he lit another cigarette. Grimes took Rutherford's place beside Detective Greerson. "So, whaddya think, Jim?"

"Well, Matt, there's probably not a chance in hell of discovering who did this without a witness." The detective was exasperated. "But I'm gonna start with who she was, where she worked, if she worked, and who may have been seen with her last. That's all I can do. Somebody had to have a motive for this murder. Find a motive and you'll likely find the killer." Again, the big cop gave quick look to the dead girl. "But I've done all I can do here."

After the three rode back to police headquarters in silence, Matt returned to the newspaper and wrote up what little he had to offer for the next edition. His biggest story of the day was the young Negro girl's murder. When Mr. Barnes read his piece about the crime, he mumbled something about the girl being found without her shoes and gave his earlobe a few thoughtful tugs. But he said nothing more while approving the copy.

---

The next two weeks flew past for Matthew Grimes. He learned that Greerson had identified the young black woman found on Cherokee Place as one Addie Faye Maddox, a onetime domestic and, more recently, a more-than-part-time prostitute. Unfortunately, the detective had no additional leads on her killer.

During that period, national stories, which renewed Matt's opinion of the world's downward spiral, continued to have top billing. On May tenth, lifelong criminal, Raymond Hamilton, was executed in Texas for the murder of a prison guard. Joe Palmer, Hamilton's partner in the murder, had preceded him to the death chamber. The following day, headlines proclaimed that a New York City bookkeeper was accused of murdering his wife and their four children, ranging in ages from nine years to eighteen months, by putting rodent poison their cocoa. His mother-in-law, herself in a hospital recovering from the effects of poisoning, declared her belief in his innocence. The case against the bookkeeper would be thrown into disarray when, later in the month, the city toxicologist announced that, contrary to a previous report by another physician, he could not find any trace of poison in the can of cocoa, a can of sugar, or in a can of tea removed from the family's home.

Even heavyweight champion Max Baer, who had been wounded by a blank cartridge fired during the rehearsal of a radio skit, was looked at with a jaundiced eye. Was the incident an accident or merely a hoax intended to promote his upcoming bout with the comparatively mediocre James Braddock? Matt could only hope that the fight, scheduled for June and one that he and Mr. Fleming were looking forward to listening to on the radio, wouldn't be canceled or postponed as a result.

To the reporter's guilt-ridden relief, the local police beat provided a fair number of stories to relate to his readers. Several safecrackers and a gang of robbers, including one woman, were sentenced following trials and guilty pleas. A number of automobile accidents on Atlanta's roadways had resulted in serious injuries and several deaths. One incident caused a great stir at the boardinghouse. On Monday night, the thirteenth of May, three stenographers were struck by a hit-and-run driver as they crossed Linden Avenue just off Peachtree Street. The driver stopped, got out of his car, and then hurriedly returned to his vehicle and drove away. The three women made note of his tag number and provided it to the police. What had caused the excitement at 71 Houston Street was that Teresa knew one of the women well and had been with the three a few minutes earlier. She had parted company with them to return to the boardinghouse right before the accident. The rest of the boardinghouse was more upset about the incident than was Teresa, who simply crossed herself and thanked the Blessed Mary that her acquaintances were not harmed more seriously.

Of most concern to Atlanta's citizenry and law enforcement alike, Matt reckoned, was the apparent sudden and forceful resurrection of a crime that most people thought had disappeared from Atlanta's streets: the offense of ride-rob. Throughout the early thirties Atlanta had seen an epidemic of what had been labeled "ride-rob" crimes, perpetrated, to some extent, by people suffering through hard times without jobs or hope, who often turned to criminal activity. The crime made driving, even during daylight hours, a hazardous adventure. In these incidents, a driver would stop their automobile at a traffic light, for example, and a pistol-wielding or knife-carrying bandit would be sitting in the seat beside them before the driver realized what had happened. The robber would then order the driver to keep quiet and to continue driving. When they reached the outskirts of town on some lonely road, the victims would be robbed, very often assaulted, and, sometimes, their cars stolen. If they were lucky, they'd be spared any further harm. Some were not so fortunate.

One such unfortunate person was a traveling salesman from Davenport, Iowa, named Max Sjoblom. Mr. Sjoblom, who'd been accompanied by his new wife on his trip to Atlanta, had stopped for a traffic light at Marietta and Spring Streets on the evening of September 22, 1934. There, Sjoblom was attacked and kidnapped by Robert Riley and Robert H. Summers, who later killed him when he resisted. The pair then dumped his body before abandoning the victim's car in nearby College Park. Both Riley and Summers were caught and convicted of the crime, with the former receiving the death penalty and the latter being sentenced to life imprisonment. At the time, the consensus was that the convictions and severe sentences for Sjoblom's homicide would bring an end to the wave of ride-rob crimes. Matt had covered the tragic case for the *Georgian* as one of his first assignments as the police beat reporter.

The thought of many people that the ride-rob scourge would then subside was a bit premature, however. During the middle week of May, Matt reported three more of the crimes being perpetrated on the city's thoroughfares. One effort was foiled when, on May 14th, a young man, holding what appeared to be a pistol, jumped into the automobile of a well-known Atlanta restaurateur. The victim, who had stopped his car in the rear of the Atlanta Woman's Club due to a punctured tire, punched the young man, knocking him unconscious, before summoning police. The would-be robber was found to be carrying part of a toy gun. The following night a man was brutally beaten and his car stolen by three men who entered his automobile at Simpson and Spring Streets and forced him at gunpoint to drive out Bankhead Highway. On Friday morning of that week, a prominent Atlanta businessman and civic leader shot a nineteen-year-old man during a struggle when he resisted an attempt by the man and a companion to rob him.

In a local item unrelated to Matt's police beat but of special significance to the local newspaper business, John Sanford Cohen, president and editor of the *Atlanta Journal* and a former U. S. senator, died during the evening of May 13th. Though Mr. Cohen was associated with a rival publication, Mr. Barnes solemnly gathered everyone in the *Georgian's* newsroom to pay tribute to a fine gentleman. Mr. Cohen's influence extended in the Atlanta newspaper business well beyond the *Journal*, Matt contemplated, and his loss would be felt by many people.

Statewide, headlines announced that two unnamed Georgia National Guardsmen would face a General Court-Martial for their role in the death of a Callaway cotton mill striker. The man's death, the result of injuries sustained in the eviction of workers from company housing, had occurred during the recent mill strike in nearby LaGrange, Georgia.

On a personal note, Matt read with pride a newspaper article about his hometown, Augusta, celebrating the 200th anniversary of its founding on May 14th. Though by Matt's calculation, based on the city's history he'd studied in school there, it was actually a celebration of it 200th *year*, having been founded in *1736* by General James Oglethorpe along the old Creek Indian trail, now called Wrightsboro Road. He regretted not being able to attend the festivities and, more to the point, not being able to take Evie with him to introduce her to his family. Instead, Matt and Evie took in a totally forgettable movie that Saturday night.

Beautiful weather helped produce heavy statewide voting on the fifteenth of May for a referendum on alcohol prohibition, setting up local option elections for wet or dry counties. Atlanta voted overwhelmingly in favor of repeal, and Mayor Key vowed to open a state liquor store in Atlanta as soon as possible.

Also on the national scene, several items provided follow-up headlines. Doc Barker was scheduled to be sentenced on the seventeenth of the month for his part in the Bremer kidnapping in Minnesota. The Federal judge in the case was expected to give Barker life imprisonment. Elsewhere, the former Barbara Hutton returned to the news with her latest husband, Count Kurt Haugwitz-Reventlow, during their honeymoon in the same hotel where she'd stayed after her first marriage two years earlier.

In international news, Colonel Thomas E. Lawrence, better known as Lawrence of Arabia, was seriously injured in a motorcycle accident Monday night, the thirteenth of May. Despite being attended to by King George's personal physician, he would die from his injuries on May nineteenth.

Meanwhile, Matt's beloved Atlanta Crackers had climbed to a game behind the league-leading Memphis Chicks and had traded between first and second place much of the first two weeks of May. The young man believed the Crackers were coming on strong, would eventually move into first place, and, then, not look back. His St. Louis Cardinals remained in the middle of the National League pack.

---

Aside from bumping into each other once at police headquarters and a lunch together at the Stars Grill, Matthew Grimes and Detective Greerson didn't see much of each other during the two weeks or so that followed the discovery of Addie Maddox's body. The blond reporter placed periodic calls to the detective in search of further information on the open murder cases with which he'd been involved. Though Greerson was working hard on the cases, nothing new had developed on any of those about which Matt was inquiring. He promised the *Georgian* reporter he'd be one of the first to know if anything broke on the crimes. For her part, Evie considered the minimal contact between the two a blessing, because she was still concerned about her boyfriend's direct, "hands-on involvement," as she termed it, in police cases. Matt tried to reassure her while maintaining his determination to go where the job took him.

Matt was surprised when the detective telephoned him at the Houston Street residence late on the night of the sixteenth. After confirming that the newspaper had not yet contacted him, Greerson invited the reporter to accompany him to the scene of a newly discovered murder victim. Matt accepted the ride along at once, of course. Greerson explained that this was not the murder of another Negro girl, but was, instead, a businessman whose body had been found in a car just west of Five Points. The detective signed off by telling his friend that he would stop by the boardinghouse to pick him up. Before he could get out of the house, the newspaper called, informing Matt of the murdered man being located. He explained to the night desk that he was on his way to the scene.

A few minutes later, Matt was sitting on the front porch swing, waiting for Jim's arrival. He fired up a cigarette. The warm night air hung heavy with humidity and was still other than an infrequent light breeze, which wafted the heavy scent of honeysuckle from the yard next door. As he smoked, he reflected on the circumstances of the telephone call from Detective Greerson. But for the topic, Matt contemplated, it might well have been an invitation to a social gathering. Even the detective's tenor sounded as if he were extending a request for his friend's attendance at a Capital City Club dinner or a Piedmont Driving Club ball. A ghoulish invitation, but an invitation, nevertheless. Matt wondered whether he was becoming too jaundiced by his closeness to the subject of someone's murder. The journalist expected a distant, clinical attitude toward a murder from a veteran detective but wasn't certain how comfortable he was with that being his outlook. He didn't have long to ponder the situation before he heard the now-familiar hum of the Hudson moving down Houston Street in the sultry night air.

Matt was standing at the curb when the car pulled up. Greerson greeted his buddy in a matter-of-fact manner as he climbed in and set his flashlight in his lap. "I figured since you've been voluntarily dragged to the murder scenes of what some might call the city's 'lesser lights,' you might want to get in on one with a little more interest to your general readership in it. You weren't busy, were you?" His tone was remote but not hostile. Matt attributed the detective's manner to preoccupation with his work and blew it off.

"Nah. Only listening to Eddie Duchin on the radio and digesting Miss Dixie's roast beef hash." Matt looked around. "Where's Rutherford?"

"He was working on something else when the call came in. He'll meet us, uh, me there. Works out for you, though, because you don't have to ride in back, right?" Matt saw a tight smile on his friend's face. With a threat of scattered showers in the weather forecast, the young man was grateful for not being in the exposed rumble seat.

"Other than the dead guy being a businessman, what else do you have so far?"

"Well, the call came in from the officer at the scene saying that the stiff's a businessman, primarily because he's apparently dressed in a suit and sitting in a nice car. I don't have anything else at this point. Could be a gangster for all I know. I've got my fingers crossed that it's Gutowski. That would save me some trouble," the detective chuckled coldly. When he caught Matt's odd glance from the corner of his eye, he went on, "Hey, look, I really don't like the slug. I especially don't like anyone who moves down to our neck of the woods and acts like southerners couldn't do anything right without 'em. Anyway, we'll see. Just thought you'd be interested, buddy."

"Yeah, sure, Jim! I appreciate the call. Could this be another ride-rob gone wrong?"

"Could be. I dunno, Matt."

The pair proceeded from Houston Street to a side road off Marietta Street, some blocks west of the main business intersection. The side street was known to be secluded after normal business hours. Greerson pulled to the curb and cut the Hudson's motor near a gathering of men around a big car parked to one side of the dark street. Both men got out of the Hudson and turned on their flashlights as they approached a gaudy Cadillac with big whitewall tires. Detective Rutherford was already standing at the driver's door of the Cadillac, flashlight in hand, examining the passenger area. At the urging of a patrol officer, the onlookers made way for Detective Greerson with Matt following closely. Matt stopped short of walking up to the driver's door. He didn't want to get in the way and wanted to avoid another clash with Rutherford.

A few reporters shouted questions at Greerson as he approached. He gave them a cynical look and advised them that, since he was an investigator and not a prognosticator, he'd have no answers for them until he'd had time to do his job. A few of the newsmen looked at each other quizzically as their inquiries subsided. As an afterthought, Greerson added sarcastically that maybe some of them needed to acquaint themselves with a dictionary. A police photographer had only then finished taking pictures of the scene. Rutherford turned and nodded a greeting to his fellow detective. Matt saw the man quickly look his way. He made no acknowledgment of Matt's presence. The two detectives began an exploration of the automobile's passenger area and the victim, looking for any clues.

*The Businessman's Cadillac*

The impatient news media people were held at bay for now. As they waited for the initial investigation to conclude, Harlan Rogers joined Matt in the throng. The two spoke briefly as they watched the detectives finish their examination of the crime scene. Harlan mentioned his intention to get a picture of the dead guy and the car, although he knew the *Georgian*, sometimes accused of sensationalism or yellow journalism, would never print a photograph of the dead man's body. Matt agreed. From his position, it appeared to the young reporter that the two detectives may have also collected a few items for evidence as they searched.

Finally, Greerson, who apparently was the lead investigator on this case, gave the newshounds a chance to view the crime scene up close. Matt joined the press scrum at the side of the death car. The *Georgian* reporter shone his flashlight into the vehicle. Inside the Cadillac, he saw a middle-aged, medium-build man lying on the front seat. He had a single gunshot wound to his left temple, at the edge of his thick black hair. The wound appeared to have blackened edges surrounding it. His grayish-white face, which sported a pencil-thin mustache, was grotesquely twisted in death. The man's eyes were a faint dull gleam under partially lowered lids. His tongue protruded slightly from between his lips. Because there was no apparent blood or brain matter splattered elsewhere in the car, Matt guessed the wound was not a through and through and, therefore, the weapon was of a smaller caliber.

The murdered man, dressed in an expensive-looking suit, had obviously been seated behind the wheel when the shot to the head had been inflicted. His upper torso had fallen across the seat toward the passenger side of the car with his right arm tucked beneath him and the other flung out almost casually through the steering wheel in a frozen gesture. The beam of Matt's flashlight also revealed an old leather satchel, which had fallen off the seat, spilling cash onto the floorboard. Exactly how much cash was impossible to tell, but Matt knew it was more than he made per month, maybe in a year. A gray homburg sat next to the satchel.

The *Georgian* police beat reporter detached himself from the news crowd at the car and stepped to where Jim Greerson stood on the sidewalk talking in a hushed voice with a uniformed officer. When they finished speaking, Matt approached Jim. "Well, it's not Gutowski. I'd know that big square head anywhere even without seeing the face."

"Yeah, I know. Damned the luck!" the big detective replied with an exasperated sigh. He suddenly seemed to Matt to be more grave than usual.

When the reporters had had enough of the grisly view, they turned to shout questions at Greerson. The newsies were like a flock of hungry geese pursuing a farmer's wife who held a handful of bread crumbs. Matt had questions, too, but preferred to stay in the background for now. In essence, Greerson advised the reporters that they'd not located a weapon yet, had no identity of the dead man yet, and had failed to locate any witnesses. He preliminarily eliminated this being a case of suicide for the present, he added, only on the basis of there being no weapon present. At the same time, he explained, that it was unlikely a ride-rob crime or a robbery because the satchel with a substantial amount of money was still in the Cadillac and the victim was still wearing a very nice watch and ring. Anyone who would have gone as far as to kill the victim, he deduced, would certainly have taken the money and maybe even the jewelry. Finally, when asked, he said he would not say anything about the weapon used, except that it was a small caliber. Then, he urged them to get whatever photographs they wanted, because the morgue's people were getting ready to take the body. With that, the gaggle moved en masse back to the car to watch the macabre spectacle.

Greerson told Matt that he would be a few minutes more before he could leave. "How's about going for a drink afterward, Matt?"

"A drink?"

"Yeah, you know, Matt, those things that adults imbibe to dilute the harshness of the reality of their daily lives."

Matt laughed sheepishly, "Yeah, Jim, I get it. I just wasn't sure what kind of 'drink' you meant or where we could get one."

The big detective shook his head slightly in disbelief, though his face was emotionless. "First, I'm not sure I buy that, Matt. Second, I'm a cop," he reminded his young friend. "I know of several blind tigers where we could find some alcohol. I'm in the mood. You in?"

'Blind tiger' was a term that had become familiar to Matt during his time at the paper, though he'd never actually been to one. In other parts of the country, he'd learned, they were called blind pigs, pour houses, and, more commonly in the big cities, speakeasies. According to some of his cohorts at the *Georgian*, compared with the ones in Atlanta, some speakeasies in other metropolitan areas were fairly sophisticated in their clandestine operation. Notwithstanding the recent vote on the sale of alcohol in Georgia, no establishments had yet opened under the new law to quench the public's thirst. For now, Matt supposed, blind tigers would continue to flourish. The young journalist was uncertain about going, but figured it to be a way to get additional inside information about the present murder case. "Yeah, sure. I need to call the night desk and give them what I have on this story so far, though, before I do anything else. Do I have time to walk down to Marietta Street to find a pay telephone?" When Jim nodded, Matt continued, "I'll be right back." With that, he turned and started trotting toward the main drag.

"Take your time! I'll be here!" Greerson called after the reporter.

Matt found a pay telephone in front of an automobile repair shop in the middle of a block on Marietta. Calling the night desk, he filled them in on what was known so far about the murder and promised to be in early to write up the latest details for the next edition. By the time he returned to the murder location, about half an hour had passed. The body had long-since been removed, and the Cadillac was being taken away. Detectives Greerson and Rutherford were only now concluding their work at the scene.

"You ready for a drink, Artie? Matt?" Greerson's voice was sullen and cold. Both men agreed. Greerson turned to his fellow detective. "Meet you at Turner's." Nodding, Rutherford made his way to his dark-brown Ford, while Greerson and Matt returned to the Hudson. Jim didn't speak during the drive to the Cabbagetown vicinity, an area Matt had often heard Miss Dixie refer to as "Chinch Row." Though no words were spoken, Matt sensed that his friend was becoming gloomier with each minute.

The detective parked up the street from a large frame house with several people quietly milling about on an expansive front porch lit by lanterns. Rutherford suddenly appeared on the street beside Greerson's door. The three made their way to the house where a bear-sized man stood on the porch by the front door. He had a big high-bridged, fleshy nose that looked as hard as nearby Stone Mountain and wore a fedora at least two sizes too small. To Matt, the hat looked like a thimble sitting on a watermelon. His uncertainty of the moment, however, kept it from being laughable. The big man nodded at Greerson and Rutherford, but gave Matt the once-over with small brown eyes. He held a hand up to the young reporter, who had hesitantly trailed the two detectives. Greerson turned back to the big man. "It's all right, Tiny. He's with us."

Tiny dropped his hand at his side and smiled halfheartedly as the three went inside.

The large front room was crowded. It contained only a few straight-backed wooden chairs, mingled with two small, worn stuffed chairs, and a small table holding a radio, from which radiated some jazzy tune. To one side of the room a wide, rough plank, supported at either end by a tall sawhorse, served as a bar. Behind the bar was a tall, rawboned man who looked as if he were beyond caring. At his back, against the wall, rested a dilapidated breakfront, on which remained only one of four original doors. Matt smiled and wondered why it was even still there. The shelves of the cupboard were filled with what appeared to be an assortment of old jars about the size of pony glasses. The room was lighted by kerosene lamps placed on high wall shelves.

While Jim walked across the room and quietly spoke to a man seated on a tall stool in the corner closest to the bar, Rutherford sauntered his way through the crowd and spoke to the barkeep. Matt watched the process, fascinated. After Rutherford spoke to him, the man behind the bar reached inside the breakfront and retrieved three of the jars, setting them on the board. From behind a door on the lower part of the cupboard, he produced a bottle of a clear liquid and poured a generous amount into each jar. The detective paid the man, picked up the "glasses," and moved back through the crowd to where Jim had rejoined Matt. As Artie reached them, he gave them a dull smile and asked, "Did you guys want anything to drink?"

Matt was caught slightly off guard by an unfamiliar sense of humor from the coarse detective. Jim snorted sourly and took two of the jars, handing one to his young companion. "C'mon." Greerson moved toward a door centered on the room's back wall. When they entered the next room, Matt realized they were in what was commonly called a "shotgun house." The style of house had a single-room-wide configuration. Rather than having a hallway, the rooms were connected by doors placed in the same location on their back walls. The arrangement was such that, if a shotgun was fired in the front door, the charge would go through all the doors and exit the rear of the house. Before tonight, he'd never been in one.

The second room, in which Matt found himself, was also lit by kerosene lamps. Matt surmised that it was one of the many older houses in the area lacking electricity. Probably, no indoor plumbing as well, he guessed. He decided he'd deal with that if and when the need arose. The space was populated by several men and women in various stages of sobriety.

The trio moved on to the next room, which in every way, was like the one they'd just left. The fourth room, at the back of the house, was less populated and quieter. Here, the men found three empty chairs, which they pulled into a small triangle near the back wall and dropped onto them heavily. They lit cigarettes and sat smoking in silence for a minute or so. In Matt's estimation, Greerson's moroseness appeared to deepen.

As if to break the mood, Rutherford raised his drink toward Greerson in a toast. "Here's to us and those like us." Jim raised his jar to his partner's. When Matt did likewise, Rutherford returned to his old form and snarled at the young correspondent, "What the hell are you doin', slick? This is a toast to those who fight crime on the streets, not those who write about it from the safety of a newsroom!"

"Look, Rutherford, me raising my glass doesn't mean I put myself in a group with you! It has to do with my respect for the job you guys do!" Matt fired back. He pulled his glass jar back to his lap and determinedly went on, "I only thought I understood what you did until I started going out to crime scenes with Jim here. I'm sure I still don't fully understand your job and all it entails. But I certainly understand it better. I think it helps me do my job better. That's all I meant!"

Rutherford didn't respond but gave Matt a baleful look. Jim, whose glass was still raised against his partner's, looked at Rutherford, and then back to Matt. "Put your glass up here, sport." His voice was cold and lifeless. Matt didn't comprehend what was behind this gloomy change in his friend. After clinking glasses, Greerson slammed downed his liquor quickly and heaved a depressing moan. Likewise, Rutherford put his drink to sleep with one punch. Matt took as large a sip of the unknown liquid as he dared. He'd tried alcohol before but this was hellish compared to that sampling. This concoction took his breath and burned all the way down, causing him to gasp and cough.

"Smooth, eh, kid?" Rutherford laughed loosely. "Turner calls this stuff 'Mountain razzle dazzle.' We call it 'block and tackle.' Ya take a drink, walk a block, and can tackle a tiger!" He smiled broadly and looked askance at his partner, whose face remained expressionless.

Trying to reestablish his manliness, Matt quickly finished his drink in one gulp. The effect may have been lost when his eyes watered noticeably and he gasped for air again. The alcohol's effect on him was almost immediate. Greerson gathered their glasses and moved back toward the front of the house, from which the level of laughter and conversation had increased with the crowd since the three men had arrived. Thursday night in the big town, Matt thought through a slight haze, as he followed Greerson's slow movements through the throng with his eyes. He turned back to Rutherford and leaned toward him. "What's going on with Jim, Artie?" When Rutherford didn't respond, Matt pressed the question. "Seriously, forget *our* problems, detective. What's wrong with Jim?"

"Aw, he gets this way every year at this time." Rutherford, too, was watching his partner as he spoke and set fire to another cigarette. He leaned forward in his chair, resting his elbows on his thighs and looked hard-eyed at the young reporter before continuing, "Tomorrow's the anniversary of his wife's death." The statement stunned the young man, but it explained some things, some earlier comments. Before Matt could express his shock, Rutherford said, "You never saw a guy, a couple so much in love. It damned near killed him when she died." His voice trailed off at the end.

"How? What happened to her?"

"Look, Matt, you can't say anything about this. Jim's very closed-mouth about it. He's still tore up over it. He won't even talk to me about it." Matt nodded vaguely. The alcohol was coming on strong. He fumbled his way to light a cigarette. "Jim and Ella – that was her name – had been married for a while. They'd been tryin' to have a kid but were having trouble. At one point, Ella was having some physical thing goin' on. They thought that maybe they'd finally succeeded in their tries for the kid. Jim was the happiest man in the world, I tell ya. When they went to her doctor to confirm it, they ran some tests and found out she had cancer. The stuff was ravagin' her body, and they couldn't do anything for her. Little less than a year later, after a very painful year of sufferin', she was dead. Jim was inconsolable. He turned mean. Seriously mean. I think when Ella died, all his feelings for people died with her. It almost cost him his job at the department. Jim had been a go-getter with a fire, a passion to make a name for himself, to climb to the top. Ella's death changed all that. The inner fire died out and his passion for anything and everyone faded. It's like anger and rage drive his investigations now."

Rutherford's face went sour. His eyes moved to the direction Jim had gone. "We used to be close. We always saw our jobs a little different, but we were great buddies. We were like this," the detective said, returning his gaze to Matt and holding up two thick fingers close together. "That died, too. Suddenly, we were at arm's length from each other. Of course, after Ella died, he was that way with everybody. Or worse. But it still bothered me. A lot." The detective gave Matt another stony-eyed look. "To be honest with you, that's part of my attitude toward you. I guess I gotta admit that I'm a touch jealous that Jim has taken to you like he has. We used to be like that." When Matt smiled at his confession, Artie's pockmarked face hardened, his body stiffened. "Say, punk, don't go gettin' no funny ideas 'bout me!" He paused and calmed slightly. "Besides, I still don't like draggin' you with us on cases! It ain't right! I'm goin' to try to stop it from happenin'! I don't think –" Rutherford didn't finish the thought. Jim returned with full glasses.

As Greerson handed them their drinks, Artie's hard face softened as he looked up at his partner. "What took you so long, Jimbo?"

"Ran into somebody who'd heard I've been looking for Gutowski. They had some inside dope for me, but we had to go outside to talk. I got a line on Gutowski's girlfriend."

"Well, that's good news, huh, Jim?" Matt blurted. As he raised his glass to his mouth, the detective merely nodded once in response. Matt's buzz was increasing in its intensity, his tongue getting thicker. He looked at Detective Greerson and carelessly, woozily said, "I'm sorry to hear about your wife, Jim."

Rutherford's face convulsed at Matt's words. Greerson froze as his face reddened, and then darkened. Over the rim of his jar-glass, he shot a hard glance at Rutherford before turning a glare on Matt, but the big cop said nothing. Rutherford gave the reporter a sinister frown with eyes boring into Matt's face. Matt swallowed hard. The three men slammed their drinks down without a word. Matt tried to shake off his screwup. He stood unsteadily and reached for his companions' glasses. "My turn to buy a round." He promptly fell back onto his chair.

Rutherford snatched Matt's glass and took Jim's. "It's mighty white of you to offer, but you'd better stay in your seat, ace. I'll get this one." He headed back to the front of the pour house. Matt, uncertain how to undo his blunder, sat quietly. From that point on, Matt vaguely remembered having another drink or two before he sank into a black pool.

Matt Grimes's eyes slowly, grudgingly opened. After a time, he sat up gingerly and found himself stretched out on a davenport in a small but neat, unfamiliar living room. Matt blinked several times, squinting in the bright morning sunlight filtering through the shear curtains hanging at the room's windows. His mind struggled between panic and apathy. The only thing he knew for certain was that he had an enormous headache and a God-awful taste in his mouth. Somehow, the fact that he was still had his clothes on gave him some comfort. He heard footsteps approaching him from behind, but his head hurt too much to turn in that direction. Jim Greerson circled the sofa and extended a cup of coffee to his young friend. Matt gratefully accepted the offering. "Where... where am I, Jim?"

"You're at my house, Matt. You seemed to have trouble holding your liquor last night. Since I instigated the whole thing, I didn't feel right just dumping you off at your boardinghouse. And you sure as hell weren't gonna get home by yourself. Either way, I didn't think Miss Dixie would have appreciated your condition. So I brought you home with me and parked you on the sofa." Greerson's moroseness lingered through his words.

"Thanks, Jim. That was swell of you. And you're right. Miss Dixie wouldn't have been happy with me like that." Taking a large gulp of the hot coffee, he went on, "I don't remember anything much after the second drink."

"Well, you had a third drink and part of a fourth before the ceiling caved in on you. At that point, Artie and I decided to call it a night." Greerson smiled thinly. "Artie was all for leaving you at Turner's. He seemed pretty steamed at you for broaching the subject of my... my circumstances. We –"

"I'm sorry, Jim. I want to blame the alcohol, but –"

"Forget it, sport. It's just something I'm dealing with." His voice was cold, distant but not harsh. The detective turned and walked to a small table and sat down to his coffee cup.

Matt rose slowly from the sofa, feeling stiff and dissipated, as a sharp pain darted through his temples. He turned unsteadily toward the table, trying to clear the cobwebs from his mind. "Anyway, Jim, I am sorry. I consider you a good friend, if you'd care to talk about it."

"I never have. Artie and some others think that's part of the problem." He got quiet for a long minute and his eyes filled with tears. "She was my whole world." Matt moved to the table in uneven steps, found a chair, and replenished both their cups from the coffeepot sitting there. He said nothing, waiting for his friend to speak, if he wanted to. Greerson's mind moved back over more than a dozen years. After another long, sluggish minute, the detective cleared his throat. "Maybe you need to know more about me to understand me better, Matt, 'cause I know I send mixed signals sometimes. To begin with, I grew up in a poor farming family over in Carroll County. Like I told you at Maloof's, after high school, I worked a year to save the money to go to Tech.

"In the fall of 1916, I packed what few possessions I had, my parents sort of packed all the hopes and dreams they had for me, and off I went to start classes at Tech. Thought I'd play baseball when I got there." A thin smile made a short struggle at the corners of his mouth. "Made the team. Things looked great. Then the war broke out the following April. Like a lot of others, I thought it was my patriotic duty to join up, so I left Tech and volunteered with some buddies from Alabama. It nearly killed my parents when I left school. Anyway, my outfit wound up as part of the 42$^{nd}$ 'Rainbow' Division. We went to France in November 1917 and to the front March of '18. I was badly wounded in the Meuse-Argonne Offensive during the fall of 1918, and I was still recovering when the war ended. That was fine with me. Even in that short excursion, I'd had enough of war." He seemed isolated in thought for a moment, and then shook his head sorrowfully, rubbing a leg. "Anyway, no more baseball playing for me.

"Our outfit finally got back to the U. S. in 1919, and I came back to Atlanta." He smiled faintly. "I started taking classes again, but I found the war had knocked some of the stuffing out of me. By the following year, my wounds had healed enough that I started working as a police officer on the supernumerary list. In 1921, I met my future wife on a streetcar. It turned out that we attended the same church, but had never spoken until that day on the streetcar." Matt shot Jim a puzzled look. "It was a big church. Anyway, when I found out she was a registered nurse, we started talking about hospitals and stuff like that, because I'd spent so much time in them recuperating from my wounds.

"We hit it off and started seeing each other regularly. She was wonderful in every way. I know it sounds corny, but she gave new meaning to my existence. It got very serious, and we wanted to get married. Ella and I decided to wait the two or three years until I was off the supernumerary list and became a full-time police officer before getting married. It was tough, though. We were so much in love, too excited." The big cop's eyes watered again. "Looking toward our marriage, I bought this place on Wellington Street because it was near her only living relative, an elderly aunt, who she loved dearly. We got married in 1925, but chose to wait awhile to start a family. She decided she wanted to enjoy some time together before settling in with kids.

"Ella," the big cop paused and swallowed hard at his first mention of her name, "was the light of my life, Matt. Everything about her..." His voice drifted off for a moment. "She loved taking the streetcar to Piedmont Park and spending the day just walking, talking, and watching people." As Jim spoke, Matt thought about the time he and Evie had spent at Piedmont. "She loved baseball as much as I did, and we'd go to Cracker's games at Ponce de Leon Park when we could. She called it Poncey. In between those Crackers' games, we'd spend time watching kids play baseball in a vacant field down the street. The neighborhood kids loved Ella and would ask her, not me, to resolve disputed plays.

After it opened, we'd go to Maddox Park and have a small picnic once in a while.

"About five years ago we began trying to start a family, but luck wasn't with us. Along the way, I was promoted to detective, and we bought the Hudson. Ella was so sentimental, though, we'd still take the streetcar to go places sometimes. She'd say that we were living the American dream, but without the white picket fence she wanted. I kept promising her one. We'd sit on our front porch, and she'd tease me about looking at and enjoying the one next door. I never got around to building that fence." He heaved a long sigh and paused. After a time, he gently jerked his head toward the front door and continued, "This house has a dogwood in the front yard that Ella dearly loved. She'd cry every spring when its blossoms dropped. She said it reminded her of snowflakes in a storm. I kidded her that she'd never even *seen* a snowstorm." Greerson sipped his coffee. His face looked pensive. Matt's shaky fingers found a cigarette in his coat pocket and awkwardly lit it as his friend spoke quietly.

"Not long after I bought the Hudson, we found out she had cancer. The doctors said there was no hope for her." Greerson's chin dropped to his chest. He didn't look up as he continued, "For nearly a year, I watched this beautiful woman, this beautiful human being waste away, suffering in great pain. And I couldn't do a damned thing about it. I was by her side every day for that year. Toward the end, she told me that death was going to be a friend to her. Cancer came into our lives and took my wife..." Tears rolled down the big man's cheeks.

Matt was at a loss for what to say, what to do. He wondered why Jim chose now to speak about all this and why him to say it to. While some uncertainties he had about the detective were being answered, those two questions remained unasked.

They sat in silence for a while before Jim spoke again. "At Ella's funeral, our pastor told me that 'it was God's will' that Ella died how and when she did." Greerson looked hard at the man across the table as his voice rose to a crescendo, "I was shocked! Pissed! I was angry beyond words, Matt! 'God's will', he said! God's will? How can a loving God allow someone like Ella to suffer and die like that? It was then and there that I turned my back on religion." He shook his head vigorously and his voice lowered. "I don't want to believe in a God who willed that a beautiful, loving creature should suffer and die like Ella had. In my rage, my attitude toward my fellow man hardened. I knew it. But I couldn't help it and didn't care. I don't see that changing either. I couldn't even *talk* about baseball after she died. Still not a happy topic of conversation for me. At first, I started drinking a lot when I wasn't on duty. Now, it's pretty much only around this date and our wedding anniversary that I get stinkin' drunk."

After another short, poignant silence, Greerson continued, "Ella's buried next to her aunt, who died in '28. They're over in Westview Cemetery, not far from here. I've never told anybody this, but I go to visit her grave a lot and talk to her," he paused, looking intently at his young friend, "and cry. But, in the last week or so,

*Entrance to Westview Cemetery*

on the way home, I've started stopping by the vacant lot again to watch a baseball game that might be going on, recalling happier days when Ella was at my side. The kids playing ball shy away from me, I think, in part because they don't know what to say to me in my grief and, in part, because word of my mean temperament since Ella's death has spread around the neighborhood.

"I can't give up this house or even the Hudson. They're part of what I have to cling to her memory with." Greerson looked up at Matt and quietly said, "Loving Ella made me want the next minute more than the last. It was a constant craving for the very sight of her." His voice drifted off. The two men sat in silence for a long time after Jim finished speaking, the detective reflecting, Matt processing.

Not until after another cup of coffee did Matt suddenly think of his job, a job that expected his participation in a morning circuit of law-enforcement agencies. He glanced at his watch and jumped from his chair abruptly, holding the table's edge for balance. "Oh, shit!" he exclaimed, rousing Jim from his reverie. "I've got to get moving! I'm late already! Barnes is gonna kill me!"

Jim raised a broad, calming palm. "If you're worried about your morning rounds, forget it. Judging from last night, I figured you weren't gonna to be up to snuff this morning. I called the paper earlier. Told them you were too sick to make the early runs, but you'd likely be in later in the morning to write stuff up. They said they'd cover it this morning."

"Thanks, Jim." The momentary panic Matt had experienced subsided, but the alarm had intensified his headache. Rubbing his temples, he looked at the big man across the table. "Say, Jim, I appreciate your sharing your background, your story with me. I can't imagine that it was easy to talk about or to relive. I'm very sorry for your loss and your pain. Just know that if you ever want to talk or... or just get drunk again, I'll be there for you."

Greerson showed a hint of a quiet smile. "First, Matt, if I *ever* want to talk about it again, I'll bring it up. As far as getting drunk goes, I'm not sure you'd survive another round like last night. But, maybe since you've had a baptism under 'firewater,' you'd be okay." Both men laughed quietly although it hurt Matt's head to do so. He quickly reached for the sides of his head again and began massaging.

While still rubbing his head, Matt tasted his tongue and shot Jim an up-from-under look. The detective was staring into his coffee cup. Sheepishly, the younger man asked, "Say, Jim, did I... did I puke last night?"

Greerson chuckled, "Yeah. Yeah, you did."

Matt laughed nervously. "In your car?"

"Well, no. You got me to stop the car, and then fell out of it." His chuckled evolved into a lusty laugh. "Lets just say that there's a rhododendron bush somewhere between here and Turner's that doesn't stand much of a chance to survive the summer."

After a brief, slightly embarrassed silence, Matt asked, "Since you mentioned me needing to write my stories, Jim, would this be a bad time to ask you some questions about last night's murder case?"

"Shoot! No pun intended."

"I get how you've eliminated robbery as a motive, what with the money and the guy's jewelry still at the scene, but how can you be sure it wasn't a suicide where somebody didn't simply happen along and decided to carry off the dead man's gun before the police arrived?"

"Well, of course, anything's possible, Matt." Greerson smiled wider than Matt had seen in the last twelve hours. "But how likely is it that someone might happen along and steal a handgun from a dead man but leave a satchel full of money behind? And what are the odds that someone who could accumulate that kind of money in this economy is going to off themselves? Besides, there are other factors to consider." He paused for a sip of coffee. "Now, I'm no Philo Vance, but my experience is that most right-handed people who blow their brains out do it with their right hand, firing into the right side of their head. This guy's wound was to his left temple area. And all indications are that the victim was right-handed." As Matt leaned forward to speak, the detective made a vague motion with his hand and continued. "My experience also leads me to believe that people tend to wear their watch on their nondominant arm because they do most of their work like catching, writing, holding, grabbing, et cetera, with their dominant hand." Matt found himself glancing down at his watch. "Wearing a watch on the nondominant hand seems to have become a custom since it's easier to check the time on the hand we use less and where the watch doesn't get stuck, dirty, or damaged. Plus, it's easier to wind the stem and to buckle the band with dominant hand that way. The dead man's watch was on his left wrist.

"People also often develop calluses on the middle finger of their dominant hand due to writing with a pen or pencil. The middle finger of the dead guy's right hand had a decent callus on it where you'd expect to find it. Maybe he was a bookkeeper or a banker. He was a paper pusher of some sort anyway. Pretty damned nice car for a bookkeeper, though, huh?" He stroked his jaw.

"Also, the men I've had contact with who carry a wallet in an inside suit coat pocket, usually carry it on their nondominant side so they can reach for it with their dominant hand. The guy's wallet was in his suit coat on the left side. Finally, and this may be a stretch, but I read somewhere that clockwise hair whorls on the back of a person's scalp tend to show that they're right-handed. At least, the odds of them being right-handed are greater. It's not an exact science, and we'll know when we learn more about the man, but he had clockwise whorls.

"I know that's a lot of coincidences, but sometimes they can add up to a fact. So, in my opinion, it was no suicide. And just so you know, my guess is that he was shot by someone standing beside the car with a small-caliber handgun while he sat behind the wheel. A small caliber might explain why no one heard the shot, which could've been lost in the noise from Five Points and Marietta Street. From the looks of it, it was a contact wound, too."

"And the money?"

The detective shrugged loosely. "Maybe a business deal was in the works. Perhaps he just didn't trust banks. Maybe it was a blackmail payoff. Who knows? Again, find the motive…"

Matt sat back and digested what he'd heard. Jim rose from his chair and poured the last of the coffee into his friend's cup. Then he made his way into the kitchen, disposed of the grounds, and rinsed out the pot. When he returned to the table, he tossed a familiar orange and white tin of St. Joseph aspirin in front of his young friend. "You'd better take some of those. It may already be too late, but go ahead anyway." As he turned and walked down a hallway, he tossed over his shoulder, "Then we'd better get moving or neither one of us will have a job!"

Shortly after splashing his face with cold water to try to come to terms with consciousness and, then, straightening his tie to look more presentable, Matt joined Jim on the porch that ran across the front of the detective's little house. When he walked up to Jim, the detective turned and nodded back toward the house. "Sorry about all that in there," he said solemnly. "Not sure why I let loose, but sorry just the same." Matt's reply consisted of a firm, understanding grasp of his friend's shoulder. They walked past the dogwood tree to the Hudson, parked in a short driveway that ran to one side of the house. As they climbed in, Matt talked Jim into dropping him off at the newspaper, notwithstanding his condition, explaining that he didn't have time to go to Houston Street and clean up first. Riding away from the bungalow, Matt saw the white picket fence in front of the house next door. As they drove toward downtown, they passed Altoona Place. Matt threw a surprised glance at the detective. Vivian and Charlie's bungalow had been only about three blocks from Greerson's place.

———

When Matt entered the newsroom, he caught the eye of Mr. Barnes, who waved him into his office. The young reporter was still trying to smooth his rumpled clothing when he closed the city editor's door and approached his desk. He cautiously stopped about two feet in front of it. Setting his coffee cup aside, Barnes spoke around a new, unlit cigar, shifting it along his lips. "How're you feeling, Matt? I understand you were a touch under the weather this morning." The editor pawed around on his desk for a match.

"Oh, I'm better now, thanks, Mr. Barnes."

"I gotta tell you, kiddo, you look like the bottom of a chicken coop." He waved a hand holding an unlighted match, "Well, never mind. You went out on that businessman's murder last night, right?"

"Yes, sir." Still a little woozy, Matt briefly ran through what they'd found and what they knew so far about the murder and the victim. As he spoke, Mr. Barnes started eyeing him suspiciously and quietly sniffing the air. Matt noticed and tried to take a casual step backward. The step succeeded. The casual part failed miserably.

"Okay," Barnes said slowly, stretching the word out as he worked the cigar around his mouth. He inhaled deeply through his nostrils and went on, "Write it up and get it to Mr. Cowart. One of the other guys – I forget which one – made the morning rounds. Not much to show, but it's been taken care of. There's —-" He stopped abruptly and stood. Leaning across the desk, he said, "Come closer, son. I want to ask you something." Matt took a cautious short step toward his boss. "Closer, boy." The young man took another hesitant step. "I knew it!" Barnes exclaimed in a low tone, as he walked around his desk. "You got a toot on last night, didn't you?" Barnes cut off whatever Matt started to say in response. "If you didn't work so hard, have so much promise, I'd..." Then the city editor relaxed and started to laugh. "You know, hard drinking is sort of a hazard of this profession. But don't let it interfere with your work, Matt," Barnes finished gravely. He put a fatherly hand on his reporter's shoulder. "First real snoot full, was it?" Matt nodded sheepishly, slowly; his head was killing him. Barnes reached around his desk, opened a drawer, and retrieved a bottle of Squib aspirin, which he handed to the young man. "Take some of these. You'll feel much better... eventually." He started gesturing again with the hand holding the match. "Now, get outta here!" he said, sniffing the air. "I wanna set fire to this cigar, and I'm afraid to strike a match with you in the room!" Barnes returned to the working side of his desk, shaking his head. "And then go get cleaned up! You're in bad need of a clean shirt and a shave! Jeez!"

Matt completed his write-up of the murder. He felt as if he were moving under water, and it was not a clean, clear body of water either. Finally, he went home to regroup before his afternoon rounds. At the boardinghouse, he received odd gawks from Miss Dixie, with whom he avoided any close contact until he'd brushed his teeth, shaved, showered, and put on a fresh shirt. Soon, he was ready to take on the afternoon, though at a slower pace than usual. Miss Dixie threw some loud "tsk-tsks" in his direction as he moved toward the front door.

In the next few days, Rhamy wormed the story out of Matt about his "missing night." The young man knew the tale would eventually make its way back to Miss Dixie. The landlady would be a bit disappointed in her young boarder's succumbing to the evils of drink, but her distress would be short-lived. She knew Matt too well. Besides, Matt rationalized, telling Mr. Fleming the tale was far easier than facing Miss Dixie with it. Miss Dixie was well aware of and could deal with the impetuousness of youth, so long as it didn't become a habit. For his part, Matt had decided that he didn't have the constitution to be a regular drinker. Soon, everything was back to normal on Houston Street.

---

Within a short time, Greerson had identified the murdered man in the Cadillac as Theodore Brewer, a local "investment adviser," as he'd told Matt, "Whatever the hell that is in this economy." The background on Brewer was thin, Greerson told him, because the man had only arrived in Atlanta in the last half-dozen years as far as he could tell. His prior place of residence is unknown for now. Wherever he'd come from, he came with enough wealth to set himself up in business and was very successful at what he did. As usual, Detective Greerson promised to keep his reporter friend up to date on the latest developments in the case.

# CHAPTER 11

# The Private Investigator

Shortly after his normal lunchtime on the last Monday of May, Matthew Grimes was in the teletype room, scanning stories coming across the wires. He hadn't eaten yet, and hunger pangs were hindering his focus on news items. As Matt was reading about the kidnapping-for-ransom of a boy named George Weyerhaeuser in Washington State, out of the corner of his eye, he saw a familiar face in an unfamiliar place. Detective Jim Greerson was wandering slowly among the reporters' desks in the city room, looking a little uncertain about his surroundings. Matt had never seen the big cop bear such an expression. The young man let the teletype feed fall back to the front of the machine and walked out into the newsroom just as Greerson, swinging his hat as he spoke, asked Brick where to find his friend. The old journalist, leaning back as far as he dare in his chair with his feet propped on a pulled-out drawer, was giving Jim a casual up and down before answering.

"Are you looking for me, Detective Greerson?"

At the sound of Matt's question, Brick raised himself erect by pulling on the edge of his scarred desk and looked around indifferently. The

# SHORTENING SHADOWS

detective turned around nonchalantly, but a thin look of relief played across his face. "Yeah, Matt! How's the boy?" Greerson tossed his thanks to Brick and put his hat back on as he wove through the array of desks in Matt's direction. Brick returned to his previous position and to whatever it was that Brick did to fill his days and rake in a paycheck. Matt slalomed his way back to his desk where the two buddies met.

The reporter sat at his desk and smiled up at his friend. He whispered to the detective, "That guy was Brick, by the way."

Jim walked between Matt's desk and the vacant one next to it. "Brick?" Jim face reflected bewilderment, as he looked back in the old reporter's direction.

"Yeah, Brick." He explained, "The night we were at Mrs. Dunbar's apartment, you told me to point him out if you ever ran into him." Greerson face was still a blank. "After I told you his philosophy about dating older women, you said you wanted to make sure you avoided shaking his hand."

"Oh! Oh yeah! Brick," Jim laughed.

The big detective leaned his butt against the unoccupied desk and picked up a handful of Gem clips. He offhandedly started making a chain of the clips. Shifting his eyes from the paper clips to Matt, he said, "It's been a while, so I thought I'd see if you wanted to grab some lunch. It's on me."

Matt absently chewed on a pencil for a second or two, and then tossed it aside. Although he was not one to pass on a meal with someone else picking up the tab, his reporter's mind was elsewhere at the moment. He leaned forward with his elbows on his desk. Looking up at Greerson, the newspaperman asked, "Anything new on the Maddox murder?"

Greerson, apparently bored with the Gem clips, dropped them on the desk behind him and leaned his long frame forward over Matt's work area. He started fiddling with the Hotchkiss stapling machine sitting

274

there. "No, not much to tell." The detective began tapping the stapler up and down with his fingers in a dot-dash fashion as if sending a telegram. Matt's eyebrows shot up as he recognized boredom in the detective's demeanor. "I talked with her daddy. He works as a sweeper at Exposition Mill. Her momma died a few years after she was born, and he's had his hands full trying to raise his four kids. Addie was the youngest. Good man. He said she just drifted away, and he wouldn't see her for months at a time. So no help there. It seems that the last person seen with her was a guy named Nathan Green. Green didn't want to talk to me, but my investigation leads me to think he was her pimp. Of course, he denies it emphatically. But he was last seen with her the afternoon before her body was discovered. Green's being with her no closer than that to the approximate time of death does me no good. And being a pimp, even if he is one, doesn't make him a murderer."

The *Georgian* reporter knew his next question might ruffle some feathers, but prodded on. "What's taking so long?" Three weeks had passed since the discovery of the girl's body, so Matt thought it was a fair question.

Greerson jerked his eyes up at Matt and stopped playing with the stapler. "Hey, smartass, it's not the only case I've got! Remember Brewer?" he snapped in a low but frustrated tone. He took a deep breath, straightened, and went on contritely, "You were there at the Maddox crime scene, Matt. You know full well there wasn't much to go on. And, besides, I'm still looking for the 'why' of it. Find the motive, you find the killer. I'm working on it." He went back to his imaginary telegraph.

Grimes nodded his understanding, "I know you are, Jim. No offense meant. Asking is my job. And, as you once told me, I've got to earn my nickels." He then hesitantly asked, "Speaking of Brewer, are you making any headway on that?"

Initially, the detective shook his head vaguely, and then seemed to catch himself and laughed. "Well, no and yes," he managed among his

Morse code efforts, "because we're still trying to get a handle on his background, but we did locate the gun that killed him."

Matt sat back suddenly, jarred by the news. "You don't say? When? Where?"

"Yeah, we only got it just this past Friday morning. A Colt .25 caliber 1908 handgun. Some rod-riding drifter found it near the railroad tracks under the Spring Street viaduct. It came to our attention when he tried to sell the thing at a hockshop only a few doors down from the police station. Not exactly sure when he found it 'cause he says he tends to drink too much, and he spent some blurry days trying to sell the thing. Anyway, because of the caliber and where he said he found it, I had some tests run. It matches the slug taken out of Brewer's noggin for the coroner's inquest." When Greerson looked at Matt's face, he read the next question there. "Sorry I didn't get to you with it sooner, kid, but I didn't get the results of the ballistics test until about an hour ago. Anyway, you still have a scoop on your rivals. Oh, by the way, that satchel in the Cadillac contained twenty-five hundred dollars."

Matt let out a short, envious whistle. "Damn! That's a lotta swag!" He quickly rolled a sheet of paper into his Remington and started typing a follow-up article with the latest developments for the next edition. As he composed, he bored on with the questions on his mind. "The Colt's an automatic. Any idea why you didn't find an ejected shell casing at the scene?" When no answer was forthcoming, Matt stopped typing and looked up into Jim's face. "Well?"

"Okay, okay. We found a copper-nickel shell casing. And the manufacturer matched the ones in the Colt found by the drifter." He returned a blank glare to the stunned look coming from Matt. "Look, we don't reveal everything to the public all at once in every case. Do you know how many crackpots come out of the woodwork in a case like this? We have to hold something back to help us separate the wheat from the chaff." Jutting his chin toward the typewriter, he added, "And you'd do me a personal favor if you'd leave out that we found the gun. Say something like the police confirmed that a small caliber gun was used in the murder... so on and so forth."

Matt saw the common sense in that approach. He shrugged and grunted, moving on to his next query as he typed. "Anything new on your search for Gutowski?"

Greerson gave his friend an odd gaze and smiled. "He did a quick fade north for a while before I could catch up to him. I hear he's back now. He keeps moving around from rathole to rathole in the Atlanta area, hiding out. The big thug won't leave town again, 'cause he's whipped over some twist from around here somewhere. Word on the street is that he can't convince her she'd be happier out West, maybe LA is what I hear. He's got it bad. I've got her name now, but she seems to have moved around, too. I'll discover where she is, and then I'll find him. It's only a matter of time." As Matt pulled his copy from the typewriter, Jim pushed the Hotchkiss away and let loose a noisy sigh sufficient to ruffle papers on the reporter's desk.

"Brother, you look like you need a diversion!" Matt laughed. "We'd better go get some lunch before you bust a gut from sheer monotony." Matt shrugged into his coat and plucked his hat from the hook on a nearby support column. The newsman made a side trip to Mr. Cowart's desk and deposited his copy before rejoining the detective, standing at the edge of a crowd of the newsroom boys. Matt's fellow journalists were razzing Brick about James Cagney's character's name in his latest movie release, 'G' Men. The character's name was 'Brick' Davis. To Matt, Greerson was observing the high jinks as if he were a small boy watching a carnival barker preview the show inside the tent. Matt nudged Jim, and the two moved toward the door. Before they reached it, Matt's telephone started ringing. The young reporter stopped short and trotted back toward his desk. "I'd better get that, Jim." Bending over his desk, he answered the call. After a moment, he threw a hand signal to

277

the detective as he said, "Yeah, hang on. He's right here." Straightening and shooting a surprised look at Greerson as he held the earpiece out, he said, "It's for you, Jim."

Walking briskly back to Matt's desk, he explained, "I gave HQ your number to reach me here if they needed me. I meant to check in before we left, so it's just as well you answered the call." He stepped around the desk, took the receiver, and picked up the candlestick phone. "Detective Greerson here." He paused, listening intently. A cold smile played at the corners of his mouth. He quickly sat in Matt's chair and returned the phone's base to the desk. Grabbing a piece of paper and a pencil from the desk's clutter, he jotted notes as he listened. "Wait! Say that again... Uh-huh... Yeah, okay. Say, is Rutherford around?" Another, longer pause followed. "Okay. Just tell him I'll meet him in front of the building in about fifteen minutes... Yeah... Okay. Thanks!" Greerson slowly dropped the earpiece onto its hook as he tossed the pencil. "Looks like we'll have to take a rain check on lunch, Matt. Another girl's body's been found on the west side of town. And this one's definitely a Negro girl," he frowned at the thought of another senseless death. Then, he smiled, as tedium evaporated from his face, and gave Matt a friendly punch to the shoulder before turning and moving toward the exit.

"Hey, wait a minute!" Matt called in a voice louder than he'd intended. His outburst ricocheting around the newsroom brought a halt to the kidding Brick had been getting. It also caused Mr. Barnes to come to his office door. In a stage whisper, Matt apologized to his city editor and let him know all was well. He then turned back to the detective when Barnes made his way back to his desk and whatever he was chewing on for lunch. "Hey, can I get an invitation to this soirée?"

"Sure! Sorry," the detective said as he stepped toward Matt's desk. "I've been so bored that I started taking off without thinking. Let's go!" Matt grabbed his pad and a pencil and shoved them in a coat pocket as Jim spoke. He quickly went to the city editor's office and explained the situation. Barnes sent his young reporter on his way and picked up a phone to make arrangements for someone to cover Matt's afternoon rounds.

Rumbling down the stairs, Matt persuaded Jim to let him drive his car this time. He explained that he didn't want to be relegated to a rumble seat again. "Plus," he said, "Rutherford can pretend he's being chauffeured, and I can pretend we're hauling him in on a charge of felony meanness.' " Greerson merely chuckled and nodded, explaining that he'd taken a streetcar over and didn't have his car with him anyway. The men made their way toward the street.

As they rode, Greerson detailed to his companion what he'd been told about the reported body to that point. A Negro female's body had been found by some kids playing over on Burokel Street near the Southern Railway tracks. She'd obviously been murdered. A uniformed officer was standing by at the scene. He explained that that was the extent of it so far.

Thanks to a minor traffic accident briefly blocking their side of Decatur Street, the Ford pulled up in front of police headquarters about twenty-three minutes later. As Matt was moving the Ford slowly to the curb, the two men saw Detective Rutherford. He was pacing the sidewalk like an expectant father, a trail of cigarette butts littering his wake. At first, the beefy detective didn't notice the significance of the car pulling to the curb. When he saw Greerson in the passenger seat, the burly detective clomped to the flivver, leaning forward from the sidewalk and placing his outstretched hands on the sill of the opened window next to his fellow officer. He cocked his chin at the driver and snarled, "What the hell is this about, Jimbo? Is this kid some kinda shadow now wherever we go?"

Greerson chuckled, dismissing his partner's grumblings. "Are you gonna get in so we can go do an investigation or are you gonna act like an ass on the sidewalk all day?"

The man standing beside the car dropped his chin between his extended arms and shook his head, nearly dislodging his Borsalino. "This

# SHORTENING SHADOWS

is bullshit," he growled. Matt and his passenger merely looked forward through the car's windshield, smiling, not uttering a sound. Grimes was slightly uncomfortable with the situation but took his cues from Greerson. Earning no response from his fellow detective after a long minute, Detective Rutherford moaned heavily, straightened, and opened the passenger door. Meanwhile, he'd garnered once-overs from several police officers making their way in and out of the headquarters building. Greerson casually heaved himself from the automobile and pulled the seat forward to allow Rutherford's bulk to make its way into the Ford's back seat. When all involved were situated, Matt pulled away from the curb and followed Greerson's direction westward through the business district then southwest to the crime scene.

When Matt turned south off Stephens Street for the one-block trip to Burokel, Detective Greerson saw a familiar dark-blue Hupmobile sedan parked by the side of the road a short distance from their destination. The detective had Matt stop the Ford briefly while he copied the automobile's tag number. As they proceeded on their way, Matt tossed a quizzical glance at Greerson, and then to Rutherford, who scowled and looked away.

Greerson had Grimes pull to the side of the street a short distance from the throng of onlookers gathering around the body's location. The number of spectators continued to grow as nearby residents boiled out of their houses to watch the goings-on. The three men scrambled from the car and made their way to the uniformed officer standing between the crowd and the dead girl. Matt veered off slightly to stay out of the detective's way while still being able to watch the proceedings. Greerson scanned the onlookers as he made his way through them to the cop. He spied someone in the crowd he was expecting to see there but looked away quickly so he wouldn't spook the man. "What have we got officer... officer?"

"Glendon Powell's my name, detective." The young cop turned his upper torso slightly in the girl's direction and briefly studied the scene as he drawled, "Some kids was playin' 'round the railroad tracks over thar when a Southern Railway worker run 'em off. They run 'cross the body of the dead Negress when they was being chased off. No idea of her name yet. Lotsa blood. Her head's bashed in and her throat was cut. I got the names and addresses of the kids and the railroad worker. Nobody else was around at the time."

"Any sign of a weapon that might have been used?"

The officer, tall and thin but with wide-set gray eyes, a thin nose, and a long chin with a cleft in it, jerked his head in the girl's direction. "Oh, yessir. There's a big rock with blood on it alayin' near the body. No knife or such, though."

"Okay. Good job, Powell. Just keep everybody back so I can –"

A sudden, excruciating wail broke the air. The pitiful cry came from an older, heavyset black woman who had only now trotted to the area. Her scream evolved into a grotesque sob, "My baby girl! Oh, Lawd, no! No, please, no! Sweet Jesus, no!" Several people simultaneously held back and supported the woman, who initially struggled to approach the body, and then swooned in the afternoon heat.

Greerson quickly made his way to the woman, who had wilted to the ground in a sitting position and was howling pitifully. Several bystanders were attempting to comfort her, while giving the plainclothesman distrustful looks. The detective knelt next to the keening woman. "Ma'am. Ma'am!" When her wails evolved to low moans but she still failed to respond, he grasped her shoulders and gently shook her. "Ma'am, I'm Detective Greerson. I need to ask you if this is your daughter. Ma'am?"

The woman didn't look up. She merely nodded fitfully as she sobbed and gasped for air.

"Ma'am, I'm very sorry for your loss," he said earnestly. "But I'm going to need to speak to you later to get your help finding whoever did this. What's your name, Ma'am?" She didn't respond. "What's your daughter's name?" The woman continued her strained, anguished gurgles as if she'd not heard the detective. He thought maybe she hadn't. The big detective stood and looked around. Greerson saw only hesitant, uncertain Negro faces staring back at him. The response was what a white cop could normally expect when asking a Negro questions in 1935 Atlanta, the result of the cops' reputation when dealing with them, he supposed. If any of them knew the girl's name, no one spoke up. Rutherford, true to form, remained at a distance, detached from the picture. Greerson asked Powell to get whatever information he could from the mother.

He then turned his attention to the dead woman who lay just off the roadway. Scanning the dark-skinned girl, the area around her, including the supposed weapon that delivered the blow to her head, Greerson could learn little beyond what Powell had already told him. As with the Maddox girl, it appeared that this woman had been knocked unconscious then dragged off the road and her throat cut. She wore what appeared to have been, at some time in the past, a colorful spring dress. The garment was now faded and splattered with dried blood. Significant, at least to Greerson, was another fact. The girl's shoes were missing. He still had one question in mind, a question that could be answered by a closer examination of the body at the morgue before her body was released to her family. When he turned away from the dead girl and moved to the street, he saw a familiar figure walking smartly away from the crowd. Greerson didn't like coincidences.

"Hey, mister!" he yelled after a departing figure. Getting no response or reaction from the man he was calling to, the big detective yelled to a uniform officer nearby, "Hey, stop that man!" Greerson started making his way through the throng toward the retreating man.

Before a uniformed officer could react, Rutherford suddenly came to life. The detective tossed his cigarette and charged hard after the black man moving briskly down the street. The well-dressed man had only reached a Hupmobile when Detective Rutherford overtook and slammed him against the driver's door of the parked car. The big black guy recovered quickly and pushed back hard off the car's body, throwing his off-balance assailant to the ground behind him. As the black man turned to face his attacker, Rutherford rapidly flicked his gun into his hand. "You bastard! I oughta blast a hole right through your ass, boy!"

The black man sneered, "*Boy*? *Boy*? I'm not the one on the ground, mister! And just how damned big do they grow the *men* where you come from?"

Leveling the gun at the black man's chest, Rutherford yelled, "You're gonna —"

"Hold it!" Greerson, with Matt at his side, had caught up to the pair and quickly stepped between Rutherford and the stranger. He faced his fellow detective and smiled thinly. "Thanks, Artie. I appreciate the help, but I kinda wanted him alive." He stared hard at the fallen detective for a long moment. When Rutherford, his gun still pointed toward the stranger, finally relaxed slightly, Greerson turned to the big black man. "I'm Detective Jim Greerson, Atlanta Police Department. Why didn't you stop when I yelled at you?"

"I didn't know you were talking to me. And I knew of no reason that you'd want to speak with me. I was only an observer like the other two dozen or so people hanging around."

"Okay, but this is the second time I've seen you at the murder scene in the last couple of weeks where a young Negro girl was killed, each in the same way. Who are you? And why are you here?"

The big stranger picked up his hat, straightened his suit coat, and looked hard-eyed at Jim, as he reached into one of his coat's side pockets. Jim didn't react to the movement, but he heard Rutherford cock his revolver behind him. Matt, who'd been standing near Detective Greerson, stepped back stiffly. Jim cut his eyes to the side and spoke calmly out of the side of his mouth. "Easy, partner. This man means us no harm." Looking back at the big black guy, he continued firmly, smoothly, "Go ahead. Get what you're going for, mister."

The man withdrew a business card and handed it to Greerson, who looked it over. It read simply, "Lincoln Mallard – Private Investigator." The card also included an Auburn Avenue address with a suite number and a telephone number.

"This you?" The man gave a single, slight nodded. "Private investigator, huh?" Greerson held the card out toward the man and asked, "Mind if I keep this?" The black fellow waggled his head slightly.

"Private investigator?" Rutherford released the hammer on his gun and holstered it as he got to his feet. "Bullshit! I ain't never heard of no such thing as a colored private investigator!"

Lincoln Mallard smiled and spoke at last, "Well, you have now." His voice was dry and cool.

"Don't go gittin' uppity with me, boy!" Rutherford growled.

When Mallard flinched at the words, Greerson made a slight hand gesture in his direction and again spoke over his shoulder. "Now, Detective Rutherford, the *man* wasn't getting 'uppity,' as you put it. He was simply stating an apparent fact." Notwithstanding the words of the big cop facing him, Mallard shot a distrustful gaze at him. Detective Greerson went on. "So what are you doing here? What's your interest in this?" he asked, as he turned and swept his hand toward the crime scene. When he did, he saw that many of those gathered were working their way from the murdered girl to his location. "Hold on a minute." Greerson decided it might be better to speak with Mallard elsewhere. "Stay here until I get back," he instructed Mallard. "And, Artie, behave yourself."

Jim Greerson flashed a wink at Matt and walked back to where the dead girl lay, watched over by the Officer Powell. The detective spoke to Powell to see what additional information, if any, the girl's mother had provided. The detective learned that her mother had given Powell the girl's name as Effie Sledge. The girl lived at home, sometimes but not most of the time. The mother didn't know where she worked or even if she worked. Powell gave Greerson the address the mother had provided, which was on a street near where her daughter had been found. When the detective didn't see the girl's mother, Powell explained that her neighbors had persuaded and, then, had helped the grieving woman return home. The officer added that someone from the morgue was on their way. Jim left him with instructions to be given to the morgue people that he absolutely needed to see the body before it was disposed of. He would be available as soon as he could get to Grady. Finally, he gave Powell instructions to go to the mother's house and ask her three specific questions. Officer Powell was to leave the answers to the questions, along with his report, on the Greerson's desk. With that, the detective returned to the Hupmobile where Matt was watching an uneasy staring contest taking place between Artie and Lincoln Mallard. Greerson laughed. "I'm glad to see that you guys made up while I was gone."

Rutherford grunted, and Mallard shot another uneasy smile at Jim. For his part, Matt was fascinated by the dynamics occurring before him. Rutherford, already unhappy with Matt's being there, was clearly miserable about Lincoln's presence, his status as an investigator, and the deference being given him by his partner. Lincoln Mallard seemed certain of Rutherford's attitude and intentions, but less so of Detective Greerson's, notwithstanding what he'd witnessed at the Maddox and Sledge murder scenes. Jim Greerson seemed unsure of the reason for Mallard's presence at the scenes of or his role, if any, in the two murders with which he was now dealing. His attitude toward the man was far different, however, than his partner's.

Greerson squared up with the black man. "Some private investigators carry a gun. Do you? Do you carry a gun, Mr. Mallard?"

Mallard paused for second, studying the detective's face. "Yes."

Extending his hand toward the private detective, Greerson asked, "Can I see it?"

"No."

"Why not?" Greerson's voice was calm and casual.

Mallard's tone was just as quiet and matter-of-fact. "Because, then I wouldn't be carrying it. You would."

The Atlanta detective dropped his hand at his side and gave the man the hint of a smile, letting the matter drift. But Greerson wanted to speak with Mallard and ask him some questions. The quandary he faced was where to achieve that. With the crowd standing around, he'd already decided that they couldn't talk there. And it was too hot to sit in a car and speak. The detective didn't want to return with the private investigator to police headquarters. Mallard was not a suspect at this point, and the stigma associated with hauling him into the station could overwhelm any frank discussion. They couldn't very well go together for a bite to eat or a cup of coffee in a "whites only" restaurant, given the current social norms.

As he weighed the options, Greerson studied Lincoln Mallard. The big detective gauged the private investigator's age to be between Matt's and his. He carried a muscular bulk beneath his bespoke suit. His broad face and a jaw of stone reflected a calm confidence even now where many of his race would feel humbled or threatened in the presence of police detectives or uniformed men with brass buttons. Although cautious, the private investigator was not intimidated in the slightest. That was probably a lot of what was pissing off Rutherford, Jim guessed with a grin. "Where do you live, Mr. Mallard?"

"Why do you need to know, detective?"

"Look, I think we need to talk, and, frankly, I'm at a loss for where to have a quiet, private conversation between a black man and a white man without going back to headquarters and without rousing curiosity or worse. You got any better ideas?"

"That's the world you've created, detective, not me."

"Well, I didn't create it either, but we can argue about that later. Right now, I'm trying to get together without a hassle."

Lincoln Mallard considered taking these men to his office, but abandoned the idea as relinquishing too much territory for now. Instead, he answered the question, "My wife and I live with her parents. But there are too many people at the house this time of day for a talk." One was too many, he decided. "And I don't want them involved with whatever you have in mind."

Jim saw one other option, though a little awkward, maybe even outlandish to some folk's way of thinking. But the circumstances were peculiar. "When you're not eating at home, where do you take your meals?" The private investigator replied with only an undecided look at the detective. "No, seriously, where do you eat?"

"Usually at Ma Sutton's place on Auburn Avenue. Ever heard of it?

"You mean the Ma Sutton's that's known for its fried chicken, vegetables, rolls, and cornbread?" Greerson grinned, "Yeah, I've heard of it."

Lincoln was taken aback slightly but quickly recovered. He spoke with a hint of derision in is voice. "Ever eaten there, detective?"

Greerson smiled and shook his head. "What say we grab a late lunch and talk there?"

Another uncertain look crossed Mallard's face. "Ma Sutton's is good with me, Detective Greerson. You'd be welcomed there, I'm sure, unlike the reverse situation."

Rutherford had listened to this exchange in silence long enough. "Hey, Jimbo, I ain't goin' to some —"

Greerson turned and shot his partner an icy stare before he could finish his thought. "Suit yourself, Artie. We'll drop you off on the way." Jim took a second to introduce the reporter to Lincoln so there'd be no confusion who was who. The two men shook hands at the introduction. "Matt, have you got any thoughts about going with us? We never did get any lunch today and here it is pushing midafternoon."

"I'm in, if it's okay. But I do need to call my boardinghouse real quick."

"You can run in and call from headquarters when we drop Detective Rutherford off." Greerson looked at the private investigator. "How about we meet you at the restaurant, Mr. Mallard?"

"See you there." He snickered, "If you get there before me, go ahead in and start eating without me."

Greerson laughed, "Thanks, but we'll wait for you."

The men got into their automobiles and started back toward the city's main business district. The Hupmobile turned off to make its way in the direction of Auburn Avenue while Matt steered toward Butler Street and police headquarters. Rutherford groused all the way about the steps Jim was taking to talk with the private investigator. "Just drag his colored ass into the station house and question him! That's what I'd do!" Rutherford was well aware of his partner's attitude toward certain words and grudgingly gave that feeling due regard. He knew Greerson was not someone to be crossed.

Greerson turned slightly and, draping an arm on the back of the seat, looked back at his partner. He shook his head vigorously. "What's the station house's attitude anytime a Negro is brought in by a cop, Artie? A guilty son of a bitch has been caught again. And that's regardless of the circumstances. You know it's true. Too much roiling for me at headquarters. Uh-uh. I'll do this my way. But I want some answers."

"You're too damned soft, Jim," Rutherford snarled. He said nothing more for the rest of the ride.

Grimes and Greerson dropped Rutherford off at the police station, where Matt called Miss Dixie about missing supper. Then, they proceeded up to Auburn Avenue and Ma Sutton's place. On the way, Matt told the detective that Miss Dixie had invited him to eat supper at the boardinghouse on Friday night, if he didn't have any other plans. Because Mr. Fleming had sworn him to secrecy about "the visit" a month earlier, the reporter stopped short of explaining what had happened and how the gun he'd given him had helped Mr. Fleming deal with the situation.

Matt guessed that, in part, the meal was probably a thank-you for that, but didn't feel he could divulge such to his friend. Jim happily accepted the invitation. Because neither Joshua nor Diane would not be present for supper, Miss Dixie had also invited Evie to join them. As he drove, Matt mulled over the idea of Evie coming face to face with the detective she saw as a "danger" to her boyfriend. However, Matt thought that he had no choice but to invite his girlfriend. He simply shook his head at the thought.

After they parked the Ford, the pair ambled through the constant hum of street chatter to the three-hundred block of Auburn and the restaurant, turning heads as they walked in this part of the city. Matt felt very self-conscious about his place in this setting. The feeling was new to him. Jim didn't seem as concerned or aware. Considering the ogling they were getting from people on the sidewalk and in store doorways, each man was silently glad that Detective Rutherford had declined the invitation.

Lincoln Mallard awaited the pair at the restaurant's front door, smiling thinly. "Welcome, gentlemen, to Auburn Avenue and Ma Sutton's," he said quietly, as he led the way through the door to the restaurant. When the three men entered the dining room, conversations stopped as all eyes turned to the unfamiliar sight of white men in their midst in this setting. Lincoln nodded to, threw hand greetings at, and spoke to some friends and acquaintances as the three walked to a table, seemingly easing the tension of the moment. He was like a politician working a crowd. The pause in the restaurant's conversational murmur was only momentary, and the chatter resumed almost as quickly as it had ended. Greerson hesitated, having forgotten that the food was served family style, which meant they were seated at a table with others. Lincoln gave Greerson an uncertain but hard look, as he pulled a chair out from the table. He was unsure of what was behind the Atlanta cop's indecision. "Is there a problem, detective?"

"No, of course not. It's just going to be difficult to talk like I wanted under the circumstances," he said quietly, nodding to the others at the table. "That's all."

The black detective was willing to take Detective Greerson at his word for now. He seemed sincere anyway. "I tell you what," Lincoln chuckled. "We'll focus on eating for now, and we can talk afterward."

"Fine by me. I'm famished!"

The three men were seated at a table with a black family, consisting of a small boy and his parents. The three men made small talk as they started a hearty and delicious meal of fried chicken and all the trimmings. Matt caught the sporadic stares coming from other diners. The little kid at their table spent more time looking at him as if he were a freak of nature than he did eating. The big reporter would uncomfortably, quickly avert his eyes to his plate when he felt the glances of the others in the restaurant. At one point, Lincoln saw Matt's reaction. He leaned close to the reporter's ear and whispered, "Not a comfortable feeling is it, Mr. Grimes? I mean being looked at as some sort of out-of-place sideshow attraction simply because of the color of your skin."

The young journalist grimaced sheepishly. "Not really, Mr. Mallard. I have to admit it."

Though showing the same self-confidence he'd displayed earlier, Lincoln was still a bit wary of the Greerson's intentions, but seemed on firmer ground, more at ease here on his "turf." "Hey, I meant to ask you guys to call me Linc. Everybody does. That is, if I'm not considered a suspect in your murder investigation, Detective Greerson. If I am a suspect, it'll stay Mr. Mallard."

At Lincoln's words, the two other adults at the table stopped eating and sat in stunned silence, staring at Detective Greerson and Matthew Grimes. The little boy looked wide-eyed at his mother, who quietly put a comforting hand on his arm. He then looked back at the unfamiliar white men seated at his table. The big cop smiled reassuringly and, with an open-palm gesture, said, "No, Linc, you're not a suspect in anything. I merely wanted to talk to you. And enjoy a fine meal. And I go by Jim." Matt also quietly offered his first name for use by their new acquaintance. The black couple went back to their food but shot lowered glances at each other and at Lincoln occasionally. The child returned to staring. This time, however, Matt was relieved to find that Greerson was the center of his interest. Given the attention they were receiving, the detective chose his words carefully. "So, how did you happen to be at the last two places I saw you, Linc?"

"Well, that's kind of a long story, if you really want to know. And you may not like what you hear."

"Yeah, Linc, I want to know. And the story is what it is. But, if you say so, it can wait a bit." The private investigator merely nodded. After a time, the family sharing the table with the three men finished their meals and quietly departed. Thereafter, the seats at the table remained unoccupied as the black man and the two white men quickly finished their meals in an uneasy silence. Lincoln Mallard had thought the restaurant probably wouldn't be conducive to the conversation Detective Greerson had in mind, but he wanted to expose the two white men to the world from his perspective. He also sought to gauge their reactions.

Later, as they stood on the sidewalk outside the restaurant gazing at Auburn Avenue in each direction, Mallard said proudly, "This is Auburn Avenue, gentlemen. The black Peachtree Street. Although it's less than two miles long, it's the hub of *our* life in Atlanta and home to more than a hundred twenty Negro-owned businesses and more than thirty-five Negro professionals, everything from dentists to major insurance companies. And," he smiled broadly, "one Negro private investigator. Of course, it does have some shortcomings. For example, you'll notice the absence of streetlights, which despite the area's significance, its traffic, and repeated promises to the contrary, the powers that be have not seen fit to install here."

"What about all the activities available on Peachtree Street and the lights of Atlanta's 'Great White Way'?" Matt interjected naively.

The black detective bowed slightly and responded with a slight edge to his voice, "Well, it's a *great way* if you're *white*, Matt." As the black man calmed himself, Jim just shook his head. Matt sheepishly nodded his understanding. Mallard continued calmly, "Don't you find at least a little irony in the fact that you two, as white men, can come into one of our restaurants and eat freely with nothing more coming about than a few stares from some other patrons? But, if one of us walked into one of your 'whites only' restaurants, it would likely end in, at the very least, a rude ejection, possibly a severe beating. And please understand that that difference stems not from a fear of the white man but from a Christian attitude toward our fellow man, even a hostile fellow man." Neither of the white men said anything.

Following a scan of the crowd strolling thoroughfare, Greerson turned to Mallard. "While I appreciate the great meal, Linc, I still want to hear your story and learn why you keep showing up at murder scenes. Can you think of anywhere we can sit quietly and talk?"

Lincoln Mallard studied the detective's face briefly and glanced Matt's way. He decided that, based on what he'd seen of them and their interaction with him thus far, taking these two men to his office was an acceptable compromise of his privacy. "Yeah, detective, how about going to my office?"

Greerson didn't ask the obvious question of why Mallard hadn't mention his office earlier. He was sure he knew the answer. And, despite having seen the man's business card, he'd chosen not to press for the invitation too early. "That sounds fine, Linc. Where is it?"

"It's in a building some farther down Auburn. C'mon," the private investigator said, leading the way.

The three men walked a distance on Auburn Avenue, still drawing occasional stares from men and women on the street. Shortly, they

## THE PRIVATE INVESTIGATOR

entered a redbrick building, the street level of which comprised retail stores and a pharmacy. Inside, the three men climbed to the second floor where Lincoln Mallard had his agency.

On entering the office through a door bearing the man's name and occupation, Mallard removed his hat, hung it on a coat stand, and motioned for his guests to have a seat as he walked around his desk. As he was taking a seat, Greerson took his hat off and held it on his knee. He ranged his eyes quickly over the office. The space was roomy and neat but sparsely decorated as offices go with minimum trappings besides the desk and chair, a telephone, and comfortable leather visitors' chairs with chromium arms. It held a bookcase with various volumes, a typewriter on a typing table, and a large file cabinet. The ubiquitous milk-glass bowl light was suspended from the center of the ceiling by three brass chains and waist-high tongue-and-groove wainscoting lined the walls. The detective noted that the photographs of several prominent Negro citizens, including Booker T. Washington, hung on the walls. Most of the men he recognized as current or deceased Atlanta citizens. One of the photographs was an older picture of a woman Greerson didn't recognize. On the desk was a small portrait of Lincoln Mallard and a woman, presumably his wife.

"Nice office you've got here, Linc. Mind if I smoke?" The detective shook a cigarette out of a fresh pack for himself and offered one to the other two men. They each accepted one. He struck a match on his shoe sole and lit his and Matt's smoke while Mallard waved the match off. Jim smiled, "Superstitious?" When the private detective only returned the smile and rolled the cigarette in his fingers, Greerson blew out the match and proceeded, "No offense, but how can you make enough money in Atlanta as a private investigator to maintain a place like this?" The Atlanta cop chose to let the word "Negro" be implied in the question.

Mallard pushed an ashtray across the desk toward his visitors. Greerson deposited the used match in it. "Well, let's just say I can and leave it at that."

Greerson plodded on to get the answers he was after. "I only figured that knowing what you do might help explain why you keep turning up at the murder scenes of young Negro women."

For a moment, Mallard toyed with a pencil on his desk, eyeing the detective. Then, leaning forward, he began, "Fair enough. Just remember that you asked. The whole thing actually goes back to the Atlanta race riots of 1906. Those were three ugly days," he said, nodding in Matt's direction, "fueled by your folks in the newspaper business printing some hearsay allegations about black men assaulting white women." When Matt started to speak, Mallard raised a controlling hand slightly and continued. "More than two dozen of my people died in the riots and many more were hurt. Remember the older man you spoke with at the Addie Maddox murder scene? The man who called himself Stitch, true name Daniels?" Greerson turned his head and glanced at Matt before returning his eyes to Linc and nodding. "That limp arm and the scar across his forehead are what he carries as reminders of the 1906 riots. His nickname, too, I guess," he sighed.

"Anyway, after the riots, Negro businesses started moving out of the downtown area, which had been fairly well integrated previously as far as business ownership was concerned. Many of them began accumulating in the Auburn Avenue area. Some prominent citizens in the Negro community at the time felt compelled to find a way to correct the wrongs being visited on their people. They basically weren't sure what they could do at that point beyond building their community economically and supporting the Negro population as a whole. Unfortunately, and not surprisingly, the white power structure wasn't about to listen to their concerns. My people did what they could, but they knew there had to be more. Nothing changed.

"Then, in 1911, along came what were called the 'Atlanta Ripper' killings of young Negro women. They stretched, unsolved I might add, over a period of at least four years with more than twenty victims, depending on whose count you follow. Again, the prominent citizens within the Negro community, people like Reverend Proctor and Henry Rucker, sought help from the authorities. They requested that the police department hire at least one Negro detective to assist in the investigation. They knew that a detective from our race might be seen as less invasive in our community and that, just maybe, it would lead to more cooperation from its members. They also believed that his presence would have sent the message that the Negro community was doing all it could to stop the murders. But, again, nothing changed. Not a thing.

"Now, twenty years later, not a single Negro has yet to be employed as even a uniformed officer by the Atlanta Police Department! Not one!" Though forceful, Mallard's voice remained calm. "Do you know what part of the Atlanta population is made up of Negroes, according to the last census? Roughly thirty-three percent. Get me? A third of the population of this city, this area is not represented by even one member of their race on the police force! For God's sake, man, the department has had *policewomen* since 1918! A Women's Bureau was set up in 1924! But no Negroes?

"I don't think there's any limit to what a Negro can achieve if given the opportunity. One of my favorite examples of that is the situation of a man named Roderick Badger. Mr. Badger was a Negro dentist here in Atlanta in the late 1800s. White dentists complained about him being allowed to practice. However, contrary to one might suppose would happen, the city council ignored the complaints of the white dentists and let Roderick Badger practice. He became a popular dentist, even with whites. The power structure can ignore reality, but they can't ignore the consequences of ignoring reality, detective."

Lincoln Mallard paused, leaned back in his squeaky swivel chair, and took in a deep breath. Matt sat, squirming in slight discomfort, watching and listening intently, moving his eyes between the black private investigator and the Atlanta detective. As for Greerson, he had nothing to say. Nothing could be said. The private investigator clasped his hands together behind his head and smiled. "So, several years ago, some prominent men and women in Atlanta's Negro community decided that they needed someone in a quasi-official capacity to watch the police department in its dealings with the Negroes of Atlanta. It's been no secret that sympathy with and even membership in the Klan has been widespread within the department. Anyway, as it turned out, I'd recently finished college, and it was known by these community leaders that I had a yen to be a police officer, although most saw it as an impossibility in this age, in this town. Oh, there were other places to go pursue my dreams, like New York City, Chicago, I guess, but my roots are here, my family and my wife's family are here. By some people's estimations, I was intelligent and full of spunk. What your friend, Detective Rutherford, would call being 'uppity.' At the same time, I could maintain a level-headed attitude to do the job. That probably factored in my favor with the decision made by my employers.

"Anyway, those same prominent citizens set me up in the private investigator business to keep an eye on how things were handled between the Atlanta Police Department and the Negro community. They got what they felt they needed, and I'm as close to being a cop in Atlanta as I'll ever get. Of course, I do other things to earn my retainer, such as hunt down folks for the insurance companies located here on Auburn Avenue. I chase down deadbeat debtors, husbands, locate missing people. A divorce case comes my way occasionally, too. That kind of stuff. My employers provided this office." He leaned across the desk toward Detective Greerson. "In fact, if you check the tag number you wrote down from my Hupmobile, you'll find that it's registered to an insurance company." When Greerson smiled, Linc smiled back and added, "Yeah, I saw that."

The Atlanta detective's smile broadened. He saw a man sitting across the desk who was smart, proud, tough, determined, and not easily intimidated by anyone. In addition, Greerson surmised, he had strength of character. All of these attributes in the right measures to do a cop's job. And maybe do it better than some he knew on the force now, he reflected. In the silence that followed, Jim got to his feet and walked to a photograph of Booker T. Washington. He read two quotes from the man that were typed and framed below the portrait:

> Nothing ever comes to one, that is worth having, except as a result of hard work. No greater injury can be done to any youth than to let him feel that because he belongs to this or that race he will be advanced in life regardless of his own merits or efforts.

And the other:

> There is another class of colored people who make a business of keeping the troubles, the wrongs, and the hardships of the Negro race before the public. Having learned that they are able to make a living out of their troubles, they have grown into the settled habit of advertising their wrongs — partly because they want sympathy and partly because it pays. Some of these people do not want the Negro to lose his grievances, because they do not want to lose their jobs.

Lincoln watched the detective closely as he read. Matt watched both men intently. When he'd finished reading, Greerson smiled and nodded. He moved to one of the windows overlooking Auburn Avenue and the late afternoon activities there. Mallard swiveled his chair slowly, following the big cop with his eyes as he walked around the room. Lincoln Mallard spoke up, "I know Mr. Washington's approach to the world isn't favored by Mr. DuBois, but I think those are two good points he makes there."

Jim nodded and moved on. "So you became a private dick watching the Atlanta PD, huh? Don't you think that our police department does everything they can to stop criminals and handle crime?"

"Honestly?" Mallard asked, to which the big cop nodded sharply. "Well, just remember that you brought it up. Hell, if the cops actually did *everything* they could, I'd be out of a job." Jim's flinch was nearly imperceptible, but Matt sensed it as he watched, and he prepared himself for the Atlanta detective's response. Mallard saw the reaction, too, but, before the big cop could say anything, he pushed on undeterred, "Look, all I'm saying is the police are bound, at least in theory, by rules a private investigator isn't. Just as in every profession, there's good and bad. Frankly, I think that some men in your department pay little more heed to the law than do the crooks. In doing my job, my biggest confining factor is Jim Crow."

"You're not saying that you'd break the law in your line of work, are you, Linc?" The private investigator merely smiled in reply. When he realized that was the only response he was going to get, Jim asked, "How long have you been a shamus? And why haven't I heard of you before now?"

"I've been doing it for about six years. The reason you've not heard of me is what I'd call 'intentional luck.' I've tried to maintain a low profile in doing what I do. I take the word 'private' in the term 'private investigator' seriously. That's the way my employers think, and I agree, it should be done. If I see or hear something I think they need to know about, I give them the information, and they take the steps necessary to bring it to the attention of the right people. Sometimes they get results, most times they don't. That's the white man's world. But I'm not there to interfere with you doing your job, detective." The black private investigator struck a match from a small box on his desk and lit his cigarette. Blowing the match out and tossing it onto his desk, he leaned back in his chair, puffing a small plume of smoke toward an open window.

Jim leaned his butt on the windowsill. "I don't run the world or even the Atlanta PD part of it." His slight irritation revealed itself in the tone of his words. "If I did, maybe it'd be different. But let's talk cases, Linc. Any particular interest in the Maddox and Sledge murders?"

"No, I'm just keeping an eye on how the police will handle them. Some folks, like your buddy Rutherford, think the investigation of a Negro's murder is a waste of their time and effort. They seem —"

"Let's get one thing straight from the start, Linc," Jim said forcefully. "I don't. There's a fiend on the loose out there somewhere, and I intend to do everything I can to find him."

"No offense intended, detective. I've seen you work the crime scene in each case, so I know how you approached them. That's why I left after a short time there. I left because it looked like you were giving the investigations a fair shake."

Greerson smiled and raised himself from the sill. He took a step away from the window and stopped. He glanced back at the wall and nodded toward a photograph hanging there. "I recognize all the people in the photographs except this lady. Who's she?"

"That's Mrs. Carrie Steele. She —"

"Yeah," Greerson nodded, smiling, "I know who she is now. The orphans' home. I just didn't recognize her in the photograph." Mallard smiled his appreciation of the cop's knowledge of his people and their history. Jim returned to his chair and leaned back in it. "Both these girls' murders have the same characteristics, the same technique. Since you know something about the cases, any thoughts or ideas about them?"

Mallard's brow furrowed. "No, not really," he smiled thinly, "not unless the Atlanta Ripper has returned after twenty years. They do appear to have been committed by the same person, though." He made a vague gesture with his right hand. "Maybe the second one's a copycat of the first."

"I don't think so. Maybe an examination of Sledge's body will help explain some things. It's being held at Grady's morgue right now. How about you going with me and seeing if anything clicks? I have a vague theory. But that's all it is, just a thought. Maybe between the two of us, we can come up with something."

"Sure! But how do you think the people at Grady are gonna react to me being there like that?"

"Let me worry about that." Jim glanced at the reporter. "Matt?"

"I hate not to go with you two, but I really need to get back to the paper and write up what I have so far," he stretched the truth. The young reporter, or rather his stomach was not up for a visit to the morgue at the moment. "Will you keep me posted, Jim?"

"As always, buddy. Do you mind dropping us off at Grady? It might be quicker than finagling with one of our cars, Linc." When the black detective nodded his agreement, Jim looked at his young reporter friend. Matt readily consented. Returning to the investigator, the Atlanta cop asked to use his phone to contact headquarters and let them know where he was going. While Greerson was making he call, Grimes briefly talked with Mallard about his background and his work.

---

Twenty-five minutes later, Jim Greerson and Lincoln Mallard rumbled out of Matt's Ford and scampered across Butler Street while Matt pulled away from the curb to return to the *Georgian-American* Building. Before they climbed the steps leading into Grady Hospital's Romanesque redbrick structure, Jim stopped Linc for a brief conversation in the shade of one of the trees in front of the building. "Listen, before we go in, you need to know that Rutherford got on the phone when I called the stationhouse and invited himself to come here for some unknown reason. He'll probably be inside. He –"

"Does he know I'm coming along?"

"No," Jim smiled, "I saw no reason to tell him." Greerson looked squarely into the black man's eyes. "Whatever he says or does, I'm asking you to let it go. I can't explain Artie, if you even *need* an explanation for him." Mallard smiled at the comment, and Jim continued, "But, if I didn't think you and I could work together on this, I wouldn't have asked you to come here. As tough as his shit may be to take, I'm asking you to. For now. Agreed?"

Mallard smiled thinly and nodded. "For now. And for the sake of the girls. Besides, I'm not one to get chased off a patch. But I need you to understand one thing about me, Jim. Unfortunately, I've had to get used to ignorant folks like Rutherford. Words like theirs don't bother me as much as does the silence of others who won't speak up against their hate." Jim's face reddened slightly, as he nodded his understanding.

Inside, the pair ignored the turned heads as they made their way to Grady's small morgue. When someone attempted to stop them, Greerson merely flashed his badge a plodded on. Downstairs in the morgue area, Jim made arrangements with a man to view Effie Sledge's body. As they spoke briefly, the attendant kept looking past the detective at the well-dressed black man accompanying him. The big cop ignored the man's obvious distaste for Mallard's presence.

About the time the attendant took the two men to a room to view Sledge's remains, Detective Rutherford suddenly rounded a corner. When he saw Mallard, he smiled sourly and growled. "Well, if ain't Boston *Blackie*? Shouldn't you be peering through a keyhole somewheres?" The attendant snickered. Mallard's face went hard, but he merely strained a smile at his adversary. Turning to his partner, Rutherford snarled, "What the hell's *he* doin' here?"

"I asked him to be here. He may be able to add something to our investigation, Artie."

"No, not *our* investigation! *Your* investigation, Jimbo! First, you drag in some punk newsie and now a dinge. I come here because I thought we was partners of a sort and you wanted my help!"

"I do want your help, Artie, but Linc here may be able to give us a different perspective on the cases involving these Negro victims."

"*Linc?*" Rutherford guffawed with disdain. "You mean like 'missing link'?"

Lincoln Mallard had stayed quiet long enough. With his fists clenched in subdued anger, but anger, nonetheless, he said between gritted teeth, "Well, I have to say that you're better read than I would've thought, detective. I wasn't at all sure you *could* read. But don't be ignorant all your life!"

Jim stepped between the two as Artie Rutherford moved Mallard's way. "I oughta break your neck!" he shouted around Greerson at the black man.

"Maybe you can and maybe you can't, detective," the private investigator replied calmly, coldly.

"You'd better show me the proper respect, boy!" Rutherford yelled, pushing against Greerson's restraint.

"Your job gives you authority, detective. Your behavior earns you respect," Mallard replied evenly.

An enraged Rutherford pushed on toward Mallard. "Why you uppity nig —" Greerson suddenly pounded a meaty fist hard on the angle of his partner's jaw. Rutherford's butt felt the cold, hard embrace of the tiled floor. Mallard froze, stunned and momentarily uncertain. The wide-eyed attendant fled the room, mouth agape. As Artie sat, rubbing his chin, feeling his teeth, and shaking his head, he looked up at his fellow detective. "What the hell did you do that for, Jimbo?"

"Let's just say you earned it from somebody here, Artie. And if Lincoln had done it, I'd have to arrest him." As Artie got back to his feet, Jim turned to look at each man and continued, "I'll thank the two of you to show each other the respect a gentleman gives as a matter of course."

Lincoln Mallard extended his hand in Artie Rutherford's direction. "I'd rather be your friend, detective." When Rutherford only glared at the black man, he let his hand fall back to his side and said without emotion, "But, if you're not interested in that, I'm prepared to be a capable and efficient enemy."

Rutherford's face convulsed slightly as he shook his head. "You talk like we're some kind of equals. Don't go gettin' that notion in your stupid brain, 'cause we ain't equals."

The tension was palpable, but before Greerson could intercede, Mallard spoke again. "Sure we are. You just haven't figured it out yet. Remember this moment, Detective Rutherford. Today the future reached out its hand to you. You should have grabbed it and held on tight for all you're worth."

The two men stared hard at each other, neither blinking nor flinching. After a long moment, Greerson, satisfied that the situation had calmed sufficiently, at least for the moment, turned his attention to Effie Sledge's remains. Pulling back the sheet covering her, he said mechanically, "Artie, help me get her clothes off."

"What? Hell, no! Whatcha want her buck nekked for?"

"Not totally naked, Artie, but I need to see if she has certain marks on her body. C'mon. Lend a hand."

"Uh-uh! Nothin' doin'! I ain't touchin'—" Rutherford stopped himself from completing the thought and worked hard at not looking Lincoln Mallard's way. "If I did, I'd have to take a bath!" he smiled at Jim triumphantly.

Lincoln Mallard couldn't help himself. "Oh, yeah. We wouldn't want you to have to do something you're unaccustomed to, detective."

Artie Rutherford immediately bowed up, fists clenched, and growled, "Your death ain't nothin' but paperwork to me, boy."

As Greerson squared up facing Rutherford again, Mallard spoke around him to the man's partner. "Boy? The next time you say 'boy,' I'd better be able to look around and see one, detective!"

Jim's fists were clinched in frustration. "You two knock it off or I'll have to stomp both of you! Get me?" Over the next minute, the other two men slowly relaxed.

"I'll help, Detective Greerson," Mallard offered and stepped to the gurney where the dead girl lay. They rolled her onto her side, and Jim started unbuttoning the back of her dress. "What're you looking for, Jim?"

"Those marks! Right there, Linc! Artie, look at this!" Greerson exclaimed, after they had struggled to slide the girl's dress down to her knees and returned her to lying on her back. He was pointing to striations on her hips and breasts. Rutherford stayed in the background.

"Okay," Linc admitted, "I see them, but I guess I don't know enough about woman to know their significance. What do they mean?"

When Rutherford snorted, Jim turned to him pointedly and asked him whether *he* knew what they meant. The detective massaged his lips with a meaty hand as he turned the question over in his mind. After a long pause, Artie reluctantly confessed that he didn't know either. Jim smiled. "Did you notice how tight the dress fit her, Linc?"

"Well, yeah, but —"

"This girl's been pregnant. And recently. I'll bet a medical examination will bear that out. The Maddox girl had the same striations. Her daddy told me that she'd never been married or had any children. Had never even been pregnant that he knew of. He did say that he thought she'd been gaining a little weight until recently. We know what Maddox did for a living. I'm willing to bet that this girl had fallen into the same life. Effie's momma will probably tell us the same story about her never having been married, having children, or being pregnant."

"But what does it mean, Jim?"

"Well, if an examination shows what I think it will, what it showed about the Maddox girl, she's had an abortion."

"Abortion?" Rutherford and Mallard exclaimed in unison.

"Yeah, an abortion. An illegal procedure. Done by someone or for someone who now wants it covered up. Maybe they figured the surest way to do that was to get rid of the girls."

Mallard asked, "How do you know about such things?"

"When my wife and I were trying to start a family, I read a lot of books, some medical, some with pictures and drawings." A slight smile broke on the big detective's face. "In some ways, I learned more than I wanted to know. So when –"

"Wait! You got an examination of the Maddox girl done? Why? By who?" Artie expressed his surprise. He'd finally processed Greerson's statement.

Greerson rubbed a thumbnail on the black stubble of his jaw and studied the girl's body as he answered his partner's question. "Ella," Jim started, paused, took a deep breath, and glanced at Linc, "my late wife, worked for a doctor who came to regard her as a daughter. He'd lost his daughter to scarlet fever, I think, or something like that. Anyway, she would have been close to Ella's age. The doctor felt really close to Ella. He'd had us over for Sunday dinners a lot. He's a peach of a guy." Jim paused and, almost imperceptibly, shook his head. He went on, "Anyway, after my wife died, he told me that, if ever I needed anything he could help me with, all I had to do was call on him. Never thought I'd have the need. But, when Addie Maddox was murdered and I saw those striations, I asked him what he thought. He told me what he'd guess had caused them and volunteered to do an examination. Maddox's daddy was okay with it if I thought it might help find her killer. My doctor friend confirmed that she'd had an abortion and said that Maddox's procedure wasn't some back-alley, clothes-hanger deal. It was done by a medical professional. I want him to check this girl, too, if he will."

"Okay, that's all well and good, but where do you go from here, detective?"

# SHORTENING SHADOWS

"Your question should be 'where do *we* go from here?' I need your help, Linc, if you're willing, but I can't pay you anything." Rutherford stirred, but said nothing.

The black man smiled and nodded. "Part of what I'm paid by my patrons to do is look out for the Negro community as a whole in whatever way I can, Jim. This *has* to fall under that heading, wouldn't you say?"

When Rutherford snorted disdainfully, Greerson prodded on, "Okay. First, I'll have this girl examined by my doctor buddy. If I'm right, it looks like we may have found a motive. I always say, 'find the motive, find the killer.' Then, we, that is, you check her background to see who her friends were, where she stayed when she wasn't with her momma, and if she was turning tricks. If she was hooking, then, we look for who may have been behind the girls' lifestyles and for who performed the abortions. To that end, I need you to check around and see what you can learn about a Negro named Nathan Green. The best I can figure is he's a pimp, was a pimp for Addie Maddox, at least. He was seen with her the afternoon she was killed. But there's only so much a white guy can get from your people, even a white Atlanta PD detective. See what you can find out. See if he had any connection with the Sledge girl, too. If my information is right, he has to know *something* about Maddox's death. He wasn't very willing to talk to me, and I didn't have much to go on when I spoke with him. Maybe he was scared. I don't know. Maybe there's someone higher up he's afraid to cross."

"Maybe he was just afraid of getting his kidneys rearranged and pissing blood in a police station basement, Jim," Mallard interjected. Rutherford snickered in the background.

Greerson bristled slightly. "Yeah, well, that's not what I'm about at this stage, Linc. Anyway, find out what you can, and we'll get back together. Now, let me make a phone call, and then let's get out of here." Greerson located the morgue attendant who'd been eavesdropping around the corner in a hallway. The attendant helped Jim locate a telephone, from which he called the doctor, and made arrangements for an examination of Sledge's body. After the phone call, Greerson gave the attendant instructions about the girl's remains and went to join his companions. He found Lincoln Mallard standing alone. Although he knew the answer, he asked the black detective, "Where's Artie?"

"I dunno. He just took off."

"Probably had something else to get to in a hurry," Jim offered.

Linc flinched. "Wait. As I see it, you're worlds apart from Rutherford in many ways, Jim, but are you gonna spend your life making excuses for his kind? You know damned well he just didn't want to be seen with me or have me in his car. He'd rather abandon you before having that happen."

Greerson shook his head and exhaled heavily. "Nah, Linc, I'm not making excuses." He gave the black man a slight shrug. "I didn't mean to insult your intelligence. Sorry." He paused before continuing with a smile, "Well, anyway it's a beautiful day for a walk. Warm but bearable." The two men turned and started toward the stairs. "Say, would a week be enough time for you to get the information we need?"

Lincoln Mallard chuckled. "If I can't get that little bit of information in a week, I need to close my office. I think I'm gonna start by checking this Nathan Green first. That might give me a better angle on the Sledge girl when I get around to looking into her background."

"Sounds great! Then, what say we meet at police headquarters at five o'clock next Monday afternoon, unless something urgent comes up, Linc? If it does, call me there."

"What say we meet at my office at the same time on Monday, instead of the police station?"

"All right with me." Greerson laughed and put a friendly hand on the black detective's shoulder as they climbed the steps, "Concerned about that police station basement, Linc?"

"Not me," he smiled in return as they moved toward the exit. "I've got nothin' to fear. Let's simply say it'd be more convenient."

They bounded down the hospital's front steps between the two large trees on either side of the entry walk. When they reached the sidewalk at Butler Street, Linc started to turn north. Jim stopped him. "It's not that far a walk back to the police station from here. Let's walk it, and I'll drive you back to your office."

"Thanks anyway, Jim, but Auburn is only a couple of blocks or so north of here. I'll walk there."

"C'mon, Linc, show me some trust and walk with me to my car at headquarters. Besides, we can talk a little on the way." Mallard smiled and nodded as the two men turned left and moved up the slight incline toward the police station.

As they crossed Armstrong Street, Mallard said, "Say, Jim, let's make sure to walk side by side." The Atlanta detective gave him a hard questioning glance as the black detective went on, "If I get ahead of you, it looks like a white man chasing a black man. If you get ahead of me, it looks like a white guy being chased by a black man. Either way, it's likely to get me a beating from some misunderstanding white bystanders."

Jim laughed heartily, but, familiar with the street here, nodded toward the block's black residences and the two nearby restaurants, each owned by a black man, one named Moses Hawkins and the other Willie Crew. "In this area, Linc, I'm the one who might be in a jam under those circumstances." Lincoln Mallard gave the detective a knowing smile and agreed. The two men moved down the street and lighted cigarettes, talking briefly about the murder cases as they moved. When Linc broached the possibility of the killings being random coincidences or the work of a copycat in the second case, the police detective dismissed the idea. He said that he thought it was the work of a single person, someone the girls knew and trusted. Knowing the line of work Maddox was in and the gossip about Nathan Green's occupation, he proposed, was why he wanted to confirm that report and brace him for what he knows. He ended by solemnly saying, "Evil is always more dangerous when it takes the cloak of familiarity."

Eventually, Linc asked his companion why his attitude toward his race was so much different from Rutherford's, finishing with, "You obviously grew up somewhere in the South just like he did. Why the difference?"

"Well, first, let me give you my opinion about something. Negative attitudes toward your people aren't confined to the South. I spent some time in a Northern state and, believe me, the feelings there aren't that much different from what you encounter around here. Sure, the Jim Crow laws down here are bad and make it worse, but the real, in-the-gut attitudes of people in other places are a lot closer to those here than some want to admit. Just remember, the 'disturbance' they called the New York Draft Riots back in '63 turned racial in a hurry. They weren't sure of the final death toll, but nearly a dozen Negro men were lynched in a five-day period and many more Negroes were hurt. Down here, unfortunately, the attitude is only more open than elsewhere. But understand that my outlook toward your race when I was growing up wasn't much different from what Artie's is now. That all changed for me during the war in Europe."

Mallard stopped suddenly and turned to face Greerson. Two men, standing across the street at the entrance to the Georgia Power Company's building at Butler Street's intersection with Gilmer Street, stopped talking and closely, guardedly watched the black man squared up with the white man. Though they saw the men, Linc and Jim ignored them. "How so, Jim?"

Greerson paused for a long moment, reflecting on his feelings and looking hard at Linc's face, which held a questioning smile. Greerson returned the smile and shook his head. Then, his face went solemn again. "What I'm about to tell you, Linc, is something I've never shared with anybody except Ella. Maybe I should have shared it. I dunno. Maybe it might make a difference to somebody somewhere sometime, but I haven't."

The detective's eyes moistened and he stared off at nothing, at nobody. "Seems I've been giving up a lot about my innermost feelings these last few weeks," he said distantly. Abruptly, he blinked and looked back at the black man. The big cop shook his head sharply. "Anyway, it's simple. My experiences brought about a change in my outlook. You see, during the war, I was assigned to the 42$^{nd}$ 'Rainbow' Division. I was badly wounded during the last days of the Meuse-Argonne Offensive. While I was recovering, I came in contact with American Negro troops of the 92$^{nd}$ Division, who'd been assigned to fight with the French army. It wasn't supposed to happen, but we crossed paths. I even got to know a few of them pretty well."

"Oh yeah? I had an uncle who fought in the 92$^{nd}$ Division," Linc beamed. "Served with Aaron Fisher." He laughed as he added, "My uncle said he got his first real pair of shoes at Camp Funston."

"Well, you should be proud of him then, Linc. The men of the 92$^{nd}$ fought hard, endured a lot, and took many casualties. Out of their experience, two common thoughts seemed to have arisen. Some say they took those casualties because they were not good at fighting, maybe even cowards. That's pure bullshit. I came to see what they'd gone through, what they'd done for a country that didn't always treat them right. Those Negro men were proud and brave. On the other hand, many Negroes and others want to brag about how the French had treated them as 'equals.' But I saw that different, too. They were treated as equals by their French commanders mostly in the sense that the French officers sent both their white French forces and the Negro American soldiers to their deaths with equal disregard, indifference for the loss of life. Of course, they did the same with the Negro troops from the French colonies. They were all seen simply as cannon fodder by their commanders." He paused briefly. "Anyway, without going into more details, the experience gave me an appreciation of who Negroes are and what they can be and can do if given a chance."

Linc looked at his companion, but said nothing. After a few seconds of silence, the black man extended his hand to Jim. As they shared a firm handshake, he said quietly, "You need to tell that story, Jim, as often and to as many people as possible." Greerson shrugged slowly, nodding. They turned and crossed Gilmer Street, moving toward the police station.

---

Earlier, as Greerson and Mallard had made their way across Butler Street to Grady Hospital, Matt drove back to the *Georgian-American* Building to write his piece on the Sledge murder. Not much else was occurring in local stories, save for an automobile accident that had injured a local couple that morning. Before working up his copy on the murder, Matt checked the wire services. The kidnapping of the Weyerhaeuser child was still a huge story. Matt also saw the account of an Alabama Negro named Jesse Owens who had set several new world records and equaled another during a Big Ten track meet in Ann Arbor, Michigan, that past Saturday. As the reporter read of the young man's accomplishments, Lincoln Mallard's words about what a Negro can achieve when given the opportunity came back to him.

Matt walked briskly to his desk and swept of his hat and coat and hung them on the column-mounted hook there. He pounded out his copy on the Sledge murder and took it to Mr. Barnes. The editor leaned back in his chair as he thoughtfully read the details. As the older man scanned the page, Matt realized that not everyone had as much concern about the death, even the murder of an everyday Negro girl, as the reporter felt the story demanded. Not certain of Mr. Barnes's reception to his angle on the account, the young man started putting forth a halfhearted apology for bothering him with it. As he was stating his case for the significance of the item, the editor, tugging at his earlobe, interrupted him. "So your detective friend thinks this murder and the one of the girl several weeks ago are related?"

Matt was taken aback slightly, but, at the same time, encouraged by the question. "Yessir. Same *modus operandi*, same race and gender of the victims. Both were Negro females. Detective Greerson's going to look into their backgrounds to see if there's a connection. We know the first girl was working as a prostitute. That may be a lead. Maybe not."

"Neither girl was found with shoes? Do I recollect that right?"

"Yessir. It may not —"

"Go down and see Mrs. LaFavor," the editor interrupted again, his tone solemn. "Tell her that you need to see everything she has on the so-called Atlanta Ripper cases from about twenty-five years ago. Look through the material. Study it so you can see if there are any other similarities." Mr. Barnes paused and gazed hard at his young charge. "Most of those girls were killed the same way as these two. And, if I recall correctly, several of those girls were found with their shoes missing. It may be a coincidence. May be a copycat. And there may be more murders before this is over. Could it be that the Atlanta Ripper, who was never caught, has suddenly emerged from prison or from a lunatic asylum and started back where he left off? Could he have just returned to Atlanta from somewhere?" Here, Barnes paused. "I don't know, Matt. Look into the older cases and keep them in mind. Might want to give the story a little of that angle. It's your story. Use your judgment, son."

"Yessir, Mr. Barnes, thanks. Funny, you know. Somebody else mentioned the Atlanta Ripper cases this afternoon, but in a different context." Matt followed Mr. Barnes instructions and spent several hours poring over the material about the old murders. The city editor was right. Some striking similarities existed. However, he only made a passing mention of the earlier crimes in his write-up. No sense in stirring up the readership too much now, Matt decided.

---

After Greerson dropped Linc off in front of his building on Auburn Avenue that Monday afternoon, the black detective returned to his office and attended to a few minor matters he was handling for one of the insurance companies located along Auburn Avenue, making follow-up telephones calls and completing a report on a missing, insured husband he'd located.

When he'd earned his retainer from the insurance company for the day, he opened a desk drawer and removed a box of cigars. Pocketing a handful as possible peace offerings or bribes, Linc left the building and walked down the street to a pool hall. As he moved along the sidewalk, it occurred to the private investigator that Detective Greerson had failed to give him a description of this Nathan Green guy and, in the rush, he'd forgotten to ask. He stepped inside the pool hall and gave his eyes time to adjust to the dimly lit, noisy establishment. Through the haze of cigar and cigarette smoke, he spied the man he was seeking. The dapper, wiry little man, who went by the name of Blue, stood across the room. Lincoln saw that he was dressed to the nines in a wide-lapelled pinstriped suit with a loud, hand-painted tie and gray spats over small, highly polished shoes. He wore a conk hairstyle. Blue's well-turned-out appearance, smooth talk, and ready supply of cash made him a favorite among the ladies. He was known to work both sides of the law and always had his ear to the ground for the latest talk on the street. Linc used the diminutive guy's knowledge and his knack for learning about people and their whereabouts as a paid source in his investigative work. No one ever thought anything of seeing the two men together, because Blue was some distant cousin of Linc's wife, Leola, although her daddy tried to put even more distance between his family and Blue's "no-account folk."

Making his way through the pool tables, the black private investigator received a few hearty greetings from sundry patrons. Lincoln Mallard was known as a square shooter in his community. Even the not-so-on-the-level populace appreciated that. The object of his search saw him coming, smiled broadly, and extended his hand. "What's the buzz, cuz?" the smaller man said energetically around a cigar clinched in his teeth. Linc mused that the cigar appeared nearly as large as one of the Black Crackers' bats. Blue's piercing black eyes shone even in the dim light.

Linc returned the smile and shook the man's hand firmly. Blue's grip reminded the detective that, while the little man was more likely to smooth talk his way out of trouble in any given moment, he was very capable of striking back when his adversary least expected it and doing some damage. Linc had seen that first hand in this establishment. The detective waved off Blue's offer of a smoke, as he glanced around the room. "Nothing much, Blue. How's about you?"

"Same ol', same ol', cuz. Just about to go get me some leg. Whatcho doin'?"

Linc lowered his voice to conspiratorial tones, but still loud enough to be heard above the din. "I need to locate somebody, Blue. Somebody unfamiliar to me." Blue nodded his understanding, as Linc added, "Name's Nathan Green."

Still nodding, the small man asked, "Which Nathan Green is you lookin' fo'?"

"What do you mean?"

"Well, there's three Nathan Greens that I knows of. One's been makin' li'l uns outta big uns on the chain gang fo' 'bout two years now." Linc shook his head. "T'other's a farmer in Jonesboro with a wife name of Selma and half-dozen kids. And the last un's a mean bastard who runs numbers here in town." Blue chuckled, "Easiest way for a cat to make a dime these days is runnin' numbers. O' course, word's out that he's branched out to runnin' a stable of girls now, too. Same white folks back him in both lines o' work."

"That last one sounds right, Blue. Do you know what he looks like? Where can I just accidentally on purpose bump into him? Any ideas?"

Blue dragged his cigar out of his mouth, looked at it, and put it back. "I knows what he look like. He's short and skinny, has a medium complexion with freckles on his face. His eyes is light green. Spooky lookin' that away. Most of all, he's just damned mean. I'm guessin' that's mostly why the white folks put him in charge of the women." Blue rubbed his hand along his jaw thoughtfully. "But I don't know his hangouts. He —" Before Blue could finish, an older man with a clipped stride approached near the two men. "Here's a brother who can prob'ly tell ya." The smallish black man took a step toward the approaching man and exclaimed. "Well, Strad! Hasn't seen you in a month o' Sundays, brother! Howzit to you?"

The older man, nicknamed for the chain between the ankle shackles he'd worn on a chain gang for many years, smiled weakly. "Hard as lard, Blue. Just hard as lard." He looked at Linc and smiled. "Mistuh Mallard, how is ya?"

Linc clapped a friendly hand on the man's shoulder and used the other to deftly fish a few dollars from his pocket. Linc shook the man's hand, slipping him the cash in the same motion. Strad's eyes showed his recognition of the gesture. "I sholy do thank ya, suh." Linc also took the opportunity to retrieve a cigar and give it to Strad, who sniffed it and tucked it into a pocket.

Blue intervened, "Say, Strad, I'm lookin' to find a lady fo' the evenin'. Where can I find Nathan Green?"

The dapper little chap's reputation as a lady's man was well known. The older man shot Blue a puzzled look at the idea of him paying for a woman's company. "Well, most nights lately, he keep hisself at Horace's place. Seem to be his base o' operatin'." Money in hand, Strad seemed anxious to depart.

Blue thanked him for the information. As he turned to leave, Strad slightly raised the fist holding the cash Linc had slipped him. "Thanky, agin, Mistuh Mallard."

"It's okay, Strad. You take care now, ya hear?" As the old man shuffled away, Linc watched him with something of a heavy heart. He looked at Strad but spoke to Blue, "You can tell me about Horace's place, right, Blue? I've heard the name, but I'm not familiar with it."

"Oh, yeah, cuz. It's a pour house over here near Bell Street. Run by a guy name a Horace Jones. At least that's the name he use now. I heared that he's had others. Anyhow, I used to go there, take a woman there ever' now and agin for a nightcap, but the place's run down a might lately. Last time I was in there, there was so many cockroaches runnin' around on the flo', I felt like I was walkin' on cornflakes. And it smelled like a fat man's drawers, too." Blue shook his head and laughed, "Hard times for ever'body, I reckon."

Linc slipped Blue a sawbuck in a parting handshake "Thanks, Blue. Not word to anybody, right?"

"I getcha! We're copacetic, cuz. But watch yo'self. This cat's a mean son of a bitch. He don't look like much o' nothin', but take care! The man ain't right! The cat be crazy awaitin' ta happen! He work for a badass, too. White dude with some kinda Hunky name I don't recollect. Both of 'em just as soon bury ya as look at ya." With that, the two men parted company.

―――

In the late afternoon, Linc pulled up to his in-laws' home in Washington Park as his wife, Leola, was walking onto the front porch. The female teacher, with whom she rode to and from Washington

High School, was pulling her gray Chevrolet away from in front of the house. The two drivers exchanged waves. Leola sat her book satchel down and lingered on the porch while her husband parked the Hupmobile. When he reached her, they enveloped each other in their arms and kissed. The passion of the moment pressed Leola's back to rest against one of the craftsman-style columns that supported the porch overhang. Their ardor had grown during their married life. Wilbert Frye, Leola's father, opened the front door and laughed, "All right you two. Come on inside and don't be scandalizing the neighbors." The couple broke from the embrace, laughing, and Linc picked up Leola's bag. The pair remained arm in arm as they entered the home, commiserating about their long days.

*Lincoln Mallard's 1934 Hupmobile 417 Sedan*

Inside, they could smell the results of Mrs. Frye's supper preparations. Mr. Frye stood by the mantel of the living room's brick fireplace, looking at the day's mail and loosening his tie. Only moments earlier, he'd arrived home from his job as a middle management actuary for a very successful black-owned insurance company on Auburn Avenue. Without taking his eyes from the letter he was reading, the older man suggested, "I imagine Mamma could use some help in the kitchen if you can tear yourself away from Linc." He smiled as he said it, but his fatherly message in his deep baritone voice was clear. Leola and Linc retreated to their back bedroom where they changed into more comfortable clothes before Linc's wife made her way to the kitchen. She joined her momma in the preparation of the family's supper. For their parts, Wilbert and Linc set the table and made small talk.

Soon, the family gathered around a repast of fried fish, red beans and rice, and collard greens seasoned with vinegar. This was one of Linc's favorite meals. "You got lucky today, Linc," Hallie Frye offered as way of explanation, "the store had croakers on sale."

Linc, his mouth full of food, merely smiled and nodded. When he'd washed the food down with a big gulp of sweet tea, he said earnestly, "I consider myself lucky every day I can come home to this house and this family." His wife reached out and squeezed his hand. His in-laws smiled at his sentiment.

"Anything new on the murders of those girls, Linc?" Mr. Frye held an avid interest in his son-in-law's involvement in the cases. Simultaneously, he was concerned about Linc's participation with a white detective, even in trying to solve the murders of black women. The older man had seen too many instances in which dealings with whites had ended badly for a black man. While he respected his son-in-law and trusted his judgment, he still had reservations.

Linc's eyes flickered from Wilbert to Hallie and back to his father-in-law. The detective knew Mrs. Frye didn't care for such talk at the supper table. However, his mother-in-law didn't react to the query. Perhaps, Linc thought, she'd given up trying to put a stop to such conversations. "No, sir. Nothing new. I'm going out a little later to track a man down who's probably involved in the case. He —"

"Oh, Linc! Baby, do you have to?" Leola interrupted.

"Yes. Yes, I do, Little Bit." He quickly, but gently responded, using the nickname he'd given her owing to her petite size, especially compared to his. Using that pet name always smoothed troubled waters. "It's only for awhile. But, yes, I have to." Linc waited until he and Leola were alone again in their bedroom before explaining where he was going and why. Linc had two motives for not discussing it in front of his in-laws. The first reason was that he didn't want his in-laws to know what type of establishment he was going to. Although they were not too straitlaced, his in-laws were among the black population who thought the nightspots on Decatur Street, which had a rough and unsavory reputation, were frequented only by lowlifes. He knew a pour house in the Bell Street area would rank in the same category with those places. Second, any hint of Blue's involvement in the matter would bring a harangue from Wilbert Frye on the waywardness and disrepute of that part of his family tree. Linc offered to take Leola along for a drink, but she balked after she'd heard Blue's description of the roaches and the rest of the ambience. Instead, she told him suggestively that she'd be waiting up for him.

At what he felt was an appropriate time, the private detective made his way to Horace's place, a block or so off Auburn Avenue. Blue's description of the place had been apt. Despite its slightly rundown condition, it was well patronized. Linc got himself a drink and wandered among the customers. Finally, when he heard Nathan Green's name called out, he turned and saw a man who fit Blue's description of his quarry, freckles, green eyes, and all. Feigning a slight case of inebriation, the private detective leaned against a nearby wall and overheard Green setting up a "date" for one of his girls, named Viola Johnson, with another patron. Linc decided that this was the man Detective Greerson was talking about, all right. And he was a pimp. No doubt about it. Linc decided not to confront the man. No sense, he determined, in spooking Green before Detective Greerson could approach him again in an official capacity. Besides, he wanted to locate this Johnson girl and try to get more information about Effie Sledge first.

The detective made his way home, weary after a long day. True to her word, Leola was lying on their bed, reading and awaiting Linc's return. The sight of her loveliness in the subdued lamp light renewed his vigor.

That evening, when Matt telephoned Evie and extended Miss Dixie's invitation for Friday night's supper, she gladly accepted. Although she'd heard a great deal about the members of the household and their activities from Diane and Matt, she'd never been to the Houston Street residence. Evie's eagerness for the occasion grew when Matt mentioned offhandedly that Detective Greerson would be there also. Because her voice took on a more calculating tone, Matt began to wonder whether getting these two people together was really in his best interest. As he returned the phone to its cradle, he recalled the words attributed to Julius Caesar as he crossed the Rubicon, *alea iacta est*. The young reporter reconciled himself to his fate.

# CHAPTER 12

# The Joy Girls

In the several days that followed his encounter with Nathan Green at Horace's pour house, Lincoln Mallard learned more about the girl named Viola Johnson. A mulatto prostitute working under the "guidance" of Green, Johnson's nickname was "Squash," owing to her light complexion. In addition, he discovered that she'd known and been a good friend to Effie Sledge, who'd also been hooking. Finally, he'd also learned where she could be found most days. Following that information, he left his office that sweltering Friday afternoon and drove to McDaniel Street in the Pittsburgh area of the city. Edging his Hupmobile slowly past the building he sought, Linc saw a woman fitting Viola's description standing on the sidewalk among a small gaggle of women. A solitary man stood among the women. The man was not Nathan Green. Viola Johnson was a tall, angular, slightly bug-eyed woman of an indeterminable age. The black investigator pulled to the side of the street about half a block from their location and cut his car's motor. In long, loose strides, he made his way back along the sidewalk to the group. As he approached the small cluster, the woman he took to be Viola departed in the opposite direction with the man in tow. The black detective moved casually so as not to "flush the covey," as his daddy would say. Like his approach at Horace's, Linc decided to collect what information he could gather better than a white Atlanta police officer might be able to and turn it over to Detective Greerson, the man with the badge.

The women, ironically trying to cool themselves with fans from a local church, turned in unison and watched Linc as he neared them. They threw smiles in his direction, but seemed hesitant to engage this unfamiliar, well-dressed black man. "Good afternoon, ladies. Hot day, isn't it?" Linc said casually, returning their smiles.

One girl, who seemed the youngest of the cluster, looked at Linc with puzzlement. "Is you a *po*-liceman?" she asked hesitantly.

An older, tall, big-boned woman defiantly stepped between the younger woman and Linc. She gazed hard eyed at the man before her, running her eyes up and down his frame. "Naw, chile! Ain't no colored *po*-liceman in dis heuh town. Wearin' a suit, must be a preachuh man. Ya be wastin' ya time heuh, preachuh man. Best be gettin' back to ya *pul*-pit." Her defiance and her words brought a titter among her fellow joy girls.

Linc, musing that this was one segment of his community where he wasn't well known, raised his hands slightly in submission. "Hey, ladies," he smiled, "I'm not here looking for trouble. I'm not a cop *or* a preacher. I'm looking for a girl called 'Squash'." When the recalcitrant woman standing in front of him furrowed her eyebrows and shot him an angry glance, he quickly added, "Nathan sent me. Said she was a friend of Effie Sledge." The mention of the pimp's name eased the tension somewhat.

The woman glanced in the direction the female Linc had taken to be Squash had traveled, and then looked back at the detective. "We was all friends a Effie's. Reckon Squash was her bestus friend, though. She ain't heuh just now," the woman said as she sidled up beside Linc, rubbed her shoulder against his, and gave him what passed for her best seductive smile. "How's about ya en me gittin' together?"

"Well, thank you kindly, but I was looking for Squash. Nathan recommended her." Linc paused slightly, trying to ad-lib his way out of the conversation and adding, "I... uh... have special needs."

The woman again quickly changed moods and pushed away from Linc. "Lawd, man, she ain't nothin' special! No mo' dan de rest a us! You gotta inj'ry or somethin'?"

"Look, I'm only following Nathan's recommendation. Maybe I'll come back later," he smiled, as he walked backward a few steps, then turned and strolled away, leaving the catcalls of the women in his wake. He needed to get back to Detective Greerson with the information he'd gathered. Monday couldn't come soon enough as far as Linc was concerned.

---

The Friday afternoon high temperature of eighty-six degrees had barely receded when the household and guests gathered in the boardinghouse parlor to await Miss Dixie's call to supper. A gentle cross breeze, spurred on by the parlor's ceiling fan, made the occasion a bit more festive. Mealtime guests were a rarity at the rooming house. As the group engaged in lively conversations, Cliff followed Detective Greerson around with his "adoring puppy" routine usually reserved for Teresa. He was obviously in awe of having a "real-life detective" eating supper at his house.

For Matt, the moment of truth had arrived. When he introduced Evie to Jim Greerson, she seemed cordial enough to those around her, but Matt detected the chill in her demeanor and her smile lacked its usual warmth. For his part, Jim certainly didn't give the impression that he noticed anything amiss as he bragged to those gathered about how much he enjoyed Matt's company and his take on cases and even suggested that he should consider joining the police department. Evie's reaction to the last comment was deflected when Melvyn interjected that he'd often considered taking up a career in law enforcement. Matt surmised that his hollow bravado was brought on by the quiet, yet decidedly pointed attention the detective's presence seemed to have momentarily drawn from Amanda. Cliff snickered at Melvyn's notion as his daddy tried deftly to stifle the boy's scorn while smiling and winking at Matt. With the lovely Teresa's late arrival in the parlor, Jim's broad handsome face looked to Matt as if it brightened. The look he'd never seen from his friend brought a smile to the Matt's face, and he made certain the two met. They seemed to strike an immediate chord with one another. Soon enough, the landlady called the group to take their seats around the boardinghouse table for a meal of fried chicken, mashed potatoes, green beans, and cornbread.

Evie ate quietly as Detective Greerson drew much of the household's attention during the meal. Cliff, especially, hung on every word spoken by the big cop. Jim was asked about his work and some cases with which he was currently involved. Matt quietly watched the detective's reaction to the praise of his work and marveled yet again at the man he'd come to know. The reporter had seen in the detective an aggregate of opposites: civility and harshness, patience and uncontrollable anger, shyness and pleasure in adoration, devotion to purpose and total disregard for those opposed to that purpose.

Eventually, the recent murder of the businessman was brought up by Miss Dixie, who lamented that decent folks weren't even safe on the streets of Atlanta's main business district. When Melvyn Briggs suggested robbery being the motive for the killing, the detective reminded him of the satchel of money left in the murdered guy's Cadillac. Melvyn blushed slightly as he conceded that the newspaper accounts *had* detailed its presence. Even so, the plump piano salesman argued that robbery still could have been the motive and that the culprit had been scared away before attaining his objective. His cherub face reddened when Amanda uncharacteristically spoke up and strongly disagreed, pointing out the satchel of money, the man's jewelry, and the dollar bill left on his body made robbery unlikely. As she finished her assertion, she blushed self-consciously and quickly returned her eyes to her plate, shooting a lowered glance at Jim. She reverted to her normal reclusive self. The detective momentarily gazed at the woman and absently agreed with her contention.

Over a dessert of lemon pound cake, the subject was changed when Rhamy Fleming jokingly asked the detective about an old yarn that had been repeated in Atlanta for years. The story was about an Atlanta Police Department rookie and a dead horse back in earlier years when finding a dead horse on the street was not uncommon, and police regulations required that they be reported immediately to headquarters. A rookie patrolman, making his rounds one day, it was told, came upon the body of a dead horse which had expired at the corner of Davis and D'Alvigny Streets, near Bellwood. Going to a nearby telephone, he called headquarters to report his find. "Dead horse at Davis and D'Alvigny streets," reported the young officer. "Davis and what?" asked the voice at headquarters. "D'Alvigny," repeated the rookie. However, he was uncertain of the pronunciation and, as it turned out, the spelling when he was instructed to spell it. "D-er-er-ah, just a minute. I'll call you back." Returning to the dead steed, the young policeman reportedly seized the body by the tail and dragged it one block north. Then, back on the telephone, he reported in a confident voice, "Dead horse, Davis Street and North Avenue." Rhamy wanted to know, once and for all, whether the anecdote was true. The tale brought peals of laughter around the table. Detective Greerson, who suddenly seemed preoccupied, gave a vague laugh and stated that he'd heard the story, too, but couldn't confirm its authenticity. When the meal had been completed, Jim Greerson seconded Rhamy Fleming's "Much obliged, Ma'am," to the amused appreciation of Miss Dixie.

As the evening was ending, Miss Dixie literally dragged Cliff into the kitchen with her to allow Detective Greerson to quietly talk with Teresa away from the group. On the front porch, Evie, Matt, Teresa, and Jim lingered briefly, staring out into the sultry night. Before departing, Greerson mentioned that he would be visiting Gutowski's girlfriend early the following week and invited Matt to go, given that he'd been involved in the case to that point. Matt sensed tension in Evie's body language at the suggestion. Nevertheless, he quickly, quietly agreed to accompany the detective.

Later, as Matt drove Evie home, she was unusually tight-lipped. Matt's attempts to draw her out with various topics of conversation, including the upcoming softball game in July between the staff of the *Georgian* and that of the *Journal*, proved futile. She simply reached out and patted his hand, concealing her marked irritation. Her not saying anything seemed very thunderous to Matt. Sensing her extreme annoyance at him, the young man let the subjects die lingering deaths and bid his girlfriend a subdued goodnight at the Nash's front door.

On his way back to Houston Street, Matt stopped at the Stars Grill counter for several cups of strong coffee served in a thick mug. When he'd arrived, the place was nearly empty. But, shortly, a few nearby movie houses let out, and the diner became crowded with people waiting out a sudden cloudburst. Matt suspected that, after experiencing the air-cooled movie theaters, some people simply didn't want to go home to languish in the unrelenting heat and humidity. The counterman had the *Ink Spots Quartet* program on the radio sitting on a shelf above his griddle. Matt could barely hear the peppy lyrics of "Swinging on the Strings" above the din of laughter and conversations. He wasn't in a lively mood, so it was all right. As the young man sat there contemplating the situation with Evie, he fished a small parcel wrapped in tissue paper from his coat's side pocket. He removed the paper surrounding a small box. Opening the box, he stared blankly at the engagement ring inside, weighing the dilemma his life seemed at the moment. After a few seconds, he moaned quietly, closed the box, rewrapped it, and returned it to his pocket. Despite the throng, Matt felt desperately alone.

One hot afternoon several days following that Friday's supper, Detective Greerson picked up Matt at the *Georgian* to go pay a call on Gutowski's girlfriend. As Matt climbed in the Hudson, Jim confirmed that Matt was carrying his firearm. The young reporter was momentarily stunned by his friend's cold tone, but explained that it had become his habit to carry the weapon with him in his car so it would be available whenever they went out together on some case. "The same rules as always apply," the detective said firmly. "Keep that gat where it is and don't do anything without my okay." Matt nodded sharply. Jostling through traffic, the big cop made clear that he wasn't sure who or what they might find at the hotel. The girl might be by herself or she might have "company." Either way, he said that he wanted to *try* to keep his visit with the woman low key. But, nevertheless, no matter what time it took, what was required of him, he told Matt he was determined to find Gutowski. Again, Matt nodded his understanding.

Greerson guided his car into Jenkins's parking lot a block or so from the Mitchell Street hotel where he'd been told he could find the girlfriend. As they piled out of the Hudson, the detective reached into the rumble seat area and retrieved two pint bottles of very good whiskey, slipping them into his hip pockets. When he saw Matt's surprised expression, Jim merely mentioned "greasing the skids of progress, if necessary."

As the two men hustled along the sidewalk, wet from a recent thundershower, Matt worked to keep up with Jim, whose stride revealed a hurried impatience. The cop filled his friend in on what he knew of the woman they sought. Her first name was Gladys with the unfortunate surname of Hooker. Ill-fated, Jim explained, in the sense that she was reported to be an overheated joy girl of some repute. Greerson continued, explaining that she had a reputation as a hard-boiled floozy. "She's been around. I don't *know* that she's a prostitute, but, from what I hear, she's only said 'no' to a man once, and, on that occasion, she didn't understand the question." They shared a laugh, before Greerson grew slightly more serous. "But don't think that, because she's a woman, she won't cut your heart out with a rusty spoon, and then go out to supper and dancing afterward." As they continued toward the hotel, Matt recalled the detective's words from the night they'd gone to the White Lantern about entering a world he'd only experienced through motion pictures or books. The young *Georgian* reporter smiled as he reflected that the "ride" with Detective Greerson since that night had been a series of such experiences.

Reaching the hotel, the two men turned in to the embrasure and pushed through the brass-edged glass doors. The registration desk was enclosed on a side wall of the timeworn lobby, past the big bronze mailbox mounted on the front wall. As they crossed the worn marble floor to the desk, a red-faced man of uncertain age peeked low from behind the pebbled-glass screen at one end of the registration counter. When he didn't reappear on their arrival at the front desk, Greerson moved to the far end of the counter where he could see the man seated at a table behind it. Matt edged his way alongside the detective. The fellow at the table was very heavyset and wore a collarless shirt and scarlet suspenders. His tiny, close-set eyes, set deep on a round, florid face reminded Matt of a burst couch. The eyes registered annoyance at the appearance of the two strangers. He groaned noisily, laid down a smut magazine of some sort he'd been sweating over, and hoisted himself heavily from his chair. His hair, which had begun a brisk retreat years earlier, was damp with perspiration in the afternoon heat. Despite the presence of a small oscillating fan humming on the table where he'd been seated, the man's fat neck glistened and his shirt was darkened with sweat at various points and at the armpits. He moved to the counter unhurriedly. The counterman exhaled long and hard, "What can ah do fo ya'll?" His voice was hollow and without energy. Despite his lethargic demeanor, Matt estimated it would take two pretty hefty blocking backs to bowl the bulky man over.

Jim gave the guy a quick, friendly smile. "Do you have a Hooker registered here?" As the fat man blanched slightly and stammered, Matt burst out in laughter. Jim looked at his companion with uncertainty. "What's the deal?" he demanded of the reporter.

Through his laughter, Matt choked out, "Think about your question, Jim."

Though his mind was racing with other things, the big cop immediately realized the double meaning his question imparted and laughed aloud. Meanwhile, the clerk was still groping for a response. Jim held up a loose hand and rephrased his query. "Do you have a Gladys Hooker registered here?"

The relieved clerk eyed the two men and shot them a washed-out smile. "Who wants to know," he drawled.

"I'm Detective Greerson from the Atlanta Police Department."

"Do tell," he responded smugly. "You got anythang sayin' such?"

The detective's smile evaporated as he drew in a deep breath and let it out silently. He reached into his coat pocket and fished out his badge. Rubbing it on his coat sleeve with a flourish, he palmed it up at the man stiffly. After studying the shield momentarily, the overweight clerk put his large, hairless hands on the marble counter and leaned over them. His belly rested conveniently on the cool stone. "Well, law or no law, this hotel has a policy. We ain't givin' –"

Without the slightest shift in the hand holding the badge under the man's nose, Greerson made a rapid, practiced movement ending with a leather-covered, thonged sap in his other hand. In one motion, he slammed it hard on the marble counter, jostling a bronze plunger bell sitting there. The sudden, loud action jolted both the clerk and the reporter. An older, grizzled man, half asleep in a Morris chair across the lobby, leaped up and made a hasty exit to the street. Detective Greerson's patience had again been quickly stretched too far. He leaned in close to the man across the counter, and spoke in a subdued, seething voice, "Listen, lard ass, I'll give you some law! I can have a dozen uniforms here in half an hour to go through this joint with a fine-toothed comb! Think they'll find anything illegal? And besides, this dump probably hasn't had a 'policy,' including one for fire insurance, since they buried McKinley! Now, I'm not asking you again! What room is Gladys Hooker in?"

The clerk straightened away from the counter and Jim's threatening form. His sloped shoulders shrugged vaguely. "She's in suite three-oh-eight." As he spoke, he reached for the counter's telephone.

Jim's sap thundered again. The man behind the counter quickly withdrew his hand. The movement was the fastest Matt had seen him make. In a low, level tone, the detective declared, "If you even try to call her, I'll make you wish you'd kept your happy ass in bed this morning! Get me?" The counterman cowered and nodded. "Now, sit back down," Jim jerked his head toward the table, "and go back to slobbering over your Tijuana bible or whatever it is you have there. And don't move 'til you see me get back off the elevator. Got it?" Another cringing nod. The guy returned to the table and sat down carefully, the way fat people often do. Despite his hangdog bearing, the clerk shot Greerson a steely eyed, hateful glare before the two men moved away from the registration desk. The clerk's nasty, defiant stare worried Jim almost as far as the self-service elevator.

Grimes and Greerson boarded the elevator, and Jim pushed the floor button. The car clanked to a crawl and eventually sighed to a stop on the third floor. The pair prowled the dimly lighted hallway, following the descending numbers above the door frames back toward the front of the building. Moving across the front hallway, Jim found the number they wanted, two from the end of the hall. Light spilled from under the door's sill. The big detective scanned the passageway. Greerson didn't want Gutowski or one of his goons to appear suddenly and catch him unawares. Matt followed his eyes, not knowing what his friend was looking for. The corridor was empty and quiet other than a radio playing behind a door somewhere down the hall. Some high-money torcher was overselling a song.

With a hand signal from Jim, the two men took up positions on either side of the door. Then, they could make out female voices and laughter coming from inside room three-oh-eight. Someone moved beyond the door, bare feet padding across a carpet. Then the men heard the sound of a drawer closing and another opening. Greerson edged to the door and knocked. The voices fell silent. No one responded to the knock. Jim glanced at Matt, and then repeated the effort, this time a quick, hard, intolerant rapping. His patience was not on ready display this afternoon. The men heard feet rustling across a carpet before a female voice sounded through the door, "Yeah? Who is it?"

"Can I speak to you for a minute?"

"You're speaking to me, mister."

The muscles in Greerson's jaw protruded in anger. But he held fast, breathed deeply, and looked at Matt, raising his eyebrows. The storm passed. His exasperated voice was just loud enough to be heard through the door. "Without the door between us, lady."

After a long silence, the door was unlocked and opened a crack. A female's piercing hazel eye peered from the opening. "Okay, mister, talk."

The detective pushed hard past the woman into the room, sweeping off his hat as he entered. Matt followed.

"Say, how do you get like that, ya big lug?" the woman exclaimed as she stumbled back into the room. She wore red lounging pajamas of heavy ribbed silk embroidered with black lotus buds. Her voice had the edgy twang of a pour-house frail. She was of medium height with dusky red hair.

"Park it on the sofa, sister," Greerson tossed as he passed her. He otherwise ignored her. The detective quickly ranged his eyes around the oversized room in the way his cautious investigator's mind led him to do. He'd try to absorb every detail for possible future reference. The woman, in turn, ignored his directions and stayed on his heels. Jim surmised that this space was the sitting room of the suite mentioned by

331

the clerk downstairs. The smell of stale cigarettes and alcohol with just a tinge of heavy perfume hung in the air. The room held a chintz-covered davenport with tables at either end, on which sat lamps with bloodred shirred shades. A tabouret sat in front of the sofa. It held a large ashtray full of cigarette butts. All had lipstick on them. A sideboard sat against a wall between two large windows. On it sat a table model radio, assorted liquor bottles with the appropriate mixers, a container of cracked ice, and several framed photographs. The windows were bounded by cretonne drapes, whose floral pattern picked up the deep red of the lamp shades. The afternoon sunlight streaming through the windows showed the dust on the sideboard. The rest of the furniture in the room consisted of a couple of straight-back wooden chairs and two bulky stuffed chairs. Although it wasn't high-class stuff, Jim thought, it was better than Vivian and Charlie had been able to accumulate. Business must be good.

A second woman sat leaned back against a corner of the davenport. She had one leg tucked under her and the other carelessly extended to the floor from under a short, flimsy, loose-fitting nightgown. Even the slack gown couldn't hide her bodacious figure. She made no effort to cover her exposed parts. In one hand she held an array of playing cards with other cards spread on the sofa before her. Her small, pretty oval face with kohl-rimmed eyes was set below wavy brown hair. A cigarette drooped from a corner of her Cupid's-bow mouth. Aside from startled eyes, her face was as blank as a pie pan. She indifferently reached to the table behind her for a large highball glass half-full of an amber liquid. She gulped it down as nonchalantly as it were an aspirin tablet.

Doors were open on either side of the space, leading to adjoining rooms. Jim moved to one of the doors with the woman he'd first encountered following closely and protesting loudly. "Whatcha lookin' for, ya big mug? There ain't nobody here but me and Doris!" The door opened to a bedroom, which smelled of lilacs and face powder. With no more than a quick glance to clear the room, he saw the obligatory unmade bed, covered with scattered clothing, and two bedside tables. Each table held a lamp with a shade identical to the ones in the sitting room. On one wall was a dressing table with a mirror for a top. Its surface was covered with cold cream jars, assorted other beauty aids, an etui, and toiletry articles. The dressing table had a kneehole and drawers like an office desk. It appeared to be maple with a single horizontal strip of a darker wood, probably cherry, inlaid across its front. A large round mirror was mounted on the back of it. A cushioned chair sat tucked slightly into the kneehole. A matching chest of drawers and wardrobe stood nearby. Again, Greerson thought that business must be doing pretty good.

As he moved across the sitting room toward the second door, Doris piped up in a strong, coarse voice over her shoulder. "My room, mister, and it's none of your business!" When she opened her mouth, the prettiness went out of her face. Despite her protests, the cop gave it a quick look. The room was much like the other bedroom, but, he surmised, with less expensive furnishings.

Jim checked a third door from the sitting room, which opened to a decent-sized bathroom. The bathroom was empty of anything noteworthy except a remarkable number of stockings and a garment he couldn't quite identify hanging over a bar mounted in the space.

For his part, Matt watched in wonder the scene before him. Brick had often joked about "lost weekends" spent in drink and unspoken pleasures at a fictional – at least, Matt supposed it was imaginary – house of ill-repute the older journalist called "Madame Foo Foo's House of Whoopee." The young reporter could only envision that this might be one of the forbidden chambers of such a pleasure palace. In his reverie, Matt found himself staring at Doris's much-exposed leg. To his chagrin, she caught him in midgawk. Without effort to cover the exposed limb, she batted eyelashes that didn't quite reach the tip of her nose and scolded him, "Take a picture, sonny! It'll last longer!" Matt blinked, swallowed hard, blushed, and moved his eyes to his companion, who he could hear laughing.

Satisfied that there was no apparent danger from the setup, Detective Greerson turned sharply to focus on the objecting chippie who followed him, giving him hell at every step. His turn was so abrupt that she bumped into him, but she stepped back and folded her arms across her ample chest defiantly. Her dead white face was that of a slightly shopworn angel but still very attractive. He sized her up as a spitfire. Matt, who had been watching the proceedings with astounded amusement, saw a shapely, redheaded man-eater.

"Well" the woman in front of Jim demanded, shifting her hands to her hips, "what gives?"

"Okay, I'm Detective Jim Greerson of the Atlanta Police Department. Which of you is Gladys Hooker?" Jim glanced over the woman's shoulder at Matt suppressing a laugh. Matt had expected Jim's use of only the woman's last name with a result similar to the one at the front desk. Jim read Matt's thought, and a smile lurked at the corners of his mouth.

"Well, to begin with, bub, don't bother with first names! Ya ain't gonna be here that long *unless* ya gotta warrant! And, if ya got one, I wanna see it! But first, let's see a badge!"

The detective arched his eyebrows, shot Matt a here-we-go-again look, and repeated the process he'd done with the front-desk clerk, but without the flourish. The redhead glanced at the badge and turned slightly to the other woman, throwing her arms in the air. "Oh, looky, Doris! We got *special* company!" she crowed sarcastically. Turning back to Jim, she snapped, "What's it to ya, flatfoot? And what is this? A shakedown? A pinch? What?"

"Nothing like that Gladys. I need your help finding your boyfriend."

"My *boyfriend*?" she blurted with boisterous laughter. "Is this a gag? You got me in stitches!" Doris sat stone-faced.

"No. No gag, gorgeous," he cajoled. "I'm trying to find Carl Gutowski."

At the sound of the name, Gladys's mouth opened and she started swearing. Matt listened, stunned. She didn't have any words that he hadn't heard before, but she fitted them together in combinations that were new to him. When she'd used up all the curse words she knew, she ran out of conversation. Then the redhead paused and studied the detective's face with a scheming look. She took the moment to regain her composure. Finally, Gladys glanced at Matt before returning to Jim and asking, "So what about Carl?" As she spoke, she walked to one of the stuffed chairs and sat on an arm, eventually, nonchalantly flopping backward into the seat with her legs still extended over the arm. Jim took hold of a straight-backed chair, moved it to where Gladys sat, twisted it around, and straddled it, facing the woman. Matt could see that this might take awhile. He sat in the other straight-backed chair and tilted it back against a side wall.

"I got nothin' to say to ya, flattie. So take your friend here and drift."

"We'd get along much better, Gladys, if you'd take that chip off your shoulder."

"Every time I take it off, wise guy, some mug hits me over the head with it! So scram! I ain't talkin' about Carl!"

"Yeah, all he ever did for her was just shove her around, copper! He's a big lunkhead with a big snot hanger!" Doris put in. Gladys flashed angry eyes at the woman. That look told Greerson what he wanted to know.

"Still got the hots for him, eh, Gladys?"

"Nah, I've dusted him off," she snorted and looked away.

The detective had watched her closely. "You're lying, dollface. Your words say one thing, but your eyes say something else. You're not a *good* liar, Gladys. You've just had a lot of practice at it." Her eyes moistened and the corners of her mouth drew down. She sat without moving for a long time. Greerson waited her out. Despite what she was, Jim found himself liking her a little. His gut instincts told him there was some good in her somewhere. Finally, the detective said, "You seem a tad bitter, Gladys. I think maybe you've had a cruel life, full of hard knocks and bad luck."

"Well, don't go openin' no relief agency for me, Mac!" she spat sarcastically. With that, she swung her legs to the floor and stood in a swift lunge, moving quickly to the sideboard. She poured a liberal measure of hooch into a tumbler and drank it quickly. Then, she was perfectly still, staring down into the empty glass.

Greerson stood and crossed the room to Gladys. The detective's hand went toward a pocket. Matt froze, jolted by the possibility that the sap would make another appearance. Instead, going into a hip pocket, the big cop produced one of the whiskey bottles and reached around her with it. "Here. No offense, but, if you're in the mood for a drink, try some good stuff for a change."

Gladys took the container from Jim, looked at the label, and smiled. She patronized the bottle and took a long drink. "I don't like answerin' your questions, buster, but I'll drink your whiskey." After finishing the belt, she turned to face the big cop and, with a feigned coyness, offered, "Pardon my manners. You wanna drink?" Jim nodded. "And you two?" she asked, indicating Doris and Matt. Each nodded with Matt saying he only wanted "two fingers" and Doris asking Gladys to mix hers with the ginger ale that sat on the sideboard. "Comin' up."

After Gladys poured another liberal measure of the whiskey into three tumblers, she handed one to Jim. Then, she took one to Matt. He looked at the drink and snorted. "I said two fingers, lady. Who are you? Bronco Nagurski?" Gladys smiled but said nothing. His gaze followed her as she walked a mixed drink to Doris, where his eyes stayed for a long minute.

Again, Doris caught his stare. "You keep givin' me the big eyeball, sonny. Wanna give me a tumble to back it up?" Her voice had a boozy edge to it.

As he blushed heavily, the young correspondent tried to recover. "No, thanks. I don't drink from a dirty glass," he said, trying to gain the upper hand. His effort failed.

Doris's mouth fell open. She dropped the cards she was holding and her foot quickly fumbled for a fallen bedroom slipper. As she tossed her cigarette to the ashtray with remarkable accuracy, she shot from the davenport past the shocked, but chuckling Gladys. Jim winced but stood firm. Simultaneously, Matt dropped his tilted chair back to the floor and rose just as Doris reached him. With fury and with the inertia of her dash behind it, she slapped his face. Hard. Despite the solid blow, a stunned Matt maintained his balance. Barely. He held onto his drink. Only just. Realizing that he'd probably earned her response, the embarrassed reporter merely stared at the woman as the side of his face turned a hot, bright red. Momentarily, she returned his glare before turning sharply and going back to the sofa. Perched on the edge of the couch, she downed her drink and shot Matt a baleful, bold glower. She lit another smoke with a flourish. Not a word was said.

As he sipped the drink, Detective Greerson kept his eyes on Gladys and broke the tense silence. "So, Gladys, back to business. Where can I find Carl Gutowski?"

The woman threw her head back and let loose with a scornful laugh. "You got any *small* questions, copper?"

"C'mon, Gladys. I need your help finding your boyfriend. It's nothing serious. I only have some questions for him."

Gladys's eyes crawled sideways in Doris's direction, then back to Jim. "Like I said, detective, I don't like answerin' questions. Nothin' says I hafta, either."

Greerson's patience was wearing thin again. After hastily setting his drink and hat down, he squared up on the woman, grabbed her arms, and threw her onto the davenport. He wasn't nice about it. Reaching for her, he fisted his hand in her hair and jerked her head back so she had to look up into his eyes. "I don't have time to stand here all day gassin'!" he yelled.

"If Carl knew I was even talkin' to you, he'd throw me out in the street!"

"Well, that's *home* to you!"

"What kind of crack is that? Take that back, you bastard!"

"The crack still goes, sister!" He tossed her head aside and stepped away.

She rebounded off the sofa and lifted her open right hand to hit him across the face. Greerson threw his arm up to block her hand, and then grabbed it and returned it to her side. "Take it easy, sweetheart. Unlike my friend there, I don't slap so easy this time of day." With that, he shoved Gladys back onto the davenport.

Her defiance remained intact. "You want somethin' from me, flattie, git a warrant! Until then, dangle and take that," she screamed, nodding toward the still-recovering Matt, "with you!"

"You make me sick to my stomach!" Greerson yelled in frustration.

"Yeah? Well, use a toilet down the hall!" Gladys shot back, throwing her head back in obstinate silence and lighting a fresh cigarette.

The detective realized he was quickly losing his temper and, uncharacteristically, his control of the situation. He knew he'd gain nothing by letting things get further out of hand. He gave her a broad, mirthless smile. "I'll be coming back, Gladys. And with a warrant. Just remember, I tried to do this the easy way. You and Gutowski *are* a match. He always does things the hard way, too. I thought you just might be a little smarter than he is, but I see that neither of you is the cerebral type." His voice was cold and hard. He turned and moved angrily to the door. "C'mon, Matt." Greerson pulled on his hat and yanked it low over his eyes.

Neither man spoke as they made their way down the hall and during the ride down on the elevator. On their way out of the hotel, the two men passed the registration desk. The clerk was nowhere to be seen. Back on the sidewalk, Detective Greerson said, "I need to get up with Linc. I hope he's had better luck than I have." As he spoke, he saw Matt from the corner of his eyes rubbing the side of his face where Doris had hit him. He was working his jaw back and forth sideways. Jim fished a pack of cigarettes from a pocket, shook one out, and held the pack out to his young companion. "Good thing Doris hits like a girl, huh, Matt," he laughed.

Matt took a smoke from the pack and groused, "Who the hell said she hits like a girl?" Jim threw his head back and burst out in laughter. Matt joined in. He'd been taught that, if you can't laugh at your mistakes, you shouldn't laugh at those of others. Detective Greerson looked at his strap watch as he crossed Mitchell Street to a greasy spoon. The five o'clock meeting time he and Linc had agreed to had come and gone. From the restaurant, he telephoned Linc at his office and made arrangements to meet him there.

---

A short time later, Matt and Jim were outside Linc's office. The private detective opened the door before they could knock. "Hey. I thought I heard you coming up the stairs. Come on in and sit a spell. Let's compare notes," he said as they shook hands. What followed was an exchange between Linc and Jim of what each had learned during the past week. The two detectives agreed that the next step would be to try to locate Nathan Green at Horace's place that evening. Linc felt compelled to apologize in advance for the state of place they'd be going to. Jim blew off the need for an apology, knowing that most drinking places in the

Negro section of town were neat and clean. When Jim invited Matt to tag along, the young reporter hesitated.

Linc's comfort level with the two men was growing, and he responded to the young man's uncertainty with a low laugh. "What's the matter, Matt? You afraid to go to a Negro pour house? Afraid somebody might take offense at your presence and attack you? Hell, the hooch will probably kill you quicker than a customer would. And, from I've learned, Horace doesn't care what color your skin is if your money's green."

Matt started to speak but was cut off by the Atlanta detective. "Nah, Linc," Jim offered through a broad smile, "I think our friend here is reliving his last visit to a blind tiger. It's an episode in his life he'd just as soon forget."

"Jim's right, Linc. I have no problem with going there. I'd hoped you'd know me better than that by now. I just don't want to wake up somewhere unfamiliar to me." Here, he smiled sheepishly, "Again."

"We'll see that that doesn't happen, Matt." Jim said, as he chuckled. Mallard nodded.

Matt rose from his chair. "All right then. Let's go!"

"What say we wait here awhile so the place has time to fill up some," Linc suggested. Matt glanced at his watch, smiled, and returned to his chair. The next hour or so was filled with small talk and conjecture about the murder cases they were working.

Although Horace's place was within walking distance of Linc's office building, he suggested that they drive his car. He had a hunch about what might transpire when he showed up with two white men in his company. They arrived at Horace's shortly before sunset, while the sultry ambience of the day refused retreat and eddies of heat still rose from the pavement. Linc parked up the street from the house, but well within view of the comings and goings. The three men climbed out of the Hupmobile, walked the short distance to the blind tiger, and went inside. As had been the case at Ma Sutton's, the appearance of the two white men caused a quiet, standoffish stir among those gathered at Horace's.

The consensus was that there were enough such establishments available in Atlanta for white folks to frequent without them showing up at a blind tiger patronized by blacks. So the white men walking into the place, even accompanied by a black man who made it clear they were with him, did not go unnoticed. Nathan Green was nowhere to be found in the crowded house. The trio decided to stay for a while and see whether he appeared.

Linc bought the first round of drinks, which came in old peanut butter jar "glasses." When Matt took a sip of the liquid, he grimaced involuntarily. Jim, more accustomed to imbibing, tucked his drink away nicely and gave no reaction. When Matt exhaled nosily as if his throat were on fire, Linc chuckled. "Good stuff, huh? I can get you a gallon of it for about a buck and a half, if you want, Matt. Some folks here call it 'scrap iron liquor.' Most just call it 'chicken liquor'."

Matt managed to huff, "Chicken liquor?"

"Yeah. Take a drink and you'll *lay* anywhere – in the gutter, on a curb, on a sidewalk." The three men shared a laugh, though Matt's sound was as much a cough as a chortle.

After about an hour, during which Matt nursed his one drink, the detectives decided that one of two things had happened. Either news of the presence of the two white men, possibly cops in the eyes of the patrons, had reached Nathan and he'd stayed away and would do so until the cops departed or he was simply not going to show by mere coincidence. On that basis, Linc and Jim decided to stake the place out from Linc's car for a while, reasoning logically that they'd be less obvious in a parked car in the dark. So, they made their way back to the Hupmobile, sat, smoked, and waited. The car's windows were down in the evening heat. From the open windows of surrounding black residences, radios bleated discordantly on various programs. Matt noticed that the *Amos 'n' Andy* program was not among them.

There wasn't much traffic, foot or automobile, on the street, so they had a good vantage point. After a bit, Greerson, who shared the front

# SHORTENING SHADOWS

seat with Mallard, turned halfway in the car seat and quietly asked, "So what about you, Linc? What's your story? Where're you from? What's your background beyond what you've already told us? I've shared a little of mine with you. C'mon. Give."

Lincoln Mallard lit a fresh cigarette from his old one, tossed the old butt out of his window, and smiled, showing white teeth even in the dim light. "Well, not much to tell really. I was born here in Atlanta. My daddy worked for the railroad. My momma was a domestic for a well-to-do white family on the north side of town. She left that and went to work for the Federal Emergency Relief Administration several years ago. I have a sister and two brothers, all older. Because my parents each worked, we were better off than some but still poor by most standards. My brothers both went to work at young ages to help out, doing whatever odd jobs they could muster. It could be tough, though, because, if my sister or I got sick, Momma couldn't miss work. The money was too dear. So one of the boys had to stay home and tend to the sick one. Even the little money they were bringing in was missed if that happened.

"My sister took Momma's domestic job when she left the white family to work for the government. The family had been good to Momma and really cared for her. Maybe it was because I was the youngest, but my parents were determined to see that I got an education." Linc sighed quietly. "They didn't want me to follow my brothers into the workplace at low-paying jobs. Momma and Daddy always hammered home the importance of an education. The family momma had worked for even paid for me to go to summer school a few years. They had the money. The husband was some sort of official for the telephone company." Matt started to say something about Evie's father and Southern Bell, but stopped himself. "It's kinda funny now, but, when I was going to school, we only had enough money for two streetcar fares among the four of us kids. My sister definitely needed the fare to get to her domestic job. So, my brother, who worked furthest from the house, would pay for his streetcar, get aboard, and get a transfer. Then he'd drop the transfer out a streetcar window to me. I'd use the transfer to catch another streetcar from different station to go on to school at Atlanta University. Life was difficult a lot of the time, but it was like our daddy always told us, 'Tough times don't last; tough people do.' "

"Anyway, I went to college and, after graduation, started my agency with the help of people I sometimes call my sponsors. My wife, Leola, and I had met while we were in school. After I got established, we secretly married, and I moved in with her and her parents. Hopefully, –"

Jim stopped him. "Why secretly married, Linc?"

"Well, Leola's a high school mathematics teacher and the schools are very touchy about married teachers for some reason. I guess pregnancies cutting into their workforce could be the reason. So we're playing their game for now."

Matt leaned forward from the back seat and, without thinking, blurted, "A teacher, huh? Which high school?"

Lincoln snapped his head around at Matt and glared in disbelief at the question for a second before responding. "Now in which the hell high school in 1935 Atlanta do you think she's allowed to teach students, Matt? Booker T. Washington High School!" His words were spoken with considerable asperity.

Matt, stunned at the power of Linc's response and at his own thoughtlessness, could only blush and look at the floorboard. "Sorry," he said feebly. His genuine regret was reflected in his eyes when he returned his gaze to Linc's face. For his part, Jim merely smiled at the reporter's naïveté and shook his head. Matt wanted to blame the alcohol, but knew better.

"No, I'm sorry, too, Matt, but only for the harshness of my response. That was a knee-jerk reaction born of years of the insensitivity of others. It had a lot more meanness to it than I meant. It's clearly unreasonable and perverse that a woman as smart and as gifted as Leola is limited in what she can do, what she can achieve, and the lives she can touch by the stupid, outdated societal norms we have to live under." He shot a smile at his companion. "I am sorry, Matt, for the tone of my response."

"Me, too, Linc. More than you know."

For a long time no one spoke, each man absorbed in his thoughts. After another hour of watching for Nathan Green with no success, the detectives decided to call it a night. Detective Greerson decided that he would probably have to use another, perhaps more ruthless approach to locate his quarry.

---

During the ensuing days, Matt and Evie didn't speak. Her icy tone the night of the boardinghouse supper had bewildered him, and he'd withdrawn some, hurt and confused. Immediately before his regular lunchtime on Wednesday, Matt was sitting at his Remington in the *Georgian's* newsroom, pounding out two relatively minor news items for the next edition. The big headlines still went to the ongoing manhunt for little George Weyerhaeuser's kidnappers and the continued adulation for the record-breaking, transatlantic maiden voyage of the passenger liner *Normandie*. At a pause in his typing, Matt looked up and saw Wilmer Nash standing at the newsroom's door. After a double take, a puzzled Matt pushed back from his desk and made his way to him. They greeted each other with a warm, friendly handshake. In light of the current situation between Evie and him, Matt spoke with an uncertain tone, "Well, Mr. Nash, this *is* a surprise! What brings you here?"

"Well, Matt, I had to come down this way to meet with some Fulton County people. Southern Bell is selling that building on the corner of Pryor and Mitchell Streets to the county for use as a courthouse annex. Thought we might grab some lunch together. That is, if you have time. If not –"

"No, no, that'd be swell, Mr. Nash!" Matt turned and glanced back at his desk. "Uh... just give me a few minutes to finish some copy, and we can go. Do you have the time to wait?"

"I'll make the time, Matt," the older man responded as he followed Matt back to his desk. "You working on anything really juicy?"

Matt spoke as he typed. "No, sir. Only a write-up about a man injured in that fire at the Cascade Theater being built over on Gordon Street and one story about a Florida fugitive arrested here by APD detectives."

"Oh, was your detective friend involved in the arrest?" The wry smile that accompanied the question led Matt to believe he understood the reason for Mr. Nash's unexpected, first-time visit to his workplace.

"No, but his partner was. Some kind of character, that one!" Matt smiled, thinking of Artie Rutherford actually capturing a fugitive. The smile was thin at best, because he was a little concerned about Mr. Nash's visit.

When he'd finished his stories and delivered them to Mr. Cowart, Matt grabbed his hat and coat off the hook and checked for his notepad and pencil. Because he'd already be out, he decided to make his afternoon circuit straight from lunch. As they walked in the warm sunshine Mr. Mindling of the Weather Bureau had promised, Wilmer Nash and Matt made small talk about the Crackers, who continued to hold first place in the Southern League. The two men decided on an eatery on Peachtree Street and found a booth toward the rear, from which both ordered the lunch special. After the waiter left with their orders, Mr. Nash leaned forward on his elbows and made an empty gesture with his hands. Matt steeled himself for what may be coming.

Evie's father explained that, while he didn't want to interfere with their affairs, he was concerned about whatever might be troubling the couple's relationship. Evie, he added, was noticeably upset about something. Matt gave the details of the problem from his perspective and put into plain words what he believed about his need to do his

# SHORTENING SHADOWS

job. Mr. Nash chuckled at the situation and related to Matt a similar issue he'd encountered with his wife in their early years together. The older man assured the young reporter that both he and his wife liked the young man and were glad that he and Evie were seeing each other. The two men parted ways with Mr. Nash promising to speak with his daughter.

---

Seeing as how the weather was nice and he'd started a bit earlier than normal on his afternoon rounds, Matt decided to walk instead of going back to the paper for his Ford Tudor after lunch. Worthy news items were virtually nonexistent as Matt made his various stops. Again, the *Georgian* correspondent made the Atlanta Police Department his last destination in hope of seeing Jim Greerson and catching up on the latest from *his* police blotter. Matt trotted up the front steps of the building and went to the press room to check for any newsworthy police reports. Coming up empty, he returned to the front desk area and asked to see Detective Greerson.

While he was waiting there, a uniformed officer brought a middle-aged man into the station. The parade of humanity that passes through those portals, Matt pondered, good and evil, hopeful and forlorn, never ceases to amaze me. The man the officer held by the arm, apparently arrested for stealing some food, reflected the reporter's thoughts. The man looked down and out, wearing a mud-speckled overcoat, despite the warmth of the day. Under the coat, he wore what appeared to be a secondhand suit, the pants of which were too short. The sole of a shoe was coming loose from a scuffed upper, and it impeded his stride some. His socks didn't match. Despite all this, he carried himself with a quiet dignity, not born of a false ego or an aura of self-importance, but in recollection of when his days had been better through his hard work. Matt swallowed hard. Things just had to get better, the young man moaned to himself.

Suddenly, Jim Greerson appeared. Shaking his friend's hand in friendly greeting, he asked, "What brings you here, Matt?"

"Doing my regular rounds. Thought I'd check to see what may be going on –"

"Say, your timing is great! Linc's on his way over. We're going to talk to that friend of Effie Sledge's he found. Maybe get a line on Nathan Green and on Effie's killer at the same time. Wanna go?"

"Sure! While we're waiting, I'll call the paper. Nothing really to report, but I'll check in with them."

"Fine! See you in a few minutes."

A short time later, Matt and Jim stood in the desk area of the police department, waiting for Linc. Artie Rutherford appeared from the detectives' area and stopped momentarily to speak to Jim. "I'm headed to the courthouse, Jimbo, since you're going out with the dinge and, I guess, the newsie." Turning to Matt, he snarled, "How goes it, punk?"

"Do you ever get tired of having yourself around, detective, like the rest of us do?"

Before Artie could respond to Matt, Lincoln Mallard pushed through the front doors, giving the detective a more desirable target for his disdain. "Well, looky here! It's Sam *Spade*! Detective Greerson tells me you're goin' lookin' for a girl named Squash. Squash 'cause she's got light colorin', right?" He guffawed before finishing with unveiled contempt, "Well, if she's Squash, that must make you Eggplant!"

The black private investigator didn't bat an eye. "You know, a punk is a punk, whether white, black, or otherwise."

Jim laid a hand on Artie's arm as he bristled. "What happened to the respect we were gonna show each other?" he asked.

Artie never took his eyes off Linc. His voice was subdued but seething. "Well, let me say just one thing! And I'll clean it up just for this *Negro*!

Nothing shapes your opinion of *Negro* people like your experiences with *Negro* people. The last three deaths of Atlanta Police Department officers on duty came at the hands of *Negro* men."

"Maybe, but how many Negro men were put down by white Atlanta Police Department officers during that time? And, just so you know, detective, that's Negro with a capital 'N' to you!"

Detective Greerson's grip on Rutherford's sleeve tightened. The latter glared at Linc for a moment. "Just remember one thing, shine, I can shoot fast and fix it faster afterwards." Without waiting, he glanced at his fellow detective. "I'll see you later, Jimbo." Artie moved away quickly and disappeared through the doors.

"So, that went well." Jim sighed sarcastically. He looked at Linc sideways. "You know, some blood may spill before this is over between you two, Linc."

"I'm afraid a lot of somebody's *will* spill blood somewhere before this problem is ever resolved, Jim. Period." The black private detective's voice was even and hard, yet hinted at regret. Jim simply nodded gravely.

After a short, weighty pause, the Atlanta detective moved on. "Okay. You ready to go find Squash, Linc? Matt's going with us."

"Ready as I'll ever be," replied Linc. He smiled at the reporter.

"Glad you can come along, Linc. Two brains are better than one."

Matt flinched. "Hey! What about me?"

"Oh, I hadn't heard," Jim tossed his head back and laughed, as the three men hustled for the door.

On the way to Jim's Hudson, Matt volunteered for the rumble seat, tentatively kidding Linc about him not being made to sit in the rear. Unfortunately, once all three were ensconced in the coupe, Jim's efforts to coax the car to life proved futile. Its motor wouldn't turn over. Jim was beside himself with frustration. Both Matt and Linc quickly volunteered to retrieve their automobiles. Being uncertain of available parking and having excellent weather, Linc had walked from Auburn Avenue to the police station. Jim didn't want to spend the time walking to another car. Confirming that their destination was the Pittsburgh section of town, he suggested taking the streetcar there. All agreed.

In due course, the three men stood on Peachtree Street, waiting for a southbound streetcar. As the car approached their location, Jim saw the location of a few passengers and a thought crossed his mind for the first time. He glanced at Linc whose face bore a peculiar look. The Atlanta detective wondered if Linc was pondering the same issue. "Follow my lead, Linc," Greerson said quietly over his shoulder as they climbed aboard the sparsely occupied streetcar. The motorman gave the black investigator a hard looked as the three men walk backed between the trolley's seats together. Jim first indicated, and then followed Matt into the last seat in the front half of the car and pointed for Lincoln to sit in the seat behind him, the first seat in the back half.

The big Atlanta cop turned sideways in the seat, laying his arm on its back and facing both men. "Now, we can talk without breaking any of their 'rules.'" The black detective smiled hesitantly. Although not afraid, he knew full well that the only person to suffer from a disturbance on a streetcar would be the Negro. For his part, Matt recognized the problem they might encounter and did not look forward to any uproar. However, he was prepared for anything. Greerson prodded on, "I'm hoping we can find this Viola Johnson girl again where you saw her, Linc. The bigger issue may be getting her to talk to me. If this Nathan Green's as mean as you've heard he is, Linc, we may –" The detective's thought was interrupted by the streetcar slamming to a halt unexpectedly. The conductor surged from his position and moved swiftly toward the three men in the middle of the car. Mallard tensed slightly. "I'll handle this," Greerson whispered over his shoulder. He turned and beamed a smile at the wiry streetcar man walking his way. The motorman wasn't the same one Matt had encountered on his way to the Crackers' opener, but he had the same nasty expression on his ruddy kisser.

The uniformed guy stopped at a point between the two seats. "Exactly what are you two doin'?" he demanded harshly.

"We're riding, sitting, and talking. Is there a problem?" Jim's voice was cool and calm.

"Not on my car you ain't! You gotta get up! Move back!" the uniformed man growled at Lincoln Mallard, pointing to the sign in the front of the car. Matt was having a flashback.

"Wait. Aren't we abiding by all your rules? I'm in front of your imaginary line dividing the car and he's behind it. And he's not sitting in front of any whites." Jim pointed out. "So what's the problem?"

"You tryin' to tell me my business, mister?" the uniformed man snarled with a cold smile. He hiked up his britches and proclaimed, "Mess with me, and I'll call the cops on ya'll!"

Detective Greerson rose from the seat, stretching his large frame to its fullest over the man and flashing his badge. "I'll save you the trouble! I *am* the cops, Buster Brown! And I'm on *official* business! Now you need to get your happy fanny back up there and drive this thing," he said, waving a hand generally around the car, "like these good people paid for you to do." The streetcar man became angrier when he saw the smile on Mallard's face, but, sensibly, let the storm pass and returned to his duties.

---

In the course of time, the two detectives and the reporter got off a streetcar onto McDaniel Street to locate Viola Johnson, also known as Squash. The motorman was still giving Lincoln angry looks when the three disembarked. The trio walked the short distance to where a cluster of black women stood. They were at the same location Linc had found them days earlier. As before, the women were fanning themselves in the afternoon heat. A woman with light complexion stood out among the group. The women were busy talking and didn't notice the approaching men until they were almost on them. When they did see the two white men dressed in suits, enough panic came over the joy girls that they started to scatter. Greerson's yell for them to stay put or else froze them in their places, apprehension marking their faces.

Among the small crowd was the defiant woman Linc had encountered the previous Friday. Her boldness hadn't waned during the intervening days. "Well suh, looks like the preachuh man done brought some comp'ny wid him dis time! I be bettin' ain't *no* preachuhs in dat bunch!"

Detective Greerson smiled but wasted no time in getting to the point. "Okay, ladies, I'm Detective Jim Greerson of the Atlanta Police Department." The women stiffened noticeably. The detective raised a wide palm to calm them. "But I don't care about what you're doing here. I'm not here for any reason, except to speak with this woman right here." As he spoke, Jim turned to face the woman known as Squash. With his words, the woman's shoulders dropped in uncertainty, while the rest of the cluster relaxed slightly. "It's all right, Miss Johnson. You're not in any trouble. I just need a little bit of information. Let's go over here to talk for a few minutes. Then you can get back to work." When the woman hesitated, Greerson took her by the arm firmly and led her toward a gap between two nearby buildings and out of earshot of the other women. Departing the group, Jim tossed back to them, "The rest of you stay here."

The defiant one called after him, "Whatcha messin' wid Viola fo'? She ain't done nothin'!"

The big cop stopped and turned slightly without releasing his grip on the young black woman. "The reason's noneya."

"Noneya?" came the insolent joy girl's reply.

"Yeah. None ya business, lady." The three men and the woman walked into an area between the two buildings as taunts from the small assembly of women followed them. Again, Matt Grimes assumed the role of observer. Jim stopped and released the woman's arm. She was tall and lean with large eyes that bulged slightly. Jim thought her eyes looked bilious. Her hair had been straightened. "Listen, Viola, I'm not looking to jam you up. I can, but I don't want to. That's up to you." He paused and pushed his hat back on his head with a hefty hand. "I understand you were good friends with Effie Sledge."

Viola's eyes watered as she cut them to Lincoln Mallard, who nodded. She quickly looked back at Jim. "Whatcha want, mistuh?" Her voice was nearly a sob.

"I'm trying to solve her murder. Part of that requires me to find Nathan Green. I understand that Effie worked for him and so do you. I don't really care about that, but I think he might know something about who killed her."

The woman's reaction led Detective Greerson to believe that his words surprised her but simultaneously confirmed something she had suspected all along. Linc glanced at the Atlanta cop. He'd seen the same thing in the girl's eyes. Jim bored in, "Effie had been pregnant, hadn't she?" The girl nodded slightly as a tear traced its way down her cheek. Now, feeling that the girl would be truthful with him, the detective prodded on. "Nathan knew about it and wasn't happy, was he?"

The light-complexioned girl slowly shook her head. "She found his disfavuh when he learnt of it. He beat her tur'ble. Acted lak that beatin' might rid her o' the baby. But Effie and her baby was tough. Nathan di'n't wanna beat her to death. She wurth too much. When the beatin' didn't wu'k, he make her go see a doctuh to be rid of it. Effie di'n't want to go to the doctuh, but she's afred." Viola glanced toward the opening between the buildings leading back to the street. "Jus' like the rest o' us. Scairt to death's all. All Effie was to Nate en his boss was money. That's all any o' us is. Nothin' mo'." Viola paused and took a deep breath, shuddering. Linc put a reassuring hand on her shoulder. "I sho' ain't gittin' in the baby way! Naw, suh! I takes *pre*-cautions. The mens don't lak it none. But not me! Uh-uh!" She paused and choked a moan. Jim listened and said nothing. "Effie was lak a sister to me. I loved that girl.

She was all the family I had." With the last words, the girl began a hard cry. Jim reached for her, but she fell against Linc' shoulder, sobbing.

In Matt's eyes, his friend showed remarkable patience in these moments. He'd shown more than the newsman had observed most other times they'd been together. Jim stood tolerantly waiting for the woman to compose herself. When her crying subsided a bit, Greerson touched her arm. Linc saw the gesture and took the girl by her arms, turning her toward the cop. "Viola," Jim said softly. After a second or so, she looked up at him. "Viola, I need to find Nathan Green. Do you know where I can find him? Do you know who Nathan works for?"

She looked up at the big cop. Her eyes held the uncertainty imbued in many Negroes talking to a white cop during that time. Linc reassured her. Finally, she spoke, "Onlies thing I know is Nathan work fo' a big, ugly white man. Nasty man. Don't know no name. Nathan, he spend a lot o' time at Horace's place." When she saw Jim and Linc shaking their heads, she continued, "But bestus I know, he stay at the Dixie Hotel. There or Performers Hotel. They both on Decatur Street. He move around sometimes. But that's bestus I know." Her head dropped to her chest. Tears flowed.

Jim reached out a comforting hand and touched her arm again. "Thanks, Viola."

As the men turned to leave, the woman spoke after them. "Mistuh, ya won't say my name to Nathan, will ya? He'll kill me."

"No Viola, I won't mention your name to anyone." He took a step back toward the woman. "But what about your girlfriends out there," he added, nodding toward the street. "Can you trust them to do the same? I'm sorry I approached you like this, but I didn't feel as if I had much choice. Do you have someplace out of town you can go? Any family? At least for a while? We'll help you get there if you need money."

"Nah. I got distant kinfolk in Amer'cus, but I cain't go back there." The black woman looked hard and broodingly at Jim. "Mistuh, if you find Nathan kilt Effie, git 'em fo' her. En fo' me." With her words, Jim's mind flashed back to that night of Vivian's plea to him. Another promise of revenge to put on his list. He merely nodded as he turned and walked away.

The three men returned to the Five Points area by streetcar. As luck would have it, they encountered the same motorman as before. The man tried hard, yet unsuccessfully to ignore the three as the two detectives sat in the same seats, as they had on the southbound journey, and discussed their next steps. The streetcar operator kept giving the trio hard, angry looks. However, on this trip, there was no confrontation. Linc and Jim ignored him.

The detective and the private investigator decided to split the two hotels Viola had mentioned for stakeout duty to try to locate Nathan Green. They agreed that Jim would take the Dixie Hotel, because it was closer to police headquarters. So that's how each man spent the rest of his week when not occupied with other matters. Linc also returned to Horace's a few evenings, just in case. Neither man found their prey. Part of Jim's time was spent getting the Hudson running again. For his part, the week's news failed to produce anything of note for Matt. Several times, he contemplated his gratitude that there was not another Atlanta Food Show on the horizon. However, he knew of one upcoming Fulton County court case that should bring some fodder for his Remington.

---

Matt telephoned Evie that Friday evening. They talked for a long time about various things. Evie seemed less distant than she had the night of the boardinghouse supper, but there was still an uncertainty in her voice. Matt asked her to go out for dinner and a movie the following Saturday night. He wanted her to have more time to consider the future of what he thought was a strong, long-lasting relationship. She accepted his invitation. He cradled the telephone still wondering if there even was a future together for them. His sleep that night was fitful at best.

# CHAPTER 13
# The Investigation Maze

The afternoon of the second Tuesday in June found Matt seated in Fulton Criminal Court amid the "legal ballet" performing the trial of Walter Cutcliff, the late Eddie Guyol's associate in crime. Cutcliff was charged with operating a lottery and with speeding. The allegations stemmed from a high-speed chase back in early April, where a high-powered car Cutcliff was in was wrecked while running from the law. The car also happened to contain a couple of sacks of lottery tickets and, according to the State, a Negro occupant at the time. Matt recalled that he and Jim had talked about the car chase the night of Guyol's murder. Because of Guyol's death, it was alleged by the State that Cutcliff was now the king of the Atlanta lottery. Seeing the big man in person confirmed in Matt's mind that he was the man with Eddie Guyol when they'd had their run-in after the Crackers' opening-day game. Matt was covering the trial for the paper, but also was present for something of a personal nature. He always enjoyed seeing guys like Cutcliff get their comeuppance.

As the trial wound down toward late afternoon with Cutcliff making a brief unsworn statement to the jury, Detective Greerson appeared in the courtroom and signaled to Matt to come out into the hallway. There, Matt found Jim standing with Artie Rutherford at his side. Jim broke into a broad, but tired grin, "I thought I'd find you here if you weren't at the paper."

Matt was surprised to see them. "What's going on, Jim?"

"We've just come from the murder of another Negro girl. Linc showed up, too. I thought you might like to know since none of your competing newspaper associates showed up."

"Where was it? Was it similar to the others?"

"It wasn't *similar* to the Maddox and Sledge murders, Matt. It was *identical*. Head bashed in, throat slit. Identical. Right down to the missing shoes. The girl —"

"Say, Jim," Matt interrupted excitedly, "some victims in the Atlanta Ripper cases had —"

"Yeah, yeah, I know," the detective shot back, edgily. "Most of the so-called Ripper's victims had their heads bashed in and their throats cut. Some girls even had their shoes missing, too. Give me credit for doing my homework, Matt." Artie smiled at the touchy back and forth between the two friends.

Matt bowed up at the sight of his smirk. "So, Artie, a *Negro* female's murdered and you go to the scene anyway? Turning over a new leaf?" he asked sarcastically.

"Aw, shaddup, punk!" Rutherford seethed.

"Artie! Matt! Knock it off!" Jim intervened wearily. Detective Rutherford hesitated and rocked side to side on his feet before walking a distance down the hall. Jim turned back to his young friend. "Hey, look, Matt, I'm sorry for my agitation. I was up most of the night looking for Nathan Green, and then went out on the murder early this morning.

I'm dog tired. That's all. Look, here's the scoop. The girl's name was Lavinia Ruffin. From what I've learned today, she was about twenty-two. Reported to be in the same line of work as the other two girls. Seems she was dragged into some weeds and killed sometime late yesterday afternoon or last night over on Gillette Avenue. Her body was discovered by two men walking to work at the Willingham-Tift lumber yard. Scared hell out of them apparently." Matt jotted hurried notes as his friend relayed the information. "Anyway, same M. O. as the others. Beyond that, about as many clues as I had on the others, which is to say none! But, on the upside, her clothes happened to be in enough disarray that I could see the same striations on her body that Sledge and Maddox had. So there's a definite connection in my mind. But brother! A corpse lying around in this heat for about twelve hours is not good for the nasal passages!"

Matt was shaking his head in thought as a fellow reporter emerged from the courtroom. "Hey, Grimes," the man called out in a stage whisper, "Judge Wood just sent the jury out to deliberate."

Matt waved his thanks and turned back to Detective Greerson. "Now, I'm only asking, Jim. Any luck with tracking Green?"

Greerson sighed, "Hell no!" Rubbing his eyes, he went on, "Neither Linc nor I have had any luck. Green and Gutowski must use the same scheme to move around and hide out. Look, I gotta get back to the stationhouse and finish some paperwork and stuff so I can go home and get what I'd like to think is some well-earned sleep. So how about we talk tomorrow?" Matt nodded. "Call me," the detective tossed over his shoulder as he departed, collecting Artie on his way.

About an hour later, the jury returned with a guilty verdict against Walter Cutcliff for the lottery charge and for speeding. Sentencing was set for the following day. Matt dodged random rainfall the next morning to get to the courthouse and see the tall, two-hundred-twenty pound Cutcliff sentenced to twelve months on the chain gang for the lottery conviction and a fine or six months imprisonment for the speeding conviction. Cutcliff, still proclaiming his innocence, vowed an appeal and posted appeal bonds. As he left the building, Matt quietly wondered whether Cutcliff would still weigh the same after he had to do some honest hard, physical labor during his chain gang sentence. A smile played across his face at the thought.

Later, back at the *Georgian*, Matt telephoned Jim Greerson. The detective had nothing to report on the search for Nathan Green and nothing new on the murders of the black girls. He relayed his belief that the status of the cases would change when he located Green. When asked, Greerson told his friend that he had nothing further to give him on the investment banker's murder. Matt pounded out the stories relating to the Cutcliff trial and the murder of Lavinia Ruffin. Although he acknowledged that there might be a connection between the murders and the medical procedure, Barnes blue penciled any reference to abortion. "At least for the time being," he said.

———

Finally, the night of the big championship fight between Max Baer, the prohibitive favorite, and the slightly older, much lighter Jim Braddock arrived. The city welcomed the sunset, hoping for a reprieve from the soaring afternoon temperatures. According to reports, the severe heat had melted fuses in a Whitehall Street shoe store, thereby setting off an automatic sprinkler system, flooding the store's window display, and ruining several dozen pairs of shoes. Adding to the discomfort from the heat was the high humidity brought about by scattered thundershowers.

The boardinghouse "family" had gathered in the parlor in quiet conversation, awaiting Miss Dixie's call to supper. Rhamy and Matt were discussing the evening's much-anticipated title fight. The young reporter felt certain that Baer would easily defeat the Irishman Braddock, but his landlord, always one to take the underdog's part, was equally convinced of a Braddock win despite the ten-to-one odds. Staying on the fringe of the conversation, Joshua revealed that he had no taste for the fine art of pugilism and didn't seem interested in the fight at all until Mr. Fleming mentioned that Baer was known to wear a prominent Star of David on his trunks. Melvyn joined the conversation in an obvious attempt to be "one of the boys," though he knew little about the sport or the match.

Teresa took Mr. Fleming's side in the discussion, expressing her hope for a Braddock win. Matt teased her that she was still upset that Baer had beaten the Italian, Primo Carnera, for the heavyweight championship almost a year to the day earlier. In response, Teresa blushed, giggled demurely, and assumed a fighting stance against Matt, who hid his face behind his arms in mock fear. The other female boarders were wondering aloud what all the fuss was over about the time Miss Dixie came to the dining-room door and announced supper. She chuckled and said that she'd prepared corned beef and cabbage, befitting her husband's pick of the Irishman to win the fight. Mr. Fleming playfully asked her whether she thought that no one in the household could smell the meal being prepared, thereby requiring her to make a formal announcement. She laughed and waved a dismissive hand at her husband as she returned to the kitchen. Those gathered laughed and took their seats at the food-laden table. When Miss Dixie quickly returned, the social time each meal presented ensued.

Diane took her usual seat next to Matt before the meal and immediately began playfully nudging his feet under the table. He accepted her actions for what they were. She was acting like a bothersome kid sister. To her surprise, Matt grasped one of her shoes with his feet and pulled it off, quietly sliding it under his chair. She tried and failed to surreptitiously locate it under the table with her feet. At once, Diane realized the embarrassment of having to explain that she'd lost a shoe during the meal, which would stand in conflict with the decorum Miss Dixie expected at her table. Diane briefly glared at Matt. For his part, Matt merely shot her a silly smirk. The young woman returned his look with a pouty expression. When this effort failed to produce the return of her shoe, she abandoned her playfulness and blushed, trying her best to pretend that all was normal. The meal ended before Matt quietly returned the footwear to its relieved owner.

After the sumptuous meal, most of the household followed its normal custom of regrouping in the parlor for a relaxing evening of reading, talking, and listening to the radio. However, Mr. Fleming, who expressed concern that the day's heat might be taking a toll on his wife, insisted that she join the others and relax in the parlor while he and Cliff cleared the supper table and cleaned the kitchen. Miss Dixie reluctantly agreed.

In a short while, Rhamy and his son joined the parlor gathering in the middle of the *Fleischmann Variety Hour* broadcast. The *Fleischmann's* program was followed at eight o'clock by the *Maxwell House Show Boat*. The time seemed to drag by. Shortly before nine p.m., Teresa, Matt, and their landlord retired to the Fleming family's smaller parlor across the hall. Despite his attempts to involve himself in the presupper fight discussions, Melvyn opted to stay in the parlor rather than listen to the fight with the others. Matt mused that his true, secret objective was to stay as close as possible to Amanda. While Rhamy warmed up the old Crosley and made sure a clear signal was coming in from WSB's radio tower atop the Biltmore Hotel a dozen or so blocks away on West Peachtree Street, Matt closed the pocket door to the hall for the duration of what he was sure would be a very short bout. As the trio settled in, Miss Dixie appeared with a pot of coffee, cups, sugar, and cream on a tray. Then, she quietly departed.

The gathering settled in by the radio. As the broadcast began, they stared at the radio's grill cloth as if they could see the fighters. What followed referee Johnny McAvoy's instructions to the contestants was, at least from Matt's understanding of the announcer's description, a battle unexpected by most fight fans. Baer seemed to take his opponent lightly while the Bulldog of Bergen spent much of his time dodging and blocking the champ's punches, especially Baer's much-touted right hand. However, the hardworking challenger appeared to win round after round by sticking his jab sharply to Baer's face. Mr. Fleming and Teresa became more ecstatic as the fight progressed. On the other hand, Matt was stunned by the champ's lackadaisical performance. Periodic whoops from the two Braddock backers brought Miss Dixie to the parlor's door several times before she resigned herself to the uproar. On one of those visits, Cliff finally joined the threesome to see what the excitement was about. Freckles followed the boy into the commotion. She went to each of the room's occupants, wagging her tail in enthusiasm, getting her ears scratched, before settling down on the floor next to Cliff. Matt's hope for a Baer win was renewed when the champ dished out a heavy barrage to his opponent in round seven, only to be frustrated when the announcer said that Baer appeared to be clowning in the eighth round by momentarily feigning an injury.

Throughout the bout, Braddock, renowned for his strong chin, weathered the storm, and he was still going strong when the final bell sounded. In the end, Braddock won a unanimous decision and the heavyweight championship title. Teresa hugged Mr. Fleming in celebration before prancing her way to Matt, giving him a bear hug and a big kiss on his cheek. Although he knew Teresa meant nothing by her actions, the episode stunned Matt almost as much as the fight's outcome had. Rhamy Fleming, grinning from ear to ear, shook Matt's hand as if the two were somehow responsible for the fight's result. Out of the blue, Matt was reminded of how someone had defined football during his playing days at Georgia: Football is twenty-two men on the field desperately in need of rest with thousands of people in the stands desperately in need of exercise.

The next morning's visits to the various news sources provided Matt with few items to write about. Returning to the newspaper, the young journalist wrote copy on two woman killed when their new car collided with a train in Newnan, a town a short distance south of Atlanta. A second article involved the seizure of a quantity of marijuana cigarettes in Columbus, Georgia, by inspectors from the Georgia Department of Agriculture. The yield was the largest single haul of marijuana cigarettes ever made in the state to date.

After speaking with Mr. Barnes about his current stories and the latest on the black girls' murders, Matt took the copy to Mr. Cowart. As he stood at the old man's desk making small talk, the telephone on the Matt's desk started ringing. He hurriedly made his way back and scooped it up by the fifth ring. "Matthew Grimes here."

"Hey, Matt!" answered Detective Greerson. His voice was calm but pressing. "We've got the report of another dead Negro girl. I'm headed out now. Interested?"

"Sure!"

"Pick you up in front of the paper in ten minutes. See ya!"

It took a second for Matt to realize that Jim had rung off and he was listening to dead air. He grabbed his coat and hat and quickly let Mr. Barnes know what was going on. "Stay in touch!" the editor yelled after him, waving a dead cigar. Barnes sensed that a larger story could be bubbling to the surface in what Matt was pursuing.

In his rush to the door, Matt disturbed the gentle slumber of Brick, who jolted awake. "Is the joint on fire?" the old reporter called to his young associate. Looking around and seeing order and calm among the rest of the staff, Brick quietly settled back in his chair.

Shortly after Matt reached the sidewalk and lit a cigarette, Jim's Hudson screeched to a stop across Marietta Street from the newspaper building. A cloud of dust rose and drifted behind the car. Matt dodged traffic and crossed the busy thoroughfare to the waiting detective.

Greerson was already pulling away from the curb as Matt closed the passenger door. "Is there a hurry, Jim?"

"No, Matt. Sorry. I'm just frustrated that these murders keep happening, and I can't seem to get any closer to stopping them. Besides," he continued as he turned left onto Spring Street, "I have a bad feeling about this one gnawing at my gut." The big cop flicked cigarette ash through his open window. His face darkened as he spoke.

"Where're we going, Jim?"

"Eads Street. Familiar with it?" Greerson glanced at his passenger, who was shaking his head. "It's just off McDaniel Street." The concern haunting Jim slowly dawned on the young reporter. "I dunno," Jim sighed absently. "We'll see."

Jim turned onto Eads, a narrow road that ran perpendicular to and to the east of McDaniel Street. He pulled the Hudson to one side, and the car's motor hiccoughed to a stop. A small crowd was gathered at the opening to a space between two houses. Jim shouted that he was the police and hurriedly pushed his way through the gathering. Matt followed at a slight distance. Before Matt could get completely through the crowd and focus on the body lying beside one of the houses, he heard a sharp crack. Jarred, he looked and saw Jim's forehead pressed against the side of one of the clapboard frame houses, his fist still against the wall where he'd struck it in frustration. Small, aged paint chips fell from the house. The aimless chatter in the throng stopped at the sudden bang. The wide-eyed face of a small black boy appeared at an open window right above Greerson's head. After a moment, the child turned away from the window and could be heard running through the house calling for his momma.

Matt continued toward his friend and casually glanced down at the woman's body lying at the feet of a black man dressed in a dark-blue suit. Matt was jolted yet again. The body was that of a thin, light-skinned black woman with straight hair. Her slightly bulging eyes were half opened but saw nothing. The side of her head had been crushed and her throat cut. Blood had soaked the sand around her head and caked her hair to her scalp. The coppery stench of blood, to which Matt had become to some extent accustomed during the past two months, wafted to him. For the first time that morning, the oppressive heat of the day overtook the journalist. He felt slightly lightheaded. Accustomed or not, Matt fumbled slightly for a cigarette and lit it to stave off the odor. As he looked from Viola Johnson's body to the well-dressed, older black man standing over her, the blond reporter heard Jim utter a low moan followed by a loud "Dammit!" The expletive echoed between the houses. The word was anguished and angry. Matt looked sideways at his friend whose eyes were squeezed shut.

The black man seemed uncomfortable standing there as he fidgeted with the fedora in his hands and spoke to Matt. "I'm Reverend Fitchett. The folks who live here and found this poor child called me. They're in my congregation. I called the police. Do you need anything more from me, sir?" Matt looked back to the pastor. He was tall and thin and had an august air about him. The distinguished effect was amplified by the graying at his temples and the pince-nez pinching the bridge of his nose and attached by a ribbon to the buttonhole of his lapel. His voice was soothing, kind, reassuring even in these circumstances.

Matt then shifted his stunned eyes from Fitchett to Detective Greerson for an answer. Jim opened his eyes, raised his eyebrows in exasperation, and inhaled deeply. He exhaled as he spoke, "No sir, Reverend Fitchett. Just, uh, let me get your name and contact information and you can go." He paused briefly before going on, "If you want to stay long enough for me to ask your congregants a few routine questions, you're welcomed to do so. They may feel more at ease speaking with me if you're present." The preacher nodded his understanding and his agreement.

As Detective Greerson pushed away from the side of the house he'd been leaning against, a familiar figure broke through the crowd of onlookers. "Lincoln Mallard!" a fairly relieved Reverend Fitchett called out.

Matt and Jim turned to see their friend approaching. "Doctor Fitchett! How're you doing, sir?" Linc glimpsed at Jim and Matt as he shook hands with the minister. The black detective saw a cautious, concerned look in the clergyman's eyes. He turned to his two white friends and nodded in greeting. "Morning, Jim, Matt." Returning his gaze to the black man beside him, he said softly, "It's okay, Reverend Fitchett. These are good men." He moved his hand between the men. "Atlanta Detective Jim Greerson and *Georgian* reporter Matt Grimes. This is Reverend Moses Fitchett, Doctor of Divinity." The preacher relaxed visibly as he hesitantly exchanged handshakes with the two men. Glancing down at the body, Linc got his first good look at the dead woman. His heart sank. "Oh no! Not Viola!"

Fitchett was taken aback slightly. "You know this young woman, Lincoln?"

"Yessir," Jim interjected in a low, dead tone, "we all knew her. She was helping us with an investigation of the murders of some young Negro girls."

"Oh, yes," Fitchett acknowledged, "I've read something of them in the newspapers."

"How'd it happen, Jim? Do you have anything on it?"

"No, Linc. Matt and I only got here a minute or so ago. We got a call from Reverend Fitchett here, I guess," Jim nodded toward the minister, "about the body being found. How did you happen to show up here?"

"After the first three crime scenes, I'd think you'd realize by now that news about the Negro community gets back to me pretty quickly. Sort of a network of information." He smiled thinly, "Some might call it an 'underground railroad' of intelligence."

Jim nodded and smiled thinly at the reference. He knelt beside Viola's fully clothed body. "Killed just like the others. Apparently, knocked out on the street and dragged in here. But, this time, a different motive." He looked up at his two friends. "This girl wasn't pregnant. She told us so only a week ago." He paused and sighed noisily. "Her shoes... she's got no shoes. Given the M. O., it's the same person or persons... but a different motive," he repeated distantly. Dr. Fitchett was fairly bewildered by the things Jim Greerson was saying but held fast and listened intently. The detective paused, and then drew a deep breath. "I blame myself for this. If I'd've found Green before now, this probably wouldn't have happened. She'd be alive." When he finished his examination of the body and the area around it, he exclaimed, "This had to have been done because she talked to us, dammit! I'm gonna hunt that son of a bitch down and –!" Jim caught himself and looked up at Reverend Fitchett. His eyes locked onto the older man's as he rose from Viola's body. "Sorry, Reverend..."

A small smile quirked at the corners of the preacher's mouth. "It's all right, young man. The Good Book tells us that, when justice is done, it brings joy to the righteous but terror to evildoers. So, justice shall thou pursue, detective."

The big cop returned Fitchett's smile. "I love Proverbs. A lot of wisdom in that book. And with a touch of Deuteronomy tacked on." Yet again, Matt was in awe of the range of Jim Greerson's knowledge. Jim made a vague motion with his left hand between the two black men. "So you two know each other?"

"Yeah, Jim. Dr. Fitchett sits on a citizen's committee I work with and, uh," Linc smiled, "do work for."

Jim rubbed his jaw for a second. "Well, nothing more I can do here, guys. Reverend Fitchett, if you have the time, let's go talk to the folks who found this girl's body." The detective quietly gave brief instructions to a uniformed officer as he left Viola's body.

# SHORTENING SHADOWS

Detective Greerson couldn't glean anything that would aid in his investigation when the four men sat and interviewed the woman who'd happened upon the body earlier that morning. The woman, a Mrs. Rosa Adams, was a stout, moon-faced, no-nonsense, motherly type. The small boy Matt had seen at the window earlier clung to her during the conversation. She'd found the body after her husband, a day laborer for the WPA had left for work that morning. Mrs. Adams had been shaken a little by the event but was obviously made of sterner stuff than most when it came to facing life's tragedies. Of two things she was certain. First, the body hadn't been there when she'd last been outside late the night before. Second, even with the windows opened, no one in the house had heard a sound during the night that might have had something to do with Viola's death.

Jim thanked Mrs. Adams and Reverend Fitchett before leaving. He gave her his telephone number in case she thought of anything else. Linc also gave her one of his business cards with an offer to call on him anytime. Jim was grateful for that gesture, because he knew full well that she was more likely to call the Negro investigator than a police department detective. Such was the way the current society operated, he reckoned. He shook hands with Reverend Fitchett and left the house.

The two detectives huddled at Linc's Hupmobile before departing the area. Matt smoked and listened in. Greerson was sure that Viola's death was the handiwork of Nathan Green. "Killing her that way put his name on it as sure as if he'd signed the body," he said. "And he had a motive." Linc agreed. After some more discussion, Jim questioned whether the information they were acting on regarding Green's possible locations was accurate. Linc told him that, because he'd had the same concerns when they continued to come up empty, he had surreptitiously confirmed that Green stayed, on random occasions, at the two hotels they were staking out. Linc added that his visits to Horace's place had had negative results.

Finally, the private investigator told Jim that he couldn't locate his best and most reliable informant for the last few weeks. The other informants he'd been using had been of no help. They discussed the likelihood that Green had learned of Viola's conversation with them and had been shaken by it. Linc expressed his conviction that, though Green was in deep hiding, he'd not left town. As they parted, the two expressed their renewed determination to find Nathan Green as quickly as possible.

Linc returned to his office by way of the Performers Hotel to check for a Nathan Green sighting. When that effort drew a blank, he decided to renew his efforts locate Blue to see whether he could be of help.

Jim dropped Matt off at the paper before returning to police headquarters. Despite his sense of urgency on finding Nathan Green, he had more than one case with which to deal at the moment. He'd swing by the Dixie Hotel a little later.

Before heading out for his afternoon visits to law enforcement and the courthouses, Matt wrote the story of the Viola Johnson murder without naming any suspects. He hoped he'd be able to fill in those blanks with a follow-up article soon.

---

Later that evening, during the *Armour* radio program and a heated game of Whist being played by four members of the household, Matt slipped out of the parlor to telephone Evie. Although Evie's telephone demeanor had warmed during the several calls that week, he wanted to confirm their date for the following night and to determine whether his girlfriend's "warming trend," as Mr. Mindling of the Weather Bureau would say, had continued. After the usual preliminary hellos and how-was-your-day niceties, Evie's voice slipped into that low sultry tone that drove Matt to distraction and roused his long-suppressed stirrings. Their conversation was long and languid.

At one point, he asked what movie she wanted to see the next night. Evie chose *Under the Pampas Moon* playing at the Paramount. They decided on supper at the Ship Ahoy Restaurant before the last screening of the movie that night. The closeness to Evie Matt had felt for some time before the boardinghouse supper fiasco reemerged as they spoke. He'd never stop caring deeply for her, but he'd felt estranged from her since that night. He knew that he didn't want their matrimony, if there was to be one, to go the way the Douglas Fairbanks-Mary Pickford marriage was headed. During their conversation, Matt reminded his girlfriend of the ball game between the staff of the *Georgian* and the staff of the *Journal* scheduled for July seventeenth. She gladly accepted his invitation to go watch him play. Evie's goodnight was as titillating as it had been before *the* boardinghouse supper. When they rung off, Matt was very happy and eager for their rendezvous.

Saturday night rolled around and Matt was walking out of the door when he heard a commotion approaching from behind. Recognizing a familiar refrain, he stepped aside and held the boardinghouse's front door as the dancing, singing Diane, wearing a sporty seersucker blouse and matching skirt, swept past him on her way to meet Dave the Dude. Diane was in high spirits, as was Matt. Because it was raining, Matt gave his fellow roomer a lift to the corner of Houston and Peachtree Street where she was to meet her paramour. He saw Dave's Brewster at the curb there and pulled up behind it. As Diane was climbing into the gleaming automobile, Matt drove past and gave a vague wave to her beau. Dave returned the gesture. Matt could only shake his head because Dave would not at least come to the front of the Houston Street residence to pick up Diane. Moreover, Diane's willingness to walk the distance in the driving rain to meet her guy surprised Matt. He could never imagine Evie tolerating such treatment.

The rest of the evening went swell in Matt's estimation, despite the ominous thundershowers the couple encountered. The seafood at the

Ship Ahoy was as good as ever and the air-cooled theater was a relaxing change from the sultriness and chaos of the stormy night. At the end of the evening, they lingered in his Ford as rain drizzled outside the Nash residence. They discussed at length Matt's job and his need to do certain things, including working with Jim Greerson, to be successful at it. Evie promised to stop pestering him about how he did it, and Matt swore to avoid any dangerous situations and to try to "stay safe," as his girlfriend put it. Because the night had gone well, Matt broached the idea of going to the amusement park at Lake Winnepesaukah that Evie had mentioned some time back. He suggested that they leave early the following Saturday, weather permitting, and make a day of it. Evie seemed thrilled with the idea. She decided that she wanted to pack a picnic lunch for them to take. Matt agreed, so it was set.

When they finally said good night at the front door, their kiss was more passionate than ever. On the drive back to Houston Street, Matt set fire to a cigarette to settle his nerves. He decided that Mr. Nash had indeed spoken with Evie. He was very grateful for her father's insight and persuasive ability. He thought again about that ring in the box, wrapped in tissue paper, and tucked away in his chifforobe.

---

The next week or so brought no satisfaction to the two detectives searching for Nathan Green. Nor was Detective Greerson able to make any progress in his hunt for Carl Gutowski. During one of their get-togethers, an exasperated Jim Greerson told Linc that he thought the earth had opened and swallowed the men. He proposed that either the pair had given up their illegal activities or they'd become more proficient at them. Linc could only nod his head in agreement with the idea and laugh grimly. The big cop decided to pay Gladys another visit to see whether she'd be any more forthcoming on Gutowski's whereabouts. Both detectives agreed that Jim would go that process alone, while Linc concentrated on Green. They parted with the continuing promise to stay in touch.

On the news front, the same period provided the young *Georgian* reporter with a few sensational tidbits, some tragic, some mere follow-ups to earlier stories. An unfortunate local woman was shot to death in her backyard when a neighbor mistook her for a burglar just before dawn on the seventeenth of June. Initially, the neighbor was held on a "blanket charge" of suspicion. The subsequent charge of disorderly conduct was dismissed by John Cones in Recorder Court on the twentieth. Mr. Cones called the shooting an "unfortunate and regrettable" tragedy.

The nationwide manhunt for the killer wanted in the April twenty-seventh mistaken-identity murder of Lester Stone at the Parkway Drive apartment building in Atlanta ended when the suspect was arrested in New York. The man, Sam Rosenfeld, had been questioned by New York police in connection with a year-old murder there. During the interrogation, Rosenfeld admitted to the Parkway Drive murder, as well as two robberies in Atlanta and two elsewhere. Not to leave any stone unturned, the Atlanta police said that they also wanted to question Rosenfeld about the Eddie Guyol murder.

In Tacoma, Washington, the legal proceedings for the George Weyerhaeuser kidnappers continued in Federal Court. On the twenty-first, one of the kidnappers, Harmon Waley, pleaded guilty to violating the "Lindbergh Law." A further element of drama was added to the events there when a Federal judge refused a guilty plea in the case of Waley's nineteen-year-old wife, Margaret. Her court-appointed attorney told the judge that he believed she couldn't be convicted by a jury, thus bringing about the judge's decision.

The afternoon of June twenty-fourth, Matt ran into Jim as the detective was leaving the courthouse. Greerson seemed a little stunned at the unexpected encounter. When Matt asked his friend what he was up to, Greerson quickly pocketed the papers he was carrying and changed the subject. "Say, Matt, I'm going back to revisit Gladys this afternoon. Since I'm getting nowhere trying to find Gutowski, I've decided to put some heat on her to get her to talk. Are you interested in taking some air over on Mitchell Street?"

Matt immediately threw in with the plan and, after a quick telephone call to the newsroom, the pair walked to Detective Greerson's Hudson and motored toward Gladys's hotel. As they drove, Jim told Matt that Rutherford had suggested that maybe Lincoln was committing the Negro women's murders to justify his existence as a black private detective. Both men shrugged off the notion with a laugh.

When they neared their destination on Mitchell, Greerson spied an older uniformed patrol officer coming out of a cheap eatery with a fly-speckled front window. "After we park," he said, "I'm gonna go get that officer. We'll meet you at the hotel door." Matt nodded. Five minutes later, Matt, Greerson and the policeman met at the hotel's entrance. Jim said, "Officer Hawley McFadden, this is Matt Grimes. Matt's a newspaper reporter," Jim winked at Matt, as he went on, "so, be on your best behavior, McFadden." Matt had encountered Officer McFadden at some time in his short career as the police beat reporter, but he couldn't recall when or where. As they crossed the lobby, Jim explained to Matt that he'd already told McFadden about the situation with Gladys. The same clerk from their previous visit was behind the registration desk. He rose slightly at the sound of their footsteps and conversation. When he peeked around the glass screen and recognized Greerson, he quickly fell back onto his chair heavily, out of sight.

At suite three-oh-eight, the detective knocked hard on the door. This time, Gladys opened the door almost immediately. She was dolled up for

373

some occasion and was apparently expecting company. Her face quickly revealed that Greerson wasn't the guy she'd wanted to see. Again, the detective pushed past her into the suite. No one else was in the room. "*Now what is it, flatfoot?*" she demanded. "I'm just gittin' ready to go out!"

"Going out with Gutowski, Gladys?" Greerson's voice confirmed that he was wasting no time this visit.

"That comes under the headin' of none of your business!" she shot back, standing toe-to-toe with Jim.

"Are you gonna help me find Gutowski, Gladys, or do we do things the hard way?"

"You give me a pain in the back of my lap! Now, git out!"

"Where is Carl Gutowski, Gladys?" he demanded, his voice hardened.

"I said, 'Git out'!"

"Arrest her, McFadden." When the uniformed officer hesitated, the detective repeated his words more forcefully. McFadden stepped toward the redhead.

At the words, Gladys backed away from the big detective, savage-eyed, shaking her head forcefully. She back until the wall stopped her. "Arrest me on what charge?" she cried.

"We'll start with obstruction of justice, Gladys. And add prostitution," came a cold, steely reply.

"Prostitution? You got the wrong number, buster! Why... I got a job... uh... in a department store... sellin'!"

"Yeah, you're selling all right, Gladys! But the merchandise you're hawking ain't available in any department store! Take her McFadden!"

The police officer grabbed Gladys, who fought his grip and pulled away. He struggled to get a better hold on her, pawing her as he tried to wrap an arm around her. "Say, what's the big idea?" she screamed as the two grappled. The police officer grabbed her as best he could to carry out the arrest. "Let go of me, will ya? Don't get so fresh! Take your hands offa me!"

"Just checkin' ya for a gun, sister," McFadden offered.

"Oh, yeah?" she jerked an arm from the cop's clutches. He still held her other wrist with his arm around the waist. "Well, that's a hot one! Try it on some rube that's just got to town, copper!" McFadden held firm. When she realized her resistance was in vain, she stopped struggling long enough to look plaintively at Greerson. "Please don't do this, detective!" she cried. Her tone softened, "Please. I'll come clean with ya!"

Greerson made a subtle motion with his hand, and the officer released his grip on the woman. "Okay, Gladys, are you gonna tell me what I want to know? Where can I find your boyfriend?"

She laughed thinly as she massaged her wrist where McFadden had grabbed it. "First off, I don't know where he is." Jim signaled the cop, who reached for Gladys. She dodged his grasp and threw herself onto the davenport, holding her arms tight across the front of her body. "No! I'm givin' it to ya straight, copper!" She relaxed, and her face took on a pitiful aspect. McFadden backed off. Gladys's voice became a sad drone. "I... I ain't Carl's girlfriend. Not no more anyways. We were together a while back. Then he met some highfalutin dame who lives on the north side of town. Out of the blue, he ain't got time for me no more! All of a sudden he's too good for Gladys! After all I done for that big lug." Her voice held the dead fatigue of hopelessness. Suddenly, Gladys's tone changed and her eyes hardened. "I tell ya, I got a raw deal!" She put her face in her hands, crying.

"Yeah. Your kind usually does, Gladys." Jim's voice had more of an edge to it than he intended. But something told Greerson that the woman was telling the truth. "What's this woman's name, Gladys?" He wasn't sure if she'd heard his question amid her sobs. He spoke more forcefully. "Help me, Gladys! Help yourself! What's her name?"

Unsolicited, McFadden put in, "Hey, why don'tcha answer the man's questions?" Greerson smiled his gratitude at his fellow officer but waved him off.

After a long moment, she spoke. "I don't know the dame's name. I swear I don't. I just know she's some bluestocking with dough and class. Her ol' man's a lawyer or a doctor or somethin' like that. But I don't know a name. I don't know where Carl is either. Honest. There's no percentage in it for me to lie to ya," she said between her fingers. She lifted her face off her hands, turned her head slowly, and looked at Greerson. Tears from her reddened eyes streaked her makeup. "I'd tell ya if I knew where to find Carl. Honest."

The detective walked to the couch and stood over the woman. "Mind if I get personal, Gladys?"

Her wet eyes flashed up at the big cop. "Whatcha been doin'?"

Greerson ignored her response and spoke softly, earnestly, "No, Gladys, you wouldn't tell me where to find Carl. You've still got it bad for him. Don't ask me why you do, but I could see that the last time I was here. You're hoping he looks you up when this classy frail throws him over." Gladys started a mournful sob, her face in her hands again. Abruptly, Jim's words were cold and lifeless. "Just so you know, he won't be in any shape to look anybody up after I find him. So don't hold your breath, angel." He glanced at the other two men, "Let's go."

As the three men reached the door to leave, the redhead stopped sobbing and called after them, "Hey, Detective Greerson! One thing I do know is that Carl knows you're after him." Her features hardened, but a cold smile worked its way onto her face. "He says he'll kill ya."

Detective Greerson was walking away. He didn't turn. "We'll see," he said quietly. The words and their tone sent a chill down Matt's spine.

Back on the street, Greerson thanked McFadden and released him to return his regular duties. Then, he and Matt moved along the sidewalk to the Hudson. Matt was perplexed. "So, Jim, you've been a cop for a while. Dealt with shit, with people like this before. What's your gut telling you now? What do you come away with from what Gladys had to say this visit?"

"I think she was telling me the truth about not being Gutowski's woman anymore. That's way too tough for somebody like her to admit, even in a lie. Now, I need to figure out who his new woman is, especially if I can't find Gutowski any other way. In the meantime, I need to catch up with Lincoln Mallard."

"My paper's put to bed for now. Mind if I go along with you?"

"No, Matt. Glad to have you. Besides, you've already come this far." Jim smiled, "And Artie won't want to join me anyway."

---

During the meeting in Lincoln Mallard's office, the private detective told Greerson that he had an informant who he thought might be able to get a lead on where Nathan Green was hiding out. After Matt agreed to keep the information off the record, he briefly explained who Blue was and his use of him. The private detective apologized for his failure to get with Blue during the time since Viola's murder, but his "regular" employment had kept him running constantly during that time. That work, he explained, included one trip to Macon and one to Crisp County, Georgia. And when he did have the time to get with Blue, he couldn't find the man. Jim assured him that no apology was necessary. He was working on more than one case, too. With Linc's promise to get back to Jim if he heard anything, Jim and Matt departed.

---

A few days later, at ten minutes after ten in the morning, Investigator Mallard pushed back from his desk and got out of his chair, stretching his large, muscular frame. His schedule that week had prevented him from locating Blue, and his available free time wasn't looking to get any better as the week progressed. He realized that he simply had to *make*

# SHORTENING SHADOWS

the time to do it. Wherever he could think to do so, the private investigator had left word for Blue to contact him as soon as possible. But, so far, no word. He pulled on his jacket from the coatrack. Linc removed his black-finished .32 caliber revolver from a desk drawer, checked it for ammo, and tucked it away in a coat pocket. He decided not to bother with his holster this time. As was his habit when he went out on the street, he grabbed a handful of cigars from the box in his desk and put them into another handy pocket. He glanced out of the windows onto Auburn Avenue and up at the sky. Rainclouds threatened the afternoon, but the rain hadn't started yet. The thermometer must be pushing the mid-80s already, he thought, as he lowered a window. The detective opted to leave his umbrella in the office and risk a downpour.

By the time he reached the pool hall frequented by his wife's cousin, the sky looked more ominous and Linc wondered if he'd made the right decision about the umbrella. As the private detective turned to enter the building, Blue nonchalantly strolled out. The dapper little man had the ubiquitous cigar screwed into a corner of his mouth. Although the question was burning in Linc's brain, he decided not to ask Blue where the hell he'd been keeping himself for the past two weeks. He needed to cut to the heart of the matter on his mind. For his part, Blue acted as if they'd last seen each other the day before. After a warm exchange of greetings, the big man quickly scanned the nearby sidewalk and got down to business. "Blue, I need your help."

Blue nodded vigorously and listened with anticipation. While Linc's money was good, the smallish black man relished more the opportunity to aid the well-known, highly respected, and better-educated detective. He, too, secretly admired Lincoln Mallard and envied his status in the black community. Though he never mentioned to others the detective's reliance on him, Blue knew that Lincoln knew. That was enough for the little man. "Yeah, I heard you was lookin' for me. I was jus' comin' to yore place. What's happ'nin', Cap'n?"

"I'm trying to find Nathan Green again. It's like he fell off the edge of the earth. I need to find him and fast! *And* it's very important that I locate him *without* him knowing I'm looking. Get me?"

"Oh, sho' 'nuf, cuz. I gets the drift." Blue slowly removed the cigar from his mouth, held it out as he looked at its glowing tip, and smiled smugly. This was a habit of Leola's cousin that Linc found annoying, but he always let it slide. "I'm hep! Small taters, I assures ya. Let me scope the terrain and gets back with ya."

After telling Blue that he could find him in his office over the next several days, Linc hurriedly walked back to his building. Blue swaggered off in the opposite direction. Linc reached the building's front door as the first heavy raindrops fell. Much later that afternoon, as Linc was finishing a report to an insurance company and preparing to leave his office for the day, someone knocked on the door. The detective dropped his pen and wearily stubbed out his cigarette in the desk ashtray, grinding it back and forth until he was sure it was out. As he approached the office door, the powerful odor of a cheap cigar wafting under the sill told him the identity of his visitor. Linc opened the door to a grinning Blue. The investigator tossed one of the little man's standard greetings at him. "What's the buzz, cuz?" he said as he stepped aside with the door and gestured the man into the office. Mallard hoped that Blue's self-satisfied demeanor brought good news on the Nathan Green front. Linc motioned him into a visitor's chair and closed the door. He returned to his desk chair.

"Well," Blue gloated as he shook out his umbrella, took a seat, and looked around the office, "like the Good Book say, 'Seek and ye shall find.'"

"I take it you've got good news!"

"Nothin' to it, cuz!" The broad, arrogant grin quickly left Blue as his eyebrows furrowed over a serious face. He leaned forward in his chair. "Ser'us business, Linc. I don't knows how long ya been lookin' for this guy, but ya shoulda came to me sooner. I had a tag on 'em 'fore yore britches touched yore butt!" The self-satisfied grin returned to the little man as quickly as it had left. Blue leaned back in his chair and clasped his hands together behind his head. His mouth jiggled the half-smoked cigar along his lips.

Linc passed on a comment on his repeated attempt to find the little man over the past two weeks. Instead, he tried firmly to cut short Blue's smug moment. "Well, what'd you find out?"

Not to be denied his minute of basking in triumph, Blue explained the circumstances before the big reveal. "Besides bein' crazy as a bedbug, Nathan's a smart, shifty cat, man. Seems he was stayin' at the Dixie Hotel. Ya know it?" Linc nodded, trying to remain patient. "But he seen some white dude sittin' in a car watchin' the place. Spooked him. So he moved to the DeMonte Hotel over on Ivy Street. That's where he be holed up now. Workin' outta there now. Checked in unda a diff'rent name. Callin' hisself Marvin Turpin." Blue paused and chuckled. "He sportin' a Cab Calloway mustache now, too. Thinks it'd be a disguise. Don't do much fo' 'em to my way o' thinkin'."

Linc gave Blue twenty dollars with his sincere thanks. As the full-of-himself little man closed the office door behind him, Linc was already dialing the telephone number to reach Detective Greerson. When the private detective had explained what he'd learned, Greerson asked whether Linc had time for the cop to come over and meet with him in about half an hour. The meeting was set.

---

Within thirty minutes, Jim Greerson was sitting across the desk from his black counterpart as they tried to put together a plan to corner the elusive Nathan Green. The pimp was obviously too slippery to be easily taken. Jim had already eliminated the idea of merely storming the hotel where he was holed up. Despite what value, or lack thereof, some people put on Negro lives, he felt such a move would put too many innocent civilians, who might be occupying the hotel or on the street, at risk. Also, he wanted to take Green unhurt, if possible. Linc had confirmed what Jim knew of Green's reputation for vicious recklessness. The Atlanta detective surmised that storming the hotel would probably lead to a shoot-out, during which police officers or Green or both could be killed. Finally, they put together a plan, most of which flowed from Lincoln Mallard's formidable mind. When they'd finished going over the details, they decided that they'd need a third person. Jim knew he'd get no help from Artie Rutherford in such an endeavor. And he didn't want to involve other officers in whom he had no confidence. He, they needed someone who would do the right thing when it was required without all the baggage of racial biases and motivations. After a brief discussion, Jim decided to ask Matt Grimes if he'd help them. Linc agreed with that idea. Jim told Linc that the plan would have to wait a few days, because he had to close another case first.

---

By Thursday of that week thundershowers had more firmly entrenched themselves into the Atlanta area, and the thermometer had risen to near the mid-90s. That evening, the Houston Street household was glad to settle in under the parlor's ceiling fan after a delicious supper of Italian beef and noodles with brown gravy followed by thick slices of apple pie, topped with Southern Dairies vanilla ice cream. The rainy darkness beyond the windows was periodically broken by brilliant lightning flashes, followed by deep rumbles of thunder as the household relocated to the parlor.

Matt settled into a chair with the sports section of the *Georgian*. The Crackers had climbed into first place in the Southern League and weren't looking back. The St. Louis Cardinals had struggled into second place behind the National League leading Giants. On the radio, a guy on the *Maxwell House Show Boat* program was crooning his way through the static when there was a hard knock on the front door. The noisy weather had kept even the ever-alert Freckles from hearing the approach of the visitor. Mr. Fleming drowsily eased from his chair and stepped to the door, a newspaper trailing from his hand. After a moment, he reappeared at the parlor door to the hall with Detective Jim Greerson. The detective, wearing a soaked, belted raincoat, bore a grim expression. Matt immediately rose and approached his friend, thinking possibly there had been another Negro girl's body found or some such crime had occurred. When he reached the hallway, Matt saw a rather stern-looking woman dressed in a dark uniform standing by the front door.

Jim removed his coat and shook the rain from it and from his hat. "Matt, I need to see you and Mr. Fleming privately, please."

Matt looked at his landlord, who seemed confounded. "Why, sure, detective," Mr. Fleming recovered, extending his hand and gesturing the way. "Let's go into the small parlor." Jim followed the older man while Matt motioned for the woman to precede him into the room.

When they were all in the family parlor, Jim turned and gently closed the pocket doors. "This is Miss Rudolph, one of our female police officers." The other two men nodded a greeting. She returned the nods and smiled vaguely. "I wanted to let you both know away from the others why I'm here. I regret the circumstances of this, Mr. Fleming, but I'm here to make an arrest in the murder of that investment adviser, known locally as Theodore Brewer, found shot to death in his Cadillac back in May."

"What? Who?" Rhamy Fleming, nonplussed, spoke louder than he'd meant to. Glancing at the pocket doors, and then back to Jim, he repeated in a softer tone, "Who is it, detective?"

"Are you serious, Jim? Someone here?" Matt cut in before the big cop could answer the landlord. His mind, too, was racing at the prospect of a murderer living under this roof. His friend had to be mistaken. "Who is it Jim?"

Greerson pulled a sheaf papers from his coat's breast pocket and tapped them with a forefinger. "The woman's name is Amanda Scott Hardin."

Mr. Fleming started to speak, but Matt laid a swift hand on the man's arm. "Amanda? You've got to be kidding! How do you get to that conclusion, Jim?"

The detective drew in a deep breath and released it silently. Somehow, he felt he'd betrayed the trust of his friend and even, to a lesser extent, Mr. Fleming, a man who'd invited him into his home and broken bread with him. "Well, it's a long story, sort of," Jim began. "Since the night of that supper here, I've been working closely with the authorities in Savannah. I've spent a lot of time looking into and learning a great deal about the backgrounds of Amanda and this Theodore Brewer fellow, whose real name, by the way, was William Housch.

"Amanda came to Atlanta from there, as you know, about five or six years ago. In Savannah, she'd been married to a Leon Hardin. From what I could gather from the authorities down there, they were very much in love and had a very happy marriage. Anyway, Leon was an officer in a fairly sizeable bank there. At some point, Leon discovered that a substantial sum of money was missing from the bank. While secretly looking into the theft, Leon also learned that another bank officer was aware of the missing funds.

"One night, Amanda's husband told her that the other bank officer, a man named William Housch, who people always called 'Dollar Bill' because of his unashamed love of money, had confessed to Leon that he was responsible for the theft. During that conversation with Leon, Housch had tearfully promised to return the money if Leon would help him cover up the theft long enough for him to make it good. Leon, always a kind and forgiving man, reluctantly agreed.

"The next thing anyone knew, William Housch, the still-undiscovered embezzler, left town on short notice, but under apparently normal circumstances. He'd told folks, everyone *except* Leon, that is, that he had to go care for an aged mother in a western state. Well, when Leon learned of Housch's departure, he also found that the money he'd stolen had disappeared with him. Leon was devastated at the betrayal. Worse yet, the efforts of Amanda's husband to help Housch buy some time led to all the evidence pointing at Leon as the perpetrator of the theft. The proof against Leon appeared overwhelming. No one believed his protestations of innocence when he told the story. No one except Amanda, of course. He was utterly despondent and at the end of his rope. One evening, Amanda came home and found that Leon had committed suicide by blowing his brains out with a .25 caliber Colt. Her husband's suicide was the final proof in everyone's mind that Leon had been the real architect of the theft. The police dropped the matter.

"With the suicide, the bank officials considered the matter closed, other than trying to recoup what money they could from Leon's estate. As a result, Amanda was left shamed *and* penniless. After the investigation and the coroner's inquest, Leon's gun was, for some inexplicable reason, returned to Amanda by the police. I can only imagine her feelings when the only thing she had left of their time together and what they'd accumulated during their marriage, was the gun with which her husband had killed himself." Jim paused briefly. "Anyway, she apparently kept it.

"A while after Leon's death, the resulting publicity about the embezzlement, and its apparent ties to Leon's suicide, a friend of Amanda's casually told her that she'd seen William Housch on the street during a recent visit to Atlanta. The friend was unaware of Housch's role in the embezzlement. The sighting was at a slight distance, the friend said, but the she felt pretty certain it was Housch. Her friend's words were enough to spur Amanda's move to Atlanta. Amanda quietly resolved to come to Atlanta to look for Housch, whom she believed had lost himself in the big city.

"It turns out that Housch, in his elaborate and lengthy planning, had gone to a Savannah cemetery in search of a particular type of grave marker. There, he found what he was looking for: a headstone that bore the name of a male who would have been about Housch's age but who had died only a few months into his life. The child had been from a fairly prominent family with sufficient wherewithal to have used a hospital for the birth, probably the Telfair Hospital for Women. In the case of a hospital birth, a birth certificate would have been registered. Having been in the banking business for a while, Housch knew what local families had been well heeled once but no longer were. With the information from the headstone, he went to the courthouse and got a copy of the birth certificate, probably from an overworked bureaucrat. With this document, he was able to obtain the necessary documentation with which to establish a new identity.

"My guess is that Amanda, figuring that even embezzlers have to go to a doctor sometime, went to work in the biggest doctors' building in Atlanta in hope of running across him. Obviously, at some point, she did. By that time, she'd changed her hairstyle and color so as not to be easily recognized by Housch in case he saw her. At least, they tell me her hair was a different color when she lived in Savannah. Ironically, he'd changed his hair color, too, and was wearing a moustache by the time she came across him. But, anyway, she definitely recognized him. I figure she contacted him, probably by telephone to assure her anonymity, told him what she knew of his past, and arranged a meeting. Again, it's just a guess, but the money we found in his car was probably what Housch thought would be a payoff for the blackmailer's silence. But the money was left behind, so blackmail money was not what the killer was after."

Matt naturally fell into his role as a newspaperman. "You mentioned the supper here that Friday night. What did that have to do with leading you to any of this?"

"When we were discussing the man's murder that night, Amanda made mention in passing of a dollar bill left on his body. I think she realized what she'd done when she said it. That bit about the dollar bill was something we'd found at the scene but didn't make public. We didn't know its significance at the time." As Matt started to interrupt, Jim raised a restraining hand. "Look, Matt, I told you that we don't always tell the world everything we find at or know about a crime scene or a crime. I guess the dollar bill left on Housch's body was Amanda's way of saying she'd recognized 'Dollar Bill' and had gotten Leon's revenge. But nobody knew about the dollar bill except a few cops and the killer. Also, the gun that we linked to Housch's killing was the one Leon had committed suicide with. We traced it back to her."

Reflective silence hung in the air for a long minute before Greerson spoke. "I need to speak with Amanda for just a minute here before I take her into custody. But the weather is too rotten to take her outside. I want to do this as quietly as possible, but it won't be a secret for long. Can I use this room and can you bring her in here?" The detective wasn't speaking to either of the men in particular. Matt started to move for the doors, but Mr. Fleming grabbed his arm, firmly but not unkindly.

"No, Matt. This is my job as head of the household." The landlord seemed to Matt to be on the verge of tears. With that, Rhamy opened the doors and stepped across the hall. In a short time, he returned with a subdued Amanda. When she saw Detective Greerson and the policewoman, she nearly fainted. The female police officer caught her and was supporting her as Matt and Rhamy left the family parlor. Behind them, Jim Greerson closed the doors.

The boardinghouse parlor came alive with quiet conversations and anxiety, but neither Matt nor Rhamy would respond to the questions being whispered. Rhamy simply put a finger to his lips while Matt merely shook his head without saying a word.

After a few minutes, the pocket doors to the family parlor opened slowly. As they parted, the household gathered at the larger parlor's opening to the hallway. A red-eyed, crestfallen Amanda walked out. She was in the firm grasp of the policewoman. Miss Dixie emitted an audible gasp and sobbed. At least one of the female boarders was crying. Melvyn, ever Amanda's ardent admirer, quietly took up a position far to the rear of the group. Josh was visibly saddened by the state in which his kindred spirit found herself. Mr. Fleming and Matt stood closest to Amanda and the police officers as they emerged.

Amanda pulled to an abrupt stop in front of Matt. The policewoman resisted her action, but, on a nod from Detective Greerson, relented. Amanda's face suddenly looked haggard and drawn. But she stuck her chin out and held her head up hard and brave. Her tear-laden eyes were sad yet fiercely determined. She spoke slowly to the police beat reporter. Her voice was tired, "I loved my husband very much. When you write it, Matt, be kind."

Matt could only look at Amanda with sympathy and nod helplessly. He reached out and squeezed her hand. "You know I will, Amanda."

Jim Greerson used his bulk to gently move the threesome on to the front door, and they were gone.

Little else was said in the boardinghouse that night. Amid the "it can't be's" and the "must be some mistake's," the gathering of residents broke up early and retreated to their rooms. That night, each person was left to his or her thoughts about the matter.

Initially, Matt couldn't drift off to sleep. His mind was spinning with the night's events. He reluctantly sat up on the edge of his bed. The young man decided that it was too hot for the bathrobe and reached for his trousers folded over the chair. Pulling on his pants in the dark, he found his cigarettes and matches on the bedside table before leaving his room. In the hall, Matt saw lamplight coming from under the sill of the Fleming's bedroom door. He quietly stepped through the door at the end of the hall and out onto the second-story balcony. The night air was sultry but at least the thunderstorms had passed. Tapping the end of a cigarette on the rail, he lit it, and waved the match out before tossing it to the yard below. Matt started woolgathering and soon found himself wondering what would make a person desperate enough to blow his brains out. The concept was beyond his understanding. He shook the thought out of his head. Then, he reflected on the idea that his detective friend had been looking into Amanda's background, suspecting her of murder, for nearly four weeks and never letting on. It dawned on the young man that Greerson might well have been at the courthouse getting the arrest warrant when they encountered one another several days earlier. It would explain the detective's curt actions with the paperwork he'd been holding and his abrupt change of subjects at the time. Jim was just doing his job, Matt reasoned. As he finished the last thought, the screen door slowly opened behind him. Mr. Fleming stepped out onto the balcony and moved toward Matt.

He leaned on the rail next to his boarder. "Mind if I join you, Matt?" he whispered, as he bit a cigar and put a match to it.

"No sir. Of course not," the young boarder replied softly, although he wasn't sure whether he really wanted company just now. But he certainly didn't object.

The two men stood in silence for a while before Rhamy mentioned that he was going to contact an attorney friend the next day to try to get him to represent Amanda. The landlord said he was hopeful based on what the detective had told them about Amanda's motive. Matt simply nodded at the possibility and sighed sadly. He knew Detective Jim Greerson well enough to know that he'd have his facts straight before he acted. When they'd finished their smokes, the two men retired quietly.

During the night, Matt thought he heard sobbing coming from Diane's room directly above his. Maybe it was from Teresa's room just to the rear of Diane's. It didn't matter really. The feeling was pretty much universal in that speck of the universe on Houston Street.

---

When the word of Amanda's arrest reached Evie from Diane the next day, she called Matt early. They spoke briefly about the circumstances of the case. Matt filled her in on all that he knew about it. He assured her that, despite working fairly closely with Detective Greerson, he'd been as surprised at the turn of events as everyone else at the boardinghouse. The subject was set aside for the present.

Several days later, Mr. Fleming quietly told his young blond boarder that he'd secured defense counsel for Amanda.

# CHAPTER 14

# Working Together

The next morning, when Matt typed his account of Amanda Hardin's arrest, he tried to be fair and balanced in his approach, but, in retrospection, he supposed he'd probably failed. He'd erred in Amanda's favor in that regard. Even so, Mr. Barnes approved the story without comment.

An hour or so after he finished the write-up, the phone on his desk rang. Matt answered it to find a hesitant Detective Greerson on the other end of the line.

"Are you mad at me, buddy?" Without waiting for an answer, the cop continued, "Look, I'm sorry for all the hush-hush dealings, but I just couldn't say anything. Even to you. I had to be sure about Amanda. And, once I was, I couldn't afford a slipup."

Matt shook off his uneasy feelings about the situation and tried to get past it. He let his hand holding the telephone's earpiece fall to his shoulder and reflected a second or two before raising it back and responding, "Nah. I understand, Jim. In hindsight, you were probably right to keep what you suspected and what you learned from me." He sighed deeply. "I might have slipped up at some point and said something and blown the whole deal. At the very least, my demeanor toward Amanda might have changed, and that may well have been just as bad."

"Let me buy you lunch as a peace offering, Matt."

The reporter looked at his strap watch. Lunchtime was upon him anyway. "Sure."

"Great!" They made arrangements to meet at the Stars Grill. The eatery was one of Greerson's preferred haunts and was fast becoming one of Matt's favorites, too.

Half an hour later, the two men were seated at a table ordering blue plate specials. In his way, Jim was as contrite in person as he'd been on the telephone. This was not a Jim Greerson that Matt was used to seeing. "Again, I'm very sorry for what I had to do, Matt."

"Well, it's done now. I understand what you did, why you did it." He smiled at the big cop across the table. "Let's move on."

"On the heels of an apology, what I have to ask you next is not going to be easy." Matt's curiosity was aroused, but, before he could ask any questions, the detective explained what Lincoln Mallard had been able to learn about Nathan Green's location. Jim added that they'd confirmed it. Then Greerson limned their plan to Matt. He finished by explaining that they needed a third person to drive the car that night and asked Matt to do it. Matt related that he and Evie had a date set for that evening and asked if it had to be that night.

Greerson explained, "Look, Linc and I are concerned that Green might sense something and pull the big flit. He seems to have that sixth sense some criminals do about trouble coming their way. If he gets into the wind again, we might never find him. I've already delayed it to take care of another matter." The detective felt it unnecessary or unwise to say to Matt what that matter was. "The sooner, the better, Matt. We need you, buddy."

Matt agreed to help. During the meal, he decided to walk to Davison's after he and Jim parted. In light of recent events, he thought breaking a date with Evie at the last minute was something that he needed to do in person.

When they were back on the sidewalk, Jim shook Matt's hand. "We really appreciate your help, Matt. I'll pick you up tonight at nine o'clock." Matt's face reflected a question, which the big cop anticipated. "It has to be after dark." As an afterthought, Greerson leaned into the blond reporter and whispered, "Oh, and bring your gun."

"Really?"

"Yeah, *really!*" Jim turned and started walking back toward police headquarters. He glanced back once and gave his friend a devilish grin.

Matt, slightly stunned at that last detail, turned and strolled north toward Davison's. As he walked, he steeled himself to tell Evie the bad news about their date that night. At least, he hoped that she would take it as much as such as he felt it to be. He decided that he wouldn't explain what was he'd be doing beyond it being work related. Matt considered it a case of not poking a bear with a stick.

---

That evening, Linc decided to tell Leola what was going on and why he needed to go out that night. Okay, he convinced himself, he'd tell her up to a point. No sense, he reasoned, in making her worry needlessly. He cautiously related what he dared as he changed into work clothes. She took what part of the plans he chose to share with her in stride. After supper, Linc disappeared into the detached garage behind the house. Leola watched from one of their bedroom windows and wondered what her man was up to. A short time later, he came back into the house carrying a cardboard box. The way he carried it, she could tell it contained something at least a little weighty. She could only shake her head at some things his profession required him to do.

A short time later, Mr. Frye was standing at a living-room window when the white detective pulled up in front of their home and picked up his son-in-law. He shook his head in concern and uncertainty as the car pulled away from the curb.

---

# WORKING TOGETHER

A few minutes after nine o'clock, Matt, with his gun holstered under his left arm, walked down the sidewalk from the boardinghouse and climbed into the back seat of a blue LaSalle sedan unfamiliar to him. Jim was at the wheel and Linc sat in the front passenger seat, so the *Georgian* journalist didn't ask any questions about the car. A sizeable cardboard box sat on the rear seat next to Matt. Again, no questions. They motored their way to a parking lot and pulled in. Jim got out, spoke to the attendant, and quickly returned to the LaSalle. After reviewing the plan briefly, it was clear to Matt why they had to wait until after sunset. He also understood why neither Jim's nor his car would meet their needs. They needed a four-door automobile. Jim had decided he didn't want to risk Linc's Hupmobile being damaged when he had access to a four-door LaSalle that had been seized from a bootlegger when he'd been arrested. Besides, he rationalized, if some well-intentioned citizen decided to get involved by writing a tag number, the car wouldn't be connected to the three men participating. Matt and Jim exchanged places in the car. Matt had never driven a car this roomy, this big. This LaSalle was a far cry from his Ford. His nerves were a bit on edge. He craved a smoke in the worst way. The young journalist settled, instead, on a piece of Wrigley.

The young reporter drove to Ivy Street and pulled to the curb at Jim's direction. He killed the headlights and cut the motor. Linc climbed out and walked a few doors south, disappearing into the DeMonte Hotel. Inside, Linc went to the front desk where he whispered that he needed to get a message to Nathan Green, who was registered there. When the tall, thin desk clerk eyed him suspiciously, Linc gave the young man a knowing smile and told him the message was for Marvin Turpin. The clerk relaxed and asked what the message was. The private detective told him to let Mr. Turpin know that his boss would be picking him up in fifteen minutes for a meeting. Turpin should meet the man at the corner of Ivy Street and Auburn Avenue. The clerk nodded his understanding and Linc departed unhurriedly.

Back outside, the black detective quickly walked to an open door of the LaSalle where the Atlanta cop passed the cardboard box to him. Box in hand, he traveled south toward Auburn Avenue past the DeMonte. "Now we wait," Jim whispered from the back seat. Matt wasn't certain whether the cop was talking to him or to himself.

The minutes slowly wound past. After a time, the black pimp appeared at the hotel's door. Jim had made sure that the LaSalle had been parked a sufficient distance from the entrance that Nathan couldn't make out the two white men inside. Another reason for waiting until dark, he mused. After a pause, during which Green carefully scanned the street, he turned and started walking toward Auburn Avenue.

"Okay, Matt, crank the car and leave the headlights off. Drive very slowly as close to the curb as you can without drawing Green's attention." Matt followed Jim's instructions carefully. Then they saw Linc walking toward them carrying the box. "Matt, try to time it so you come up beside Green just as he gets to Linc."

The next few seconds went by so fast, with so much commotion, Matt could not have imagined it. He timed his arrival beside the pimp perfectly. As they approached that point, Linc stepped toward the buildings facing the narrow sidewalk, forcing Nathan Green to move closer to the street. As Linc completed this maneuver, he dropped the box in Green's direction with a crashing result. Green jumped away from the box and still closer to Ivy Street and yelled at Linc, "Watch it, nigger! Get out the way!" The words were still hanging in the air as Jim threw the sidewalk-side rear door open and Linc charged for it, collecting the stunned, smaller Green as he ran. The design of the LaSalle's rear wheel fender extending forward into the door area proved a small impediment, but the combination of the force of Linc's bulk and the surprise of his victim overcame the minor obstruction. Also pivotal in pulling off the maneuver was Jim grabbing Green by his collar and dragging him into the rear seat of the car. It took a few seconds for the pimp to collect his senses. In that time, Linc was in the car with the door closed behind him, and Matt had the LaSalle moving as rapidly as reasonable down Ivy Street.

Jim had their captive in a chokehold with his arm. However, Green's free arms were viciously fighting as Linc tried to pat the man down for weapons. As they struggled, Green was able to draw his legs up closer to his torso. He was trying to reach for one of his shoes as the car stopped at the intersection with Auburn Avenue. When Matt glanced back and saw what the pimp was trying to do, he quickly reached for his gun with his business hand. The driver turned and stretched his arm out as far as he could toward the back seat, pointing the .45 automatic within mere inches of Green's heart. "Nah, you're not that dumb," he cautioned softly, but with a cold resolve that surprised even Jim Greerson.

The black pimp froze as his eyes widened. His neck held firmly in the crook of Jim's elbow, Green cast a sideways look at Jim, and then at Linc, who was now able to run his hands rapidly over the man's motionless body. The private investigator removed a large straight razor from one of the pimp's socks and a large caliber revolver from a coat pocket. Otherwise, the search came up empty. Matt reholstered his gun and returned to his driving duties.

Jim tightened his hold momentarily. As Nathan choked, the big cop said into the man's ear, "Hello, Nathan. Remember me? Are you gonna behave now?" Getting no immediate response, Greerson squeezed the man's neck even harder, producing more strangling noises. "Listen, asshole, I don't care if you're ever able to speak again after tonight. Or, for that matter, if you even live or die. You're looking pretty good for the murder of Viola Johnson. With the evidence I have, it's a short step from there to three other murders. Now you might escape a date with the hot seat on one murder, but not four. Cooperate. Talk to me, and I'll let Boykin know you helped the police. He'll listen to me if I say you should get mercy, Nathan." Jim turned Green's head to face him as he spoke.

The lights from a nearby building momentarily flooded the car. Looking at his face, Jim decided that the pimp had basilisk green eyes. He could see what prompted Viola's and the other girls fear of him. Jim tugged on Nathan's newly acquired mustache with his free hand and smiled.

Suddenly, Linc flashed the straight razor up where Jim could see it in the flickering light as the LaSalle passed illuminated buildings. The Atlanta cop's eyes widened. "Well, well. What do we have here, Nathan? A straight razor? The kind of weapon that could be used to slash a young woman's throat? You're looking better and better for all four murders."

Their captive gargled what sounded like surrender. Detective Greerson eased his hold slightly on Green, who coughed and gulped air. Jim directed Matt to keep driving for a while. He didn't say it, but he wanted more time with Green before he took him to headquarters. The detective was concerned that the word might get out about Green's arrest before he could learn anything further about whom, if anybody might be involved in these killings with Green. Also, he didn't want anyone on the force to see him questioning the pimp either. If asked, Greerson would have said it was more of an issue of caution than a lack of trust of his fellow police officers. That's what he'd have said anyway.

When the Atlanta detective asked Green about the murders, the suspect shook his head in defiant silence. "Well, we can do this one of two ways, Nathan. You can talk to me here and now or we can go to police headquarters, and you can talk there. And you *will* talk, believe me." He asked, after a pause, "You ever pissed blood, Nathan?" As he asked this, Jim looked at Linc and smiled broadly. "We've got a basement that's made for scum like you. Just ask Mr. Mallard here." The captive glanced at Lincoln Mallard with pleading eyes. Jim interrupted the silent plea, "Oh, but don't look to him for help. This is out of his hands."

While this had been going on in the back seat, Matt had driven the LaSalle to a parking lot a few blocks off Peachtree Street. Matt jumped out and quickly spoke to the attendant, who was savvy enough to take the reporter's money and walk away. When he returned to the car, Nathan Green was pleading his case. Looking from one detective to the other, he breathed heavily, "Look, man, I didn't kill all those girls. That was somebody else —"

"Somebody else who wanted to keep their stories about forced abortions quiet?" Linc prodded roughly.

"Yeah. That's right. That's who kilt 'em!"

Linc slapped the man hard only to get his attention. "And who was that person, Nathan?"

"I can't say. I —"

"Can't or won't?" Jim made the same polished, complicated movement Matt had seen him make that night in the White Lantern restaurant. His Colt finished in his working hand. Green's eyes bugged out when he saw it. Greerson struck the pimp fiercely on the side of the head with the gun. The pimp emitted a girlish scream. His chin dropped to his chest as a large weal formed. "That somebody didn't have the same reason to kill Viola. She wasn't pregnant and never had been. No, the motive for that murder was that she'd talked to us about you! That means you, Nathan, killed her!" Greerson's voice took on a more subdued, icy tone. "You'll stand for her murder. Like I said, maybe the others, too. If you're smart, you'll tell us who killed the other girls if it wasn't you."

Blood dribbled from a corner of Green's mouth and from his nose. "He'll kill me if I say anything. I ain't sayin' nothin'." Greerson placed the Colt, barrel down, on the pimp's knee and pulled back the hammer. Again, Nathan looked to the black man sitting beside him.

Linc smirked at the man and shook his head. "Yeah, don't look to me for sympathy, Nathan. I have nothing to offer a man who played a hand in the killing of young Negro women, whether he's black or white." Linc nodded to the Colt. "And I don't care if you ever walk again."

Green tried in vain to pull away, jerking his head back and forth briskly. "Wait! Wait!" he choked. Green looked up at Detective Greerson.

"What if I give you the name of the croaker who done the abortions? He's some old white dude. Don't mean nothin' to me. Can't hurt me none. If he puts the finger on somebody, that's on him."

Jim pondered the convoluted logic of Green's thought process for a second. Maybe he could kill two birds with one stone. He could get a doctor, who's been violating the law, off the streets and possibly get to the murderer through the doctor, too. If, for some reason that didn't work, he could always return and have another go at Nathan Green. He pulled the Colt back from the pimp's leg, released the hammer, and reholstered it. "Okay, Nathan, give me a name. Who's the doctor?"

"I only heard it one time. But the name I heard was a Dr. Perrine."

"Dr. Perrine?" The pimp nodded forcefully. "If this turns out to be a lie, Nathan, you'll wish you'd never been born."

"That's the name! Honest! But that's all I know of 'em."

At that point, the LaSalle's occupants, except Nathan Green, relaxed to some extent. Jim told Matt to drive them to police headquarters. While he took his prisoner inside, Matt and Linc sat in the car and waited. At the jail, Detective Greerson had Nathan Green booked in for the murder of Viola Johnson and for suspicion of murder in the three other cases. The two other men sat in the car, becoming stuffy in the sultry night air, even with the windows open. They talked briefly and laughed about how the events of that night had unfolded. Linc and Matt spoke of their backgrounds and found a few common interests they shared. First among them was hunting, although neither man had gone out in quite a while. They also both enjoyed baseball a great deal. Matt told Linc about the concern his girlfriend had about him working with Detective Greerson. Linc chuckled and confided that felt compelled to withhold some information about their "excursions" from his family, too. They shared a laugh at their commonality. After a point, the conversation lagged, and they sat in silence and smoked until Detective Greerson reappeared and drove them home.

# WORKING TOGETHER

On the drive, the two detectives discussed their next steps. Jim Greerson was determined to locate this Dr. Perrine and pay him a visit at the first opportunity. Linc begged off going, explaining that he had let several things slide during this time and he desperately needed to catch up on his work. Jim expressed his understanding of Linc's situation and added his sincere thanks for all the work he'd done so far. Especially, he told Linc, he was grateful for the plan he'd devised to grab Green. He chuckled and told his companions that he'd never snatched a suspect off the street like that before. They laughed. Linc made certain that his Atlanta detective friend didn't take him "off the team" completely. He made clear that it would only be for the next several days that he'd be tied up. That was the understanding between the two men. When Greerson looked to Matt, the young police beat reporter was on board with going to visit the doctor. Again, Jim complimented both men on how they'd handled the Nathan Green situation.

A short time later, Greerson pulled the big LaSalle up in front of the Frye home. Jim grabbed Linc's arm as he started to get out of the front passenger door. "Okay, Linc, I have to ask. What was in the box?" Matt pulled himself forward against the back of the front seat, in expectation of the answer.

Linc smiled broadly, showing his handsome white teeth. "Well, I needed something to give the box weight to make Green move away when I dropped it. But, at the same time, I didn't need to be too burdened by the weight. I simply appropriated a few bricks from my father-in-law's garage. They're left from when he built this house." Both men looked past Linc at the neat craftsman-style brick home behind him. Linc closed the LaSalle's door, moved along the front walk, and bounded up the steps. Matt moved to the front passenger seat, and the big car moved gracefully down the street.

Detective Jim Greerson spent the next two days, including what would normally have been a day off, getting as much information as he could about Dr. Perrine, whose first name he determined was Clayton. His investigation also revealed that Dr. Perrine had been a very well-to-do, well-thought-of physician once. He had what one might have called a silk-stocking medical practice. The good doctor had been the personal physician to many of Atlanta's prominent families. Further, some important people traveled to Atlanta to be treated by him. Over time he became fairly wealthy, but, like many people in his position, the doctor lost almost everything in the stock market crash. Shortly thereafter, apparently distracted by his financial woes, Perrine made a fatal mistake during a relatively routine surgery and lost a patient on the operating table. Unfortunately from the doctor's perspective, the patient had been a member of one of those very important Atlanta families. A review of the case left no question that the doctor was guilty of malpractice, and he'd been very publicly sued. Before long, the word spread and his high-class clientele abandoned him completely, his medical practice evaporated. As a result, he sank further into financial doldrums. Simultaneously, his standing in the community at large eroded. Greerson would hazard a guess that Dr. Perrine's rapid, downward spiral led him to places he never thought he'd visit, to activities he'd probably once thought repugnant in the extreme.

---

Monday morning, the first of July, Detective Greerson met with his superiors and explained his case, what he'd learned thus far, including Dr. Perrine's purported involvement. He laid out his plan to confront and possibly arrest the physician. The detective was told to hold off on approaching Perrine until "others" could be consulted about the situation. By "others," Jim knew that his superiors meant those further up the food chain, including the politically well connected. He was very frustrated about the possibility of interference with his investigation, not to mention a potential leak of information to Dr. Perrine. But he could only bide his waiting for an answer while the politics played out. A week passed with no further word to the detective to proceed. It seemed that Dr. Perrine still had many influential friends, who didn't see the need to bring a floundering white doctor to additional disgrace when the case "only" involved the deaths of Negro prostitutes. So the process of waiting out the political shenanigans continued for the Atlanta detective.

---

Meanwhile, Detective Greerson received a tip from an informant that Gutowski could be found at a house a few blocks off Capitol Avenue on the south side of town. Jim, Artie, and Matt, with his gun tucked under his left shoulder, bundled into the Hudson and tore down to the address in question. Matt, again relegated to the rumble seat, was also again thankful for fair weather during the ride. After carefully approaching, and then entering the structure, the trio found nothing but an empty, fairly dilapidated house. Even so, a few items remaining there gave evidence of a hasty exit by some unknown person. Unidentified, that is, except from Jim Greerson's perspective. Greerson found a few crumpled Kool cigarette packages. The brand was relatively new and not widely favored yet. Kool was, however, the brand that the detective knew Carl Gutowski smoked exclusively. In addition, the detectives located some loose .45 caliber rounds. Gutowski never carried any other caliber handgun.

As they waded through the house's debris, Matt stumbled upon an interesting discovery. Wide-eyed, he held up a booklet and said to no one in particular, "I have a question. What's this?" When Greerson reached his side, he saw a butcher's handbook, demonstrating, among other things, the way by which to dismember a carcass. Rutherford saw the publication and let out a guffaw, suggesting that somebody had decided on a better way to dispose of their victims. Artie followed his comment with a self-satisfying belch. An icy finger traced its way down Matt's spine. Jim expressed his frustration at missing his prey yet again by putting a fist through the lathing and plaster of the nearest wall.

---

The first Saturday night in July, Evie and Matt had a date to go out for supper and dancing. After dropping Evie off at the end of the evening, Matt drove to Houston Street as a thunderstorm rolled across the city. Reaching the boardinghouse, he saw a familiar maroon and black Hudson parked at the curb. He glided his Ford to a spot behind it. The big reporter slid out of his car and hustled up onto the porch as the torrent continued. Shaking the rain from his hat, Matt speculated that Greerson was probably there to scoop him up for another crime-scene visit. He opened the front door and entered the hallway, hanging his hat on a wall-mounted coat hook there. Romantic music came from the Philco in the parlor. Turning into the dimly lighted room, Matt found Teresa Rossetti and Jim Greerson sitting close on the divan and talking softly. While Matt was stunned, Jim jumped up as if caught in the act of some dastardly crime. Teresa merely flashed her alluring smile and said nothing. Matt Grimes quickly realized that Detective Greerson had *not* come to the residence to see him. The younger man waved a restraining hand to his friend, made greetings in passing, and moved on to the kitchen from which light shone and food preparation sounds sprung.

Despite the late hour, Miss Dixie was fussing over frosting a cake. Matt approached her and, head nodding back toward the front room, asked in a conspiratorial tone, "What's with those two in the parlor?"

"Oh, that. Jim and Teresa got back from their date a little bit ago. They just can't seem to say goodnight. Isn't it sweet?"

"Date? What date?" Matt looked toward the parlor again before returning his stunned eyes to Miss Dixie. "How long has this been going on?"

"Well, this was their second date." She moved the frosted cake to the metal cake saver on the stove. Matt leaned back against the side table and crossed his arms over his chest. A broad smile played across his face as he waited. Miss Dixie turned back to her boarder and, wiping her hands on a dish towel, continued, "Jim came by the house a few days after the situation with Amanda and talked to Rhamy and me. He said he'd wanted to ask Teresa out after he met her at that Friday night supper here but had thought it best not to do it until his investigation of that man's murder was done."

Miss Dixie paused briefly in contemplation before continuing, "Anyway, he wanted to know if we'd have a problem with him showing up here and asking Teresa out. He was so sweet, standing there with his hat in his hands. Of course, we knew he'd had a job to do when it came to Amanda's arrest. And as much as the whole thing with Amanda hurt, we'd never stand in the way of Teresa and him. We told him we were fine with it, and it was up to Teresa from that point. They've been talking on the telephone almost every night since then. They may have met for lunch a time or two. I'm just not sure." She stepped softly to the door and glanced down the hall toward the parlor. She looked back at her boarder and smiled broadly. "Seems Teresa's more than fine with it."

"That son of a gun! He never let on! I swan that man can keep a secret!" He looked at his landlady intently. "Miss Dixie, you have no idea how big a milestone this is in that guy's life." Swearing her to secrecy, Matt gave Miss Dixie an abbreviated background on Jim and the loss of Ella. She put fingers to her lips, and her eyes watered at the telling.

A few minutes later they could hear Jim leaving. Shortly, Teresa appeared at the kitchen door to say goodnight. By Miss Dixie's and Matt's estimations, she almost glowed with happiness as she turned and quickly climbed the stairs. Another page in the book of life at the Houston Street boardinghouse had turned.

---

Finally, after a heated meeting with his superiors early on the morning of July eleventh, Detective Greerson was given the go-ahead to proceed with his investigation of Dr. Perrine. As Jim planned for his meeting with the doctor, Artie told him in no uncertain terms that he wanted nothing to do with arresting the prominent doctor for the deaths of some "colored trash." Jim, though angered by it, was not surprised at Rutherford's attitude and shrugged it off. He knew who *would be* interested.

About midmorning, Jim telephoned Matt, who was typing the few local but minor stories to be found on the Atlanta police beat. Again, Matt was facing national stories that were of greater consequence than anything in Atlanta and its vicinity. The wire crime stories still captured the headlines. Jim explained his plans to meet and confront Dr. Perrine with the allegations after lunch. Finally, Jim asked, "Do you want to take some air on the north side of town?" Matt felt certain that he could get someone to cover his afternoon rounds, so he readily opted in to the scheme. The two men agreed to get together at the Stars Grill and grab a bite to eat there before heading out to meet with the good doctor.

A short time later, Matt carried his copy into Mr. Barnes's office. His editor scowled and expressed his dismay at the lack of "meat for the readers to sink their teeth into" from the crime beat perspective. Matt, becoming more comfortable in his role, merely shrugged. Then, he described what the police had determined thus far about the murders of the Negro prostitutes, including the indications of abortions. He further explained the opportunity he'd have that afternoon to be present at the questioning of a doctor who had possibly performed the abortions and, therefore, was likely connected to the girls' murders. Mr. Barnes perked up considerably. Flicking cigar ash off his vest, the editor exclaimed, "By all means, stick with the story! If this breaks, it'll be front-page stuff! We'll beat the town on it!" Barnes said he'd have someone cover the afternoon circuit. When the editor excitedly mentioned sending a staff photographer, Matt convinced him that it wouldn't be a good idea at this stage. Barnes calmed enough to allow the two men to agree that there'd be plenty of opportunity for photographs if and when the doctor was formally charged.

---

An hour or so later, the journalist and the detective met under the vertical sign over the sidewalk at the entrance to the Stars Grill. While they ate a quick meal in the cafeteria, Detective Greerson went over what he'd learned about Dr. Perrine so far. He finished by grousing about how difficult it was to get information on the average citizen. Jim said he'd had to call in some IOUs and ask some huge favors to learn as much as he had. When the big cop finished his rundown of the doctor, Matt sat dumbfounded. He wondered how much more information his detective friend had expected to get about a complete stranger in such a short period.

After the meal, they hustled to Greerson's Hudson parked nearby. When Matt said he was going to miss riding in the LaSalle, Jim playfully poked him in the shoulder, laughed, and told him to "gut it out." As they drove north out of the city, Matt asked where they were going. Jim explained that the doctor had given up the offices from which he had once practiced. Exactly where he'd performed the abortions, if he'd performed them, was unknown at the moment, the cop told Matt. But Perrine was now more or less a recluse in his home on West Paces Ferry

Road. Chief Poole had told Greerson that the area was rapidly becoming an exclusive niche for the very well-to-do families in Atlanta. Perrine had built the home several years before the crash, the detective had learned, and it was all he had left, at least for now. Whether he'd keep it was a matter of conjecture. The wolves were at the door. Meanwhile, Dr. Perrine was said to be trying to keep up appearances.

After a time, the two men were driving along the meandering thoroughfare of West Paces Ferry Road, crossing gentle hills and small valleys. The two men saw a few homes, tending more toward mansions really, along the road. Those to be seen were on expansive, wooded tracts sitting majestically on either side of the street.

Eventually, Jim turned in to a long, curving driveway, which quickly changed from concrete at the street to flagstone as it sloped up to the residence. The Perrine home was a large, square two-story place of old red brick with leaded windowpanes across the front. The wide flagstone driveway continued under a porte-cochere that passed through to the rear of the mansion. A low wall of the same brick ran to the side of the covered area and continued down the side of the yard beside the driveway. Espaliers grew here and there along the extensive wall topped with a white stone coping. The pass-through provided a glimpse of a garden in the rear of the home. A multicar garage sat off to the side behind the home. The garage had rooms located above it, and a shiny Buick sat in front of one of the doors. Jim smiled when he saw the car, because, when he was younger, he'd always heard the adults call a Buick a "doctor's car." A walkway of the same flagstone led from the driveway over two terraces to the front door. In a way, the mansion reminded Matt of some homes built by northern polo players who'd come south to the county immediately across the river in South Carolina to pursue their sport. There, they'd established what was known as the Aiken Winter Colony.

The two men eased out of the Hudson, collected themselves, and climbed the walkway to the massive front door. Detective Greerson flattened his thumb against the button located to one side of the entry. A melody of deep chimes sounded somewhere within. After a minute or so, an older man, wearing dress slacks and a collar-attached dress shirt without a tie, opened the door. He smiled and greeted the pair standing there, "Good afternoon, gentlemen. May I help you?"

"We're here to see Dr. Perrine," Jim said in a friendly way that belied his feelings and his intent.

"I am Dr. Perrine, sir."

"I'm Detective Jim Greerson of the Atlanta Police Department. This is Matt Grimes. We need to speak with you about a matter that has come to the department's attention. Your name has come up during an investigation."

The doctor's shoulders dropped immediately at the detective's words. His face bore a disheartened aspect as he guardedly said, "Oh my." But, just as quickly, he recovered his superior air and seemed to resign himself to deal with whatever might be coming his way. "Won't you come in, gentlemen? I'll be glad to help in any way I can," he lied. "We can speak in my library." Dr. Perrine opened the door wider as his visitors entered the large foyer. After closing the door, the older man turned and led the way. "I apologize," he said over his shoulder, as he moved through the home, "for the time it took me to answer the door. But I'd almost forgotten that it's the servants' day off," he lied again.

The men walked past a rather ornate staircase on one side of the entry vestibule to a wide hallway covered with a thick carpet runner concealing the sound of their steps. They walked through zones of silence before entering a walnut paneled room filled with old, dark furniture. It had thick wall-to-wall carpeting. Large windows at one end gave a fuller view of the garden hinted at from the driveway. An opened window offered the smell of moist earth as if the garden had been recently watered. Bookshelves lined the wall through which they'd entered and a second wall. Books filled the shelves. A large stone fireplace dominated the

407

fourth wall in the room. Over the fireplace mantel hung the oil portrait of a beautiful young girl. The portrait, illuminated by a hooded light above it, Jim surmised, was of a member of the Perrine household. Dr. Perrine gestured his visitors into two leather chairs as he walked around a large desk and sat in a comparably sized chair. The desk, whose back was to the windows, was a hand-rubbed walnut affair.

"Do you mind if I smoke, doctor?"

The doctor smiled and reached for a pipe from the stand on his desk. "Why, no. Not at all. In fact, I'll join you, detective." As he spoke, Perrine pushed a cigar humidor across the desk. "Won't you try one of my cigars, gentlemen? Though I tend to lean on a pipe more often than not, I have them specially wrapped for me and imported from Cuba."

Not anymore you don't, thought Greerson derisively. "No, thank you. I'll stick with my usual brand of cigarettes."

The doctor glanced at Matt, who lifted a cigarette he'd retrieved from a fresh pack and shook his head slightly, smiling. The older man chose a briar pipe from the stand, looked at its bowl, and frowned. He proceeded to knock ash from it. A clump of residue missed the ashtray and fell to the desk where it crawled in the draft from the opened window. Ignoring the ash, Dr. Perrine started packing tobacco into the pipe's bowl. The ritual of lighting up gave the two visitors a moment to observe the doctor more closely. Jim knew him to be in his late fifties, although he looked older. He was of average height and tending toward a paunch. His face was drawn and listless. When he tried to flash a smile, it appeared only briefly and looked as if it were forced. The touch of gray showing at his temples on both sides of his head ran along the bottom fringes of his hair and met in the back. Jim thought it gave him an undeserved distinguished look.

Where Matt saw a figure worn down by his circumstances, Jim saw a man dealing with the torment of a voice in his head telling him that he'd done something wrong, if not morally, then legally. Most true criminals didn't have that voice, Jim believed, or, at least, didn't listen to it.

As he puffed his pipe to life, Dr. Perrine gave Jim his best "I have no idea why you're here" look. Then, he put it to words. "Gentlemen, I have to state my surprise that my name would come to the fore in any type of police investigation. I've not been the victim of any type crime, I can assure you."

Jim cut to the core of their business with the older man. "Well, you see Dr. Perrine, during my investigation, your name has emerged not as a victim of but as a perpetrator of a crime. The case I'm working –"

"Why that's preposterous on the very face of it! I'm a well-respected member of this city!" Perrine exclaimed as his face turned a deep red. "I have powerful friends in high places in Atlanta and in the state! I don't have the slightest idea –!"

"Well, let me ask you this, doctor. Have you ever performed an illegal medical procedure?"

"I'm sure that I don't have any idea what you're talking about, detective! See here, I won't have you come into my home and –!"

Jim suddenly threw his hand up stopping the doctor. "That dog won't hunt, doctor." Perrine tossed a supercilious sneer at Greerson. Jim Greerson had seen that condescending smirk on too many swells who thought that they were dealing with someone beneath them. The detective had never taken kindly to haughty attitudes from anyone, especially from those with no true basis for such a play. "Those powerful friends you had once have gone the way of your medical clientele. And before we dance around the subject too much, doctor, let me make it clear that the crime in question is that of performing abortions."

The doctor's face blanched. He was visibly jolted as he stared at the black perpetual calendar and pen set on his desk and took a deep, quivering breath. Leaning forward with his elbows on the desk, he started to speak but only made a negligent gesture with his left hand before steepling his fingers. His forehead came to rest on his fingertips. The lull that followed was a vacuum. Detective Greerson was prepared to wait. The fragrance of gardenia drifted through the open window. The only sounds were the ticking of a clock on a nearby table and the rhythmic swinging pendulum from a large grandfather clock they'd passed in the hallway earlier. Finally, the older man looked up as a brief, tired smile washed over his drawn face. "Sir, you have all the subtlety of a political cartoonist from the opposition party. I take it you have some measure of proof to back up your allegations."

"Yessir, I have witnesses directly connecting you to at least three abortions," Greerson bluffed. "It would have been bad enough if it had stopped at the abortions. But the three girls were murdered to cover up that offense. So the crimes go beyond mere illegal medical procedures."

Initially, the doctor said nothing. He dully fingered a few papers on his desk. Jim waited and Matt observed. Finally, Perrine's eyebrows drew together in a tight frown. "I don't suppose it would do any good to state my belief that sometimes a doctor might do something because he felt it was a woman's right to have the final say about what happens to her body." He looked at the detective intently, hoping for a glimmer of understanding.

"Don't bother trying esoteric arguments with me, Doctor Perrine. My job is to enforce the law. Right or wrong in the eyes of a medical man, performing an abortion is against the law in this state. Besides, these three women didn't have the final say about their bodies, as you put it. The three abortions I'm investigating were all done against the women's will."

Another poignant pause hung in the air as Perrine gazed intently, sorrowfully at Greerson. "You don't understand, young man, how my life has been devastated in the last half-dozen years."

"Oh, I know your background, doctor. I know how you've suffered financially. The fact —"

This time, the doctor interrupted, "What you speak of, detective, is merely the numerical aspect of what has happened to me. Financial losses, losing your livelihood are one thing. Losing your status is quite another. I am no longer welcomed at my clubs. I can longer show my face at the Capital City Club, the Piedmont Driving Club, the Dogwood City Club, to name a few. Friends no longer call. Invitations are not extended. Or accepted, for that matter. How can you possibly understand how demoralizing that is to a man in my position?"

"So you turned to crime?"

The doctor winced at the word. "It's a distasteful story. Back... I no longer had a medical practice, Detective Greerson. My source of income gone and my savings and holdings wiped out by the misfortune on Wall Street, I was at my wits' end." Jim noticed that the doctor omitted any reference to his malpractice woes and the resulting devastation to whatever residual wealth he might have held at the time. Perrine was continuing, "I was near pulling a Brodie, I think is the phrase in today's parlance. Out of desperation, I had to borrow money from a less-than-reputable person. I'm not given to calumny, sir, but I believe that to be a fair assessment of the gentleman. When I couldn't repay him, the man threatened me." Here he showed another tired smile. "He found me somewhat immune to physical threats given my dire situation.

"Then, he threatened my daughter. My daughter, Mildred," the doctor explained, nodding toward the portrait over the fireplace, "is all I have left, sir. This man seemed to know a great deal about Mildred, which stunned and frightened me. I begged him to leave her out of the whole sordid affair. For whatever reason, he backed off his threats against her. Finally, he made a proposal to me by which, with very little effort on my part, I could wipe the loan off his books, as he put it, and earn a modicum of income with which to maintain all of this," he said as his eyes swept the room.

His gaze fell on the girl's portrait once more. "At present, even Mildred is a source of conflict for me. I've spoiled her, sent her to the best schools, given her a superior education. Now that brilliant, willful mind of hers comes back to torment me with her careless ways, her deliberate disregard for my wishes. But she's all I have left." The doctor took in a deep breath and let it out silently. His eyes clouded up. "Anyway, God help me, I took him up on his proposition. I'm a weak man, detective," he chuckled woefully. Even his laughter held the sound of a building caving in on itself.

Suddenly, the doctor opened a drawer. Alarmed, Jim stood quickly. As Matt watched intently, the big cop moved hastily but gracefully, with ease, around the desk. The doctor removed a match folder from the drawer, which he closed just as quickly, and relit his pipe. Jim moved back away from the doctor but didn't return to his chair. He leaned his backside against a nearby table and crossed his arms. The doctor looked up at him. "Hardship makes morality more fungible." He took a long drag on his pipe in contemplation. "What now, detective?"

"Well, doctor, even with the evidence I have, I'm not going to arrest you at this time. I'll go back and finish my investigation first. But we'll see each other again soon. I promise you that. Meanwhile, stay away from any surgeries."

Perrine's eyes watered. He hauled in a breath and raised his rounded shoulders. "What do I do now? How do I cleanse myself of the harm that I've caused?"

Greerson straightened, ready to leave. "How about the old phrase, 'Doctor, heal thyself'?" Matt got out of his chair.

The older man shook his head slightly. "And how do I go about that, Detective Greerson?"

"Why don't you start with a huge, prolonged Murphy's drip, Doctor Perrine? Or maybe a high colonic would serve you better."

The doctor's eyes flashed his recognition of the cop's sarcasm and bile. He sighed wearily. "Well, at least your efforts will most likely free me from the clutches of Carl, even if it has to be by my incarceration," he said softly.

Jim Greerson and Matt Grimes looked at each other in astonishment. Greerson shot a hard-eyed stare at Perrine. "Carl?" he asked with bated expectation.

Fidgeting with his pipe, the doctor responded, "Yes, Carl. The lowlife from whom I borrowed the money. Carl Gutowski. Are you familiar with the man?"

Jim tempered his excitement at this development and leaned over the desk toward the doctor. "Yeah. Yeah, I know the man. And I need to talk to him as soon as possible as part of my investigation. Do you know where I could find him right now? Keep in mind doctor, that I would consider it a huge step toward helping yourself in this matter if you can tell me where to find Carl Gutowski!"

"No, I don't know where he might be. If I did, I'd most definitely tell you, detective. I despise the very ground the man walks on."

"Whatever you do, Dr. Perrine, don't lie to me about this. Where can I find Gutowski?"

"I have no earthly idea, detective. Please believe me. I would certainly tell you if I knew, because, as I said, I would do anything to be removed from under his thumb."

"Do you know anyone else who might help us locate him?"

Doctor Perrine shot Jim a puzzled glance. He seemed to be turning something over in his mind. Finally, he sighed, "No, detective. I can't help you on that count, either."

"Okay, Dr. Perrine. We'll go for now. If you think of anything that may help me find Carl Gutowski, please call me immediately at this number." Jim jotted his office telephone number on a pad from the doctor's desk. "Remember, any help you can give me in that regard will make things easier for you. As I said, we'll see each other again soon. Don't bother getting up," he added with a touch of disdain. "We'll see ourselves out." With that, he turned and started toward the front door. Matt followed closely, leaving a despondent Dr. Perrine in his library. Matt heard Jim mumble "That son of a bitch!" and Carl Gutowski's name several times under his breath as they traversed the hallway to the foyer.

Just as the two men reached the front door, a beautiful woman, dressed in tennis togs and casually carrying a racket, was making her way down the staircase. Both men recognized her as an older version of the girl in the library portrait. She was a long, hungry brunette, swinging lean thighs. Tall and built to proportion, the woman had curly black hair and soft, intelligent sea-gray eyes, which she fixed intently on Jim's. She stopped her descent in midstride, but said nothing. After a pause, Jim turned his gaze from the woman, jammed his hat back on his head, opened the door, and disappeared through it. Matt followed close on his heels.

"Wow!" Matt exclaimed softly as they descended the walkway. "Did you see that darb? What a dish! Did you see those pins of hers?" Even though Jim didn't appear to be listening, Matt finished the thought. "Brother, she could make a bulldog break his chain!"

As they climbed into the Hudson, Greerson was still muttering to himself. He sat behind the wheel for a brief time, contemplating the situation. He turned in the seat to face his companion. Matt had been watching the detective with uncertainty. "You get this, Matt, right?

"Yeah, Jim, I get it. Gutowski's behind the abortions these women had. Which means he's most likely behind their murders, too. Right? If he didn't commit them himself, he had Green do them. Or somebody. He's the boss who Green's protecting!"

Greerson nodded and turned back to the steering wheel as a late-model Auburn convertible sedan zipped past them and drove through the porte-cochere. The pair in the Hudson watched the red car, with its top down and its spare tire mounted over the rear bumper, make a wide, sweeping U-turn when it reached the paved area in front of the garages. The Auburn sped back and screeched to a stop at the bottom of the walk leading to the home's entrance.

Ignoring the Hudson, the pale, red-haired driver looked toward the front door, through which the brunette stepped nonchalantly. She descended the flagstone walk in sylphlike movements, swinging the tennis racket. Once she reached the Auburn's passenger door, she cast her cool, steady eyes on the Hudson's driver. A warm come-hither smile played at the corners of her mouth. The driver reached across the seat and opened her door. She dropped into the convertible's seat with her eyes still fixed on Jim. As the guy in the Auburn spoke to her, she glanced at him and smiled broadly. After a brief kiss, the Auburn dropped back into gear and moved quickly down the driveway. The tall brunette glanced back at the Hudson one last time before they disappeared. Jim spoke suddenly in a harsh voice, "The woman's nothing but a piece of fluff, Matt."

Neither man spoke much during the drive back to town. Detective Greerson weighed what he'd learned from Dr. Perrine. Many pieces of his cases fell neatly into place. He had all the more reason to find and deal with Carl Gutowski now. With this new information in mind, Jim figured the goon had to answer for the death of Charlie, his treatment of Vivian, *and* the deaths of at least three young women. Periodically, Matt would glance sideways at his friend. The set of the big cop's jaw told the young reporter all he needed to know about where Jim's thoughts were.

---

Greerson made a point of going to visit Green in the lockup as soon as he returned to police headquarters. He confronted Green with Dr. Perrine having given up Gutowski as being behind the abortions. Therefore, the detective told the pimp that he'd concluded that Gutowski was his boss. The startled, frightened look on Green's face confirmed what the detective suspected. The black pimp, recognizing that he no longer needed to keep quiet on that front, reluctantly acknowledged Gutowski's roll in the illegal medical procedures. When the detective pressed him harder on the murders of the women, Green quickly added, "It was Gutowski that kilt all the girls after I got 'em to the places you found 'em. Hit 'em with a baseball bat and dragged 'em into the bushes where he finished 'em off. 'Cept one. I don't remember which one. But he forgot his bat. So he hit her with a big rock afore killin' her. But I swear I didn't *know* he was gonna kill 'em."

The big cop leaned over Green, sitting on a shelf-bunk. The sharp smell of disinfectant filled the air, assaulting their nostrils. "First, even if you didn't know Gutowski's intentions with the first girl, which I don't believe for a second, you sure as hell knew what was gonna happen to the others!" Greerson paused and stared hard at the prisoner. "And, second, I'm not buying that story when it comes to the killing of Viola Johnson. The only one of you two who had a real motive for her murder was you, Nathan. You found out somehow she'd talked to me about you. You couldn't tolerate that. She had to be an example for the rest of your women." His voice was cold and hard. "I'll tell you again, Nathan, cooperate with me. Don't be a chump. I'll let Boykin know you were a helpful witness, and he needs to go easy on you." The detective leaned in closer to Green. "Where's Gutowski?" When the black man shook his head vigorously, Greerson grabbed him by the collar and punched him hard in the face. The inmate reeled backwards down on the thin mattress. The big man jerked him back up again.

A turnkey strolled past the cell. Green shot a pleading look at the man, who said casually, "Don't be attackin' the detective, boy," before he walked away. Nathan looked back at Jim, who smiled wickedly.

Despite more questioning and threats, Nathan Green would not budge on his story about Johnson's murder. Greerson decided to change subjects to an extent. He knew that he could always come back to Green later about Johnson murder. "The shoes, Nathan. What about the girls' shoes? Why were they taken after the girls were murdered?"

Initially, the little man shot a defiant, blank look at the detective. When Jim drew back his fist, Nathan winced and quickly exclaimed, "Gutowski thought it'd be funny! Said he read about somebody doin' that in the past when they kilt a girl! Thought it'd be funny, that's all!"

That Gutowski would try to make a joke in the deaths of three young women infuriated Detective Greerson. And either Gutowski was involved in Viola Johnson's murder or Green decided to continue the cold-blooded gag. "Tell me where I can find Gutowski, Green!" The man looked back at the detective with a blank stare as if he'd not understood him. Another punch from Jim's burly fist brought forth nothing. "Where is he, Green?" Nathan's expression didn't change. He clammed up. When Jim drew his fist back again, the pimp screamed that he had no idea where Gutowski could be found. The detective didn't believe him, but he recognized that, when he's not taken by surprise, the little man was as tough as Mallard had said he'd be. He was no weak sister, the detective had to admit, and he'd hold out. Disgusted, Jim shoved the man back on the bed hard. "Just remember that Old Sparky is waiting for you if you want to take all four murders, dumbass! Think it over!" The detective left the jail angry and frustrated.

# CHAPTER 15
# Needed Killing

The following Sunday evening, Matt was at the parlor card table, watching Diane and Cliff work on a jigsaw puzzle. In the background, an orchestra played a smooth version of "Blue Moon" through the Philco. Matt momentarily thought of Vivian and wondered how she was doing. Teresa appeared at his side and bent to whisper in his ear. "Matt, Jim's on the phone and wants to talk to you." Her voice carried far enough for the resident piano salesman, seated nearby, to hear. He released a resounding surly grunt, which brought sad, subdued smiles to the other faces in the room. Melvyn had been unhappy with Detective Greerson since the night of Amanda's arrest. Every time Jim appeared to pick up Teresa for a date or he telephoned her, Melvyn would make a sour face. Often the grimace would be accompanied by a derisive sound. Despite the facts involved in her case, which saddened the household in general, Melvyn despised the detective for removing the alluring Amanda from his life. Jim was gracious enough to ignore his plump antagonist.

Matt walked to the telephone table in the hall and picked up the receiver. "Hello, Jim."

"How's the boy, Matt?"

"I'm good Jim." The reporter chuckled. "Say, I notice that you never ask Linc, 'How's the *boy*?' Any particular reason?"

"Anybody ever tell you that you're a smartass, Grimes?"

"On occasion," the blond journalist snickered. "Just giving you a hard time, my friend. What's up?"

"Say, I've been giving this Perrine business a lot of thought. I still can't lay hands on Gutowski and don't have much to go on. So I figure I'd go back up there tomorrow afternoon and play a hunch. Because you were with me on my first visit, I wondered if you might want to go along. Besides, you seemed kind of smitten with the daughter, and I'm counting on her being there. Whaddya say?"

"Sure thing, Jim," Matt replied while trying not to sound too enthusiastic. "I'll zip through my afternoon rounds and check in with the city room. Then, we can go. There's not been much to report on the local police beat lately anyway. Tomorrow'll probably be the same. Will that work?"

"Sounds fine, Matt. Where do you want me to meet you? Want to grab a bite to eat first?"

Matt said that lunch sounded good, and the two men agreed to meet at the Tasty Toasty Sandwich Shop again, because it was within easy walking distance of the Houston Street house. Matt chided his friend to try to avoid being followed by another goon this time.

---

The young journalist parked his car at the boardinghouse when he'd finished his afternoon circuit. He made the short walk to the sandwich shop in time to meet his friend. Over lunch, Matt asked Jim about his seeing Teresa. Returning to his old form, the detective was closed-mouth about his personal life. His face split in an enormous grin as he did admit that he was happier than he'd been in a long while.

An hour later, the Atlanta detective and the *Georgian* reporter were cruising toward West Paces Ferry Road. Jim explained that he'd been reflecting on some things the doctor had said about his daughter, like her willful mind, rebellious nature, and careless ways. Those things, combined with what Gladys had told them about Gutowski's new girlfriend being a bluestocking from the north side of the city, led him to think that Mildred might be the hood's new, unnamed girlfriend. The detective suspected that maybe the daughter was fooling around with Gutowski in a rebellious splurge to upset her father. He restated that it was only a hunch, but he was going to play it. However, Matt couldn't conceive of someone like the woman he'd seen with the tennis racket going for someone like Gutowski under any circumstances.

Soon, they turned in to the driveway of the Perrine residence. After parking the Hudson, the two men approached the front door. Before Jim could ring the doorbell, the red Auburn roared to a stop at the foot of the flagstone walkway. The flame-topped man was behind the wheel. Mildred Perrine rode close beside him. She smiled coyly when she saw the two men waiting at her front door.

Mildred and her red-haired escort climbed out of the Auburn and casually made their way up the flagstone walk. "I don't think Daddy's home right now," she offered as she walked past the two visitors to the entrance. She turned back to Jim. Mildred was wearing a white blouse with a gray suit that brought out the gray of her eyes. A matching hat sat firmly atop her head of curly black hair. She took her hat off, rumpled her hair, and smiled. "At least, I didn't see his car out back when we drove up."

"That's all right, Miss Perrine. I really wanted to speak with you anyway. I'm Detective Jim Greerson of the Atlanta Police Department. This," he said indicating his companion, "is Matt Grimes." The woman opened the door and stepped inside without responding. Jim thought she was playing it very aloof. Her redheaded companion pushed past Jim and Matt to Mildred's side in the doorway. Detective Greerson was annoyed by the action but let it slide. "Do you mind if we come in for a minute, Miss Perrine?"

"Why, no. Please do come in. We can talk in the sitting room. I don't want to use the library in case Daddy returns," she volunteered. "That's more or less the center of his universe now. And please call me Mildred." The woman, who Jim estimated to be a few years his junior, had a soft, husky voice. Matt found her more alluring than before.

With the Auburn's fair-skinned driver following her closely, Mildred led the men to a room off the main hallway. The large room, whose hardwood floor was partially covered by a thick area carpet, held an expensive, oversized sofa and two matching chairs. They were arranged to face a fireplace and were separated from it by a large coffee table. End tables held lamps with leaded-glass shades. Mildred carelessly tossed her hat onto the seat of a chair and drew her gloves off. The gloves followed the hat. Her suit coat was the last of her clothing to find its resting place there. The brunette invited her visitors to take a seat as she bent to turn on one of the lamps. Jim remained standing next to the mantel over the fireplace but pointedly lobbed his fedora onto her clothing in the chair. Matt kept his hat in his hand but followed Jim's lead and took up a position standing beside one of the stuffed chairs. Casting a tolerant glance at the two strangers, the attractive woman moved soundlessly across the room to an intricately carved sideboard, standing on tall legs, against one wall. Jim assumed it to be an antique. He did until Mildred opened the two center sections of its top. A large, fully stocked bar rose from inside the piece and came to rest level with its surface. She turned gracefully and asked, "Anyone else care for a drink? I'm simply parched." All three men threw in with the idea. "What'll you have, detective?"

Jim smiled. "That looks like some friendly scotch you have there. I think I'll become acquainted with that, thank you. Straight, please." Mildred's companion snorted jeeringly. Jim, already annoyed with the man's presence, started to say something but let it drift. He needed things calm at the moment. When Mildred turned to him, Matt joined in Jim's whiskey selection. The woman finally looked to the red-haired man who echoed a choice for scotch. "Fine, Hunter, I'll have the same, but on the rocks" she said evenly. "Do the honors, please." Her words were less a request and more an instruction from a woman accustomed to getting her way with men, particularly, this one. She expected the service. He was used to giving it.

In Hunter's expression, Matt could see the instantaneous conundrum he faced: the desire to keep Mildred happy versus the reluctance to serve those he saw as his lessers. Jim saw it, too. The big cop watched him as he slowly, reluctantly moved to the sideboard and started pouring the drinks. Decked out in sporty worsted slacks, a blue collar-attached dress shirt, and a jaunty coordinated sweater vest, Hunter tried to exude an air of nonchalance as he set about his assigned duties. The guy was unscarred by hard work, in Jim's estimation. He was the pedantic sort of fellow Jim knew all too well. The redhead was the type who acted as if he'd read Shakespeare without being forced to.

Mildred moved to the coffee table by a route that took her close to where Greerson stood. The perfume of her skin came to him as she passed. At the table, her long, precise fingers removed a cigarette from a holder. The woman also picked up a cigarette lighter. She handed Jim the lighter, held the cigarette to her lips, and waited behind bedroom eyes. The detective glanced over her shoulder at Hunter busily making the drinks. He wondered whether the flame-topped man had any idea of the "dance" occurring just across the room. Jim moved his eyes to meet Mildred's. A faint smile lifted the corners of her mouth as she waited. He made her wait. After a time, he snapped the lighter to life and held it up but away from her cigarette. She looked at him smoothly and leaned to the flame. After taking a deep drag on the cigarette, Mildred blew the smoke at the cop's face. He stared at her through the haze. Matt watched with rapt interest as the scene unfolded. He still thought Mildred was a knockout and imagined how she would light up the dance floor at one of the City Club affairs.

The piquant woman let loose a low, laconic laugh before retreating to the large chesterfield. She nestled back among the throw pillows just as the dutiful Hunter delivered her drink. He went about distributing the cocktails to Jim and Matt before sitting next to his female companion. Mildred looked up at Jim. "Now exactly what was it you wanted to speak with me about, Detective Greerson? I had assumed your business was with Daddy."

Jim sipped his drink and sat the glass on the mantel. He stuck a match on the fireplace stone and put it to a cigarette. The time had come to play his hunch. "Tell me about you and Carl Gutowski, Mildred."

She hesitated. "Well, the man is a business associate of Daddy's."

"No. That's not what I said. I'm asking about *you* and Carl. *Your* relationship."

The brunette looked at Greerson with mild disbelief. "What? There is no *relationship* between Carl... Mr. Gutowski and me." She fluffed her hair carelessly and looked away as if uninterested in the topic.

"You'll have to forgive me if I don't believe you. You have –"

Hunter sprang from the sofa toward Jim. Standing toe to toe with the larger man, he growled in an oily voice, "Now see heuh, suh." He glanced back at Mildred and smiled, proud of his stand on her behalf. "Ahm not gonna allow Miss Perrine to be called a liah or to be subjected to scurrilous accusations!" he drawled.

Jim looked at Hunter with contempt. He impressed the big cop as one of those people he encountered on occasion who had a swollen sense of self-regard, feeling their money gave them sway, both psychologically and physically, over others. At the same time, they tried to imitate what they believed to be the airs of old southern gentility. "And ahm not given to wastin' my breath, suh," Jim mocked. When the red-head's body became rigid, the detective continued in a stiff, edgy voice, "This is police business, sonny! You need to stay the hell out of it!"

Trying to gain control, Hunter quickly reached out and put his hand hard on Jim's shoulder. Oh, Hunter, bad move, thought Matt. The reporter felt certain that the closest Hunter had ever come to a fist fight was a Cagney movie.

The redhead's voice rose. "Perhaps you don't know who ah am! You should –"

As Hunter spoke, Jim looked at the hand woodenly, and then slowly returned his gaze to its owner's face before interrupting. "*Perhaps* you're tired of having the use of that arm, Hunter," Detective Greerson said in a small, flat voice. Hunter blanched and released his grip. He smiled a little crookedly. Matt noticed that his left leg shook visibly inside his trousers. There followed a silence with barbs on it.

The hush was broken by Mildred, who put her cigarette on an ashtray and quickly moved to the red-haired man's side. "Hunter, it might be better if you run along." The man turned to protest, but was cut off. "I'll be fine. The detective only wants to see what I know about one of Daddy's business associates." She glanced past Hunter to Detective Greerson. "That's all. Now run along, and I'll call you later."

The man tried to again to reclaim the room. "But ah feel the need to stay heuh for youh well bein', Mildred." Despite his attempted bravado, he sounded beaten, disheartened.

With the condescending air of a schoolmarm dismissing one of her charges, Mildred took him by the arm and led him from the room, saying as they walked, "Please, Hunter, it'll be fine. Now you run along." He shambled away in shock, and the pair disappeared down the hall toward the front door.

After they'd gone, Matt looked at Jim and smiled. "What a charmer!" he whispered. Jim merely nodded. Words came to his mind but died unsaid.

A minute later Mildred returned. "I'm sorry about Hunter." She sniffed dismissively, "He has his uses." She might have been speaking about a footstool or clothes hamper, Jim reflected. The tall brunette walked to the detective and leaned in close so they were practically touching. She reduced her voice to a husky, sultry whisper. "Men have all kinds of uses, detective." She smiled seductively. "So do women."

"You're throwing it away, lady. I'm here strictly on business," Jim said softly.

Mildred leaned in closer, "I'm only saying we could have some fun together." Her voice in Jim's ear was a clean, dry whisper. The hint of liquor on her breath was lost in the fragrance of her skin.

"Never gonna happen," he whispered in response.

She pulled back suddenly but with grace and released a low, rich laugh. "Forget I mentioned it."

"It won't take a minute."

A padded shoulder lifted slightly and fell. As she crossed to the sofa, Mildred asked in a tone that ignored the previous few seconds, "Now what were you inquiring about, detective?"

"I want you to tell me about Carl Gutowski. Will you tell me about *you* and Carl?"

Mildred's lips and mouth conveyed a mixture of distaste and impatience at the question. The big detective looked at her with a level, unsmiling expression. Returning to her place on the chesterfield, she reached for her scotch and, raising the glass to her lips, watching Jim, finished the drink. She swallowed the liquor thoughtfully. Another silence. This time with tension. Jim was prepared to wait. Matt found a chair from which to observe this vignette. As he sat, the striking brunette gave him a fleeting, sideways look. The blond journalist lit a fresh cigarette with his old one, which he stubbed out in an ashtray. Sighing quietly, Mildred made a noise with the ice in her glass. She looked pensive. She glanced sideways at her abandoned cigarette wisping a tiny thread of smoke into the still air. The woman touched her slim, delicate neck caressingly but in a manner more contemplative than seductive.

Then, she flicked her eyes back at Jim. Her face went hard, her demeanor resolute. "There's not much to tell really," she said without too much conviction. "It was just a crazy episode. I accidentally met him here once as he was leaving after a visit with Daddy. Though we'd never met, he acted as if he knew me, knew all about me really. I knew nothing of him. Frankly, he aroused my curiosity. He was such an unusual sort. Later, when I mentioned meeting Carl, Daddy warned me to have nothing to do with the man." She smiled. "That only roused my interest all the more. We saw each other for a while. He was different. We had some crazy fun together. But I'm afraid he took the whole affair more seriously than did I. The dope wanted me to *marry* him. *Marry him*!" she emphasized with some *hauteur*. "I wouldn't marry that oaf if he were the last man on earth," she said casually. "And if he claimed to be, I'd demand a re-count."

"A clever phrase, Mildred, but I hear that you two are *still* pretty hot and heavy. Something about you bowing your neck against your daddy's will. I also hear Carl's still trying to get you to run off with him."

"Do I look like the kind –?"

"Don't ask me to describe your kind, Mildred."

Mildred's gray eyes snapped at Greerson. The detective braced himself for an attempted slap that never came. Instead, she surged to her feet and went past him to the sideboard where she poured a drink and drank it quickly. She followed that with another. The woman picked up a siphon of charged water and turned back to face the detective. For a moment, Matt thought she was going to throw the bottle at his friend. Suddenly, she gasped and flashed her big gray eyes at the door to the hallway. Dr. Perrine had quietly stepped into the edge of the sitting room.

"I thought I heard voices as I came in." He nodded across the room. "Hello again, detective. Mr. Grimes." The voice emerged from his mouth slowly, like a condemned man trying to climb down from a tumbrel. The two visitors returned his greeting, nodding a "Dr. Perrine" in the older man's direction. Perrine cast a weary smile at his daughter. "How are you, my sweet?"

"Oh, I'm just fine, Daddy! We're only having a little talk. How are you?"

"I'm... I'm fine, darling." The doctor looked sadly at Jim Greerson. "I'll be in my library if you need me." He walked away slowly.

When her daddy was out of earshot, Mildred quickly tucked away another drink. Her eyes slowly filled with tears. "Poor Daddy. I'm so worried about him. He's so lost since he can't go back to his clubs. He truly misses his times at the Capital City Club, the Piedmont Driving Club, and, for whatever reason, that stick-up-its-ass Dogwood City Club. I simply don't understand it all."

Detective Greerson surmised she was in the dark about her father's criminal activities and how they related to Gutowski. Again, he suspected that Gutowski was merely an example of a spoiled child wanting so desperately something she's been told she cannot, should not have. But the detective had a point to this soiree, and he wasn't reaching that objective this way. He head nodded toward the scotch bottle at her elbow. "Pace yourself, lady. You haven't told me what I came here to learn."

Initially, Jim's comment was rewarded with a freezing look. Defiantly, Mildred turned to the sideboard and poured herself another, more generous libation. Lifting her glass in salute at the detective, she smiled and gulped it down. "I can hold my own, detective!"

Spoiled brat, the detective mused again. "Fine, Mildred. You're your own woman. You can hold *your* own and, apparently, someone else's, too. Go ahead! Take it from the neck, for all I care! Now, what about Carl?"

The answer was a long time coming. When she spoke, her voice had plenty of frost. "Carl turned out to be long on promises, short on performance. It was an oddly ungracious allusion. Polysyllabic words seemed to offend him. In short, he was a dance-hall sheik." Her tone was not quite haughty, but vain and smug. Slamming her glass down, she continued, "After a few laughs, I gave him the air," she added, dusting her hands together and chuckling. "Carl wouldn't accept it. He kept phoning and showing up. Said he couldn't live without me," she laughed louder. "But he's still alive as far as I know."

"You're right," Greerson said in a flat tone. "He's not dead. Yet." Mildred's eyebrows arched as she showed a passing flicker of emotion. "Where can I find Carl, Mildred?"

She shrugged when he looked at her. "I don't know for certain. He's been moving around for some reason. The last time we spoke he said he was going to be staying with some people whose name I don't quite recall." She paused in contemplation. "Their name was, uh, Blalock, I think." She paused again. "Yes, it was Blalock. He said he'd be staying at their house. I don't know where they live, though." A quick, perceptive look passed between Matt and Jim. The Blalock House was a name familiar to both. Though neither of them had been inside, they knew of its reputation. "I don't care anyway. I've had a change of heart about Carl."

Detective Greerson looked at the attractive brunette and said flatly, "Was it a change of heart or a choice of evils, Mildred?" Those gray eyes flashed in anger again. Jim threw his cigarette into the fireplace and stood tall. He ignored the rage in her eyes. "You know, Mildred, your daddy told me you've had a superior education. Maybe, at some point, you read some of the writings of Aristophanes, the Greek poet and playwright. He's supposed to have said 'Youth ages, immaturity is outgrown, ignorance can be educated, and drunkenness sobered, but stupid lasts forever.' "

"You bastard! How dare you! Get out of –!"

A resounding crack from somewhere in the back of the home stopped the woman in midscreech. For a split second, the three people gaped at one another before Detective Greerson bolted through the sitting-room door into the hallway. Matt and Mildred started after him. "Stay here, Matt!" he yelled over his shoulder. "And keep her with you!"

Matt struggled to restrain the tall brunette from following Jim. He watched the big cop amble to the closed library door. Greerson was certain he knew what he'd find on the other side. He felt no need to rush.

Glancing back over his shoulder at the hysterical woman thrashing about with his friend down the hall, he opened the door. Entering, he saw Dr. Perrine draped across his desk at an odd angle as a large crimson pool spread from beneath him over its surface. The detective saw immediately that the doctor was dead. The left side of his head had been blown away. Blood, skull fragments, and brain matter were strewn from the dead man across the room toward the fireplace and the portrait of his beloved Mildred. Jim closed the door quietly and approached the desk. A .45 caliber automatic handgun lay near the doctor's right hand. Perrine's face was badly distorted in death. Circling the scene, Jim saw the contact entry wound on Perrine's right temple he'd expected to find. He also noticed an opened drawer, the same one from which the doctor had removed the match book during their first visit. He speculated whether the gun had been there at the time. Jim also mulled over whether the gun, Gutowski's caliber weapon of choice, had been given to Perrine by the goon for some reason. Dr. Perrine hadn't struck the detective as a .45 caliber kind of mug.

Under the edge of the desk's black pen set, Jim saw a handwritten note. Blood spatter stained the page, and the spreading pool crept closer to it. Momentarily, the detective questioned whether suicide cases ever considered the possibility that their final act might obliterate or, at the very least, make more grotesque the message they sometimes felt compelled to leave. He guessed that, if they'd been thinking straight, maybe they'd have chosen some option other than they did. As he reached across the doctor's body to rescue the note, he could hear Mildred's frenzied cries down the hall. Greerson didn't envy Matt the job he'd been left with. He gently pulled the note from beneath the pen set and read it:

> I am very sorry for the harm I may have caused. I love you very much, Mildred. You remain the only thing in my life that has any meaning. But I cannot face the degradation of being sent to prison.

Detective Greerson looked down past the note at the dead man. He drew a long breath and let it out silently. *The old man thought I was here to arrest him*, the big cop mused sadly. Laying the note aside, he picked up the telephone and made the appropriate phone calls to report the incident.

A short time later, Mildred, Matt, and Jim were in the sitting room, waiting for the police to arrive. The detective had refused to let the woman go near the death scene, despite her screeching demands. Instead, she nursed another drink and smoked between crying jags. Occasionally, she would put her face in her hands. "Daddy's dead," she'd sob between her fingers.

By the time the authorities had arrived and were completing their required tasks, it was dark. When Jim felt he'd given all the information he could to his fellow detective and the coroner's representative, he and Matt left the home to return to police headquarters. They paused at the Hudson, now accompanied by several other vehicles on the flagstone driveway. Leaning on Jim's heap, Matt passed a cigarette from a fresh pack to his friend. He lit both smokes. The two men looked back at the residence. Light leaked from draped windows. Jim said wearily around his cigarette, "Some day, huh, Matt?"

The reporter shook his head in sad astonishment at the events that had evolved that afternoon. He puffed a swirl of smoke and watched it float up in the dim light. "I gotta tell you, Jim, I really feel sorry for Mildred. What a mess."

"She'll land on her feet. Her kind always does."

"You think?"

"Yeah, she'll be back in the gutter now." Jim's voice cut through the night like a silver stiletto. Matt looked at him in disbelief. The statement was unnecessarily cruel, in his estimation. The detective couldn't see the reporter's face clearly in the dark, but guessed his reaction. In answer to his look, he continued, "It's all right, Matt. She knows all the warm places." After another brief, stunned silence from Matt, an unmoved Greerson added, "Look Matt, I know that sounds harsh. I'm sympathetic to a point. But, if you want to be a tease or go on the make and crawl between the sheets with scum like Carl Gutowski, especially if only to be rebellious, my compassion ends. 'Like a gold ring in a pig's snout is a beautiful woman who shows no discretion.' " Matt cocked his head in puzzlement. "Proverbs. Anyway, she and her old man put themselves in this situation."

Matt shrugged off the detective's disdain for Mildred Perrine. "Well, what now, coach?"

Jim tossed his cigarette to the ground and crushed it with his shoe. "I only hope Mildred's right about Gutowski staying at the Blalock House. But, as bad as I want to lay my hands that square-headed son of a bitch, it's too late to go to the there tonight. Besides the fact that it's been a long day, I have to chin with some higher-ups first, because the joint's in another county. I don't mind stepping on toes, but I'm gonna step lightly once in a while."

"What if they say no?"

"They won't. It won't look too good to the public if they let a killer, even the killer of Negro women, get away with multiple murders. There are rumors swirling around about a possible grand jury investigation of the police department in the next several months. The higher-ups won't want to add this to the list of issues. The timing couldn't be better for me."

"Yeah, there's been a rumor flying around the *Georgian's* city room about a grand jury probe of the police department coming soon. I've meant to ask you about it."

In the darkness, Matt couldn't see Jim's facial response but sensed a frown. "Won't affect me any," the detective said evenly. "Let's go."

Back in the city, Greerson drove Grimes to the boardinghouse. He told Matt that he'd telephone him after he'd spoken to the powers-that-be about collecting Gutowski from the Blalock House. The cop walked with his friend to the front door in hope of seeing Teresa. As luck would have it, the dark-haired beauty was in the parlor, writing a letter to her family in Florida. She and Jim broke into broad smiles on seeing each other. While Matt toddled off to bed, the couple escaped to the front porch swing.

---

The next morning, Detective Greerson tried to get a meeting with his chief, but the man was unavailable until midafternoon. Mustering patience, the big cop worked through his morning routine. At one point, he telephoned Linc and Matt. He brought the former up to date with the events and the results of the visits to the Perrine mansion and his plans going forward. The latter he made aware of the delay in his planned meeting. Mallard asked to be included in any trip to the Blalock House to locate Gutowski. Despite any racial problems that might ensue from his presence there, he assured Jim that the Negro community would take it as a step in the right direction regarding race relations in light of the Negro women's murders. That, he argued gently, was in addition to the fact that he thought he'd earned the right to be present at the conclusion of the case. Jim chuckled and told the black investigator that he couldn't dispute that point. Matt made the same request for inclusion in what they hoped would be the capture of Gutowski. He also sighted his work in the case and the dependability he'd shown thus far. Despite his concern that there may well be gunplay involved, Greerson agreed to include his young friend. The Atlanta detective promised to call each man when he had an answer.

To fill part of his waiting time, Greerson talked at length to one of his fellow detectives, Arkell Rutledge, who'd grown up in Clayton County, the location of the Blalock House. Arkell had also worked at the resort in some capacity in his youth. Jim was familiar with the establishment but only to an extent. Without letting on why he wanted to know, he gathered as much information about the place as possible.

Greerson knew that the Blalock House was an old three-story clapboard resort hotel on Jonesboro Road in Clayton County, southeast of Atlanta. He'd driven past it enough to recall that its high-peaked roof ran from back to front, where it covered a wide porch across its facade. The porch's roof was supported by freestanding columns, reminiscent of the plantation homes of yore. The building sat very wide and very deep on a horseshoe-shaped drive off the main road. Several old trees with whitewashed trunks stood in the oval formed by the driveway. A filling station and repair garage was located across the road from the hotel. That much he'd seen passing the place on Jonesboro Road.

Blalock House's reputation was that of a rather dilapidated relic that had once been an escape for Atlanta sportsmen who reveled in the fishing, hunting and golfing there. For those who cared to bring their family, there'd been activities for them, also. The expansive property boasted a spring-fed lake that flowed into a nearby river, which ran through the resort's multi-acre property. Both the lake and river were formerly used for fishing and boating excursions. In bygone days, the owner had kept the property stocked with quail, and the lake was a perfect spot for in-season duck and migratory goose hunting. A now-aged golf course was located nearby.

As time had marched on, the establishment's reputation eroded with age, as had its amenities. The hotel and its attached tavern, which extended as a sizeable one-story el from the left side of the main structure, were in a state of disrepair with chipped and peeling white paint. Some windows were missing one or both dark-green shutters. Other shutters hung precariously by sheer willpower. The resort hotel had more recently become a haunt of ne'er-do-wells, seeking to remove themselves from the Atlanta and Fulton County jurisdictions for a short time, as well as for traveling salesmen on shoestring budgets, and a few widows living on insurance proceeds.

Rutledge filled Jim in on more details about the Blalock House, particularly the inside layouts of both the hotel and the tavern. He explained that the tavern had served as the hotel's restaurant in its heyday, but had now been converted to a roadhouse. An area for automobile parking, he pointed out, was located around and behind the tavern. Jim decided that he may be getting more facts than he needed, but he didn't want to stop Rutledge's flow of information. As Detective Rutledge drew out a floor plan on a sheet of paper, he indicated the location of the tavern's direct access to the hotel lobby and the main entrances to both the roadhouse and the hotel lobby. The detective finished by saying that the whole operation was under the protection of a powerful county politician, who owned it through a straw man. The setup was run, in turn, by an older couple somehow related to the politician.

During this rundown, Artie happened along and conspicuously listened in on the conversation. When Rutledge had finished, Jim thanked him, but blew off his question about why he was seeking the information, saying he was planning an extended weekend and only wanted to know more about the place. As Arkell Rutledge walked away, Rutherford leaned into Jim. "So what's up, Jimbo?"

"Nothing, Artie. Just a natural curiosity about something. That's all."

"Bullshit!" Artie whispered hoarsely, glancing around the detectives' area before looking intently at Jim. "I know you better than you wanna think, partner. You're up to somethin'! Now what's the lowdown?"

"It's nothing, Artie. Just forget it."

"Not on your life! You're givin' me a lot of hooey, Jimbo! The harder you try to give me the brush, the more I know somethin's up! Does it involve rough stuff?"

Jim looked over both shoulders. "All right, all right! Pipe down!" he said in a conspiratorial tone. "Something *is* in the works. And, yeah, it could well turn into a rumpus. But I've gotta get approval for my plan first. So, in the meantime, keep your chin buttoned! Okay?"

"Include me in the play and you gotta deal!" Jim smiled and nodded. Artie was always up for a tangle with a hard number, he mused. The harder, the better. Since getting to know the big man, Jim had learned that Artie joined the police department with the idea that the work would be more like law enforcement in the Wild West. Since he learned the truth about the job, he'd been sorely disappointed and annoyingly bored at times.

About half-past three that afternoon, Detective Greerson sat across the desk from his chief. The barrel-chested man that Jim had to convince of his plan listened intently. When Jim had finished explaining his take on the facts of and his scheme to finish the case, the chief knocked ash from his smoke and looked sideways at Greerson. "Now don't go gettin' that big brain of yours workin' overtime just yet, detective. You've got a lot of circumstantial evidence against Gutowski, I'll grant you. But, with Dr. Perrine dead and this Green boy not talkin', that's all it is. Circumstantial."

"Here's the deal, chief. I can connect Dr. Perrine with Gutowski. Even the daughter can testify to that. Chances are good I can locate the surgery where Perrine performed the abortions, and then get a witness on that end. I just haven't had the time to do it yet. It's a surefire bet that he didn't do them at his home." The detective was ticking the items off on his fingers as he spoke. "I have a medical witness who can testify that three of the dead girls had undergone the procedure. Gutowski was who Green answered to for the girls he was running. So Gutowski was Green's boss. Green has refused to talk, I think, because he was afraid of retribution from the big goon. Once Gutowski's in custody, I know I can make... um... get Green to talk," he finished with a somewhat awkward grin. "Besides, Green knows if he doesn't cooperate, he looks real good for all four murders and a date with the hot seat."

The chief pondered the situation for a minute. "You say and I hear that this Gutowski is mighty bad business, a hard number. How many men are you gonna take with you?"

"Well, I think Artie and I can handle this guy easy enough. He's a rowdy, but not that tough a mug." Jim smiled wickedly, before going on, "What's more, I can't risk word of the play getting out. The owner of the joint Gutowski's holed up in is too well connected. Chances are he knows of and approves of some of his hotel's residents."

The chief studied Jim's face for a minute. "You know, you've changed a lot over the last several years. Sometimes, I'm not sure who you are anymore, Jim." Greerson looked down at the tops of his shoes. The chief was right, of course, he reflected. "Listen, you're a good detective, but you're also a little too headstrong at times. That can be a good thing. But it can also get you killed. And I don't like goin' to the funerals of my men."

"Then don't come, chief," Greerson sat flatly, looking fixedly at his boss. "Look, chief, the Chinese have a saying: 'Life is lighter than a feather; duty is heavier than a mountain'. I'm gonna do my duty to bring a murderer to justice." He emphasized his last words to put a cap on his argument. They were intended to make the chief realize that, to oppose his plan to bring Gutowski to ground, might not sit too well during a future grand jury probe of the department.

"Okay, Jim," the chief relented, "go to it. But I want a full report on the operation when you're done. Be careful. Don't do anything foolhardy. And don't get any civilians hurt, okay?" Jim nodded, thanked the chief, and shook the man's hand before he left his office.

When he reached his desk, Jim was met by Rutherford. When Greerson only smiled at him, Artie demanded, "Well?"

"We're a go," he said quietly and smiled.

Artie maintained a soft, though impatient tone. "Well, what is it? What's the caper?"

"We're gonna pinch Carl Gutowski for the murder of Charlie Newsome." Artie smiled broadly. For whatever reason, there was no love lost between Rutherford and Gutowski, either. Jim chose to save the most distasteful aspect, at least to Artie, for last. "And for the killings of those three women."

"What?" his voice rose. Jim raised his hand quickly and glanced around the room. Rutherford returned to hushed tones. "You're kiddin' me, right? Say, is that smoke investigator gonna be involved in this?" When Jim didn't answer right away, the big cop protested, "Aw, c'mon, partner!"

Jim quietly suggested that they take a walk to discuss the situation. When the two men were finally in an open area between some buildings near police headquarters, Greerson stopped, retrieved a cigarette, and turned to offer one to Rutherford. Artie put a match to both smokes as he eyed his fellow detective warily. Neither man spoke. They stood there for a moment in that tableau as Jim gathered his thoughts. "Look, Artie, I put up with a lot from you on the job." When his fellow detective started to protest, Jim raised a quieting hand and continued, "But I know you've had to put up with a hell of a lot of crap from me since... well, you know." Rutherford nodded his understanding. "But here's the deal. Gutowski's good for those Negro women's murders and, I honestly believe, for Charlie Newsome's, too. I'm gonna bring him in with or without your help. And, whether you like it or whether you know it, a lot of what I have on him for the other three killings is the result of Lincoln Mallard's work. He's gathered information that neither of us could have gotten from sources we could never have hoped to use. So, yeah, he's in. I'm asking you to think of this as going after Gutowski just for Newsome's murder, if that helps you deal with it. But I need your help, Artie." Rutherford remained silent. "So that's the deal. Period. There'll be lots of kudos to go around for an arrest in the Newsome murder and, with you still sort of being on the chief's shit list, it can't hurt you." A long silence hung in the air between the two men. "Well, whaddya say, Artie? Are you in or are you out?"

Rutherford blew out a long plume of smoke, which drifted up into his squinting eyes. For a long minute, the detective wrestled with the idea, still undecided. Finally, he said, "All right, Jimbo. Just keep that dark meat away from me. Agreed?"

"Fine, Artie. I can't change you at this late date. Just don't cause trouble while we're working it."

Rutherford stiffened at the words. "Whoa, partner! I don't need no *changin'* as you put it. To my way of thinkin', you been hangin' around the wrong sorts of people too much lately. That's what the problem is. So lets us get that straight right here and now."

"Okay, Artie. You've got your approach, and I've got mine. Fair enough?" Rutherford gave Jim a halfhearted nod. "And just so you know, Matt Grimes is going, too." Another protest from Artie was stopped short by a hard-eyed glare from Greerson. "He's dependable and he's been involved in a lot of this case. Sometimes, I might add, when I couldn't find you to go out on it with me. So he goes. I'll take responsibility for both Mallard and Grimes. Period." Artie shook his head in silence. On that uneasy impasse, they returned to the office.

Back at his desk, Jim called Linc and Matt to let them know what time he'd be picking them up to take the air out on Jonesboro Road. He reminded both to bring their guns. Detective Greerson had decided to use the LaSalle, the only car that he could quietly get his hands on which would hold the four men in his group, plus Gutowski, *if* he were at the Blalock House and *if* he came along peaceably.

———

Linc put in an appearance at home after work only long enough to grab a bite of supper and to let Leola know he had some work to do later.

Assuming that this work had something to do with the white men again, his father-in-law merely shook his head in concern.

Greerson and Rutherford appeared at the curb in the LaSalle a few hours before sunset. When Linc climbed in the back seat and bid them hello, Rutherford only grunted. Jim greeted him while elbowing his partner firmly in the ribs out of Linc's view. Greerson confirmed that the investigator was carrying his weapon.

The big blue car pulled up to the front of 71 Houston Street a short time later. The young news hawk came out of the house and climbed into the back seat beside Linc. He was carrying a thermos of black coffee compliments of Miss Dixie. Artie made a wisecrack about his landlady sewing a name label into his clothes for him, too. Matt was too tense to get into it with the coarse detective then and ignored the barb.

Before they left the boardinghouse area, Jim retrieved the sketch of the floor plan Detective Rutledge had made for him. In the low light of the LaSalle, he went over it using his flashlight and limned his plan to the other men. Basically, he wanted to use Matt to go into the hotel and confirm that Gutowski was staying there and in what room. Afterward, Jim would locate and confront the man. Meanwhile, he needed Artie and Linc to cover the exits to make certain the gorilla didn't make an escape. As a Negro at a "white's only" establishment, he recognized that Linc's involvement would have to be limited but nonchalantly covering the front entrance from the car should not provoke any problems. Artie snarled a smart-assed remark suggesting that Linc sit behind the wheel of the LaSalle and pretend to be a chauffeur. Rutherford's comment drew another sharp elbow from Jim.

*The Infamous 1934 LaSalle 350 Sedan*

439

# SHORTENING SHADOWS

The private investigator responded that, *if* he were doing the chauffeuring, Rutherford would sure as hell be walking. With that bit of tension in the air, Jim took the opportunity to remind them that they absolutely needed to work together to pull this off. As he spoke, Greerson looked at all three of his companions. Grimes nodded and glanced at Mallard, who nodded. Linc, in turn, looked at Rutherford, who gave no indication of noticing. When the tension eased, they finished a brief discussion of the scheme and departed Houston Street for the Jonesboro Road hotel.

In the fullness of time, they reached their objective. As Greerson pulled into the hotel's driveway and parked some distance from the front entrance, the men saw a trim, light-skinned Negro boy shining the chromium of a long, sleek roadster parked under the trees in the center of the semicircular drive. The trees stood in what was now a weed-wild garden, weeds that somehow thrived in their shade. The boy sung as he worked fast to beat the fading light. His singing in the distance sounded like a soft drone. Artie thought to say that there was a Negro who knew his place, but he'd already grown weary of Jim's elbow.

The four men climbed out and gathered at the LaSalle's trunk. Before Matt could turn to move to the hotel, Detective Greerson grabbed his arm with one last warning in a low, deadpan voice, "I get that you know how to use that gun, Matt, but whatever you do, don't put yourself in harm's way. If it goes to shit, get out fast! If you can't for some reason, just remember you dictate who fires the first shot!" The big cop looked hard at his young friend. "There's nothing glorious in dying for nothing." The urgency in his voice drew Matt up short. The younger man could only nod his understanding before cantering toward the hotel's front entrance. A frisson of excitement coursed through his body. He moved forward with such calm as he could muster. The remaining three men watched him hopefully.

Jim turned to Linc and started to speak. Linc saw the look on the cop's face, read his thoughts through it, and cut him off. "You don't need to say anything to me about being careful, Jim. My uncle always says that bombs and bullets are colorblind, unlike some folks." Greerson nodded gravely.

Climbing the few steps to the wide porch, Matt passed through double oversized screen doors. The two large oak doors of the entry way stood open to allow whatever breeze might filter into a grand lobby that he mused was only slightly smaller than Ponce de Leon Stadium. The young man momentarily looked around the sizeable space. The lobby rose two stories to a mezzanine level with a U-shaped balcony, accessible from the first floor by a set of stairs climbing from right to left and across the back wall.

On its two sides, the balconies that overlooked the lobby led to rooms on the sides of and toward the front of the hotel. A balcony across the back wall on the second floor opened to two hallways running on each side and to the rear of the building, apparently providing access to interior and exterior rooms on either side of the hotel. Those corridors were set in slightly from the side balconies, indicating slightly deeper rooms than those toward the front of the hotel. The back wall of the second floor was also the location of a set of stairs leading to the third floor. Several old fans were suspended from the lobby's ceiling and slowly stirred the warm, stuffy air. Four old-fashioned chandeliers also were suspended from the ceiling.

The lobby's wide floor space was covered by a worn maroon carpet and littered at various points around support columns with heavy, overstuffed chairs and settees, covered in tattered paisley brocade. Included in the groupings were occasional tables holding gold-colored lamps at least two decades out of style. The memories of the once-grand place drew back into remoteness with time.

As Matt started to walk to the registration desk on the right side of the lobby, he saw a row of telephone booths lining the wall on the left. He decided that electricity was probably the Blalock House's first concessions to the march of time. The telephone booths were its last. He got it in his head to modify Jim's plan slightly. The young journalist walked nonchalantly to one of the booths. When he did, he saw the short hallway that ran perpendicularly from the lobby to the tavern. Matt entered a phone booth and closed the folding door behind him. Dropping a coin in the slot, he dialed the operator and asked her to connect him to the Blalock House.

Shortly, the desk phone started ringing. It reached Matt as a murmur coming through the closed door of the booth from across the lobby. The young blond adjusted the mouthpiece and turned his head to see better the front desk. The clerk, a thin man with short brown hair, answered the phone. Advising the man that his boss had directed him to deliver a package to Mr. Gutowski, he asked for the hood's room number. The man offered to take delivery of the package at the front desk. When Matt explained that it had to be handed over in person, the clerk told him that Gutowski was registered in room two-oh-one, but that he wasn't in his room. As Matt's heart began to sink and his mind started to spin, the man added that Carl was in the bar. The clerk thoughtfully asked Matt whether he wanted him to get Gutowski to the phone. Matt declined gratefully, telling the man that he'd find Carl when he got there. He thanked the man and cradled the receiver. The reporter waited a minute or so until the man at the front desk was otherwise occupied before leaving the booth and making his way out through the screen doors into the night. He hustled back to the LaSalle where the three men waited. As they ditched their smokes, Matt was fumbling to get one lit.

Matt explained what he'd done and learned. He also assured Jim that Rutledge's layout of the lobby and stairways was dead on. "That's perfect!" Greerson exclaimed in a whisper. "Okay, here's what we'll do.

Artie, I need you to cover the back entrance. It leads to the parking area and that's most likely the direction Gutowski'll run if I can't get the thug pinched. Linc, you stay near the front door or as near as you can to keep him from coming out that way." Jim and Linc ignored a muffled snort from Artie. "But be careful. This mug's nobody to take lightly. Matt, I need you to go to the desk and keep the clerk occupied while I get up the stairs to the second floor. It may not be a problem, but I'm not prepared to take a chance at this late stage.

"Once I'm upstairs, Matt, give me ten minutes to get into Gutowski's room and look around. Then, I need you to go into the tavern and locate the mug. Ankle past him slow enough for him to get a good look at you. He'll remember you and that 'love tap' of yours from the White Lantern. Then get the hell out of there. Get to somewhere around the lobby where you can watch for him but he can't see you. My guess is that, when he sees you in the tavern, he'll panic at least enough to hightail it back to his room either to hide out or to pack his bags for a big flit. After he goes upstairs, if he goes upstairs, stay where you can see the lobby in case he tries to make a break back through the tavern. If he tries to go out the tavern, just yell like hell. But don't confront him. He's too dangerous when he's cornered. Get me?"

"What if he just hauls ass directly out from the tavern without going to his room? What then?" Artie asked.

"Well, I'm counting on him being so comfortable in this hideout that he doesn't have everything he thinks he needs with him at all times. He'll need to get back to his room for *something* he wants to take with him if he has to leave here. A gun, maybe, or something," Jim answered the detective in a hopeful tone. "If not, I'm counting on him coming in sight of you, Artie, in the parking area as he heads for a car."

The three other men nodded their understanding of their roles in the scheme. While Rutherford made his way around to the back of the hotel, Mallard, Grimes, and Greerson moved toward the front entrance. Linc dropped off some distance before they reached the porch. The black boy, finishing his work on the roadster, stopped and stared at the well-dressed black man accompanying the two white men in suits. As Jim entered the building and Matt waited briefly on the porch, Linc walked to the boy and made casual conversation about the car the young man was polishing. The entire time, he kept a wary eye on the front doors.

Jim entered the hotel and took a circuitous route to a picture postcard stand at the bottom of the staircase on the lobby's back wall. He casually looked at several offerings. Matt walked in shortly thereafter and ambled to the front counter. The man, who had answered Matt's call earlier, sat behind the counter in a Boston rocker with a crocheted antimacassar over its back. As he rose from it to come to greet the young man, the rocker gave out a homey squeak. On closer observation, Matt realized that the desk clerk was older than he had initially contemplated. He had sallow skin. Where Matt thought he'd seen a lean man, he now saw him as gaunt, sparse of hair, and with narrow features. Behind one cheek a substantial amount of chewing tobacco was tucked away. The reporter took up a position to keep the clerk's back to Jim. The two men at the desk made small talk about the weather before moving on to the possibility of hunting on the hotel's property. The old man had a chronic rattle in his chest as he spoke. Over the clerk's shoulder, Matt watched Jim repeatedly remove a postcard from the rack, glance at it, and then return it before picking another. All the while the detective would cut sideways glances toward the front desk.

At one point, the old man stopped talking abruptly and turned away from the counter. He spit out his chaw. As Matt watched, a tangled mass of brown fiber sought an unseen spittoon down somewhere behind the counter. Matt heard it hit the receptacle like a wet rag. Suddenly, Detective Greerson quietly hustled up the stairs. Matt caught the movement out of the corner of his eye. Seemingly unaware of Jim, the old man ran the "cleansing" finger of a purple-veined hand inside his cheek and spit again. He shook his head and smiled down at the object receiving his expectoration. "That gaboon is takin' a beatin'. Sorry 'bout that, young feller."

"That's all right. Been around tobacco all my life," Matt chuckled, as he watched Jim reach the top of the stairs and turn to move on to the balcony so he was out of sight of the registration counter. In truth, Matt had never seen such a quantity of tobacco leave a man's face at one time. If it wasn't a world's record wad of chewing tobacco, Matt mused, it was a damned good average. The young journalist glanced at his watch to mark the ten minutes Jim had said he'd need. As he did, the old man cut another huge plug and tucked it into his face. After a few seconds, the old clerk switched his chaw to the other side of his face and spit. Again, he made contact with the large spittoon behind the counter. Matt decided he didn't necessarily want to be around for the disposal of this load. He thanked the man for his help and excused himself. As he turned to leave, Matt reckoned that *all* semblance of the refinement, which had once graced the Blalock House, had faded with the grandeur of this relic of bygone days.

Crossing the large space, the blond reporter decided the best observation post he could have after his visit to the tavern would be the inside of one of the telephone booths. Matt glanced at his watch and, having nine minutes to wait, opted to monitor the time in one of the large stuffed chairs there. From that vantage point, he watched Greerson make his way along the balcony above the reception desk. The big cop was scanning the room numbers posted on the doors as he moved toward the front of the hotel.

———

Detective Greerson prowled the balcony looking for room two-oh-one. He found the room in the hotel's front corner. No light shown under the door's sill. He looked down and saw his young friend sitting in the lobby below, watching him. Quickly pointing to his strap watch, he held up the fingers of both hands. Matt nodded his understanding and recalculated the time he must wait before going to the tavern.

Greerson stood to one side of the door and rapped loud enough to be heard inside the room but not so loud as to draw attention from below. No one answered his knock. He took a piece of hard celluloid he always carried and eased it between the jamb and the lock. As Jim pushed hard toward the door's hinges, the celluloid pressed against the slope of the spring lock, which snapped back. The door gave way. Still standing to one side, he pushed the door open slowly. Only dead air greeted him. Jim stepped inside quickly and flattened himself against the open door. He moved slightly and closed the door slowly. Without the lobby light spilling into the space, he decided, the musty-smelling room was as dark as a foot up a bull's ass.

Greerson snapped on his flashlight and shone it around the room. In its strong beam, the detective saw an unmade bed with a side table and lamp sitting between two windows on the far wall. To his right, on the front wall of the hotel, a dresser with a mirror was placed between two more windows. A table-model radio, two scotch bottles, one a dead soldier, and a few glasses sat on top of the dresser. The number of glasses led him to deduce that Gutowski may have company staying with him in the hotel but not necessarily in the same room. A stuffed chair with a standing lamp beside it sat in the corner immediately to his left. In the beam, he could also see the grimy woodwork, cracked window shades, and curtains of dirty cotton lace. Jim guessed the bedsprings probably stuck into your back, too. A few clothing items littered the floor. The room was warm and oppressive.

The detective moved to the bedside table. Other than a couple of packs of Kools and a folder of matches, its only drawer was empty. He ran his hand beneath the pillow and the mattress. Nothing. Jim quickly, quietly walked to the dresser. Holding the flashlight in the crook between his neck and shoulder, he pulled out the dresser drawers and rummaged through the clothing they held. In the second drawer down, he found a .45 automatic tucked beneath some BVDs. Greerson removed the magazine and cleared the gun's chamber, catching the round in his hand. He emptied the magazine and put all the rounds in his coat pocket before replacing the magazine in the handgun. The detective returned the .45 to where he'd found it in the drawer. In the bottom drawer, he discovered a satchel containing a substantial amount of cash. Jim left it where he'd located it.

Detective Greerson threw the flashlight beam on his watch. In the few minutes he had left, he fanned the reminder of the room but found nothing of interest until he moved to the chair. As he walked across the room, the flashlight's beam caught something unusual standing in the corner behind the chair. Jim stopped short. The light revealed a Louisville Slugger baseball bat smeared with a dark-brown stain. He made a mental note to collect the bat as evidence later. Detective Greerson sat in the deep chair and waited in the dark.

---

At the ten-minute mark, Matt rose from the chair and made his way to the short hallway that separated the hotel's lobby from the tavern. Passing doors marked "Office" on his left and "Kitchen" on his right, he found the swing door entrance to the bar. The murmur of voices and music came to him from beyond the door. Bracing himself, the crime beat reporter pushed the door open and walked in. The tavern was bigger than he'd expected, and he didn't see Gutowski right away. A bar ran along the length of the wall to Matt's right. High-backed booths lined the far wall and most of the one to his left. Tables and chairs were scattered around a large floor area with a small clear spot immediately in front of him, presumably for dancing. No one was using it at the moment. A Seeburg Selectophone, blaring some tinny tune, occupied the corner just to his left. A fair number of customers littered the bar stools and occupied the tables. None of them were the man he sought. Neither was he in the booths on the far wall, the occupants of which Matt could see clearly.

Matt eased to his left and walked slowly along the booths on that wall. His mind raced as he moved, uncertain of the reception he might receive. He only hoped that the hooligan wouldn't start any trouble with so many witnesses present. As the occupants of the third stall came into view, he saw Gutowski facing away from him. Initially, Matt couldn't see the face. He didn't have to. He'd know Gutowski's square head anywhere. The big lug was sitting with two other men, drinking and talking loud and animatedly. One of the men across from Carl offhandedly glanced up at Matt as he passed. The man was smoking a huge cigar, the stench of which assaulted Matt's nostrils with a wallop. In Matt's opinion, it smelled like someone had set fire to a croker sack full of cow manure.

The young newsman walked a few more paces before turning around and moving slowly back toward the door he'd entered. As he passed Gutowski's booth again, the gangster looked up at him. His brain registered a face. With a look of mild shock, his jaw dropped open. Matt returned his gaze and shot a mirthless smile his way. He hoped that his grin would have the desired effect. Matt had decided to be about as inconspicuous as an outhouse in a front yard. He quickened his pace to some extent after he passed Gutowski's crew and even more after he went through the swing door into the hallway. The sound of the music died away behind him as he marched down the short corridor. He hustled as inconspicuously as possible to a phone booth in the lobby and closed its door behind him.

Shortly, Gutowski appeared and moved across the space rapidly. Matt pulled as far back into the darkened booth as he could when he saw him.

The hood was constantly prowling his eyes around the area as he made his way to the front desk, where he stopped and spoke briefly in subdued tones to the clerk. He turned and scanned the lobby again before moving to the stairs. Matt was certain that the phone booth was neither deep nor dark enough to escape the bad man's fierce glare. Gutowski bounded up the stairs. Matt was stunned at the speed with which the big man made the ascent. Then, he jogged heavily down the balcony to the door Detective Greerson had entered earlier. After groping with a key as he looked around, Gutowski opened the door and went into the room. Matt stepped out of the phone booth and waited, uncertain what to do next.

---

As Detective Greerson sat in the blackness of the room, he heard heavy footfalls on the stairs, and then along the balcony. They stopped just outside the door. The shadow of someone standing there spilled under the sill. A key fumbled in the lock. The door opened slowly. The big goon moved into his room, and the door clicked shut behind him. He continued across the room in the darkness to a front window. Gutowski pulled the lace curtains aside and moved the window shade slightly to eyeball the view, which looked out onto the dark, deserted road in front of the hotel and across to the well-lighted filling station. He released the shade and let the curtains fall together again. Suddenly, he knew he wasn't alone. Before he could react, Detective Greerson, sensing the man's instinct, flipped on the floor lamp beside the chair where he sat.

Gutowski jerked and turned quickly. Then, regaining his composure, he stared steely eyed at his visitor. After a few seconds to size up the situation, he growled, "What gives? How'd you get in here, peckerwood?"

"I came in through the mail slot."

Gutowski cast a glance at the door. "Oh, okay. I get it. I'll have to teach that ol' man a lesson."

"Your days," Greerson snarled, "of teaching anybody anything, especially women and old guys, are over." He voice was flat and lifeless.

"Says who? You got no jurisdiction here, copper!" Gutowski growled.

"My jurisdiction is where my badge is, jerk. Who's to say different?"

The hood mulled something over and flashed a small mirthless smile. "Let's talk, detective." He made a motion with his right hand. "Mind if I smoke?"

"No, I don't mind. Just make slow, easy moves, Carl. Keep your mitts where I can see 'em."

As the goon eased his right hand toward his lapel, Greerson casually removed his weapon from its holster and held it on his knee. When the detective made his move, Gutowski let his hand fall empty. He shot Jim that baleful grin again. "I just realized I got no smokes on me. There's some in the drawer here. Mind if I get one?"

"No, Carl. Just take it easy. While you're lighting up, tell me something. Did you kill Charlie Newsome?"

Gutowski had started reaching for the second dresser drawer down when he stopped and looked back at the cop. "Kill Charlie Newsome?" the big hood smirked and sarcastically went on. "Gee, I dunno. I'll have to check my diary, detective." Before Jim could respond to his answer, the gangster made an unexpectedly quick move into the drawer and produced the .45. He pointed it at Greerson and pulled the trigger three times in rapid succession. All he got for his effort was dry clicks. Gutowski looked at the gun vacantly.

The detective raised his gun slowly and aimed it at the big goon's midriff. Reaching into his coat's side pocket, he retrieved the .45's rounds and dropped them at his feet. "You're probably wondering about these. Now, grab some air, punk! I'm taking you in, Gutowski. You can leave like you came in or go in the trunk of my car."

The big hooligan dropped the gun. A thin, hard sneer crossed his lips, as his eyes grew cold and dark. "Son of a bitch!" He looked down at the .45, and then across the floor at its ammunition. "I didn't have time to feel the difference in its weight." Gutowski returned his gaze to Greerson. "But you're not takin' me anywhere, copper. It's not in the cards," Carl snarled defiantly.

Greerson's voice was cold and dispassionate. "It's a new deal from a cold deck, Carl."

Carl mulled that over for a second before saying, "Well, I'd still like that cigarette." Jim nodded his approval and made a cautioning motion with the barrel of his gun. Gutowski carefully retrieved a pack of Kools and a book of matches from a coat pocket and lit the smoke. He tossed the cigarette pack and matches onto the dresser. A twisted smile worked on the corners of his lips. "You got nothin' on me for Charlie's killin', gumshoe."

"Well, I've got enough. Besides, you're good for the murders of three Negro women in addition."

"Bullshit! I read about those three. Nigger trash's all they were. You can't tie them to me!"

Jim's jaw tightened in anger. "You know, even with all I went through during the war, I never really got to like killing people. But, with you, Carl, I'm willing to make an exception." He paused and let his rage dissipate. "Nah, you don't even come close to being worth it." He gambled on the news about Dr. Perrin's suicide not yet reaching Gutowski. "No evidence, Gutowski? Well, I've got Dr. Perrine's testimony about how your loan sharking, and then blackmail brought about their abortions. Mildred will testify to your connection, too." To add to the goon's discomfort, Greerson put in, "She doesn't think too much of you, by the way." Gutowski shifted slightly. "And then I've got Nathan Green's story about how you knocked the girls out with that baseball bat before you killed them," he said, jerking his head to the object behind him, "to cover everything up. No, I'd say I've got a good enough case to send you to Milledgeville for a date with the hot seat."

Carl snarled scornfully, "Send a white man to the chair for some nigger trash? No grit jury would do that! Ever!" The goon slowly moved one of his feet forward half a step as he spoke.

Greerson waved his Colt menacingly at Gutowski's midsection. "Now, like I said, put your mitts up high and empty!"

Gutowski pulled his foot back and raised his hands slightly. "Listen, detective, you're a reasonable sorta mug. I've got a satchel in a drawer here that's holdin' somewheres between four and five thousand bucks. It's all yours. Just walk away. Forget you seen me."

"*Between* four and five thousand? Having trouble counting, eh, Gutowski? I'd've thought a lug as big into the numbers racket as you are would have learned how to count and add better by now. No, I'm not after your money. I'm after you! Now, get 'em up, Carl!" The man raised his hands higher. At Gutowski's indication of surrender, Greerson did something uncharacteristically careless of him, something he couldn't explain to himself afterward: he reholstered his gun. Then, he started to get to his feet. "You need –"

In one deft motion, Gutowski reached for his mouth with his left hand and snapped the burning cigarette at the detective's face. Greerson moved his head slightly, and the butt passed over his shoulder. At the same time, the hooligan drew a .45 from under his left arm and tried to take aim at the cop. Greerson was already reacting. He charged low from the chair. Leaving his feet in a dive, he crashed his right shoulder into the Carl's chest just as the automatic roared twice over his head. Gutowski stumbled, his free hand pawing the air like a blind man. A third shot from the .45 found the ceiling. The detective's left hand grappled for the gun while he tried to gain some measure of control over his assailant with his right. As they wrestled, Greerson delivered several short terrific jabs to the thug's chin. When Jim finally wrested the .45 from the hood's hand, it tumbled and slid toward the door. Gutowski mustered all his strength then and delivered a hefty fist to the side of the detective's head. The blow was barely enough to knock the big cop off the top of him. Before Jim could regain his footing,

# NEEDED KILLING

the big mobster scuttled across the floor to the door, gathering his gun as he moved. Gutowski ran out of the room, slamming the door behind him.

---

After Gutowski had disappeared into the hotel room, Matt waited and watched from the hotel lobby. Everything remained quiet for a few minutes. During that time, Matt saw Mallard enter the lobby, carrying a large box and being led by a little old white lady, who nodded to the desk clerk as she passed. The pair crossed to and climbed the stairs. They then took the next flight of stairs to the third floor and disappeared. Shortly, the young journalist heard two loud gunshots in swift succession. A split-second later, a third blast rang out. Several more seconds passed as Matt stood frozen before Carl Gutowski's room door opened and he burst through it, slamming it behind him. The big mug's eyes ranged the lobby below. As he ran, he spied Matt and raised his gun at the young man. Matt jumped behind a support column before a potshot was thrown in his direction. Wood splintered near Matt's face. He heard the rumble of the goon's footsteps. The blond reporter glanced from his hiding place as Gutowski sprinted into the second floor's far hallway.

---

Jim Greerson regained his feet and dashed for the door, drawing his Colt as he moved. A gunshot rang out as he reached the door. Opening it carefully, he made certain Gutowski had moved away. The big cop was angry enough with himself for his earlier careless move. He was intent on not making another. The balcony was clear, but he could hear the thunder of Gutowski running. Jim stepped out of the room and scanned the lobby as he trotted along the balcony rail. Below, Matt appeared from behind a damaged column. Greerson immediately

453

understood the nature of the last shot he'd heard. His determination to put a stop to Gutowski intensified. Matt waved at him indicating the hall closest to Jim leading to the rear of the hotel. The detective approached it cautiously. Powder smoke reeked in the air.

---

No sooner had Gutowski vanished down the hallway than Matt saw his friend emerge from the gangster's room with his gun drawn. A wave of relief swept over the young reporter. When he realized Jim was looking his way, Matt signaled which direction the hooligan had gone. Matt watched Jim slow his pace as he reached the corner where the balcony met the corridor. The detective pressed himself against the wall and glanced quickly around the corner before disappearing into the poorly lighted passage. Matt started galloping up the stairs two at a time. Before he reached the second floor, he heard the two men, who'd been sitting in the tavern with Gutowski, charge into the lobby. He stopped and glanced sideways in their direction. They immediately saw Matt on the stairs. The one who'd been smoking the atrocious-smelling cigar yelled at the young man. As he was shouting something the crime beat reporter couldn't quite make out, the man drew a handgun and fired at Matt. The wall just beyond the journalist's head recorded the hit with an explosion of plaster and lathing. A woman, who'd been approaching the front desk, screamed and fell to the floor. The desk clerk dropped behind the counter. In the chaos, one of the men knocked over a side table, breaking a lamp. Matt finished his ascent of the stairs four at a time. Ducking into the second-floor hallway at the top of the stairs, he threw himself against a wall a pulled his gun from its holster. Suddenly, he felt like a clay pipe in a shooting gallery.

---

As he stood on the hotel's back porch, which overlooked a parking area, the blast of a gunshot came to Artie Rutherford through the screen door there. He quickly drew his weapon and stepped into the back hallway. The detective couldn't tell exactly from where the report had come, but he thought it was somewhere above the first floor. The hall lighting's dim, a bit tricky, he muttered to himself as he listened intently. He believed he heard running coming from the second floor, so he turned and started up the staircase that ran along the back wall. Shouts and the loud discharge of a second shot came from somewhere toward the front of the hotel. The gunfire caused Artie to stop momentarily when he was about halfway up the steps. He weighed the situation. Suddenly, Carl Gutowski appeared at the head of the stairs above him. He was wearing a .45 automatic in his right hand. Before the big cop could react, the gangster swung his gun on him and fired. Initially, Artie Rutherford didn't feel the bullet, which struck him above the elbow and jerked his left arm back. When Artie raised his gun to return fire, Gutowski was already sprinting away. The big detective shook off a sudden explosion of pain in his arm and continued up the stairs cautiously, his weapon leading the way. He heard a door open and close quietly somewhere on the second floor.

———◆———

The faintly lit hall was empty as far as Greerson could tell. Low-light, burned out, and missing bulbs made the area difficult to reconnoiter. But he could make out a tall hutch against the wall some distance down on his side of the passageway. The detective couldn't tell whether Gutowski was using it for cover. His gun raised and at the ready, he skulked slowly along a wall of the corridor, expecting an encounter with Gutowski at any second. An older man opened a door behind Jim and stuck his head into the hall. The Atlanta detective turned quickly and, sizing up the situation, whispered coarsely, "Get back in your room and lock the door!" Wide-eyed, the man complied in short order.

Before the big cop could start moving again, a gunshot sounded from the lobby behind him. He looked beyond the older man's door toward the lobby momentarily. From somewhere in that direction and below him came a babel of confusion: shouting, running, doors slamming, and the sound of breaking glass. Jim was looking back toward the lobby and weighing his options when a single gun blast sounded from down the hall toward the rear of the hotel. Concerned that Gutowski was possibly on a killing spree of innocent people in the hotel, Greerson decided to continue on the path the goon had run. Before he could turn back and resume his trek toward the rear of the hotel, he heard a door close quietly in that direction. His head snapped around, but it was too late to detect where the soft sound had come from.

---

As Matt held his gun in readiness and flattened himself against the wall behind him, he breathed in the stillness. He listened to his breathing, not panting, but slightly labored. The young man had never been as keenly conscious of his own breathing before. He hoped it would continue for a long time. The reporter wasn't scared, just anxious. Every little thing took on an enormity of its own. Like a squeaking tread on the staircase. Suddenly, Matt could hear at least one of Gutowski's men slowly climbing the stairs toward him. The guy was failing miserably at using stealth in his moves. Suddenly feeling exposed in his current location, he abruptly had the urge to leave, to move. He started backing slowly down the hall toward the rear of the hotel, waiting for one or both of his adversaries to round the far corner. It took him nearly a minute to reach the back intersection of the halls. It felt like half a day.

---

At the moment two coins were pressed into his hand, Lincoln Mallard heard the first sharp crack of a shot being fired somewhere downstairs. The noise jolted him and the little old lady at his side. The black private investigator instinctively reached for his gun. He touched its cool grip under his arm and, looking down at the already-alarmed woman, hesitated. When the second shot roared, he took the gun from its holster and squeezed the butt down at his side. At the sight of the black man with a gun, the older woman howled her way to the far corner of the room and cowered in fear. His quick attempt to calm the woman couldn't get through her bawling. Linc turned and left the room with the old lady still shrieking.

Once he'd closed the room's door behind him, shutting off the woman's wails, he heard noises toward the rear of the hotel, he moved along the third-floor hallway in that direction. Another shot rang out, this one somewhere in front of and below him. He silently descended the back stairs to the second floor. At the bottom of the stairs, he turned in to the corridor only to find a bulky man framed against the dim hall lights and facing him. Linc and the second man each immediately assumed a firing stance with their weapons raised to shoulder level. Just before squeezing his trigger, the private detective recognized the silhouette of a Borsalino. "Detective Rutherford! It's me, Lincoln Mallard!" Linc called out in a gruff whisper. The Atlanta detective relaxed, lowered his gun, and walked to where Linc stood. When they were side by side, Mallard said softly, "That was close."

"Closer for you than me," Artie grunted. Linc was shaking his head almost imperceptibly when both men heard someone quietly making his way along the far passageway. They exchanged fleeting glances, and then carefully move in that direction.

As they crept, the two men passed a small credenza and a straight-backed armchair sitting to one side of the hall. A large, faded print of a horse-mounted plantation overseer in a cotton field hung above the credenza. The artwork was illuminated by a hooded light above it. Linc elbowed Artie, nodded in its direction and whispered, "Anybody you know?" The big cop made a sour face. In the illumination of the artwork, Mallard noticed for the first time that Rutherford was wounded. When he pointed to it, Artie only waggled his head strongly as if it were nothing. They moved on. Before they reached the junction of the two halls, the readily recognizable figure of Matthew Grimes quietly backed around the corner, still facing the direction from which he'd traveled.

"Matt!" Linc whispered. The reporter started, and then quickly turned, relieved to see the two men. "What's happening?" the black investigator inquired. Matt quietly but excitedly pointed toward the hallway he'd just left.

---

When Detective Jim Greerson heard the door close, he thought it was in the hall he was on but wasn't quite sure which of the one of the dozen or so rooms it belonged to. Now, Jim heard low voices coming from the passageway crossing the back of the hotel. He eased down to the corner and edged a look around it. At the back concourse's junction with the far hallway, he saw Artie, Linc and Matt together. Something down that passage back to the lobby held their attention. Considering his companions' location, Greerson was now certain that Gutowski had slipped into one of the rooms he'd just passed. They would surely have seen or heard the big goon had he run that far. The alarm would have been raised. Whatever the three were dealing with, he told himself, they could take care of it. He felt compelled to continue his search for Gutowski. Because of where he'd been standing when the door clicked shut, he eliminated the first four rooms on the hall closest to the lobby area. After a quick count, he decided that that left eight rooms which he had to clear. Turning back, the detective started retracing his steps in the lobby's direction.

———

As Jim Greerson made his way to the third door of the eight rooms he needed check for Carl Gutowski's presence, a solitary figure ascended the back stairs to the second floor. On reaching the top step, the second of Gutowski's two men crouched by the newel and spun back toward the three figures he spied at the far end of the run. Having lost track of Carl in the melee, he and his partner had determined that they were going to take on and drop these mugs, whoever they were. He waited for his partner to make his move at the lobby end of the side passageway. Unseen by him, his associate was edging around the corner into the hallway at that point. A large handgun was in his working hand. Matt peeked around the corner and watched silently. The man obviously means to bring serious harm to anyone in his way, Matt reasoned. He recalled Jim's admonition about who dictated the first shot. Even so, the reporter made his mind up to give the miscreant a warning before shooting that the man had not offered him.

Using the corner of the halls' intersection as a shield, Matt raised his arm to the level of his shoulder and sighted down it. The gun felt very far away. "Hey! Don't make me shoot!" the young journalist yelled. His shout startled his two companions and the hoodlum squatting by the staircase. At the far end of the hallway, the object of Grimes's aim squared up and started to raise his automatic. At this point, Matt didn't hesitate. His gun jumped three times. All three shots found their mark. The front of the hood's shirt was a sudden mess of blood. Firing twice into the floor as he fell, he plunged to the ground, dead before he landed.

Simultaneously, the man crouched by the staircase post straightened and raised his big, black automatic toward the three men, two of whom offered him clear shots. In that split second, Linc saw the gangster stand with his gun raised. Seeing the danger, he pushed Rutherford, who had his back to the gunman, hard toward the back wall. As he did, the private investigator leveled his revolver at the goon. The big cop fell to the floor unaware of Mallard's motive for the assault. He angrily jumped up to confront the black investigator. As Artie rose, Linc and the hood engaged one another in a chaotic, short, incredibly loud firefight. Artie started to raise his weapon in response to the assailant's fire. During the exchange, Linc was spun violently to the left by the concussion of a shot, which struck him slightly above the waist on his left side The wound was through-and-through. Linc regained his firing position and used every one of his handgun's .32 caliber rounds to bring the criminal down. But the man didn't drop before his gun pulsed and roared until it was empty. His gun wasn't empty before Matt was struck in the shoulder by a bullet as he turned to face Linc and Artie. The shot knocked Matt back against the wall. And the magazine hadn't poured out completely prior to Artie taking three hits to his chest and abdomen area. The big detective fell hard.

When it was over, cordite fumes hung in the air. The hallway was deathly silent. When the quiet struck Linc, he imagined for an instant it was the kind of utter stillness that his uncle had tried to describe experiencing during the war following an artillery barrage.

Matt slumped against the wall and slid to the floor, clutching his right shoulder, leaving a blood smear as he went down. He lost control of his gun hand and the .45 tumbled to the ground. His eyes and mouth were twisted opened in sharp pain. Blood ran down his arm inside his sleeve, then across his drooping hand where it dripped from his fingertips.

After determining that Matt's wound didn't appear life-threatening, Linc went to Artie's side. In the dim light, he saw that the man's injuries were far more serious, but there was nothing he could do for the big cop. Blood covered the entire front of Rutherford's shirt and crept from beneath him. After a long, sluggish minute, Matt recovered enough to crawl to the fallen man. Artie looked up at the black man by his side and tried futilely to say something. His teeth were stained crimson with blood. Rutherford looked down at his bloodstained shirt and swallowed hard. Then, he saw Linc's wound and struggled to speak. "We both bleed red." Matt looked for a response from Linc, who merely nodded. The police detective's breath became shallower and more labored. "I... I didn't know... why." He looked at Linc intently. "Thanks, Linc." His face slowly changed to the quiet, empty face of a dead man. Linc closed his eyes and started muttering quietly to himself. Matt looked at him and started to speak until he realized that the black man was praying, the vitriol that had flowed from Rutherford forgiven but not necessarily forgotten.

---

Detective Greerson took up a position at the side of a room's door. This was the third of the eight rooms he needed check in his search for Gutowski. He reached over and rapped hard on its surface. His knock was met with three quick blasts from a gun, causing sizeable holes in the door at chest level. Nice pattern, Jim thought sarcastically. Okay, this is it! He stepped back and hit the door with his leg out straight. The jamb splintered and door flung open hard, struck a piece of furniture or something behind it, and bounced back toward the detective. As the door was ricocheting, the detective heard a volley of gunshots sounding from the direction of his companions. He knew there was nothing he could do for them at this stage. Greerson dove low through the door toward the left side of the room as two more explosions sounded from somewhere in the dark room. He rolled away from the opening and came up on one knee next to a bed and in a firing position, his eyes prowling the room quickly. The light from the hallway, as dim as it was, still shone enough to reveal the faint figure of Carl Gutowski hunkered in a back corner, using the second bed in the room, as best he could, for a shield.

The detective, hidden in the room's darkness, heard a soft, awkward breathing noise at his knee and realized a person was lying there. When he reached out with his free hand, he realized it was a female. As his eyes adjusted to the low light coming from the hall, he saw that her face was a morass of bloody pulp. The dim light showed that a thin rivulet of blood trickled from one ear. At least she was alive, he thought. Then, Jim saw a man's body tangled in the covers on the bed. In the low light, he saw blood on the man's face. He couldn't tell whether the figure on the bed was still breathing.

Having sighted the gangster, Jim ducked his head below the level of the bed, while keeping a watchful eye, and whispered, "Okay, Gutowski, by my count, you've used up what rounds you had in the magazine, assuming the thing was full to begin with. Maybe there was one in the chamber, maybe not. I'm gonna figure there was. Maybe you were carrying an extra mag, maybe not. I'm guessing you weren't. So, that would mean you've got one, maybe two shots left. I'm gonna stand up and square off with you, you son of a bitch. If you got 'em, use 'em, cause I'm sure as hell gonna use mine!"

"That's not copacetic, copper! You can probably see me, but I can't see you!" Gutowski's voice was strained and panic-stricken.

Before he could respond to Gutowski, the detective heard a rattle, a spent sigh, and then silence from the woman on the floor beside him. His anger intensified, but his voice remained low and seething, "I'm gonna fix that for you, Carl! I'm gonna stand in the doorway so you can see me. Now that's fair, right? That's more of a chance than you gave Charlie Newsome or Addie Maddox or Effie Sledge or Lavinia Ruffin, right? Or these poor people," he followed up, nodding in the dark to the room's two occupants as if Gutowski could see him, "whoever the hell they are! That's more consideration than you showed Vivian or Mrs. Dunbar, you bastard! So, here goes, Gutowski!" As he spoke the last words, Greerson leapt into the doorway. Almost immediately, Jim realized the big criminal was pulling the trigger of his big automatic and getting nothing but those clicks again. "Still miscounting the trumps, eh, Carl?" Greerson chuckled nastily. The hoodlum threw his handgun at the silhouette of the cop. Jim moved slightly and the gun rattled into the hall behind him.

Gutowski let loose a raging snarl like a wounded, cornered animal and charged the detective. Jim quickly reholstered his gun and braced himself for the impact. The two men fell to the floor in a tangle of limbs and snarls. Greerson rapidly gained the upper hand and crawled on top of the goon's abdomen, using his legs to pin the man's arms at his sides. Despite heavy punches from the detective, Gutowski continued to struggle and buck but to no avail. Once he'd subdued Gutowski to that point, Jim reached to the bed and retrieved a pillow. He placed it over Carl's face and pulled a .25 caliber Arizmendi Protector from his coat's side pocket. Shoving the gun's muzzle deep into the thick cushion, he fired three quick shots. Feathers blasted from the pillow and filled the air as Gutowski stopped struggling. The room fell quiet in the silent, looming presence of death. The detective exhaled long and hard. That bit of business done, Jim wiped the gun clean of prints and tossed the untraceable weapon onto the bed before shredding the pillow with angry, determined hands. Then, he found and turned on a light and set about helping the injured occupants of the room, if anything he could do would help.

———

Nearly a dozen men appeared where Linc and Matt knelt beside Detective Rutherford's body. The group included the old clerk from the registration desk, who told Matt that he'd already called for the police and for an ambulance. The latecomers grumbled their surprise at seeing the well-dressed Linc working with Matt as an ally amid the chaos. Because only their dead companion was a law-enforcement officer, the men refused to allow the pair to look for Detective Greerson, despite their demands to do so. Linc and Matt openly expressed their concerns for the cop's well-being and tried to break away to search for their friend. The locals steadfastly refused to allow it and, instead, forced the two men outside to await the ambulance and the authorities. Several other men, they were assured, would follow them with Detective Rutherford's body.

By the time Grimes and Mallard emerged from the building, a ground fog coming off the nearby river had enveloped the grounds surrounding the hotel. The full moon pushed its way through the haze and made some objects appear whiter than they actually were. The group stopped abruptly on the porch. The desk clerk asked Matt where their car was. With the answer, the locals guided the two men to the LaSalle where they forcibly sat Linc and Matt on the big car's wide running board. The hoarse croaks of bullfrogs and chirps of crickets sounded loudly in the night air.

It wasn't until they sat together at the car that Linc realized that he somehow still clutched the two coins from the old lady in his left hand. Matt heard Linc laugh softly. It had an icy ring to it. When Matt asked the reason for his chuckle, Linc showed him a shiny dime and nickel the woman had paid him for carrying a box to her room. The investigator laughed thinly, "She must have been installing a safe or something in her room. I know that was the heaviest damned box I've ever carried. She was going to get the kid shining the car to haul it for her, but he couldn't even lift it. So she 'hired' me. Anyway, she told me I'd been a 'good boy' and paid me the fifteen cents for my effort. I did it because I figured it was one way to get into the joint unobtrusively." He paused, and then laughed quietly again. "Fifteen cents! I think I'll buy myself an annuity!"

A thought occurred to Matt. "What's the date, Linc?"

The private investigator looked at the luminous dial of his watch. "Well, seeing that it's after midnight, today's Wednesday, the seventeenth."

Matt chortled. "I'm supposed to play in a ball game against the *Journal* this afternoon."

Linc motioned toward the young man's right shoulder. "Not with that, you won't."

"Yeah, and I'm *really* looking forward to facing my girlfriend with this wound."

Because Linc had heard of Evie's misgivings about Matt's working with Detective Greerson, both men chuckled quietly. Linc turned serious. "Let me say this one thing, Matt. You acquitted yourself well tonight."

"Me? You saved me and... you saved my life tonight, Linc. Let me say thanks while I'm thinking about it."

"No problem," Linc sighed. He looked toward Artie's body. "I'm afraid it just wasn't enough."

"Certainly not because of a failure on your part, my friend."

Any momentary mirth they'd felt had long since faded as Matt and Linc looked back at the hotel's entrance, glowing indistinctly in the fog and spilling cold, gray light onto the porch. They wondered aloud whether Jim was all right and where he could be. The locals approached, unceremoniously dropped Artie's sheet-wrapped body in the oval formed by the driveway, and walked away. The old desk clerk returned with some cloth material and safety pins. He explained that he was going to fabricate a sling to support Matt's shoulder until the ambulance arrived. He made no mention of tending to Linc's wound. Matt leaned back against the front fender and winced in pain while the old man worked. As he fitted the fabric around Matt's shoulder, the man glanced up through the fog at the moon. "Looks like we won't be ahavin' the same excitement as last night with that lunar 'clipse." His voice seemed strained to make small talk.

"Seems we've upset a few people hereabouts," Matt suggested to the old man.

# SHORTENING SHADOWS

He gave Matt a hard-eyed stare and shifted his chaw before returning to the chore at hand. "Well, the locals here don't cotton much to big-city folks comin' down and shootin' up our establishments, scarin' hell out of our wimmen folk." He shot an up-from-under glance at Linc, and then moved his eyes to Matt. "And I'll tell ya, young feller, I'll quit blowin' on the fur and git to the hide. Ya come down here doing it with some kinds of *your* folks and *our* folks git a powerful more upset than usual."

"This was a police matter, sir."

"Ya asayin' yore friend there's a *po*-lice officer?" the man asked, nodding toward Linc and spitting to the side.

Linc started to say something, but Matt continued, "No, but we were working with the police on police business. That man over there under the sheet is a police detective. There's another one around here somewhere, too. And police, that is, *right* police don't like people helping fugitives and gangsters hide from the law, either."

The man stopped his efforts abruptly and dusted his hands. "Don't know nothin' 'bout that."

"And, just so you know, mister," Matt quickly added, jerking his head toward Linc, as the old man straightened, "I'll take this man any day of the week over most other men I've ever met!"

Linc smiled. The old man frowned and quickly moved away. The two men on the running board watched him shuffle back to the hotel's front door. Before they could take their eyes away from the entrance, a familiar figure came out. The man started walking toward the LaSalle with a purpose. Jim Greerson emerged from the pewter mist and gained definition.

An ambulance and two county sheriff's cars pulled into the hotel's driveway as Jim moved up the slight incline toward them. Linc and Matt painfully stood as he approached. Linc called out, "Man, we're glad to see you, Jim! Are you all right?"

"Yeah, I'm fine," he said wearily, shaking Linc's hand, and then Matt's left hand gingerly. "Looks like you two are a little worse for wear." Greerson paused for a second. "Where's Artie." He got a long silence. Jim's face took on a pleading, sorrowful aspect.

Finally, Matt nodded to the body. "He didn't make it, Jim. One of Gutowski's guys got him. The same mug clipped both of us, too."

As Matt spoke, Detective Greerson spun and looked toward the blood-soaked sheet. He let out a soft whimper. "Damn!" he whispered. "Artie was a good cop." After a pause, he continued, "Misguided in some ways, but a damned good cop."

"Did you find Gutowski?" Matt asked.

"Yeah. He's deader than spats." Jim showed a drained, thin smile.

Grimes gave his friend a questioning look. "How?"

"Well, he didn't die of old age, Matt." The reporter turning the idea over in his mind did something to his face. Greerson read his thoughts through that face. "Matt, it's like the old joke in some outlying counties about the three possible "verdicts" in murder trials: guilty, not guilty, or needed killin'." Recalling the detective's promises to Vivian and Viola Johnson, Matt's glare remained stoic, piercing. Jim added, "Look, think what you want. I'm guided and bound only by my conscience." He paused and signed heavily, "I am answerable exclusively to my own conscience and judgment."

Explanations didn't matter in the end.

Ambulance personnel gave preliminary attention to Matt's wound, putting his right arm in a sling to better support the shoulder. Then, grudgingly it seemed, they tended to Linc's wound. Afterward, they loaded the two men and Artie Rutherford's body, into their vehicle. Before the doors closed, Jim walked to them. He shook their hands again. The big Atlanta detective told them he'd catch up with them later, after he dealt with the local authorities and reported to his chief. As the doors were closing, he looked sorrowfully at the sheet covering Detective

Rutherford's body. Greerson heaved a big sigh and made a vague motion with a hand. To Matt, the movement seemed as much a "thank-you" as a "farewell."

Linc and Matt sat in silence for a long time after the ambulance departed the Blalock House. Matt's shoulder felt large and hot as it rested in the sling. His eyes revealed sharp lights of pain, and he put his head back with his eyes squeezed shut as he dealt with the throbbing ache. He opened his eyes slowly and watched Linc, who showed little or no effects from his gunshot wound. The private investigator checked his weapon and reholstered it. Then, he examined the hole in his suit coat where the thug's round had torn through it. He shook his head in something akin to disbelieve and chuckled. Matt observed Linc closely, wondering what thoughts might be going through his mind. The black man suddenly became aware of Matt's stare and looked over at him. They smiled at one another. This is a man, Matt considered half ashamedly, that I probably wouldn't have given a second thought to three months ago. Tonight, he pondered, I found myself standing up for the man, giving him preference in my heart and mind over any number of other men to have at my side in a tight spot. Beyond feeling that he owed his life to Linc, Matt respected him. The young reporter wanted to know what Linc liked and didn't like, what he did when he wasn't "investigating," what made him tick.

After a while, he broke away from contemplations of Linc. Lost in thought, he focused on the bloody sheet covering Detective Arthur Rutherford's body on the floor of the vehicle. Maybe Jim was right. Maybe Rutherford had been a good cop. Much about his personality seemed to blind others to that perception. He could be a nasty son of a bitch, but he *did* die trying to bring justice to bear.

Grimes's contemplation drifted to his friend, Jim Greerson. He liked and admired the big detective. He was a good, tough policeman. But what made a cop a *good* cop in the world Jim was forced to inhabit? The young journalist couldn't help wondering what had happened to bring about Carl Gutowski's death at the detective's hands. Repeatedly, the blond reporter replayed the earnest promises Jim had made to Vivian and Viola. He wanted to think the best of Detective Greerson, but... He moved his head from side to side forcefully and tried to shake the thoughts.

As the ambulance jockeyed through early-morning traffic toward Grady Hospital, Matthew Grimes realized that, in the last several months, he'd passed through a portal of sorts, had done things he'd not thought himself capable of, had seen and heard things he didn't fully understand, recognized problems that had yet to be dealt with. Rhamy Fleming had been right. Some unsettled issues in the country were like dark shadows on the land. Some of those problems would be resolved, too quickly for some, not swiftly enough for many, and never for still others. One man couldn't do it alone, he believed, but it was a start. Clocks ticked off the minutes and hours, but in many ways time stood still. The sun rose and the sun set, but the shadows remained. They were shadows that would be, had to be shortened with time, and, in time, made to disappear. And it would take everybody's efforts and understanding to dissolve them. Life is changing for me and for many others, he contemplated, and that change will be permanent. If not now, soon. Hopefully.

THE END

# GLOSSARY

**Ankle** — Walk, as in "Ankle past him slow."

**Back-window** — Skip out, escape

**Bangtail** — Racehorse

**Batty** — Crazy, loco, weird

**Beezer** — Nose

**Bindle punk** — Chronic itinerant misfit and criminal, called such because they carried a "bindle," the bundle in which a hobo carried all his worldly possessions

**Blind tiger** — A location where liquors and alcoholic beverages were sold illegally; also called blind pigs, pour houses, and speakeasies.

**Bluestocking** — An educated woman who is interested in books and ideas

**Brace** — Question, grab or shakeup somebody, especially to get them to divulge information; also to prepare, steel, or fortify one's self or something

**Bug, the** — Numbers racket, illegal lottery

**Button your chin** — Keep quiet; also, pipe down

# SHORTENING SHADOWS

**Butts** — Cigarettes; also gaspers, smokes, coffin nails

**Can** — Bathroom

**Chifforobe** — A combination of wardrobe and chest of drawers

**Chin** — Conversation; chinning is talking

**Chinch** — Bedbug

**Chisel** — To swindle or cheat; a chiseler is a perpetrator of such deeds

**Chump** — A stupid or foolish person

**Clammed up** — Refused to talk, kept quiet, uncooperative

**Copacetic** — Okay, fine

**Croaker** — Doctor

**Conk** — A hairstyle popular among black men from the 1920s, which called for a man with naturally "kinky" hair to have it chemically straightened using a relaxer

**Crazy as a bedbug** — Another way of saying loco, crazy

**Dangle** — Leave, get lost, scram

| | |
|---|---|
| **Darb** | Something remarkable or superior, often referring to a woman |
| **Dead soldier** | An empty bottle, as in "Two scotch bottles, one a dead soldier." |
| **Dinge** | A black person (with racist connotations); also smoke, shine, dark meat |
| **Down in the mouth** | Depressed, feeling low |
| **Drift** | Get lost, scram, leave; also can mean to let go of, as in "Matt let it drift." |
| **Etui** | A small ornamental case or box, often holding jewelry or toiletry items |
| **Fade** | To go away, get lost |
| **Fan** | Search, rummage through, rifle |
| **Flame-top** | Redhead |
| **Flash** | Flashlight |
| **Flatfoot** | Cop; also a Flattie, copper or gumshoe |
| **Flit** | Move quickly from one place to another, disappear, escape |

| | |
|---|---|
| **Flivver** | A Ford car in particular, or any car in general; also a heap, crate, bucket, boiler |
| **Fluff** | Arm candy, for show only |
| **Frail** | A woman; also a twist, jane, broad, dame, doll. A dish or a looker is an attractive version of the same gender |
| **Frill** | A girl with the connotation of one who is easy or cheap; also a floozy |
| **Gaboon** | Spittoon |
| **Gag** | A joke or trick |
| **Gams** | Legs, especially a woman's; also pins |
| **Gat** | A gun; also rod, heater, iron, roscoe |
| **Give the air** | Brush off, break up with, dump |
| **Gorilla** | Muscular man |
| **Grab (a little) air** | Put your hands up |
| **Grifter** | A huckster or a con man; a lowlife |
| **Grub** | Food |

| | |
|---|---|
| **Gun play** | Shoot-out, gunfire |
| **Hard number** | Tough guy, hard guy |
| **Hash house** | Cheap restaurant; also greasy spoon |
| **Hatchet man** | A killer or gunman |
| **Heart balm** | Generally refers to money received in a Breach of Marriage Promise (Breach of Promise) suit |
| **Heel** | Undesirable man, jerk, lowlife |
| **Hep** | Wise, clued in |
| **Hooch** | Liquor, booze |
| **Hood** | From hoodlum, a criminal of some sort; also hooligan, goon, gangster, mobster, thug |
| **Hooey** | Nonsense, baloney |
| **Hot seat** | Electric chair; also Old Sparky |
| **Jake** | Fine, okay, acceptable |
| **Jam** | Trouble, a tight spot |
| **Joe** | Coffee, as in "He had a growing need for a cup of joe."; also java |

| | |
|---|---|
| **Joy girl** | Prostitute; also a chippy, pro skirt, happy lady, sleepy-time girl, streetwalker, lady of the evening, roundheels |
| **Kisser** | Mouth, face |
| **Meat wagon** | Ambulance |
| **Miscount the trumps** | Misinterpret or misunderstand a situation, overlook something |
| **Mitt** | Hand |
| **Mob** | Gang |
| **Mouthpiece** | Lawyer; also shyster |
| **News hawk** | Newspaper reporter; also newsie, newshound |
| **Lam** | Flee hastily, as in "The frail I saw through the window must've taken it on the lam." |
| **Lid** | Hat |
| **Lousy with** | Full of, brimming with |
| **Lowdown** | The details, a rundown, the skinny |
| **Lug** | Man, guy |
| **Moniker** | Nickname |

| | |
|---|---|
| **Mug** | Man or face |
| **On the make** | Playing somebody, out for an act of mutual good feeling |
| **Paw** | Grab, grope, fondle |
| **Percentage** | Advantage, motivation, angle |
| **Pinch** | Arrest |
| **Play** | Column space, reporting; also can mean a gambit, plan, scheme, business, or procedure, e.g., "Having a second man along would certainly help his play." |
| **Pull a Brodie** | To jump from a high place, e.g., a bridge, building, etc. Derived from Steve Brodie, who jumped off the Brooklyn Bridge in 1886 |
| **Punk** | Generally, a lowlife |
| **Puts the finger on** | Identifies, names |
| **Racket** | Job, caper, scheme, business, game |
| **Rube** | An uneducated person who is usually from the country, a bumpkin |
| **Rumpus** | Disturbance, excitement, dust-up; also tangle |

| | |
|---|---|
| **Sap** | A blackjack |
| **Sawbuck** | Ten dollar bill; a fin is a five dollar bill |
| **Shamus** | (Private) detective. Also referred to as a private dick or gumshoe |
| **Sheik** | Lothario, a man whose chief interest is seducing women |
| **Slug** | Bullet |
| **Smack** | Slap, punch |
| **Smart up** | Get wise to something |
| **Snatch** | Kidnap |
| **Sore** | Angry or upset with |
| **Squawk** | Complain, harp at someone |
| **Swag** | Money, goods, valuables, as in "That's a lotta swag!" |
| **Swell** | Good, fine, nice |
| **Swells** | People of high social position or who are dressed in the height of fashion |
| **Tabouret** | A small portable stand or cabinet |

| | |
|---|---|
| **Take it from the neck** | Drink from the bottle |
| **Take some air** | Go for a ride, leave, go outside |
| **Tijuana bible** | Small eight-page publications of cartoon erotica that became popular during the 1930s |
| **Torcher / torch singer** | One who specializes in singing songs of unrequited love |
| **Weak sister** | Pushover, as in "He was no weak sister." |
| **White of you** | Decent, good of you |
| **Wisecrack** | A joke or jape |
| **Yap** | Mouth |
| **Yegg** | Safecracker who can only open easy safes or, generally, a tough character |

# About the Author

Tom Woodward is a retired Coast Guard Commander, having served twenty-six-plus years in a combined Navy and Coast Guard career. Upon his retirement, he moved to the Atlanta, Georgia, area, where he worked for over twenty years as an assistant district attorney, retiring recently from his position as a senior assistant district attorney.

He now stays busy doing volunteer work and writing. His previously published book, *Loose Ends*, is a collection of short mystery stories.
Contact the author at
Tom.Woodward71@gmail.com

Made in the USA
Lexington, KY
10 May 2016